OFF THE RECORD

Jennifer O'Connell

NEW AMERICAN LIBRARY

New American Library
Published by New American Library, a division of
Penguin Group (USA) Inc., 375 Hudson Street,
New York, New York 10014, USA
Penguin Group (Canada), 90 Eglinton Avenue East, Suite 700, Toronto,
Ontario M4P 2Y3, Canada (a division of Pearson Penguin Canada Inc.)
Penguin Books Ltd., 80 Strand, London WC2R 0RL, England
Penguin Ireland, 25 St. Stephen's Green, Dublin 2,
Ireland (a division of Penguin Books Ltd.)
Penguin Group (Australia), 250 Camberwell Road, Camberwell, Victoria 3124,
Australia (a division of Pearson Australia Group Pty. Ltd.)
Penguin Books India Pvt. Ltd., 11 Community Centre, Panchsheel Park,
New Delhi - 110 017, India
Penguin Group (NZ), cnr Airborne and Rosedale Roads, Albany,
Auckland 1310, New Zealand (a division of Pearson New Zealand Ltd.)
Penguin Books (South Africa) (Pty.) Ltd., 24 Sturdee Avenue,
Rosebank, Johannesburg 2196, South Africa

Penguin Books Ltd., Registered Offices:
80 Strand, London WC2R 0RL, England

First published by New American Library,
a division of Penguin Group (USA) Inc.

First Printing, September 2005
10 9 8 7 6 5 4 3 2 1

NEW AMERICAN LIBRARY and logo are trademarks of Penguin Group (USA) Inc.

LIBRARY OF CONGRESS CATALOGING-IN-PUBLICATION DATA:

O'Connell, Jennifer.
    Off the record / Jennifer O'Connell.
    p. cm.
    ISBN 0-451-21645-8 (pbk.)
    1. Women lawyers—Fiction.   2. Rock musicians—Fiction.   I. Title.
    PS3615.C65O27   2005
    813'.6—dc22   2005009433

Printed in the United States of America

Designed by Ginger Legato

PUBLISHER'S NOTE
This is a work of fiction. Names, characters, places, and incidents either are the product of the author's
imagination or are used fictitiously, and any resemblance to actual persons, living or dead, business
establishments, events, or locales is entirely coincidental.
The publisher does not have any control over and does not assume any responsibility for author or
third-party Web sites or their content.

The scanning, uploading, and distribution of this book via the Internet or via any other means without
the permission of the publisher is illegal and punishable by law. Please purchase only authorized electronic editions, and do not participate in or encourage electronic piracy of copyrighted materials. Your
support of the author's rights is appreciated.

Because she listened to music while vacuuming, and as a result I learned every word to every song on Elton John's *Yellow Brick Road;* because she gave Barbra Streisand a run for her money while singing along to *A Star Is Born* on our car's eight-track tape player; because we'll never know what really happened to the Sade concert tickets my dad insists she threw in the garbage and she insists he misplaced;

for my mom, with love.

Those who wish to sing always find a song.

—SWEDISH PROVERB

BOSTON GLOBE MARCH 21, 1990

Will the Real Janey 245 Please Stand Up?

By Jeffrey Lee,
Boston Globe staff writer

So who is the elusive Janey 245? If you asked Barbie Klein, a cashier at the 7-Eleven in Billerica, she'd tell you it's her. But so would Kate Dowd, a Las Vegas dancer who says she once gave Teddy Rock a lap dance on his way through Sin City. And Susan Lane, a school bus driver in Bethesda, Maryland. And Tracey Barry, a Miami hotel clerk who claims she met Teddy Rock when he visited her hometown of Daytona Beach during a college spring break.

"Teddy's never been to Daytona Beach, and he didn't even attend college," says his publicist, Steven Michaels.

Then why does Janey mania have so many women staking a claim on the name?

"What woman wouldn't want Teddy Rock to write a song about her?" points out Michaels from his office in uptown Manhattan. "Teddy is famous, he's successful, and there are a lot of women out there who would love to be the person who started it all."

And start it all she did. When "Janey 245" hit the airwaves last September, it was an instant hit. Even today, six months after its release, the song continues to conjure up strong feelings among fans.

"I was moving into my dorm and a guy down the hall was blaring his stereo. I heard the beginning of 'Janey 245' and stopped in my tracks," recalls Dawn Larson, a freshman at Boston University majoring in communications. "That song was played over and over again all semester and nobody ever got sick of it. If it came on the radio right now, everyone would stop what they were doing and sing every word. That's the type of song it is."

While Teddy and his camp of managers, promoters and publicists refuse to identify the real Janey behind the song, there are lots of women who'd like us to believe it's them. And so, until Teddy decides to fill us all in on the real woman who inspired his hit song, the question remains—Will the real Janey please stand up?

CHAPTER ONE

*P*resent Day

"Are you watching it?"

I cradled the cordless phone against my shoulder and kicked the front door shut, careful not to leave a black skid mark from my polished heel. Or piss off Mrs. Winston across the hall.

"Watching what?" I asked, rifling through the pile of bills and grocery circulars falling from my arms as I made my way through the darkened living room. I tossed my keys in the direction of the coffee table and heard them land on the hardwood floor with a jangle. My hand felt for the lamp to shed some light on the situation. The next time I saw a commercial for the Clapper, I really had to write down the number.

"*Off the Record.*" The voice on the other end of the phone held a hint of exasperation, as if the first thing every person did after thirteen hours at the office was race home to watch hour-long specials devoted to has-been rock stars. Only in Andy's world. "Turn on Music One. Now."

I laid my briefcase on the sofa, reached for the remote control positioned on the southeast corner of the coffee table, and flipped on channel 42. A bleary-eyed musician in a black baseball cap was earnestly explaining to the camera how he found inspiration.

"Yeah, so?"

"Do you know who that is?" Andy asked.

Just in time to make me seem less like the boring lawyer Andy viewed me as, and more like the cool sister he wished I was, a caption with the singer's name flashed on the screen between the stubbly shadow on his chin and a patch of chest hair.

"Apparently that's Teddy Rock. So what?"

"Just listen," Andy assured me. "You won't believe it."

I watched the thin, weathered rocker talk about the first hit that changed him from a shy midwestern boy into a superstar. I remembered the song, "Janey 245." It was on everyone's radio my freshman year at college and would forever be associated with my first taste of independence.

"I'll never forget her; she changed my life." A slow grin spread across Teddy's full lips as he remembered Janey.

"That's you," my brother broke in. "You're Janey 245."

"What are you talking about?" I moved in nearer to the TV set and kneeled in front of Teddy Rock for a closer examination. From what I remembered, he'd been the *it* boy back when "Janey 245" was in serious rotation on MTV. Since disappearing into the black hole of one-hit wonders, Teddy had grown older, but no less gorgeous. His glossy black hair was shorter, but still floppy, managing to make him look like a disheveled Johnny Depp, complete with razor stubble and aquamarine eyes that always looked like he was squinting—or trying to picture you naked.

"That's Theodore Brockford—Teddy Rock. He wrote 'Janey 245' about you. Listen."

As fourteen-year-old concert footage streamed across the screen, a younger, shirtless Teddy Rock belted out the chorus to "Janey 245."

> *You made a man outta me,*
> *You opened my eyes and made me see*
> *What it means to be alive,*
> *Janey 245*

While the song played uninterrupted in the background, the interview with the latter-day Teddy continued. The camera's previous close-up had been replaced with a full shot of Teddy reclining on a leopard-print couch in faded, frayed jeans and a vintage Ramones concert T-shirt. He wore them both well.

"That's ridiculous. Besides, he can't be Theo Brockford. I always thought Teddy Rock was older." Weren't famous people always older? That way you never had to really feel inferior or wonder why the hell someone you were old enough to babysit in junior high was on the cover of *Fortune* magazine sitting on the pile of cash he made after taking his Internet company public.

"He's thirty-two. Same as you. He said Janey was a neighborhood girl he went to school with. She had blond ponytails and wore rainbow leg warmers on her scrawny legs."

"My legs were not scrawny, and every girl wore rainbow leg warmers back then," I reminded him.

"But not every girl was named Janey. And not every girl lived at 245 Memorial Circle."

I was shaking my head from side to side before I realized that my gesture of denial would go unnoticed by Andy, who was six blocks away and most likely sitting in his fully loaded La-Z-Boy enjoying a cold beer. He was wrong. There was no way the chain-smoking former heartthrob waving around a filterless Camel like a sparkler was the kid who lived across the street from us growing up.

I sat back on my heels and tried to reconcile the little boy who lived in the quaint Cape Cod house with the guy on TV talking about his rise to fame and the requisite spiral into booze, drugs and women.

"Jane?" Andy interrupted. "Are you still there?"

I had to admit, it did sound awfully coincidental. But it was also circumstantial. I wasn't even a litigator and I knew Andy's argument was flawed. Any first year law student could shoot holes in his theory and yet I was supposed to buy into Andy's inane conclusion, no questions asked.

"You think I'm Janey 245?"

"No doubt about it," Andy told me, convinced.

I was the girl with the big dreams and the stars in my eyes, the free spirit who gave him wings and taught him to fly? Okay, so the lyrics weren't exactly poetic, but with its blaring guitar riffs, and a chorus that sucked you in and had you singing at the top of your lungs, the song had been a hit.

"That song was huge."

"Number one for ten weeks in nineteen eighty-nine," Andy informed me, once again digging into his deep knowledge of all things trivial and useless. This was a guy who could recite the Cubs home game schedule by heart even before tickets went on sale, but if asked his own social security number, would draw a complete blank.

"There's no way that song's about me. I barely remember the guy."

I tried to recall moments when Theo and I exchanged furtive glances, afternoons when I rode my bike down the sidewalk in front of his house and we stole glimpses of each other and shared a smile. But nothing.

As far as I could remember, Theo was just an average kid who sat by himself on the school bus and stared out the window from the moment he cocooned himself in the last row of seats until the double doors opened and deposited us on the middle school's front steps. He definitely wasn't the kid you thought would become a famous rock star. That'd be Jimmy Shaw. Jimmy used to instill fear on the dodgeball court while girls sat on the sideline watching him run around in his white painter's pants and faded black AC/DC T-shirt. Every day we waited like beauty contestants to find out whom Jimmy would ask to hold his lunch money so he could launch skin-stinging throws at cowering opponents.

No, Theodore Brockford was no Jimmy Shaw. I didn't even know Theo was moving until that day in sixth grade when a moving van pulled up in front of his house and he failed to show up at the bus stop.

"He never acted like he noticed me," I mumbled, my eyes searching the nineteen-inch screen for some clue as to why Teddy Rock would remember me. The rock star reached for a glass of water and dramatically squeezed his eyes shut and winced as he gulped. Probably just a habit after too many years of vodka straight up.

"Do you ever wonder where she is?" the interviewer's smooth voice asked offscreen.

"Who?" Teddy turned toward the camera as if he'd forgotten anyone was there.

"The girl, Janey 245."

"Oh, her. Yeah. All the time." Teddy tipped his head to the side and let a smoke ring slowly escape between his lips. "I kinda wonder *what if?*"

What if?

"Jesus, Jane, what'd you do? Show the kid your training bra or something?" Andy laughed at his own joke. "Maybe you don't remember him, but you obviously made quite an impression on our little Theo. You're like Roxanne and Layla—you're famous!"

Only Teddy Rock wasn't exactly Sting or Eric Clapton. In fact, for the past twelve years he'd barely been in the same league as Tiny Tim.

"A muse—to Teddy Rock of all people. What will the firm's partners think of our little straightlaced Janey now?" Andy asked.

I stood up and smoothed the creases from my pants. My suit had just come back from the dry cleaner and I was hoping to get another wearing out of it.

"Nothing. I'm not about to go around claiming that I inspired a Teddy Rock song."

"Not *a* Teddy Rock song, *the* Teddy Rock song."

"Yeah, well, wasn't he in jail or something?" I headed into the kitchen and absentmindedly opened the freezer door, only to be greeted by frostbitten cardboard boxes and a few empty ice cube trays.

"He was never convicted. Besides, he's trying to make a comeback."

"He only had one hit song. That's not a whole lot to come back to."

"It's enough to get him on TV," Andy reminded me. "You know, I bet they'd love to interview you, too. You should call the network and tell them who you are."

I turned back toward the living room and rested my elbows on the cool granite of the breakfast bar, watching Teddy's life continue to unfold in another four-minute segment.

"Yeah, I'll be sure and do that, Andy." Right after I chuck my legal career down the toilet and pursue a future in the yoga arts.

"You've gotta lighten up, Jane. Listen, I have to run. One of the bartenders got sick, and I told Sam I'd be there by nine."

I know, that's why I've gotta go."

"Tell Sam he should can your ass once and for all."

"Tell him yourself. He keeps asking when you're gonna stop by. He's got it in his head that you're some big-shot attorney who can't find the time to remember the little people."

Andy had to be making that up. Sam would not think that. Would he? "He never said that."

"So, I'm adding some color commentary. Seriously, he'd like to see you."

I glanced at the green digital numbers on the microwave clock: 9:36. Sam was too nice for his own good—and for Andy's.

"You'd better go. And tell Sam I'll stop by," I added.

"I'm sure he'll feel privileged," Andy replied before hanging up.

Although it killed me to admit that there might be a grain of truth in anything Andy said, he was right. I hadn't seen Sam in months and I couldn't help but feel a pang of guilt. Only it was worse than guilt and stronger than a pang. I felt downright ungrateful.

Sam was one of the few links we still had to my dad, and even though his best friend was gone and we weren't family, Sam was always willing to stand in for the father we'd lost. Birthday cards in lavender and pink envelopes always found their way into my mailbox on my birthday, Christmas gifts were always carefully wrapped and placed under the tree at my mom's house, and when I graduated from law school Sam sat in a folding chair in Harper Quadrangle for three hours on a steamy June morning, his view of the podium obscured by the enormous bouquet of flowers he patiently held on his lap. And here I hadn't seen Sam in months.

Still, there never seemed to be a good time. Maybe I could stop by the bar after work tomorrow night. Then again, with a litigator from our Washington, DC, office flying in to prepare for the Farnsworth case, I'd have to play it by ear. If not tomorrow, definitely the next day. Or the next.

I briefly debated whether I should even bother popping a tray of frozen macaroni and cheese in the microwave, or just bag it and go straight to bed. It was almost ten o'clock—and another Stouffer's gourmet dinner didn't exactly make my mouth water, no matter how pretty the photo on the box. I'd just grab a bagel on the way to the office in the morning. Besides, in six weeks I'd have my partnership review and all the skipped dinners and early mornings eating bagels at my desk would be worth it, not that forgoing microwave dinners and bowls of cornflakes was the greatest of sacrifices.

On my way to the bedroom, I flipped off the TV and bent down to pick up the fallen mail that created a trail to the front door like breadcrumbs. It wasn't until I was undressed and about to step into the shower that I realized I'd been humming the familiar chorus of "Janey 245" the whole time. Damn, that song was insidious!

> *I remember ruby lips and satin skin*
> *That made this mama's boy wanna sin,*
> *I reached to touch your wanton thighs*
> *To look into your melting eyes,*
> *But you were gone, our night was day*
> *I felt for you, but you'd slipped away*

As the warm water of the shower slid down my legs, I tried to see the wanton thighs Teddy Rock described. They weren't bad thighs, but *wanton* would imply that they'd been touched recently by more than the slippery lining of a wool suit, which I knew not to be the case. In fact, it had been more than a year since I'd broken it off with Perry and accepted my fate as one of the perpetually sexless. And ruby lips? Not unless they were stained from the cherry Slurpees.

And to think that I could be Janey 245.

My brother had really outdone himself this time. In high school Andy caught an episode of *America's Most Wanted* and convinced himself that our music teacher bore an uncanny resemblance to an escapee from a Louisiana prison. Taking his cues from Sonny Crockett and Ricardo Tubbs, Andy even tried to bait Mr. Frankenmeyer into confessing his crimes. Wearing a black T-shirt, his white cotton blazer, and RayBans, Andy confronted the unsuspecting Barry Manilow—obsessed music teacher with a Black & Decker hydraulic nail gun, the escaped serial killer's weapon of choice. He thought Mr. Frankenmeyer would break under the stress and Andy would save us all from a bloody death, but apparently without the Ferrari and mariachi sandals, Andy's interrogation techniques were less effective than his Miami brethren would let on.

Instead of a confession and a medal of bravery from the Westover Police

Department, Andy got suspended for removing the nail gun from the wood-shop classroom. Then my parents banned him from watching *Miami Vice,* and the rest of us were stuck hot gluing memory boxes for the rest of the year while Mr. Frankenmeyer took an extended mental health vacation.

No. There was no way Teddy Rock could have written that song about me. He barely knew me, and Janey 245 sounded nothing like me. The Janey in the song was a woman who didn't follow the rules, someone who mesmerized Teddy Rock and then broke his heart. Confusing me with the girl in the song would be like confusing bad, bad Leroy Brown with Charlie Brown. Impossible. And, he wondered *what if?* Please. The only thing Teddy Rock was probably wondering was where he contracted a raging case of herpes.

ROLLING STONE SEPTEMBER 1989
REVIEWS

Teddy Rock/Rock Hard

KICK RECORDS ★★★★

Singer-songwriter Teddy Rock fills his debut, *Rock Hard*, with a raw combination of vocals, guitar and lyrics that take you on a musical experience that rivals a roller coaster. Not only does he put his talent out for you to hear and feel, he wants to take you on a ride. There are no safe pop ballads here, as Rock grabs you in the very first seconds of the album with the delayed and echoed chords of "Janey 245," a song that has no trouble lifting off. "You opened my eyes and made me see what it means to be alive," Rock sings in "Janey 245," propelling a chorus that's pure radio bliss. The song may be about a girl, but the honest vocals and thrashing riffs give new perspective to what could have been a predictably radio-ready cut. Rock can belt out the highest shrills you've ever heard, such as those on "One Too Many," or go deliberately deep, as demonstrated on the slow burner "Not Tonight." Rock's complex chords and distinct sound are impressive, challenging listeners even as they're tapping their feet. Couple that with his singing talent, and you have a musician who knows how to hold your attention.

CHAPTER TWO

"Jane, Weston will be here any minute. We all set?" Arthur waited in my doorway for an answer, his Rolex tapping against the metal frame as if ticking off the seconds until I responded. Time was money, after all.

"I sent him copies of the trust documents last week, and we're meeting with Kitty tomorrow afternoon," I reported, with the obedience of a soldier responding to her commanding officer. The only thing missing was a salute.

Arthur grinned. "That's my girl."

A senior partner referring to me as a girl would probably be considered the kiss of death anywhere else, but Arthur didn't mean anything by it. I was his girl—the only woman he'd recruited out of my law school class, and now the star of the firm's estate planning and administration practice, who was poised to exceed her target billable hours and the expectations of Olivia, who made me promise that in her absence I'd take over where she left off. Sure, I was Arthur's girl, but I was also his cash cow, and bottom line, when Arthur and the other partners looked at me, they didn't see boobs and a uterus. They saw dollar signs.

Dollar signs. Of course.

That had to be what Andy was thinking when he decided that I was Janey 245. In fact, Andy probably had the whole thing worked out already. First Teddy would come looking for his long-lost childhood love, and then, upon finding her, would whisk Janey and her brother off to his palatial mansion in a cherry red Ferrari. Of course, the mansion would have a room where Janey's brother could crash, a stocked refrigerator, and a kidney-shaped pool out back where he would entertain the numerous groupies who'd find him irresistible once they discovered he was practically related to Teddy Rock.

"Any more news from the granddaughter's camp?" Arthur asked, jarring me away from the cushioned lounge chairs that I imagined were dispersed around Teddy's pool. The landscaping in my office, which consisted of an anemic spider plant crawling precariously along my bookshelf and a potted ficus cowering in the corner, left much to be desired after I'd pictured Teddy's slate terrace and the cascading waterfall that filled his black-bottomed pool.

I shook my head. "Not yet."

Arthur slapped the heel of his hand against my door. "Any chance this will get settled before it goes to court?"

"Settled?" I practically spit out the word, and it hung in the air, along with the implication that Kitty had done something wrong—or, more likely, that I had done something wrong when I drew up the trusts. "Kitty has no reason to settle. There shouldn't even be a lawsuit."

"Tell that to the granddaughter's attorneys." Arthur ran a hand along the length of his silk tie, inspecting the paisley for traces of his daily veal parmesean from Italian Village. "Don't worry; Weston will take care of everything."

What, me worry? What did I have to worry about? My biggest client was being sued by her seventeen-year-old granddaughter, a trust-fund baby who thought going to court was merely an occasion to add a new Hermès bag to her collection. After all, Martha Stewart had made court appearances look downright fashionable.

Arthur dabbed at his tie and then savored the pale red sauce he'd collected on the tip of his finger. "God, I love their Bolognese."

He held his hand out for me to take a look and for a minute I thought he was going to offer me a taste.

"I'm not worried," I assured him, attempting an airy tone. Instead I sounded defensive. I didn't do *airy* well. It was one thing to want to win; it was another to appear to take it personally. Even if I did.

"We won't lose," I repeated, not allowing myself to think otherwise.

This wasn't about my ego, not that ego was frowned upon in the halls of Becker, Bishop & Deane. In fact, it was practically a prerequisite. And it wasn't even so much about my upcoming partnership review, although that certainly added irony to the situation. It was about doing what's right. It was about doing exactly what my father had forgotten to do.

"It's out of your hands now, Jane." Arthur shrugged and continued to examine his tie, probably looking for a spot of the cheesecake he had for dessert. "Your work is solid and I trust the outcome will be in our favor. Kitty knew what she was doing when she picked you; her estate is in safe hands."

Arthur winked at me and left, leaving me to bob uncomfortably in the wake of his words.

Solid. Reliable. Safe. All the qualities you'd want in an attorney entrusted with Kitty's fortune. But Arthur sounded like he was describing a minivan, not a woman. And definitely not the Janey in Teddy Rock's song.

As I sat behind my substantial mahogany desk in my ergonomically designed Herman Miller chair, surveying an office that was about as bland and devoid of character as a hospital waiting room, I almost laughed out loud. The idea that Teddy was thinking of me as he sang his song and rocked his leather-clad hips into a microphone stand until he practically faked an orgasm on stage wasn't just amusing in a vague, abstract sort of way. It was hilarious.

How could Andy think I was Janey 245? I was a family van designed to maximize safety, not a turbo Porsche. Then again, how could the guy on TV be the little boy who lived across the street from us growing up? Teddy was as sexy as hell—if you liked that sort of rock-star-bad-boy thing. I never would have guessed that Teddy Rock was Theo Brockford. The skinny kid in the Toughskins corduroys sure had filled out.

I always figured rock stars were the cool, popular kids in school, or at least the tormented outsiders who wore jean jackets and work boots way before the Gap made them trendy. Back in middle school, even I was more likely to be a rock star than Theo Brockford was. My friends and I were invited to all the cool boy-girl parties, the invitations arriving in our mailboxes under the guise of celebrating someone's birthday or a holiday. We all knew the parties were really an excuse to sneak spiked punch and play kissing games that had us pairing off in darkened closets and bathrooms. We'd spend hours in our bedrooms preparing for those parties, picking out just the right Fair Isle sweater and wide-wale cords, our curling irons in overdrive as we twisted the hot barrels over and over to the beat of Duran Duran's "Hungry Like the Wolf."

Jimmy Shaw even lured me out to the garage during one of those parties and tried to feel me up, which resulted only in making my stomach turn over as the sambuca and fruit juice we'd pilfered from the liquor cabinet tried to make an impromptu exit on the backseat of Karen Dowd's father's Chrysler. Jimmy's near-successful attempt to get to second base was definitely the sort of thing that earned a girl rock-star status. The next year I was even elected to student council, and while I'm sure my ingenious fortune cookie campaign that included slips of paper imploring students to VOTE FOR JANEY had something to do with it, my association with Jimmy Shaw sure didn't hurt.

At least Teddy didn't mention that young Janey was bowlegged. It was one thing to be described as a free spirit with wanderlust, but it was another to be remembered as the girl who could almost pass a Nerf football between her knees—a fact I knew only because Andy once held me down on the front lawn and tried. Not that I believed Janey *was* me, as Andy insisted, but the bowlegged thing would have been a dead giveaway.

If it were true, which I seriously doubted, I had to give Teddy some credit for an active imagination. I could picture him bent over the table at some hole-in-the-wall café, a veil of cigarette smoke hanging over his head while he scribbled the now-infamous lyrics with a dull number two pencil and tried to imagine little Janey Marlow as a grown woman.

One thing I was sure of: Teddy definitely wasn't imagining Janey seated in a twelve-by-twelve office engrossed in LexisNexis searches on the implications of taxable gifts, only sporadically catching glimpses of the steel and glass skyscrapers outside her window when she remembered to look up from her desk. This Janey wasn't exactly enticing mama's boys to sin. In fact, it was my job to make sure they didn't.

I should have pushed the idea of Teddy out of my head, eliminated it from the realm of possibility once and for all, but instead I sat back, kicked my feet up on my desk and briefly let myself toy with the idea that Andy was right. Well, I didn't actually kick my feet up on my desk. I slipped my heels off first so I wouldn't scuff the stained mahogany, and then I rested my toes against the beveled edge so I wouldn't disturb the stacks of papers organized on the desktop. But, still, in the seven years I'd been sitting behind this desk, it was the closest I'd come to kicking my feet up. And it felt pretty good.

If what Andy said was true, I'd have a salacious little secret that I could enjoy in some perverse way, like how Olivia must have felt when she'd wear a red garter belt and push-up bra under her suits to gain an edge during negotiations. Even though she was the only one who knew that just below the waistband of her tailored skirt a few rhinestone butterflies were perched on a flimsy net thong, Liv said it made her feel a little bolder, and even a little wicked.

Although I preferred the term *responsible* to *straightlaced*, which conjured up images of uptight librarians gleefully charging kids for their overdue Judy Blumes, Andy's question kept repeating in my head: What would the firm's partners think of straightlaced Janey now?

"Jane?" a voice called from my doorway, startling me and my stockinged feet—bunioned big toe and all. Litigators always did enjoy the element of surprise.

"Hi, Drew." I quickly swung my feet off the desk, jammed them into the shoes hiding underneath and hoped it wasn't obvious I'd been reflecting on the negotiating impact of flimsy net thongs.

"Am I interrupting something important? You seemed pretty focused on what you were doing." Drew pointed to the notes I'd jotted down before he disrupted me.

I glanced down at my desk blotter, where I'd been absentmindedly scrawling the numbers 245 over and over in black ballpoint pen. I attempted a look of lawerly concentration and then assured him that my important work could be put aside. "That's okay; I can take a break."

Drew entered my office and took a seat in the armchair across from my desk while I discreetly covered my blotter doodles with a well-worn yellow legal pad.

Although we'd been introduced at the firm's holiday parties, Drew Weston and I never shared more than a few words at the open bar before continuing to mingle. Unlike the aforementioned boy-girl parties, the purpose of the firm Christmas party was kissing of another sort, the kind that landed on the asses of partners and was hoped to have an impact on end-of-year bonuses.

Now that Drew Weston was seated in my office wearing khakis and a sport coat, his blue oxford casually unbuttoned at the neck where normally a partner's tie would be tightly fastened in a perfectly symmetrical Windsor knot, I understood why Olivia had once had a thing for Drew. And why she'd warned me about him.

"I don't think I've ever seen you without a band playing 'White Christmas' in the background." Shouldn't he be wearing a gold chain around his neck with one of those Italian horns dangling against a mat of chest hair?

"Or Mitzi serenading Arthur with her karaoke rendition of 'Santa Baby,'" Drew reminded me. "I was afraid you wouldn't recognize me. I left my candy cane tie at home."

Not only did I recognize Drew; I was trying to picture him fending off the drunken advances of half the female staff at the going-away party Becker, Bishop & Deane threw when the firm moved him to DC. From what Olivia remembered, just about every administrative assistant, paralegal and first-year associate was smitten with him. There'd even been a rumor that Drew and the firm's temporary receptionist had a little rendezvous on the copy machine during the going-away party. Now, that was definitely something Teddy's Janey would do. She'd probably even push the ENLARGE button just to spice things up.

But Drew didn't seem to be sizing me up for a spin on the firm's self-collating Xerox. Instead he looked past me and stared out my office window. Not exactly the reaction I'd expected from a man willing to go en flagrante on a piece of office equipment.

"I was thinking we could begin by reviewing the Farnsworth trust documents and Kitty's gifts to the foundation," Drew stated, more interested in the view out my window than the scenery sitting in front of him. "The basis of Darcy's lawsuit requires that Kitty lacked the authority to transfer funds."

Mighty businesslike for the guy Olivia had described. Maybe he was just warming up. Maybe legal jargon was his attempt at foreplay.

"Okay," I agreed, thinking that even a little display of appreciation would be nice. Last night I'd picked out a suit that would send the message that my interest in Drew was purely professional, but to not even elicit a little flicker of interest? My bunion could not be that much of a turnoff.

"Once we've gone over the documents, I'd like you to"—Drew continued to outline the work ahead of us, but it all sounded like the unintelligible sounds the adults make on *Charlie Brown* cartoons. Not even one lingering glance? Olivia had made it sound like Drew wasn't exactly discriminating in his taste of women.

And here I'd rehearsed a snappy comeback in preparation for Drew's unwelcome advances. Okay, so it wasn't exactly snappy, and it was more of a kind rebuttal along the lines of *I'm flattered, but I don't mix business with pleasure.*

God. My snappy comeback sucked. But, still, I would've at least liked an opportunity to try it out. All that preparation for nothing.

Instead of giving me the Drew Weston I was expecting, he'd walked into my office and outlined a legal war plan without even stopping to waste time on the pleasant small talk that usually accompanied these types of meetings—*the flight was fine, the traffic from the airport wasn't so bad, love the new furniture in the lobby.*

Drew slapped his hands on his knees and stood up. "Ready to start?"

So, there it was. No come-on, no breathy proposition. Drew was more interested in the case than in making time with the firm's most billable associate.

"Sandy's got a conference room all set up for us."

"Great."

By the time I'd pushed my chair back and reached for my notebook, Drew was already on his way out the door.

On our short walk down the hall at least six people stopped us to shake Drew's hand or pat him on the back and make some good-natured joke about how they thought the firm got rid of him years ago. He accepted the well wishes graciously, if uncomfortably. I didn't know who the hell Olivia was thinking of when she gave me the lowdown on Drew Weston, but he was nothing like what I'd expected.

I knew I shouldn't say anything, but when we finally reached the conference room I couldn't help myself. I liked to get down to business as much as the next person, but that whole scene in my office just didn't make sense.

"Did we get off on the wrong foot or something?" I asked, pulling out the chair beside Drew and taking a seat at the conference table.

He looked surprised. "Not at all. Why?"

What was I going to say? That he should have made a pass at me by now? "No reason, I just thought . . ." I let the sentence trail off without knowing how to finish it. I just thought, what, that he should have lived up to his reputation? "Forget it."

At this point, I might not have known what to expect from Drew, but he certainly knew what to expect from me. Arthur had summed it up so nicely— solid, reliable, safe. Drew was only three years older than I, but he was still a partner. A partner who'd be deciding my professional fate in six weeks.

I pointed to the collections of files neatly laid out on the conference room table. I'd meticulously prepared everything I thought he'd need. "That pile includes all the papers pertaining to the Farnsworth Foundation. That one contains all the correspondence and filings from the granddaughter's attorneys, and this one is filled with press clippings." I held up a brown accordion file. "They're arranged by local and national coverage." I would have made one hell of a Boy Scout.

"Press clippings?"

"The suit is getting a lot of local media interest, not to mention that article in *Fortune* last month."

Drew took the file from me and pulled out a stack of newspaper articles. "I'm assuming the media has tried to get quotes from you?" he asked, without looking up. Was he so disinterested in me that he couldn't even bother to face me when he spoke?

"No comment," I repeated, just as I had every time a reporter called my office asking questions.

"*My family has managed the estate as if I were a child,*" he repeated verbatim, reading from an article. "*I've been betrayed and it's just not fair.*"

"Oh, it's fair all right," I cut in and reached for a manila folder. "In fact, you'll see in the documents that Kitty had full authority to transfer assets out of the family trusts at her sole discretion."

"*Poor little rich girl.*" Drew held up an article from the *Chicago Tribune* and mimicked the headline. "Did Darcy Farnsworth hire a PR firm?"

"I wouldn't doubt it." From what I could tell she also had a trainer, a stylist, and a personal shopper.

Drew slipped the article back into the section marked LOCAL and slid the accordion file toward the center of the table. "It sounds like you don't like Darcy very much," he observed, quite accurately.

"She *is* suing my client," I replied, pointing out the obvious.

"People sue people all the time. That's how Becker, Bishop & Deane pays the bills, remember?"

Drew was right, but I hated this. I hated the idea that Darcy was dragging Kitty to court, and I hated the idea that it could be my fault.

"I could never be a litigator," I told him. "You probably thrive on stuff like this."

"I don't know if I'd say I thrive on stuff like this, but it's definitely a high-profile case. And I like to win."

"Is that why you're a trial attorney?"

Drew didn't answer my question; instead he stood up and shrugged off his blazer before sitting down and rolling up his shirtsleeves. "Shouldn't we get back to work, Jane?"

Something was definitely not right. If this was the same Drew Weston Olivia described to me, then he obviously had some sort of split personality disorder. "Have I done something to piss you off?" I asked.

"Not at all. Why?"

"Because you haven't said two words to me that weren't directly related to Kitty's case."

"I just assumed you'd be anxious to get started," Drew answered. What was I going to say to that?

"Well, yes, but we've never worked together before and I just thought maybe we should get to know each other a little since we'll be working closely for a while."

"That's fine with me, Jane. I was just under the impression that you were all about work."

"And I was under the impression that you were all about play," I replied, immediately regretting saying out loud what had sounded like such a great line in my head. Excellent snappy comeback; wrong audience. I was talking to a partner, for God's sake.

Drew swiveled his chair toward me. "Excuse me?"

"I just meant . . . Why don't we start over."

Drew leaned back in his chair and stared at me. Was he sizing me up or debating whether or not to report my comment to the disciplinary committee? I couldn't tell.

"Maybe that's a good idea," he finally agreed. "To answer your question, no, I'm a trial attorney because my status as a star Little League shortstop for the parks and rec team didn't exactly translate into major league success. My mother tells everyone that I've just taken my penchant for arguing with umpires and traded in home plate for the witness stand. She says that no matter which side I'm arguing, I think I'm right."

"My father used to tell me that if I argued the opposite of what I believed it would make my own argument stronger," I admitted, hoping to put us on common ground. We weren't off to the greatest of starts.

"Was he a lawyer, too?"

I nodded. "Mostly real estate closings, that sort of thing. He had his own practice in my hometown."

"Is that why you went to law school?"

I felt like I was in a car that had gone from zero to sixty in mere seconds. When I suggested we get to know each other, I meant small talk along the lines of how we liked our coffee, not questions about our family histories and career choices.

I shifted in my seat and hesitated for a minute before answering. "Not really. That was more my mom's doing." Or, more accurately, a result of my mom's undoing. Unfortunately, my mother had to deal with my father's death and the discovery that he had taken very good care of his clients' interests but somehow had forgotten to take care of ours.

Drew frowned and shook his head seriously. "Look at us, holding our moms responsible for our own poor choices."

I opened my mouth to tell Drew that wasn't what I meant when he broke out into a smile.

"I was just kidding, Jane."

"I knew that," I lied. "Of course you were kidding." This time Drew didn't smile and it was obvious that he was seriously questioning whether or not I could take a joke. I attempted a smile, even though there was nothing funny about the fact that Drew unnerved me. It wasn't just that he was someone I needed to impress before my upcoming review. And it wasn't even that he wasn't living up to his reputation, although that did throw me a little. No, it was that Drew Weston had managed to make me feel out of control in a situation I should be in control of. Kitty Farnsworth was my client, after all. He was in my office, on my turf. So why did I feel like I was trying to catch my balance on shifting sand while Drew remained on sturdy ground?

The phone on the credenza rang and I stood to answer it while Drew continued sorting through the documents. As soon as Sandy announced that Andy was on hold, and he *really* needed to talk to me, I contemplated hanging up on the spot.

"He said it was an emergency," my assistant assured me. Andy tended to consider his own personal crises emergencies for everyone within a fifty-mile radius. Andy's past emergencies have included an urgent need to retrieve the White Castle frisbee he left in my car, news that he'd taught his neighbor's parrot to recite "There once was a girl from Nantucket" and, my personal favorite, the desperate call I received when Andy discovered that his afternoon *Charles in Charge* reruns had been canceled.

A second later, Sandy transferred Andy onto the line.

"You're up early," I observed, checking my watch. It wasn't even two o'clock yet.

"Not by choice," Andy answered, his voice muffled under what was undoubtedly rumpled sheets and stale cigarette smoke.

I turned my back on Drew and the conference table and discreetly cupped my hand over the mouthpiece. "Company last night?"

"She wanted to go out for breakfast."

"What did you tell her?"

"Egg allergy and lactose intolerant."

The truth was, Andy's only intolerance was with women who expected more than a granola bar tossed in their direction as he pointed toward his front door.

"Look, I'm busy. I'll talk to you later," I practically whispered, but obviously not quietly enough.

When I replaced the receiver, Drew looked up from the legal pad he'd been scribbling on. "Boyfriend?"

"Brother."

"Is he a lawyer, too?"

I sat down and tried to think of a suitable description of Andy. Slacker? Freeloader? Arrested adolescent? "Bartender."

Drew set his pen on the table, suddenly interested in my brother, who poured drinks for a living. "Oh, yeah? Where?"

"A bar up on Southport. It's owned by a family friend."

"Well, I'll have to check it out. It's been a while since I spent some time in Lincoln Park."

Drew Weston at Sam's Place? I doubted it was his speed. From Olivia's description I'd always pictured him in dance clubs telling women to call him Drew Diddy, while trendy music pulsated in time to an orchestrated light show.

"It's not exactly a hot spot," I explained. "It's more like a tavern with three bowling lanes in the back."

"Sounds like fun. I should have known that wasn't a boyfriend," Drew added, continuing to sort through the documents.

Now it was my turn to swivel a chair. "Why's that?"

He looked up. "I didn't mean anything bad by it. It's just that you have quite a reputation around here as a workhorse, and I can't imagine that leaves much time for anything else. It's no big deal, Jane. A lot of people are like that."

A workhorse? Was that better or worse than a minivan? "A lot of people are like what?" I asked, waiting for Drew to elaborate. I'd never been on the receiving end of an equine metaphor before.

He twirled a pencil between his fingers like a baton and observed me silently for a few minutes before pushing his chair back from the table and swiveling to face me. If we kept this up, all our swiveling would rival an E ticket ride at Disney World.

"If I had to guess," he started, about to offer up his assessment of the woman sitting before him, "I'd bet that all the dollar bills in your wallet are right side up, presidents facing forward in ascending denominational order." He didn't give me a chance to answer before continuing. "You make lunch plans with your friends but always cancel because something more important comes up at work. The pillows on your couch are arranged at forty-five degree angles, you always give a cab driver directions because you think you know the best way to get where you're going, you believe there actually *is* a right way to hang toilet paper and take it upon yourself to remove and rearrange any non-complying rolls, and that bartender brother of yours who's still in bed at two in the afternoon probably wonders how his conscientious sister even shares the same gene pool."

Had he been spying on me? This guy was good. And he wasn't done.

"You make your bed every morning, even if you're running late and it means you'll miss your bus, because you know you won't be able to concentrate all day with the comforter bunched up at the foot of the mattress. And the clothes in your closet follow the colors of the rainbow, starting with red at one end and stopping with purple at the other."

"Hold on," I interrupted. "You're off on the bus thing, I take the train to work. And my closet does not look like it should have a pot of gold at the end of it." What I didn't say was that he would probably be right if my closet were filled with anything besides bland work suits.

"Really?" Drew scratched his chin and feigned deep concentration before pointing to the pad of paper in my lap. "I bet you hate it when people rip sheets of paper out of your notebooks and leave that curly fringe stuck in the wire binding," he continued his cross examination.

I glanced down at the notebook in front of me, its wire binding free and clear of any lingering fringe.

"And you never shared your notebook paper in school, did you?"

Wrong! I was so glad he finally missed the mark that I almost jumped up and yelled, *I object!* "Actually, I did share my notebook paper. Quite often—fringe be damned. Sometimes I also borrowed someone else's pencil even if it had bite marks on the sides."

"I'm a little surprised." Drew grinned at me. "You've thrown me a curveball, Jane Marlow. Maybe you're not as predictable as I thought."

"Maybe not," I agreed, grabbing his number two pencil and placing it between my lips as a demonstration of my impetuous nature. I couldn't actually bring myself to bite down hard enough to leave behind a dental impression, but I hoped Drew couldn't tell.

He was so sure he knew people like me, but Drew definitely didn't know that he could be sitting across from Janey 245. That very thought was my own version of Olivia's butterfly thong. Ordinarily I wouldn't even consider repeating office rumor, but what the hell. Drew may be good, but Janey could be good, too.

"I'm not the only one with a reputation around here," I announced, my face partially obscured behind my notebook. I was feeling brave, but not that brave.

"Uh-oh. I don't know if I like the way that sounds, but go ahead."

"What client code did you use on the Xerox when you and the temp celebrated your pending departure on the copier?" I asked, my eyes still on my notebook.

"What?" Drew croaked, choking on the word.

"You had to input a code to make copies, so I was just wondering who you charged it to. Or maybe you just used the code for general office work?"

Drew crossed his arms over his chest and leaned back, waiting for me to continue. "I don't have any idea what you're talking about, but I have a feeling I'm going to enjoy the explanation."

An explanation? Wasn't my allusion enough? Now I was supposed to describe in detail what supposedly transpired between a partner and a receptionist? If I was going to back down, now was the time to do it. But that was probably exactly what Drew expected me to do.

"Well, rumor has it you and the firm's temporary receptionist got up close and personal on the Xerox machine at your going-away party," I explained, carefully phrasing my answer.

"That's nuts, not to mention the fact that it's also sexual harassment. And you believed it?"

"You believed what you heard about me," I pointed out in my defense.

"That's because, for the most part, it's true!" Drew laughed. "I guess now I know why the cleaning staff seems to spend an inordinate amount of time disinfecting the copy room."

"So, it never happened?"

"No, Jane, it never happened. She was a nineteen-year-old part-time student who pulled me aside and asked for some free legal advice, something to do with a landlord who wouldn't fix her mother's radiator, I think," Drew explained. "She wanted to know what she could do, not if I could do her."

"Really?"

"Yes, really."

At least that would explain why he wasn't making any moves on me. The thought made me feel a little better, although I wasn't exactly sure why. "Well, then, I guess you're not the only one who is surprised."

"I guess not." Drew bowed his head in mock defeat and turned his chair back toward the table. "You can keep the pencil."

She may have worked beside Drew for two years before the firm sent him to DC, but Olivia was all wrong about him. And Drew was all wrong about me. Well, maybe not *all* wrong. So I was organized. So I took my responsibilities seriously. So Andy was probably spawned in a test tube in some laboratory where they were attempting to discover whether someone could truly live like an adolescent his entire life. Drew's perception of me as some regimented control freak was misguided. He didn't get it. Just like Andy didn't get it. Somebody had to step up and take care of things. I couldn't help it if that someone was always me.

"So which is it?" Drew asked, looking up from the folder in front of him.

"What?"

"The direction the toilet paper should hang on a roll. Which way is right?"

I didn't have to answer. I knew I *shouldn't* answer. But there was a right way and there was a wrong way. And I knew the difference.

"The sheets should hang over the roll, not under."

Drew smiled at me and nodded. "I'll try to remember that the next time I encounter a situation where I'm called upon to replace an empty toilet paper dispenser."

This time I didn't say anything. After living with Andy and a childhood of empty cardboard rolls, I was too busy being impressed with the knowledge that Drew actually replaced the toilet paper at all.

✳ ✳ ✳

Around six o'clock, Sandy ordered our dinner, and Drew and I continued to pore over the hundreds of documents between forkfuls of pad thai. As the hands on the clock circled around again and again, the hallway outside the conference room's open door was less and less traveled until eventually nobody passed by at all. By eight thirty I was sure that Drew and I were the only two people left in the office. Even though yesterday I thought that I'd be fighting off an overzealous Drew, today we'd spent almost seven hours together and there wasn't one moment all day that suggested that Drew saw me as anything other than a colleague. Or, come to think of it, a minivan.

"What are you humming?" I finally asked, unable to concentrate. I'd gone over the same sentence six times and still didn't have any idea what I'd read.

Drew looked up. "Was I humming? I'm sorry, that's obnoxious. I'll stop."

"Thanks." Even though I knew the answer, I couldn't resist asking, "So, what were you humming?"

"Just this old song from college. I was watching Music One last night as I packed, and I can't get this Teddy Rock song out of my head."

"'Janey 245'?"

"That's the one."

I knew it was completely unlikely and outrageous to even think about, and I might not resemble Janey 245 now, but who knows what Teddy saw in me when I was a kid? I was even considered the creative child in the Marlow family before Andy decided that taking photography classes and calling himself an artiste was one way to get around having to act like everyone else. I remembered the plaster of paris Parthenon I made in fifth grade, an exact replica complete with Doric columns made from cardboard paper towel rolls—it had even garnered praise from the school principal. It was right before Teddy moved, actually. Could that young girl really have inspired a song?

"Teddy Rock lived across the street from me growing up," I told Drew.

I watched him and waited to see whether he'd make the connection. I even sat up a little straighter, wondering whether Drew would point out how, now that I wasn't slumped over the conference table nibbling on my pen cap, I reminded him of the Janey in the song.

But he never did. Instead, Drew continued reading the file in his hands, oblivious to the possible presence of a muse in his midst. "That's pretty cool," he answered, not even bothering to stop scribbling notes.

At nine o'clock we called it quits. As Drew said good night and disappeared behind the elevator doors, I was sure that never once during our seven hours together did it occur to him that I could be Janey. Or that I could be wearing a red garter belt and rhinestone butterfly thong under my navy blue suit. And for some reason, some completely illogical, unfathomable reason, that really bothered me.

MEDIA ALERT FOR FEBRUARY 22, 1990

Teddy Rock Takes Home Awards for Best New Artist and Song of the Year at 32nd Annual Grammy Awards

The 32nd Grammys were welcomed back to Los Angeles with a spectacular show at the Shrine Auditorium. Forty-seven million viewers watched at least part of the three-and-a-half-hour telecast, where newcomer Teddy Rock took home two awards. Rock accepted awards for Best New Artist and Song of the Year, for his number one hit "Janey 245," amid enthusiastic cheers.

"I'd like to thank the fans and everyone who supported me from day one. I couldn't have done this without so many people behind me," said Rock as he held his awards. "This is more than a kid from the Midwest could have ever dreamed."

Teddy Rock's debut album, *Rock Hard*, has sold over 1,000,000 records since its release in September 1989.

CHAPTER THREE

"**W**hy aren't you at the bar?"

Andy was kind enough to finish his mouthful of pizza before answering. "I'm off tonight, but I promised I'd go by and help close the place." He shook his head at me. "I knew you wouldn't stop in and see Sam like I asked you to."

"How do you know I didn't?"

First Drew, now Andy. Why did everyone think they could predict my actions with the precision of the Hubble telescope?

"Please." Andy looked down at my briefcase and then patted the over-stuffed chenille pillow propped under his elbow. Needless to say, it was no longer propped up at the forty-five degree angle I'd left it in this morning. "I like the new pillows. I got a little pizza sauce on the corner of this one, but it should come out. And before you tell me that there's a bottle of Spot-Out under the sink, I should tell you that I already know and I'll take care of it when I'm done eating."

It was no secret that Andy treated my refrigerator as his own personal takeout window. Or that he preferred my apartment to his own. That I have furniture where he has futon cushions and a La-Z-Boy, and utensils where he keeps plastic sporks left over from KFC takeout has something to do with it. "I thought I gave you my key for emergencies only."

Andy held up the half-eaten slice in his hand and kicked his bare feet onto my coffee table. "It was an emergency. My fridge was empty and I was starving."

I slipped out of my heels and walked into the kitchen to pour a glass of wine and retrieve the bottle of Spot-Out. "So, is that the only reason you're here? To eat my food?"

"Not the only reason, but a good one. I also thought we could talk about an idea I had, since you couldn't find the time to talk to me when I called today."

"And which idea would that be? The one where you decided to join the pro bowler's tour after winning the Pints and Pins tournament at Sam's? Or the one that has you taking juggling classes so you can hire yourself out as a clown for children's parties?" I tossed Andy the bottle of Spot-Out and he caught it midflight but didn't make a move to actually take off the cap and clean the sauce from the pillow.

"Hey, Olivia said she'd hire me."

"Olivia would hire the entire cast of Ringling Brothers if she thought it would make the twins sit still for more than three minutes." I pointed to the bottle of stain remover he'd placed on the coffee table next to his beer.

"It can wait. I dabbed the spot with some beer as soon as it happened. Here." He patted the cushion next to him. "Take a load off."

Andy eyed me eyeing the stain. "It's killing you, isn't it?" He cupped his hands around his mouth megaphone-style. "Step away from the stain, Jane," he commanded.

I resisted the urge to douse the spot and joined Andy on the couch, but not before placing a coaster under the sweaty beer bottle that had already created moist rings resembling the Olympic logo along the edge of the table. I rested my head on Andy's shoulder and looked straight ahead at the TV.

"Look, there's your boy." Andy brushed the pizza crust crumbs off his lap onto my rug and pointed to the TV, where Music One was rerunning Teddy's episode of *Off the Record.*

Not that I could concentrate on Teddy. I kept picturing the HandiVac tucked away in the hall closet a mere ten feet away.

"Just don't look down, Jane," Andy instructed with the even tone of someone trying to talk a jumper off a ledge. He placed his hand on the top of my head and held it there. "You can do this, they're just crumbs. People ignore them all the time."

I reluctantly let the weight of my head sink into his shoulder and we watched in silence as the interviewer asked Teddy about the making of his first video.

"You don't think it's weird that fourteen years ago he never mentioned who Janey 245 was and now he can't stop talking about me—I mean her?"

"Do I think it's weird that Teddy Rock had half-naked girls throwing their underwear at him and he didn't stop to talk about his childhood crush?" Andy shook his head. "Are you kidding me?"

"I wasn't a childhood crush, just the inspiration for the song." Maybe. Possibly.

"The guy's trying to make a comeback, of course he's going to talk about the only hit he ever had."

Video clips showed Teddy onstage, bending down to sweep his hand across the outstretched fingers of screaming female fans. The guy was all show. Every movement of his hips, his coy smile and the winks that sent the girls in the crowd into fits of hysterics seemed choreographed. It reminded me a little of that *Brady Bunch* episode where some record guys turn Greg into Johnny Bravo—complete with suede fringe jacket, love beads and those amber-tinted sunglasses the size of saucers. Like the fabricated Johnny Bravo, Teddy may have only been eighteen years old, but he played the part of rock star like a seasoned professional.

"Do you think he remembers Dad?"

Andy shrugged, and my head bobbed up and down. "I don't know. Maybe."

Theo was long gone by the time my dad died, but he had to remember how we'd play soccer on the front lawn every night during the summer. Even though my father spent a long day reviewing sales contracts for houses with leaky roofs and buckled linoleum floors, Andy and I wouldn't even let him go inside to change out of his work suit. He'd always end up tossing his suit jacket across the hood of the car and then take off kicking the soccer ball with his loafers, his tie flying over his shoulder like a kite tail. After listening to our cheers and screams, other kids in the neighborhood would come over and play with us, but I don't remember Theo ever being one of them.

Andy grabbed the remote control and turned down the volume, reducing Teddy's concert footage to a silent movie. "So, I was telling everyone at work last night that my sister was Janey 245—you would have thought I'd said you were a porn star."

"Only you would consider that a compliment."

"Anyway, I came up with an idea to get more people into the bar."

"How's that?"

"I was thinking maybe we could have a little promotion, have you there talking about Teddy or something."

"I'm not even going to justify that idea with an answer."

"Maybe make up a few T-shirts," he continued, ignoring me. "I wonder if I could get Teddy to show up."

"I said no."

"What's your problem? I'd kill to have some hot babe sing about me. Or even a few hot babes—maybe the Go-Go's, when they were younger, of course," Andy explained, lest I think he'd want to see a bunch of forty-year-old women naked. "I don't know why you're so against this. If I were you, I'd want everyone to know."

Of course he would.

"You know, in college *Playboy* came to campus looking for women to audition for their Women of the Ivy League issue."

"No way!" Andy practically screamed, as if he couldn't believe I'd been holding out on him for all these years.

"Way."

"You're not about to tell me that they picked you, because if I was fantasizing about my sister in some bleached blond wig I'm going to be sick." Andy covered his mouth and pretended to gag.

"No, you idiot. I didn't pose."

"So, they didn't pick you?"

"I never auditioned, Andy. My point is, here were these intelligent, interesting women taking their clothes off, and for what? Fifteen minutes of fame? So they could be drooled over by a bunch of horny guys who can't get laid?"

"No harm, no foul," Andy reasoned, completely missing the point.

"I've worked hard to get where I am, Andy, and I'm not going to risk it for a little meaningless attention. There's no way I'm letting anybody know about this."

"That's too bad. Sam thought it was a great idea."

That was hitting below the belt, even for Andy. "The bar can't be that slow."

"It's just a bunch of Sam's friends nursing draughts and a few unsuspecting stragglers. I don't know what he expects. Have you seen the jukebox?"

Not in months, but no need to help Andy pack my bags for another guilt trip.

"Are things really that bad?"

"Sam had to let Bruce go."

Andy did have a tendency to exaggerate, but if Sam let Bruce go, things had to be worse than I'd thought. Bruce was a fixture behind the bar. He was the one who used to serve me Shirley Temples and pretend to cut me off if I started getting silly after I'd had a few too many. As weird as it was, that bar was a piece our childhood. As much a part of our Saturday routine as Conjunction Junction, the little guy who was a bill sitting on Capitol Hill, or that round yellow guy with the toothpick legs who used to extol the virtues of cheese while spearing it with his cane. I wasn't ready for Sam's Place to fade away like everything else. But there had to be something I could do that didn't require publicly declaring I was Teddy Rock's muse.

"Maybe there's something else we can do to help." I started to get up from the couch, but Andy reached over and pulled me back onto the cushion, where I landed on the remaining pizza pie.

"But a promotion is the best idea. We could call it *Janey 245—Live!* Kinda like Elvis."

"Look, I've had a long day." I stood up and peeled half the pie off my suit, where it left four pieces of greasy pepperoni clinging to the seat of my pants.

"Maybe *Viva Las Janey?*" he suggested, as if the only thing I objected to was his working title.

"I can't think about this right now, Andy. I've got processed meat sticking to my ass."

Andy reached over, removed the pepperoni from my suit and proceeded to eat them. "Okay, but will you at least come by and see Sam? The bar's really got him down."

"I'll try to stop by tomorrow after work," I offered.

"No trying, Jane. Promise," Andy ordered and held up his right hand, his pinky crooked and waiting for mine in exchange. I knew I should. I wanted to, but with Drew in town for the lawsuit . . .

"Andy, you know I can't—"

"Take time out of your busy life to visit the guy who thinks of you as the daughter he never had?" he finished for me. "No excuses. Promise."

For someone who had the self-control and focus of a five-year-old with ants in his pants, Andy was unrelenting when he wanted something. Which is exactly why my mother went out and bought him a dirt bike after he went on a hunger strike and swore he wouldn't eat until he was straddling his own Kawasaki. Of course, Andy stashed a box of Snickers bars under his bed so it wasn't like he was going to waste away, but my mom gave in, and just as she predicted, Andy wound up in the hospital with a broken leg after he tried to jump our neighbor's wood pile Evel Knievel–style and ended up crashing into their wrought iron patio furniture instead.

I gave Andy my hand and hooked his pinky just like when we were kids. "Pinky promise."

When he let go of my finger, Andy reached into the back pocket of his jeans and pulled out a crumpled fluorescent green paper. "Check this out." He unfolded the paper and smoothed the creases with his fingertips before laying it out flat on the coffee table. "I was thinking that Sam's should get a softball team together this summer. All the other bars do it—McGee's, Kincaid's, Four Farthings—and this way we can get some exposure for the bar and have the team come by after games for drinks. Great idea, huh?"

I reached for the flyer and read Andy's recruitment ad for Sam's Sluggers. It was as if overnight my brother had turned into a marketing savant. Andy avoided work at all costs, and here he was coming up with promotions and sponsorship opportunities.

"It sounds good," I admitted, for once unable to poke holes in one of Andy's ideas. It was a little disconcerting, this side of my brother. What was next? Would he forgo the belated birthday cards with bare-assed cartoon characters saying sisters were from Uranus for poetic Hallmark cards that arrived on time and wished his lovely sister a happy day?

"So far we have four players, including me. All I need is four more by Saturday and Sam's Sluggers is ready for our first game."

Pleased with himself, Andy unmuted the TV and went back to watching *Off the Record*. He didn't even attempt to hide the satisfied smirk spreading across his face.

But I knew that look. I'd seen it plenty of times as a kid. And I knew Andy was up to something. I just hoped it didn't have anything to do with me dressing up in a white rhinestone pants suit and blue suede shoes.

* * *

Andy took off around eleven o'clock, and I fell into my nightly routine. I thought about calling Olivia to tell her about Drew, but the twins would already be in bed and she'd kill me if I woke them up. Not because they needed their sleep, but because Liv needed hers. Once I was showered, moisturized and clad in my terrycloth robe, I ran my finger along the suits hanging in my closet and tried to decide what to wear tomorrow. It had to be something appropriate for our meeting with Kitty, yet an outfit I could wear to the bar without looking totally out of place. Andy was doing his part to help save the bar, the least I could do was spend some time with Sam.

Instead of the organized, color-coded rainbow Drew assumed hung in my closet, I was faced with a nearly monochromatic range of navy blues, blacks, grays and even a few browns for good measure. It was almost ironic that the wardrobe of a trusts and estates attorney could also double as the uniform of a funeral director. Andy loved to point out the similarities of both professions.

Maybe tomorrow I should try something a little different, like the teal-colored A-line skirt and the gold chain-link belt that Olivia handed down to me after she had the twins. After three years of trying to get down to her pre-baby fighting weight, Liv had finally given in to the added inches around her waist. I was the lucky recipient of several designer castoffs, which Olivia reluctantly parted with after I promised to return them the minute she got back her twenty-nine-inch waist.

Trendy suits and fashionable accessories—is that what it took to catch Drew Weston's attention? Is that why he didn't even think of me as he hummed Teddy's song? Was it that hard to believe that I could have wanton thighs?

Over on the TV stand in the corner of the bedroom, my favorite Weather Channel anchor warned of a warming trend. Yes, I had a favorite Weather Channel anchor. Drew would probably have a field day with that little detail, too.

I finally picked out a silk cream blouse paired with a navy chalk-striped pants suit and placed my favorite sling backs at the foot of my bed. Watch out, world! Jane was really going out on a limb with that one! But what were my options? I was choosing between houndstooth and pinstripes, not latex and leather.

I set my alarm clock for five a.m. and turned the lamp's dimmer switch until it clicked off. As I lay in bed thinking about Andy and the day's events, the yellowed light from the streetlamps cast a warm glow through my open window and I could make out the silhouette of my suit hanging neatly against the closet door. It created a somber shadow, a headless form without any life.

In the darkness I listened for the sound of cars passing, for cabs discharging their passengers on the sidewalk two stories down. But all I could hear were the cool chords of a guitar and Teddy Rock's voice singing about a woman who was nothing like me.

Farm Aid 1990 Brings Together Family Farmers and Artists

Indianapolis, Ind.—At a sold-out Farm Aid benefit today, 24,000 concertgoers demonstrated their support for struggling family farmers. At the concert, family farmers from across the country joined founders Willie Nelson, John Mellencamp, and Neil Young and a lineup of star-studded artists, including Teddy Rock.

"Teddy Rock's participation today demonstrated the true reach of our message," said Farm Aid organizer Sophie King. "When one of today's most influential rock musicians takes time out of his busy schedule to perform for free, it raises the visibility of the event and the cause."

Teddy Rock's set included three songs off his platinum-selling album, *Rock Hard*, including the hit "Janey 245," which received a standing ovation.

CHAPTER FOUR

Drew was in a closed-door meeting all morning with his litigation team, and by ten o'clock my presence had yet to be requested. Although Arthur kept assuring me that I had nothing to worry about, I felt a little like I was the one on trial, like I was waiting for Drew and his team to issue their verdict—that I'd screwed up. Because as much as I was certain that Darcy didn't have a legal leg to stand on, I couldn't help but wonder whether maybe I'd made a mistake. I could live with a lot, but I couldn't live with repeating Marlow family history.

"Sandy, any news from Drew?" I asked, standing beside her desk with my half-empty coffee cup.

Of course I knew Sandy hadn't heard anything from Drew, but it gave me a reason to carry my coffee mug out to her and make a show of finishing what was left in the cup. Which gave me a reason to walk down the hall to the coffee room to refill, which just happened to mean I'd pass the conference room where Team Drew was dissecting my documents like crime scene investigators searching for that one piece of incriminating evidence, that spot of blood only visible under some special ultraviolet light.

Not that I was paranoid.

"Nothing yet." Sandy kept her eyes fixed on the pages of a motion she was transcribing for another attorney. "I'll let you know, though."

"You need any coffee?" I asked, tapping the side of my hollow mug for sound effect. "I think I'll go get a refill."

Sandy's fingers continued to fly over the computer's keyboard, but this time she looked up from the loopy black writing filling the pages she'd propped up on a metal stand. "Um, no. But thanks anyway."

"Okay." I turned to leave and added, "I'm going to stop by the ladies' room on my way."

The rapping of computer keys halted and I knew I'd gone too far. It was one thing to get up and walk all the way to her desk just to ask whether Drew had called. And it was even okay to offer to bring her some coffee. But it was another thing entirely to publicize my bathroom intentions to her as if she should send reinforcements in after me if I didn't make it back safely.

Sandy gave me an approving nod and, from the way the corners of her mouth were trembling, I could tell she was struggling to keep from laughing at me. "Well, have fun."

"Need anything?"

This time she lost the struggle and attempted to disguise her chuckle with a feigned coughing attack that ended with her wiping a tear from the corner of her eye. "I guess you could bring me a tissue."

"You got it."

Halfway to the bathroom, I passed the closed door of the conference room. I looked down the hall to my left and then my right before placing my ear as close to the door as possible without looking like I was playing amateur detective. Nothing, just a few mumbled voices I couldn't make out. What if I'd really done something wrong or overlooked a detail? What if Darcy really did win her lawsuit? How would I explain making such a huge mistake when I should have known better?

I considered holding up my empty coffee cup and placing it against the door so I could listen better, only I couldn't figure out how to explain a coffee-cup ring on the wood if someone happened to spot me acting like Inspector Clouseau. Instead I crouched down by the door handle, squeezed my eyes shut, and attempted to invoke the hearing powers of a bionic Jaime Somers.

"Jane? What are you doing down there?"

I looked up directly into a tangle of nose hair swirling around the nostrils of our managing partner.

"Is anything wrong?" Arthur asked.

"Just looking for something I dropped," I quickly explained and started groping the green berber carpet in search of something, anything. Damn cleaning service was too diligent for its own good.

Arthur bent down and joined me in my hunt for the nonexistent. "What are we looking for?"

Thankfully, just as I thought I'd have to pick up some loose carpet fibers and claim I'd lost the lint from my belly button, something pricked the palm of my hand.

"This." I held up a small, wirey item.

Arthur frowned. "A staple?"

"Sure. Sharp little weapons, these staples. Wouldn't want anyone to get hurt, create all sorts of workers' comp issues. Better safe than sorry, right?"

"Sure. Right." Arthur reached out and held on to the door handle as he stood up. "You know, Jane, maybe next year you should throw your hat in the ring for floor fire captain. We could always use someone with your vigilance and perception."

Apparently there were a few new features on this year's minivan. Vigilance and twenty-twenty vision.

"I'll be sure and do that, Arthur," I called out, already on my way back to my office, staple in hand. Along with a still-empty coffee mug.

"Hey, whatever happened to my tissue?" Sandy asked as I passed her desk.

"Sorry, they were all gone."

Sandy smirked, this time not even attempting to hide it. "Sure they were."

I'd had a close call with Arthur, but I didn't give up. Although I should have.

By the time I announced my fourth trip to the bathroom, the conference room door still hadn't opened, I wasn't any closer to knowing what was going on with Drew and his team, and Sandy must have thought I'd developed a bladder infection.

I had to accept the fact the if Drew had any questions, he knew where to find me. I just didn't know whether that was a good sign or a bad one.

At three thirty the conference room was all set up for our meeting with Kitty. The coffee decanter was filled with a fresh pot of Starbucks coffee, and a platter of assorted Danishes and fruit was laid out on the sideboard as if this were a pleasant social affair rather than a conversation about a two-hundred-million-dollar lawsuit.

When I first started at Becker, Bishop & Deane, discovering leftovers from client meetings was a huge bonus. Danishes, bagels, deli platters, even hot trays of sliced tenderloin and herbed potatoes if it was a big-ticket client and the partners' wives were out of town or just shitty cooks. If it weren't for the remnants from client meetings piled in the kitchenette at the end of the day, I probably wouldn't have eaten at all my first year as an associate. I was also probably the most regular lawyer in the firm thanks to my habit of consuming picked over, stale bran muffins for breakfast, lunch and dinner.

"I guess Sandy is going under the assumption that Kitty isn't on Atkins," Drew observed, removing a cranberry scone from the tray and taking a bite. "Want one?"

"No, thanks." I waited for Drew to mention the case, but he was busy with his scone.

"Have to say, I'm not a big fan of scones," he told me, taking another bite. "I never quite understood the appeal of a hard, dry pastry with fruit. Give me a cheese Danish any day." Drew lifted a napkin from the stack and wiped his hands. "Muffins are good, too, but only if they're bad for you. None of that whole grain stuff masquerading as a muffin."

At this rate, it seemed as though we were going to dissect the entire family of baked breakfast goods before he decided to tell me about this morning's closed-door meeting.

"So are you going to tell me your verdict?" I finally asked.

Drew looked confused. "My verdict?"

"Yes, your verdict." Was he doing this on purpose?

"I'm assuming you're talking about our review of the trust documents."

I nodded and braced myself for his answer. "Is it my fault Darcy's suing Kitty?"

"You know, for someone who claims she could never be a litigator, you sure are eager to assign liability." Drew put down his half-eaten scone and reached for another napkin. "We didn't find anything wrong with the documents, Jane. They were fine."

I let out the breath I'd been holding and expected to feel relieved by Drew's news. Maybe even experience a little satisfaction. So why was I more irritated than euphoric? The documents were fine.

Fine? That wasn't exactly a ringing endorsement.

I reached into my mental tackle box and started fishing. "So everything was in good shape? No problems?"

"Not that we could tell. Like I said, they were fine." He wasn't taking my bait. Drew didn't offer any glowing adjectives to describe my work. No praise for my astounding legal mind. Just a four letter word. Fine.

I hoped fine was good enough to win in court.

"How'd you ever get Kitty as a client, anyway?" Drew asked.

"We met at the Architecture Foundation's gallery."

Depending on the audience, this story could have two versions: the first illustrates a savvy associate who made a calculated decision to land a client worth serious billable hours; and the second is a tale of serendipity, which is closer to what actually happened. The truth was, I didn't so much convince Kitty as accidentally bump into her. It hadn't occurred to me until later that day that while I was marveling at the varied architecture of downtown Chicago, Kitty was probably counting the buildings that comprised the Farnsworth empire.

"And you didn't know she was Kitty Farnsworth?"

"I thought I recognized her, but she introduced herself as Katherine, so I figured she didn't want to make a big deal out of it. We started talking and by the time we left the gallery she'd given me her card and told me to call."

"Why you?"

"Why me?" I repeated.

"Yeah. Kitty must have lawyers all over her all the time. Why'd she pick you?"

I'd asked myself the same question plenty of times, but I'd never actually asked Kitty. I guess a part of me knew the answer, but it wasn't the response people wanted—they all figured I'd pursued Kitty with a vengeance and given her the Becker, Bishop & Deane sales pitch over dinner at an expensive restaurant.

When we'd met at the gallery, Kitty and I were standing over a scale model of downtown Chicago, each building exactly replicated to just a fraction of its real size. Kitty pointed out her favorite building, a twenty-story art deco structure that her late husband purchased right after they were married. I told her that my late father had his first job out of law school in that building, and Kitty was more surprised that we shared a similar loss than she was that we shared an interest in the same concrete and steel building.

I don't usually go around telling people about my dad. It's not exactly cocktail banter, and if it does happen to come up there really isn't anywhere to go from there except stories about ailing incontinent grandparents or, if someone's really desperate to keep the conversation going, the day they discovered Fido didn't actually retire to a farm in the country. Not to mention that when people first find out that my dad died when I was seventeen, their faces fall with concern or understanding and then freeze as they wait for my next move. Their eyes look up a little and linger on my face, trying to determine how I'm going to proceed. Their interest is piqued at that point, and although they know it's morbid, it's still curiosity. They won't come out and ask the question, but they'll wait in silence until I offer it up. How?

Fiery car crash? Debilitating disease? Freak accident?

But it was nothing that dramatic. In fact, it was downright common, and yet every time I told the story, my explanation didn't begin to convey the horror of the moment my father's body slumped over our holiday dinner.

Gordon Marlow died of a heart attack. A seemingly healthy forty-three-year-old man who jogged regularly and could hold his own on a tennis court dropped dead on our dining room table while brandishing a carving knife and meat fork intended for the fifteen-pound Thanksgiving turkey still steaming on the platter in front of him. The whole scene was disjointed now, but what I remembered most vividly were the sounds that seemed to punctuate the event, always occurring just a moment after the action that caused them, as if I were watching a movie with a Foley artist whose timing was off. The shattering glass when the Lenox gravy boat tipped over, the jangle of the silverware jumping off the linen napkins as he fell over onto the table, my mother yelling that the grease was going to stain his shirt before she realized that he wasn't getting up—I heard every noise in succession until the paramedics arrived and wheeled him away. And then I heard the silence.

But when I told Kitty about my father, it was different. She didn't have to *act* like she understood what it was like to lose someone. She knew what it was like firsthand.

"I don't know why she picked me," I told Drew. "But I do know that I want to make sure she doesn't regret her decision."

"This is personal for you, isn't it, Jane? Is it because she's a spoiled little rich girl? Is that why Darcy bothers you so much?"

"No, it's not the money." Drew gave me a skeptical look. He probably thought I was jealous of Darcy Farnsworth. Hell, who wouldn't be jealous of a seventeen-year-old who didn't have to worry about how she was going to pay for college or how her mom was going to pay the mortgage or even how she'd get to her tony private high school every morning—that's what drivers were for, right? But it wasn't the money. Really. Whether Darcy Farnsworth inherited two dollars or two hundred million dollars didn't impact me one way or the other.

"If it's not the money, then what is it?" Drew asked.

I'd never been asked to put it into words before. It was enough to dislike Darcy because she was suing Kitty. It was enough that she was publicly contesting the trusts and foundation that I'd busted my ass to create. And I could really hate her for doing all this so close to my partnership review.

But once Drew forced me to say it out loud, none of those reasons came out. "It's that she feels entitled to security. Darcy has everything and she still wants more."

I thought my answer would satisfy Drew, but he wouldn't let it drop. It was as if he knew there was more to it than that. I suddenly had an idea what it must be like to be up in the witness stand in front of Drew Weston. Darcy Farnsworth didn't stand a chance.

"She doesn't have everything, Jane. She's seventeen years old and she's suing her grandmother. Her life sounds pretty screwed up to me."

I rearranged the Danishes, filling in the void left by Drew's scone. "Anyway, Kitty's going to be here any second. Are we all set?"

Drew studied me for a minute and, like every good litigator, knew it was time to leave his line of questioning. Instead of pressing the issue he surveyed the table and nodded. "All set, minus one cranberry scone."

But at quarter after four, there was still no sign of Kitty. And, due to the fact that Drew hadn't eaten lunch, there was also a Danish missing from the sideboard.

"This is weird, it's not like Kitty to be late." Once again I rearranged the contents on the platter.

Drew wasn't concerned. "It's only been fifteen minutes. She'll be here."

"No, she won't," Sandy announced, walking into the room and over to me. "Kitty just called. She's not feeling well and wants you to call her tomorrow to reschedule."

"Is she okay?" I asked. Kitty had never canceled a meeting on such short notice and I wondered whether Sandy wasn't telling me more because Drew was in the room.

"She says she's just coming down with a cold or something." I waited for Sandy to give me a sign that there was more to it than that, but instead she simply collected the coffee carafe and snacks and left the room.

"I guess we're done here, then," Drew announced. "But before you leave, there is one more thing."

Here it was, what I'd been waiting for. Now Drew was going to tell me that my work could have been better, that there were ways I could have ensured that the trust documents couldn't be challenged. I knew *fine* wasn't good enough. It never was.

"What is it?" I asked, frozen in my spot as I braced for his answer.

"Do you think you could ask Sandy if she'd bring back the plate of Danishes? I'm still starving."

When I returned to the conference room to check on Drew it was already past six o'clock and he had loosened his tie and rolled up his shirtsleeves, preparing for another long night.

"I'm going to take off; do you need anything?" I asked, peeking my head into the quiet room.

Drew flashed a look at his watch. "It's a little early for you, isn't it?"

"I have a family commitment," I explained, using every ounce of willpower I had not to offer to cancel.

"This family commitment wouldn't happen to involve the bar on Southport you told me about, would it?"

"Actually, it would," I admitted.

"There's nothing here that can't wait until tomorrow. Would you mind if I tagged along? Otherwise I'm in for another night of hotel cable TV."

I had two choices. I could make a big deal about it really just being a night for family, or I could tell him to grab his coat and meet me by the elevators. I knew which answer he probably expected.

And that's why I picked the one he didn't. "Sure, if you want to, but it won't be very exciting, probably just us and a couple of Sam's friends."

Drew stood up and grabbed his suit jacket from the back of his chair. "Sounds great. It beats watching reruns of *Sanford and Son* on TVLand."

TVLand? Now it was my turn to be surprised. Olivia had always made me think of Drew as more of a pay-per-view porn kind of guy.

CHAPTER FIVE

Play-Doh. Coppertone suntan lotion and that white paste you used to scoop out of plastic tubs with wooden Popsicle sticks. There are some smells that conjure up such strong memories that if you close your eyes, you'd swear you were right back in a specific place in time.

No matter where I am, the smell of Drakkar puts me back at Winter Carnival with Jay Whitney, sitting around the ice sculpture on the Green drinking peach schnapps out of a thermos while we listened to an a capella group sing "Shamma Lamma Ding Dong." I could be on the el on my way to work and a businessman brushes against me as he pushes on to the crowded train, or just entering the elevator after someone left his trail of cologne behind like a calling card, and I can practically taste the peach schnapps and feel my toes begin to tingle as frostnip sets in.

It was that way with Sam's.

The moment I stepped through the front door, the pungent smell of the white vinegar Sam used to clean the pitted wood floors transported me back to when I was a little girl and my dad would hoist me onto a stool to drink Shirley Temples at the bar, while he and Sam talked about football and basketball and friends from high school. Sam was always moving around the room, filling the tub behind the bar with ice or replenishing the self-serve popcorn machine he kept in the far corner, and my dad would just keep the conversation going as he trailed along behind him.

Right after my dad died, Sam's was the only place I could go and feel sane. I saved up our times at Sam's the way I'd saved my father's gravy-stained shirt, folded in my closet, the buttons still missing where the paramedics had ripped it open to begin CPR.

But then, when the facts started to unfold and day-by-day life as we'd known it was chipped away, going to Sam's chafed more than it soothed. The same scuffed, unvarnished floors and green vinyl stool cushions stopped feeling comfortable and started looking old and worn. The bar that once felt alive seemed to have grown aged and tired. There was something missing. Some*one* missing. And I never looked at Sam's quite the same way again. I started weaning myself from the bar until I dropped by only occasionally. And so now, having found reasons to stay away, when I do walk through Sam's front door, the familiar scent is even more startling, jarring me back there with my dad. I remembered the exact stool with the wobbly leg, the nicks and carvings that patrons absentmindedly etched into the bar with the edges of stray bottle caps, and the way the neon Budweiser sign reflected off the bar and bathed it in a red glow.

I rarely asked anyone to come to Sam's with me, and I've never invited anyone from work to the bar, except Olivia, but she didn't count. Two days ago it wouldn't even have occurred to me to ask Drew to Sam's, and here I was in a cab with him winding our way through the streets of Lincoln Park. I'd come a long way, baby. Well, maybe not a long way, but I'd definitely made a step in Janey's direction—without even giving the cab driver directions, although I'd gotten the feeling that when we got in the cab Drew was waiting for me to map out our route with the precision of a GPS navigation system.

"So, how do you feel about living out of a suitcase for the next few months?" I asked, practically pressing my heels through the floor mat to keep from landing in Drew's lap as the cab swung around a double-parked car. The backseat was downright cozy compared to the conference table we were used to.

"I'll let you in on a little secret, but you can't tell Arthur, because I'm banking on some sympathy around the office." Drew leaned over and lowered his voice as if the taxi driver couldn't be trusted with the information he was about to impart. "I'm looking forward to it."

I gripped the headset in front of me as the cab took a hard right onto Southport. "Are you a big fan of those mini bars of soap or something?"

"Well, I like mini soaps as much as the next guy, but actually I'm glad to be here for baseball season. I already have tickets lined up for some games at Wrigley Field. Do you go to many games?"

"I used to, when I was a kid. Not so much anymore."

As we sailed toward an intersection at Mach speed, about to run our sixth red light, the driver must have had a crisis of conscience—either that, or he noticed the police car stopped across the intersection in the southbound lane. The cab's wheels stopped midrevolution as the driver gripped the steering wheel, thrust his body back into the seat and applied all of his three hundred pounds to the brake pedal. Just as I was about to be hurled into the front seat, Drew's left arm instinctively flew out across my chest and saved me from being impaled on the roach clip dangling from the rasta beads entwined around the rearview mirror.

"Sorry about that," Drew apologized when we came to a complete stop and his hand was precariously perched atop my left breast. Of course the driver didn't say anything as he continued to sing along to his Bob Marley. "It's a reflex I inherited from my mom. She was the human seatbelt."

"Believe me, I'm not complaining." I tried to catch the driver's eye in the rearview mirror to shoot him a dirty look, but he was happily thumping out a Bob Marley beat on the fur-covered steering wheel. "If it was a battle between me and the windshield, I think the windshield would win."

"Anyway, maybe we'll have to get you out to a Cubs game," he offered, picking up right where he left off.

I mumbled something that sounded like *Sure, maybe*, and Drew continued talking about how much he missed Chicago in the summer. Not that I was listening anymore. All I could think about was the way he'd flung himself across me. That must be one hell of an arm to keep 130 pounds from propelling into the dashboard. He must work out.

All of a sudden I was hyperaware of Drew's leg pressed against mine, his thigh muscle tensing and then relaxing as he braced himself for red lights. The harder I tried to ignore it, the more difficult it was to overlook. Flex, unflex. Flex, unflex. Drew was off and running about how much he missed playing volleyball at North Avenue beach, and all I could picture were those thighs. Which got me thinking about Drew bent over the copier with the temp.

We'd laid those rumors to rest and now I was sitting in the back of Hell Cab practically replaying them with me in the costarring role. And I couldn't even blame Drew, who seemed oblivious to the fact that I kept nodding without actually knowing what the hell he was saying. When Olivia had me convinced that Drew was the office make-out king, I couldn't help but imagine him doing all sorts of sordid things. Now what was my excuse?

Quite honestly, imagining anyone in our office as anything other than a coworker had never been a concern before. Most of the guys around Becker, Bishop & Deane were either hypercompetitive associates who were more likely to screw you figuratively than literally, or married partners with pancake asses and an acute awareness of the financial impact extramarital affairs had on divorce settlements.

Sure, office affairs happened. Olivia actually met Bill at the firm before he left to join the corporate side of things. She said sleeping with a coworker was more of a fringe benefit than anything else. The firm didn't offer any sort of reimbursement for fitness club membership and she figured sex in the office served the same benefits—stress relief and a cardio workout, if you did it the right way. She'd even lobbied for a juice bar in the lunchroom.

Olivia dated a coworker and her world didn't turn upside down—at least not until she found out she was pregnant. If I wasn't up for partner, and if I was someone who'd do something impulsive just because the last time Perry and I had sex he got a leg cramp and had to ice it down with a bag of frozen peas before we finished, then I could do it, too. At least I'd like to think I could.

"So, what do you say?" Drew asked, waiting for my answer to a question I'd obviously missed.

"Sounds good," I replied, with no idea what I was agreeing to.

When the cab slowed to a stop in front of Sam's Place, I took a twenty-dollar bill out of my purse and caught Drew sneaking a peek inside my wallet, where the presidents were all facing me in upright ascending order just like he'd predicted.

Damn. I closed my wallet and attempted to conceal the bills as I passed the money to the driver.

Drew stopped my hand in midair and pushed it back toward my lap. "No way, you were nice enough to let me tag along. This one's mine."

He watched as I replaced the twenty in my wallet, intentionally stuffing it somewhere between the singles and the fives in a display of daring indifference.

"You must be feeling reckless tonight, Jane," Drew commented, eyeing my wallet.

"Watch out, I just might charge drinks and not pay the balance in full at the end of the month."

Drew grinned and sat forward to pay the driver. "Take it easy, Jane. I don't want you to hurt yourself."

He handed over his own twenty-dollar bill and opened the door to leave. "Is there some sort of event going on?" Drew asked as he held open the cab door and waited for me to file out behind him.

"I don't think so." I looked up at the ROK96 banner strung over the plate glass windows of the bar and the people slowly filing in through the front door. "Andy didn't mention anything."

"Then what's up with the van?" Drew pointed up the street, where a white ROK96 van was parked a few spaces away from the bar, a red and blue splash of paint on its side proclaiming WHERE CHICAGO ROCKS.

I shrugged and peered past the staggered line of twenty-somethings, trying to catch a glimpse of Andy inside the doorway.

"Since your brother works here, do you get to go to the head of the line?"

"That's never been a problem," I told Drew, falling into place behind a guy wearing a Cubs hat. "I've never seen the bar this crowded before."

We stood there in line watching the condensation forming on the plate glass windows running the length of the parfront. Inside the packed room, small droplets of water slid down the glass until they collected along the window ledge and formed a growing puddle at the base of a familiar green flyer taped to the window. Sam's Sluggers was still actively recruiting.

When we finally made it inside Sam's, the air was hot and humid. Bodies pressed together in front of the bar calling out their orders.

"This place isn't exactly the quiet hole-in-the-wall you had me expecting," Drew commented, trying to make his way past a cluster of people who'd decided to stop and rehash yesterday's Cubs loss.

"What are all these people waiting for?" I wondered out loud.

"It's not what they're waiting for, it's who." Drew practically had to yell above the noise of the crowd as he pointed to a ten-foot banner strung behind the risers of a makeshift stage. WELCOME CHICAGO'S OWN JANEY 245.

"What the hell——" I muttered, blinking at the banner.

"What?" Drew asked, turning his ear to me. "I couldn't hear you."

I didn't bother repeating myself because I had already spun around and was scanning the room for my brother—behind the bar, by the jukebox, down the hall toward the bathrooms. Anywhere he'd be hiding. And he had to be hiding. Because he had to know that I'd kill him for this. And if he didn't know it before, he'd certainly know it once I found him.

I finally spotted Andy over by the waitress station holding court for two giggly girls. The oblivious grin on his face meant he obviously hadn't seen me walk through the door.

"Andy." I called out his name, but he was too busy entertaining the cropped-top duo. "Andy," I shouted again, this time cupping my hands around my mouth so my voice would carry. Andy looked over at me and waved. He said something to the girls that set them off on a fit of laughter and left his harem behind as he headed toward me.

"So, what do you think?" Andy asked when he reached us. "Pretty cool, huh?"

"Cool? Are you kidding me?" I cried.

"They're all waiting for you." Andy raised his hand and caught the attention of the man onstage. The guy, who had to be one of the on-air personalities judging from the attention the girls were giving him, waved back and then tapped his watch impatiently. "I told you this would work."

"Andy," I warned.

"Jane," he imitated me and pointed toward the bar, where Sam caught us staring and shot me a thumbs-up. "Look, you said you wanted to help Sam, and this is the best way."

"I made a mistake."

Andy shook his head at me. "Jane, you don't make mistakes."

"I told you we'd come up with something else. I can't do this now." I turned toward the door but Andy reached out and grabbed me, as if I could have escaped through the crowd even if I wanted to.

"You can't leave," Andy insisted, holding on to my shoulder. "Look at Sam."

Behind the bar Sam was busy ringing up bottles of beer and shots, his fingers flying on the oversized round keys of the old-fashioned register. Andy called out and Sam looked past the customers waiting six deep for their orders and winked at me without even pausing.

"There's no time to come up with something else, Jane. Time is running out. Tell her she can't leave," Andy pleaded with Drew. "I'm Andy, by the way."

I took a deep breath, inhaling a lungful of cigarette smoke that was about as cleansing as a forest fire. "This is Drew Weston," I introduced politely. I'd forgotten that Drew had a front-row seat to my meltdown. That couldn't bode very well for the woman who, just fifteen minutes ago in the cab, was playing monetary Russian roulette. "Drew, this is my brother."

"Hey, nice to meet you." Drew flagged over a waitress making her way toward us with a tray held high above her ponytailed head as she attempted to keep a round of shots from tumbling onto unsuspecting patrons.

"Oh, my God, is that Natalie?" I asked, knowing full well that there couldn't be too many waitresses wearing overalls and a faded maroon University of Chicago Medical School T-shirt.

"Yeah, once the place started filling up I figured we needed a waitress."

"Jeez, Andy, I'm surprised you didn't call Olivia, too."

"I did, but she couldn't get a babysitter on such short notice. She was really bummed out she wouldn't get to see Janey."

I bet she was.

"Hey, Jane, you like?" Natalie asked when she reached us, spinning around so I could get the full effect of the green canvas apron tied around her waist. "Sure beats scrubs."

"You didn't have to do this, Natalie," I told her.

"Actually, it's not so bad. I think I've earned almost ten bucks in tips."

"I'll have a Budweiser," Drew ordered, and Natalie took a pen out of her apron pocket and started jotting down his selection.

"She's not a waitress, Drew. She's a doctor. This is my friend Natalie."

"Hi, Natalie. Is the health care system so bad our physicians are moonlighting as waitresses?"

Nat shrugged and slid the pen behind her ear like a seasoned service professional. "Delivering babies, delivering drinks, there's more in common than you might imagine—either way your customers still get pissed if you drop their order on the floor."

Drew and Andy laughed.

"Go take care of the paying customers, Nat," Andy instructed. "I'll handle Jane and her date."

Nat curtsied for us and spun around to leave. "Whatever you say, boss."

My hand reached for Andy's head and I pretended to pick something out of his hair. Instead I grabbed his earlobe and made a concerted effort to keep a smile on my face even as I spoke through clenched teeth. "Andy, Drew isn't my date, he's a partner in my firm, which is why we really can't be doing this right now."

"Is this some sort of promotion or something?" Drew asked, pointing to the stage.

My fingers let go of Andy's lobe and he looked from Drew to me, waiting to see if I'd filled my date in on his theory. "Yeah, you could say that," he answered, stepping back from me a few feet until we were a safe distance apart. "Jane is Janey 245."

I only had a second to catch Drew's jaw falling open before Andy grabbed me by the elbow and started pulling us through the crowd.

"Sam is going crazy trying to keep up with all the orders," Andy tried to whisper in my ear, but in this crowd even a whisper had to be shouted. "Can you believe this? I had no idea it'd be this big when I called the radio station."

"How'd this happen so fast?" I asked.

"I called ROK96 yesterday when I had the idea and told them they'd have an exclusive if they could get over here tonight. After that, I'd be calling their competition. It was genius. They jumped on it."

"Andy, I want to help, I really do, but we were going to come up with something else," I practically pleaded with him when we finally reached the bar.

"I know, but what was I supposed to do? I already had the whole thing set up."

"Call them and tell them no. Tell them you were wrong, there is no Janey."

"Come on, and miss all this?" Andy grinned and swept his hand around the room. "Look at Sam; this is the happiest he's been in ages."

Sam did look happy, cracking jokes as he handed over drinks and accepted cash in return.

"You're Janey?" Drew asked me when he caught up with us at the bar.

At this point there didn't seem to be any use in denying it. "Apparently so."

"That's amazing." Drew almost looked impressed. Which was a little disturbing. I could draw up a trust for a multimillion-dollar client, establish a foundation and contribute to the donation of serious sums of money to worthy causes, and all Drew could say about it was *It's fine*. But being Janey 245 was amazing?

"It's not something I usually tell people."

"Then I'm flattered you brought me here for Janey-Palooza. And I thought we were just going out for a few beers."

Me, too.

"Nice trophies." Drew was squinting at the row of gold-plated bowlers lined up on the shelf over the cash register.

"Those are mine," Andy told him, pointing to the three trophies toward the end of the shelf. "Pins and Pints tournament champion three years running. It's kind of a family tradition. Those four over there were my dad's."

"Bowling not your game?" Drew asked me. "I don't see your name up there anywhere."

"We don't let Jane bowl anymore," Andy explained, as if I wasn't capable of answering for myself. "My sister has a competitive streak that isn't pretty. A few years ago she practically tackled our Guinness sales rep to the ground when he bowled a strike and Jane was convinced he'd stepped over the line. We practically had to stop the tournament to mop up the blood, everyone kept slipping."

"That is *not* what happened," I cut in, but Andy just nodded at Drew and crossed his heart with an earnest index finger.

Andy handed Drew a beer, which he took and quickly raised for a long gulp. I should have ordered something. With what seemed like six-hundred-watt spotlights clipped onto the beamed ceiling over the stage, and a packed bar that probably hadn't used central air-conditioning since Sam bought the place, I could feel droplets of sweat begin to percolate on my neck. The crowd had grown so thick I could practically smell the bratwurst the guy standing next to me had for lunch. I've never been a fan of processed meat, and the stench of brats wasn't doing anything to change my mind.

"Jane hasn't been here in a while. She says she's too busy, but I think it has something to do with her being a sore loser. Not that it isn't difficult being some hotshot estates attorney for people who want to die without the tax man breathing down their necks."

"Really?" Drew answered, enjoying Andy's description of my job.

"Oh, yeah. If Jane was arrested for murder, I wouldn't assume she was innocent until I found out if the victim had an estate plan, because if he didn't, there's no way Jane would let the poor son of a bitch die."

I ignored Andy and turned to Drew. "Are you sure you want to stay?"

"We just got here." Drew held up his half-full Budweiser and looked from me to Andy as if trying to decide whether we could really be related. "So, who's that?" Drew pointed to a black-and-white photo leaning against the wall between two of the trophies.

"That's our dad. He was Sam's best friend. They took that the day my dad passed the bar exam and Sam bought this place. Sam jokes that the only bar exam he ever wanted to take would require knowing the difference between a Bloody Mary and a White Russian."

"Hi, Jane!" Sam called out from behind the bar. "Andy, can I get a little help over here?"

"Hey, Drew, we could use some help. Ever work a tap before?" Andy asked hopefully.

"Are you kidding me?" Drew looked almost excited by the idea. "And to think my mom said being in a fraternity wouldn't give me any employable skills."

"Great. Go behind the bar and tell Sam you're helping out." Andy turned to me and took my hand. "They're ready for you. Come with me." As Andy led me toward the stage, I glanced back at Drew, already standing beside Sam taking orders.

I did my best to avoid the hot ashes dangling from cigarettes, but as Andy pulled me through the sweaty crowd, it was impossible to steer clear of the glass bottles and plastic cups bumping against me. Beer splashed against my shoulder and drops from vodka and tonics landed on my arm, leaving behind dark stains that I made a mental note to tag with a pin and report to my dry cleaner.

I tried to shake him loose, but my little brother had at least four inches and seventy pounds on me, and there was no way he was letting go of my hand. He dragged me through the crowd and up the two steps to the platform stage, where he pushed me in front of the DJ.

"This is Janey." Andy handed me over and waved farewell before I could object.

"Janey." The DJ inspected me, starting with my tits. I would have been pissed if it didn't so happen that, at barely five foot four, the DJ was practically eye level with my B cups. "Well, it's nice to meet the inspiration for one of my favorite songs. I'm Doug, or as I'm known to our listeners, Big D."

He held out a hand for me to shake, but I didn't reciprocate. Playing at being Janey with Drew was one thing. Playing Janey for a bar full of people was another. How was I going to pull this off? "Yeah, I've heard of you."

"And I've heard of you, only I didn't know it was you."

"Join the club," I muttered.

"So, Janey—"

I wanted to correct him, to tell him that my name was Jane, when I noticed Natalie waving to me from a table in the corner. And there was Drew working beside Sam while Andy poured more peanuts into the brown wooden bowls on the bar. Everyone was doing their part to help Sam. "Yes, Big D?"

"We're just going to have a little informal interview. We'll be live in a few minutes."

Andy had won. It was the Kawasaki dirt bike incident all over again. "Great," I agreed. "Let's get started."

Big D leaned over to the technician and whispered instructions before the music faded out and the crowd turned their attention to the stage.

"Welcome to Sam's Place," Big D roared into his microphone. A wave of cheers and applause rose from below us. "Come on, is that the best you can do? I said, welcome to Sam's Place!" he roared again, even louder. The crowd followed his lead and turned it up a few decibels.

"I'm Big D, and tonight we're here with someone who, until now, we all thought was a figment of Teddy Rock's imagination."

On cue, the opening chords from "Janey 245" blasted out of the speakers positioned on either side of the stage.

"Here she is, Chicago's very own Janey 245."

A surge of applause and cheers filled the bar and seemed to build until it spilled over the stage like a tidal wave. There were even a few whistles, and I'm not talking the timid pucker-your-mouth, whistle-a-tune kind. These were the type of deep, loud whistles that required the strategic positioning of fingers and a set of strong masculine lungs. The types of whistle usually reserved for sports teams and women on the verge of disrobing.

"So, Janey." Big D turned to me and attempted to throw an arm over my shoulder, an attempt that, due to the fact that I was a good four inches taller than him, was unsuccessful. "You want to be called Janey, right?"

"Right." I stooped down to give the vertically challenged DJ another shot at my shoulder, and he gladly seized the opportunity. After all, Big D was just doing his job. Janey wasn't a heartless bitch.

"Janey, over here!" someone called from the audience and then assaulted my pupils with a blinding burst of white light that left me seeing flashes that could rival a Fourth of July celebration. Andy never mentioned photographers. What was next? My name in lights on the Goodyear blimp?

Big D turned to the audience and raised his hands. Like Pavlov's dogs, they obediently shouted their approval in return. Loudly.

I scanned the crowd, an indiscernible bunch with one thing in common. They wanted to see Janey. I was watching ninety complete strangers cheering for her. For me. There were ninety strangers chanting my name, an ob-gyn slinging beers like a St. Pauli girl, and one amused partner from Becker, Bishop & Deane watching from behind the bar as the surreal scene unfolded before him.

"So, Janey," Big D continued once the noise died down. "I don't think I'm going out on a limb here if I tell you that you're not exactly what I imagined when I pictured the girl who captured Teddy Rock's imagination. You look more *plain* Jane than *insane* Jane."

I stopped myself from pointing out that he was more Mini Me than Big D.

"And you're a, what?" Big D continued tapping his chin in an attempt to jog his memory. "An undertaker or something?"

An undertaker. Lovely. I was being made fun of by a physical and mental midget who called himself Big D. So much for giving him a break.

I stood taller and watched Big D's arm fall off my shoulder. Janey might not be a bitch, but she wasn't stupid, either. She wouldn't let Big D turn her into the evening's comic relief. To paraphrase a dirty dancing Patrick Swayze, *Nobody puts Janey in a corner.*

I reached for Big D's microphone and shared custody of the device while I announced confidently, if a little too loudly, "No, I'm a lawyer."

The speakers crackled and the cheering abruptly halted. There was no deafening applause, no encouraging whistles. Just mutterings and stares that made me feel like each person in the audience was remembering every bad lawyer joke he or she had ever heard. Not the response I was going for. "I'm an attorney," I clarified, hoping the alternate term was more palatable. But Big D had already taken the microphone back and my clarification hung in dead air space.

"An attorney with wanton thighs and ruby lips, I didn't know they existed." Big D kneeled beside me as if inspecting the length of my leg. Luckily his view was obstructed by my suit jacket. And the hands I had clutched by my sides. "How about a look at those thighs, huh, Janey? Come on, guys," he prompted the crowd. "Don't we want to see the thighs that inspired Teddy?"

I stood frozen, watching Sam laughing behind the bar as he handed over four Heineken bottles to outstretched hands.

This wasn't about me, I reminded myself. We were doing this for Sam.

I had a choice to make. Up until now I'd been playing with the idea of Janey, toying with it to show Drew I wasn't so predictably mundane. I could continue dipping my toes, testing the waters, or I could dive in. Janey sure as hell wouldn't be standing next to a lecherous Smurf letting him run the show. She'd turn the tables. She wouldn't hide behind a suit of armor, even if that suit was a tasteful navy blue Tahari pinstripe. She'd expose who she was. She might even expose a little skin.

And that's when something inside me clicked. Somewhere between watching my brother and friends pitching in to help save the bar I remembered, and the cheering faces dotting the audience, something changed. I wasn't the girl who sat cross-legged on her lavender gingham bedspread cramming for final exams while her classmates were dancing to "Love Shack" at senior prom; the girl who thought her new role as fatherless daughter and scholarship student meant she was supposed to care more about AP English than being elected to the prom court; the girl who wouldn't let herself admit that she really wanted to have her picture taken in the artificial gazebo at the Renaissance Banquet Hall. Tonight, that all changed. Tonight I was prom queen. Tonight I was Janey.

I held my nose and prepared to swan dive—or belly flop.

"Can you hold this?" I slipped out of my blazer and handed it to Big D. He held my jacket in his puny hands while I undid another button on my shirt. "That's better. All this talk about inspiration was making me hot." Once the double entendre rolled off my tongue, I couldn't believe I'd actually said it. From the look on Big D's face, neither could he.

"Yes, it is, Janey, it's getting downright steamy." Big D flashed the audience a mischievous grin.

A round of whistles and cheers surged up. I couldn't even look in Drew's direction, but I thought I heard Andy cheering the loudest.

"Okay, well, then, why don't you answer some questions for us, Janey. We're all curious about the real Janey 245. Were you in love with Teddy Rock?"

"In love with Teddy Rock?" I repeated, buying myself some time. There'd be no wading here, it was time to jump right in. "I guess you could say that if you wanted to."

"Oh, I think I see a little spark there, people. Did you see it?" Big D asked the crowd, encouraging them. "So, with his new album coming out soon, are there plans to reunite?"

"I haven't seen Theo, um, Teddy in years," I quickly corrected myself. The crowd let out a disappointed murmur. "But of course I'd love to see him again," I added, feeling obliged to give them a little hope. "We had some good times."

"What do you remember most about Teddy?"

The real answer would definitely not work here. "There's so much, I hardly know where to begin. Besides, it's not polite to kiss and tell, right?" I shot Big D a conspiring look. Janey was on a roll now. What was next, serenading the bar with my own rendition of "Happy Birthday, Mr. President"?

"Sounds juicy; you'll have to fill me in on those details when we're off the air," Big D stage-whispered, smirking at the crowd while he waited for their laughter to die down. "Well, then, tell us—'Janey 245' was the most requested song of nineteen eighty-nine here at ROK96. Were you shocked when you heard it on the radio the first time? Did you know that Teddy's love anthem was written for you?"

"I had no idea." *I still don't,* I wanted to add, but didn't. Instead, I watched Sam's fingers working hard to keep up with all the cash being pushed across the bar. "I was in college. And he'd changed his name. But you know, I always saw a little bit of myself in Janey. It was my brother, Andy, who finally figured it out. He's down there by the bar." I pointed to Andy and he held his hands up in the air and waved to the crowd. That ought to get him laid tonight. He owed me one. Wait a minute, I was up onstage giving Big D an interview with Janey 245. Andy owed me two.

"Do you have a message for Teddy if he's listening right now?" Big D asked.

"I guess I'd have to say, you know where to find me."

"Well, we're all hoping for a reunion, aren't we, people?" Another round of cheers and applause filled the bar. "Teddy and Janey together again. With his first new album in ten years due out in ten weeks, Teddy can probably use all the inspiration he can get. Thanks, Janey, this was a lot of fun." Big D reached up to pat me on the shoulder and then turned to the crowd. "How about having Janey sing a verse of her song for us?"

"I'm really not much of a singer without shampoo in my hair and my loofah microphone," I answered regretfully above the noise of the crowd, almost sounding coy.

Big D laughed at me. "Come on, just one little chorus?" he pleaded, holding the microphone out and waiting for me to take it.

I looked into the crowd of unfamiliar faces, all the people who didn't know Jane Marlow. They didn't know what to expect from me, how I should act and talk and behave. All they knew was that I was Janey 245. And I had a license to decide what that meant.

I took the microphone from Big D and wrapped my fingers around the warm metal base, feeling its weight in my hand. I closed my eyes and took a deep breath before making my public singing debut. "You opened my eyes and made me see what it means to be alive, Janey 245."

"Let's give it up for Janey!" Big D cried out when I'd finished.

That wasn't so bad. I'd heard worse. I bowed to the applauding crowd.

"That was great; thanks, Janey. We've got ROK T-shirts for everyone, and maybe we'll have a chance to talk with Janey again a little later. In the meantime, here's the song you've all been waiting for, Teddy Rock's 'Janey 245.'" He pointed to a technician managing the computer console and the beginning of "Janey 245" blasted out of the large black speakers flanking the stage.

I took my suit jacket from Big D and made my exit stage left, where Natalie was waiting for me with a shot of tequila.

"I know tequila isn't exactly your drink of choice, but I figured you could use it."

"Thanks." I took the tequila and downed it. "Oh, my God, do people really order this stuff?" I gagged, wiping my mouth with the back of my hand.

"I think it's the aftereffect they like more than the taste." Nat handed me a paper cocktail napkin, as every good waitress would. "I've got to hand it to you. When Andy called and told me all this Janey stuff, I didn't believe him. But you were pretty good up there."

I glanced back up at the stage, where just a few minutes ago I was belting out my namesake song—quite well, if I did say so myself. "I was, wasn't I?"

Nat placed the empty shot glass back on her tray and rolled her eyes. "Don't be going all Britney Spears on me. I said *pretty* good. I wouldn't quit my day job if I were you."

I pointed to the spilled beer drenching the front of her apron. "You should talk. Come on, let's go see Sam."

"What, no tip?" she asked. "Man, they're right about you lawyers being cheap."

"I'm not just a lawyer," I reminded her, tossing my blazer over my shoulder and attempting my best, and only, diva impersonation. "I'm famous—I'm Teddy Rock's muse. I'll have my people call your people and maybe we can work this tip thing out."

"Sure, sure." Nat shook her head at me and laughed before heading over to a thirsty-looking foursome at a nearby table. "That's what they all say."

I tucked the blazer under my arm and started to thread my way through the crowd, my head down as I searched for the path of least resistance. Which, given the fact that there wasn't an empty spot in the entire place, wasn't easy.

I didn't make it past the first table before I was surrounded by fans eager to talk to Janey. People kept tapping me on the shoulder or excusing themselves from conversations to perform an introduction that inevitably began with *I loved your song*... A few even brazenly stood in my path until I was forced to either stop and talk to them or steamroll over their bodies like the defensive line for the Chicago Bears.

I couldn't walk three feet without someone shouting out my name, and at first it made me uncomfortable, like those snap-crotch leotards my mom always made me wear as a kid. They never felt quite right, and I was always tugging at the elastic, conscious of the fact that at any moment a snap could come undone and spring up toward my belly button like a window shade. But if you gave it a chance, eventually you forgot that you were wearing metal fasteners over your underwear. And by the time I was halfway across the bar, Janey was fitting me just fine.

Instead of ignoring the enthusiastic greetings, I waved every time I heard someone calling out *Janey*. I answered questions, from the ridiculous (Q: Is it true Teddy stuffed rolled-up tube socks in his pants before going onstage? A: I'm not sure, but I knew plenty of girls who stuffed their bras with knee-highs, so anything's possible.), to the absurd (Q: Did Teddy ever ask you to go on tour with him? A: I did learn how to play a mean recorder in music class, but my repertoire was pretty much limited to "Mary Had a Little Lamb" and an improvised version of "Row, Row, Row Your Boat.")

I made up funny anecdotes about growing up next to a future rock star and acted flattered and humbled every time someone recalled exactly where they were standing the first time they heard "Janey 245." When my one-liners and quick comebacks had them in stitches, I decided it was the perfect time to excuse myself and move on to the next group. Always leave them wanting more, right?

Everywhere I turned I found myself surrounded by enthusiastic listeners, my witticisms falling on highly receptive ears. They laughed! They cried! They couldn't get enough. They gave me two thumbs up and five stars. I was a hit. Everybody loved Janey.

Twenty minutes later I finally made it to the bar, where Sam and Andy were waiting for me like a homecoming committee. "Hi, love," Sam said, giving me a kiss on my forehead. "Your brother's idea worked, if you can believe it."

"That was awesome!" Andy wrapped his arms around my waist and lifted me off the ground until my feet were dangling.

I avoided looking over at Drew, who was behind the bar pouring a draft.

The dull crash of bowling balls striking pins in the background briefly drowned out the lyrics of "Janey 245" still lingering in my head.

"You were great, Jane, thanks. Wish I could stay and talk but, as you can see, I've got to get back behind the bar." Sam gestured toward the line forming in front of Drew. "Andy, we need another case of Bud from the back," he ordered, pointing to the cooler door.

When Andy and Sam were gone, I didn't have any other choice. I wedged myself between two bar stools and waited for Drew to finish serving a round of shots. "Having fun?"

"That'd be an understatement." He tossed a beer mug in the air and caught it behind his back. "Watching TV movie marathons of *Cocktail* finally pays off."

"Look, I didn't know Andy planned all this. I'm sorry."

"Sorry? For what?" He slid the now-full beer mug across the bar, where an eager pair of hands caught it and passed a five-dollar bill in Drew's direction.

"My brother has this crazy idea I'm Janey 245, and Sam's bar is kind of struggling, so . . ."

"Well, it was obviously a great idea. You've got a packed house."

I followed Drew's gaze out toward the stage, where everyone who came to see Janey was drinking and laughing and having a great time. Even Natalie, Drew, Andy, and Sam were having fun with all this. I had to admit, it wasn't so bad.

"Hey, I'm going to have to steal your free labor," I told Andy when he returned from the cooler. "Drew and I should get going."

"Sure. Hey, Drew, thanks a lot for helping out." Andy balanced a case of Bud bottles and attempted to shake Drew's hand as he stepped out from behind the bar. "Do you play softball? We're getting a team together."

"Are you kidding me? You may have the bowling trophies, but softball is my game."

"Drew's only in Chicago for a little while," I told Andy, trying to give Drew an opportunity to let him down easy.

"I'll be here for the next month at least," Drew reminded me. "Would that work?"

"That's cool. We'll take what we can get. Our first game is Saturday at the fields on North Avenue. We're coming back to the bar afterwards to celebrate our victory."

"I'll be there," Drew confirmed. "Are you playing, Jane?"

"I wasn't planning on it," I admitted.

"Well, maybe you could come and cheer us on."

"Or be our mascot," Andy added, hauling away the case of beer.

"Muse, mascot, is there any limit to your talents?" Drew asked, trailing behind me as I made a path toward the front door.

I turned to answer and bid farewell to Janey's adoring crowd, my hand in the air waving like a just-crowned beauty queen. And that's when I saw her. And she saw me.

And I had a feeling I was about to be dethroned.

Teddy Rock Stalker Arrested Again

BY BRADLEY ROSE

A woman previously arrested for stalking Teddy Rock outside the rocker's home in Malibu, California, was again apprehended for the same reason on Monday, according to the Associated Press. Lindsey Sue Boyd, 29, was booked at about 12:30 a.m. Monday and jailed on $150,000 bail.

"She was arrested for stalking as well as violation of probation for a previous stalking arrest," Los Angeles County Sheriff's Sgt. Robert Maxwell told the wire service.

Boyd's rap sheet in relation to Rock is extensive. The Missouri resident was first arrested in November for stalking the artist outside his residence in the beach community. Prior to the second arrest, she was under court order to stay at least 300 yards from his home and avoid contact with him. Last February, Boyd went to jail for violating that order and last month pleaded innocent to contempt of court and violating a court order after she sent a letter to Rock from her jail cell.

Teddy Rock is currently preparing for the release of his second album and was unavailable for comment.

CHAPTER SIX

"Jane?" she called out, pushing her way past the cluster of people loitering by the entrance.

I thought maybe I could duck out the door before she reached me, but a couple making out in the doorway blocked my quick exit.

"Jane?" her voice called out again, this time from just a few feet away. I tucked my hair behind my ears and took a deep breath before turning around.

"Hello, Darcy."

"God, it really is you. I thought it was, but—" She shook her head in disbelief and fixed her eyes on the shirt buttons I'd undone on stage. "I can't believe this."

She wasn't the only one. "What are you doing here, Darcy?"

"I came to see Janey 245 with my friend's older sister—so I guess I came to see you. It's unbelievable."

How was it possible that Darcy would show up at Sam's tonight? And how was it possible that the little kid I was talking to at Kitty's birthday party last year had grown into the girl standing before me?

I glanced down at the floor and glimpsed Darcy's feet, which were tucked into a pair of sequined flip-flops—no, make that standing before me with perfect raspberry polished toes and a sterling silver toe ring. The braces were gone and she must have gotten contacts, because I'd never noticed the long lashes hidden behind the wire frames of her glasses. And those boobs, where'd they come from?

"Jane?" Drew came out from behind Darcy, where he'd been watching our awkward exchange.

"Drew, this is Darcy Farnsworth, Kitty's granddaughter." I gestured toward Drew. "Darcy, this is Drew Weston."

Drew extended a hand. "It's nice to meet you, Darcy."

As people pushed past us, I continued the introductions. "Darcy, Drew is the lead attorney on your grandmother's lawsuit."

Darcy licked her already glossy lips and held on to Drew's hand a little longer than necessary.

I stepped between them before Darcy could go on and on about how unbelievable it all was. "We really shouldn't be talking, Darcy."

"They're not going to disbar you for talking to me, are they, Jane—Janey? If anything, I'd think you'd be more worried about Arthur catching a glimpse of your karaoke routine."

I thought of that old commercial—never let them see you sweat. Kind of hard to do in a packed bar where it's over a hundred degrees.

I decided to ignore the karaoke remark, even though I thought there was a big difference between singing somebody else's song and singing one that was written about you. "Actually, I don't think your attorneys would appreciate you talking to us, either."

I tried to appear threatening, but how worried could she have been? I was the one who underwent an onstage thigh inspection.

"Does your father know you're here?" Drew asked, coming to my rescue.

Now it was Darcy's turn to sweat. "Why? You're not going to tell him, are you?"

She turned to me and we studied each other for a second, each of us trying to figure out who'd be more busted if we got caught—Darcy by her dad, or me by Arthur.

"I think you should probably go home now." Drew tipped his head toward the door. "You're underage, and we wouldn't want to create any trouble for the owner, would we?"

Darcy considered Drew's suggestion and must have decided that the wrath of her father beat that of the firm's managing partner. I wasn't so sure she was right, but I was glad she didn't know enough to call Drew's bluff. Getting outed by someone who actually pastes mini jewels on her toenails would be too much for me.

"Come on, Courtney, this was getting boring anyway." Darcy turned on her flip-flopped heel, but not before adding, "Your brother's really cute."

I watched Darcy and her princess posse strut past the front window, just checking to make sure she'd taken Drew's veiled threat seriously.

"Don't worry, they're gone," he told me.

What was I going to say? He'd just saved me from certain career suicide. "Thanks."

"No problem." He led the way to the door and I followed. "So, that's our Darcy."

"The one and only."

"Well, I wouldn't worry too much about her telling her father she ran into you. I can't imagine he'd be too thrilled to find out his seventeen-year-old daughter was in a bar."

Drew was probably right, but Darcy's remark about Arthur stuck with me. I passed through the door Drew held open for me and turned to him once we were outside on the sidewalk. "I'd really appreciate it if you didn't mention this to anyone at the firm. For obvious reasons."

"You just better hope no one listens to the radio. Big D seems to be a pretty popular guy."

"Yeah." I stood there on the sidewalk listening to the music drift out the door every time someone entered the bar. "Just please keep this to yourself."

"Sure, if that's what you want."

I fought off the urge to make him pinky promise. I figured after being put to work behind the bar and witnessing an impromptu performance by Janey 245, he'd been exposed to enough of my family's idiosyncrasies for one night.

Once I got home I had plenty of time to think about the evening's turn of events. In a Janey-inspired moment of courage, I'd decided to invite Drew to Sam's and show him that I wasn't all that he expected—and did I ever show him. And Darcy, too, who ended seeing a show she'd love to tell her father about if it didn't require getting herself in trouble in the process. I'd even practically sworn Drew to secrecy so nobody at the office would discover what Darcy had so eloquently pointed out—the unbelievable fact that I was Janey 245.

Not exactly a typical Wednesday night.

But Andy's idea had worked. Sam's was packed. And getting up on stage and playing Janey wasn't as bad as I'd thought it would be. I'd held my own with Big D, and everyone in the bar couldn't wait to talk to me when I left the stage. I couldn't really explain it, but there was a certain allure to being Janey, as if it gave me license to do things that I would never even consider on my own. If you didn't count running into Darcy, the night had actually turned out okay. Besides, nobody listened to the radio anymore; they all had iPods and MP3 players and music they were pirating off the Internet. No one was going to find out.

Although I didn't forgo my nightly flossing—going out on a limb was one thing, but proper dental hygiene was another—I decided to go to sleep without even picking out tomorrow's outfit. I was Janey. And Janey wouldn't need to plan out her outfit the night before. She was a fly-by-the-seat-of-her-pants kind of girl.

I climbed into bed and closed my eyes, letting the sound of the crowd's cheering lull me to sleep.

CHAPTER SEVEN

Usually I'm at the office before the administrative staff, and almost always before our receptionist. But the little change to my nightly routine threw me off. Not only did I not pick out today's suit, I forgot to set my alarm, and when you add the two together, you end up with a lawyer who's over an hour late for work.

When I stepped off the elevator, Tara was already seated behind her elegant semicircular reception desk. She seemed to light up when I arrived, and before I could even get close enough to say hello, Tara waved and called out a cheerful, "Hi, Janey."

Now, it could have been just my imagination, but I wasn't usually the recipient of cheerful greetings from Tara. She was more the type to give you a bored nod while she Googled old boyfriends on the computer and pretended to be swamped with important duties. Usually when I passed by her later in the day, she'd give me a perfunctory *Hello* before going back to her typing or adjusting her telephone headset so it didn't interfere with her blowout. I probably should have known then that something was different. Instead, I chalked it up to a rare good mood and headed toward my office. But it wasn't just Tara.

It was as if everyone I passed in the hallway smiled a little longer, or greeted me with just a little more familiarity in their voices than usual. I couldn't put my finger on it, but there was an imperceptible change in the office, like the wind shifting direction. And, unfortunately, by the time I reached my office, I had a sick feeling that I knew why.

Sandy would know what was going on. I had to find her. Now.

I started out for the coffee room and was about to enter when I spotted two women hovering over the coffeepot—one of them with Tara's chunky caramel highlights. From the hushed voices and giggles coming toward me, I just knew, *knew*, Tara was enjoying herself too much to be talking about the dark roast. I ducked beside the refrigerator and listened.

"He's way hotter than those lame boy bands around today. But I just don't get it," Tara explained, reaching for the coffeepot. "Why Jane?"

She knew. And if Tara knew, then by the end of the day everyone in the office would know—if it even took that long. She could decide to save everyone a lot of trouble and send out a companywide e-mail—even though that was a little too efficient for our Tara.

I had two choices. I could come out from behind the refrigerator and face the music, so to speak. Set Tara straight about what happened last night and hopefully stop any speculative rumors in their tracks. Or I could retreat, regroup and figure out my next move. It was no contest.

Even if I told Tara I was helping a family friend, explained that the bar needed the publicity, it wouldn't do any good. All she'd hear was that I got up onstage and, during a live broadcast, announced I was a lawyer who didn't kiss and tell. My only saving grace was that I didn't mention the firm's name.

I withdrew into the hallway and double-timed it out of there. Every time I heard an approaching voice, I bobbed and weaved like Muhammad Ali until I found cover behind an open door or empty cubicle. But once I reached my office there was nowhere to hide, because loitering in the doorway, Robert from the mail room was waiting for me.

"Yo, Janey," he called down the hall when he saw me peek around the corner.

While I cautiously made my way toward him, I took a quick glance over my shoulder to see whether anyone caught Robert's call.

"Sandy wasn't at her desk, so I decided to wait for you," he told me before handing over a FedEx package. "All the guys in the mail room think it's so cool that you're Janey 245."

"Thanks, Robert," I replied weakly and took the orange and blue envelope. Still, he didn't leave. Instead Robert held his hand in the air and waited for me to slap his palm.

Reluctantly, I raised my hand and returned his high five, the smack of skin echoing down the empty hallway. What was next? Would they be writing about me on the men's room stall? I ducked into my office and quietly shut the door.

Soon everyone in the firm would know. I was the woman who led a rock star astray. Me! Suddenly Drew's promise to keep last night to himself no longer mattered. He never intended to keep it quiet. He'd sold me out.

My phone rang, and I thanked God for caller ID. It was an outside number I knew—not Arthur. I grabbed for the receiver and picked up the blinking line.

"What's up, Liv?"

"What's up? Are you kidding me? Andy calls last night and tells me Teddy Rock wrote a song about you, and you're asking me what's up?"

"Liv, I'm screwed. Tara knows what I did at Sam's and she's telling everyone in the office. Arthur is going to shit."

"Calm down," Liv counseled, readily accepting her role as someone older and wiser. "How does Tara know?"

"Drew Weston must have told her."

"Drew? How does Drew know?"

"He was there. I took him to Sam's with me."

"Why'd you do that?" she asked, trying to make sense out of the situation. "That's not like you."

Of course it wasn't like me. That was the whole point of bringing Drew in the first place—to do something he wouldn't expect me to do. Seeing any colleague outside the office was awkward enough, no less bringing someone to Sam's. The first time I ran into Arthur outside the office, Natalie and I were waiting in line at the movies. There he was in blue and green plaid Bermuda shorts, a Nike T-shirt and Birkenstocks. I'd never quite pictured Arthur as an athlete, so the Nike shirt was enough to throw me off, but the Birkenstocks— they ruined me forever. Arthur could be wearing a pair of three-hundred-dollar wingtips and all I could see were the ten coiled, hairy monkey toes inside his black dress socks.

"It doesn't matter," I told her. "That's not the worst of it."

"It gets worse?"

"Darcy Farnsworth was there. She saw the whole thing."

"Wow." I could hear Liv cringing. "That is pretty bad. Boy, when you decide to shake things up, you really go all the way, don't you?"

"Liv, what am I going to do?"

"Look, Arthur loves you, and he can't argue with the hours you bill—he's made a fortune off of you. You'll probably just get a stern talking-to."

"You really think so?"

"Sure." She didn't sound all that convincing. "Come on, take a deep breath."

I closed my eyes and inhaled loudly.

"That's better, isn't it?" Liv asked.

"A little," I breathed out, hoping Olivia was right.

"It will be fine, really. Would you rather trade places? I've been negotiating a precarious peace treaty between two dueling dictators all morning."

"No, thanks. I don't know how you do it," I admitted, picturing George and Ethan adamantly refusing to give in, no matter how skillful Olivia's bargaining ability. I mean, this was a woman who once negotiated a merger between an importer of olive oil and an exporter of bottled water. You'd think ten years spent in the quagmire of legal maneuverings would have prepared Liv for twins. "What are they arguing about this time?"

"You tell me—could Elmo kick Barney's ass or does the esteemed dinosaur's sheer size give him the advantage?"

I thought about this for a moment. "I'd have to vote for Elmo. He seems more agile."

Olivia lowered her voice. "Secretly I think so, too, but you do understand that as an enlightened mother, I must encourage their unique points of view even if I just wish Mister Rogers would snuff them both out for good. If I have to listen one more time to Ethan inform George that Elmo is really a girl named Emily, I swear I'm just going to tell them there's no such thing as Santa Claus—I don't care how many years of therapy I'm paying for."

"They just turned three. They'll outgrow this."

"Yeah, but what will grow back in its place?" The distinctive sound of water rushing out of a toilet and then trickling back in to fill the bowl punctuated Olivia's profound musing. No wonder we'd had more than thirty seconds of uninterrupted conversation—Olivia was hiding out in the bathroom. "We on for lunch today?"

"Shit, did we have lunch plans today?"

"Don't say it," Olivia warned, knowing where this was headed. "Come on, I want to hear the lowdown on Teddy Rock and your coming-out party last night."

"Please, don't say his name, and let's just forget about last night. I don't want to think about Teddy Rock or Janey ever again." I rubbed my temples, trying to smooth the throbbing vein that was on the verge of popping out of my head at any moment. "Besides, I can't leave the office with all this going on, not to mention Kitty's case."

I picked up my Palm Pilot and started tapping, looking for another day to reschedule our postponed lunch. "What about tomorrow—assuming I still have a job?"

"Today is Natalie's day off. I don't think the fair doctor could make it tomorrow. Besides, you canceled on us last time."

My fingers paused midtap and hovered over the glass screen while Drew's words replayed in my head. *You make lunch plans with your friends but always cancel because something comes up at work.* Was I really that bad? And, almost worse, that obvious?

"Can we do it today at eleven?" I almost wished Drew was there to witness my flagrantly un-Jane-like behavior. Not that I cared any longer what he thought of me.

"That works for me. The only thing I've got to schedule around is Gymboree and naptime. What'll it be? Cheesecake Factory?"

"Great. I'll meet you guys there at eleven—and I meant what I said. No talk of last night or Teddy Rock."

Liv reluctantly agreed and emerged from the solitude of her bathroom. "I'll call Nat. See you at eleven."

I flipped open the heavy leather desk calendar Arthur gave me every year for Christmas. He hadn't quite embraced the idea of digital organizers, and I hadn't embraced the idea of telling my managing partner that I didn't need a ten-pound faux alligator–embossed book taking up space on my desk. So, every year I thanked him, replaced last year's gift with the new one, and used the otherwise blank pages to keep a running tally of my billable hours.

I quickly turned to the familiar page clearly identified by the thin gold satin ribbon bookmark attached to the book's spine. And there it was. Decision day.

My partnership review was scheduled at almost the exact midpoint of the year, which meant that I should have completed at least half of the twenty two hundred hours I was expected to bill annually. My fingers worked their way backward through the pages until I reached yesterday, where I'd scrawled the number 1302.5 before leaving last night. It was only May and I was more than halfway to meeting my target, but I doubted that would sway Arthur very much when he heard about last night's exhibition.

"Jane." Sandy tapped lightly on my door a few times and opened it a crack. "Arthur would like to see you in his office."

I didn't require a hall pass, and there wasn't a hard wooden bench against the wall outside his office, but from the way Sandy relayed Arthur's message, I felt as if I was being called into the principal's office. Without even asking, I could tell from the pained look on Sandy's face that she knew. I imagined Sandy had the same look as someone sent to summon a defeated gladiator into the lion pit. Unfortunately, the only armor protecting me from a gruesome demise was my Max Mara suit.

I passed Sandy and walked proudly down the hall, determined to take my punishment like a grown-up. On my way to Arthur's office, I passed Michael Sullivan, head of our intellectual property practice. I straightened up and pulled my shoulders back. "Michael." I nodded and tried to look like I was calculating taxation rates in my head instead of making my way to Arthur's office to be scolded like a naughty child.

He nodded in return. "Janey." Janey. Not Jane. Not just a polite hello. Freaking Janey! I looked back at Michael, but instead of catching the back of his thinning blond hair I caught a glimpse of him checking out my ass.

That was it. I decided to make a quick detour.

"How could you do that to me?" I demanded, slamming the conference room door behind me. "How could you tell Tara about last night when I asked you not to?"

"I didn't tell anyone, Jane." Drew answered calmly, barely even registering a reaction to the door still reverberating in its frame.

"You must have told someone. Tara's giving me looks like I'm some sorority sister she wants to do keg stands with, Michael practically just slapped me on the ass on his way down the hall, and now Arthur wants to see me in his office."

Drew didn't answer. Instead he reached across the conference table for the newspaper. "Have you seen this?" he asked, thumbing through the pages until he found what he was looking for. "That's probably not the best picture. I thought you looked better in person."

I grabbed the paper out of his hand and looked down to find a black-and-white photo with the caption HERE'S JANEY! taking up one-quarter of the entertainment page.

There I was. Onstage. With Big D cheering on the crowd while I stood next to him looking like I'd just found out I had a yeast infection.

"I'm sorry," Drew apologized, even though none of this was his fault. "I guess I'm not the only one who knows now."

I didn't even attempt to read the article. There was nothing it could say that would make this any better. In fact, it could only make it worse. Darcy didn't have to tell her father. He'd find out just like Kitty and every one of my clients—by reading this morning's news. "I'll take care of it," I replied more calmly, my voice hiding the fact that my heart was running a marathon in my chest.

I took the long way to Arthur's office to give myself some extra time to prepare an explanation. I had to figure out how the executor of a billion-dollar estate gave Teddy Rock an invitation to sin.

At least I didn't find out about the *Sun-Times* article from Arthur. That had to give me some sort of advantage. Although at the moment, I wasn't sure what that could be.

When I arrived at Arthur's door, I could see he was on the phone. Although only the high back of his leather chair was visible from where I stood in the hallway, two wingtips were propped up on his credenza and the black corkscrew of the telephone cord was stretched across his desk.

I knocked lightly on Arthur's door and he swung around to face me and waved me in. I'd decided that the best defense wasn't the best offense. In this case, begging forgiveness was probably my best option. So much for taking it like a grown-up.

When he finally hung up, I didn't even wait for him to start in on me.

"Arthur, I'm so sorry," I apologized.

Arthur slowly nodded, acknowledging my obvious regret as he unwrapped a strawberry lollipop. Last year he quit smoking and took up Dum Dums. "I've got to admit, Jane, I was more than a little surprised when I picked up this morning's paper."

"You have to know I'd never do anything that would put the firm's reputation in jeopardy," I continued, the words tumbling out over one another. "You have to know that, Arthur."

"We've never had one of our associates show up in the entertainment section of the *Sun-Times* before, Jane." Arthur lodged the lollipop in his right cheek as he spoke, looking like a lopsided chipmunk. You'd think this would be distracting, but, like everyone else in the firm, I was used to it by now. Besides, the idea that my career was circling around the toilet bowl at the moment was more than enough to keep my attention.

"I realize that. My brother organized a little surprise for me last night at his bar. I swear I had no idea what he was up to."

"From what I've heard, it wasn't so little. A few people said you were on a radio show, too." Arthur held up the *Sun-Times* on his desk, as if putting forth a piece of evidence. "So, tell me, what's this I read about you dating this Teddy Rock fellow?"

"I didn't date him, Arthur. We knew each other as kids."

"It says here that he wrote a song about you." Arthur thumbed through the paper until he came to the page he was looking for. "Interesting song."

Arthur cleared his throat and placed the two half-moons of his reading glasses on his nose before reciting the lyrics on the page in front of him.

> *Even without touching, I felt your skin*
> *Calling me, taunting me, time to begin*
> *I took your hand, let you lead me astray*
> *Willingly let you have your way*
> *And now I close my eyes, bringing you back to me*
> *Like the stars we wished upon, only a memory*

He stopped reading and peered over the rims of his glasses. "Sounds like you were more than just friends."

"Arthur, we were barely friends. I guarantee that there will be no more stunts like last night. I'll call Kitty and other key clients to explain. I'm not going to put my practice at risk," I assured him.

"Risk?" Arthur stood up and came around to my side of the desk. He sat on the corner and crossed his arms, his feet dangling in midair like a child's. "I was thinking of it as more of an opportunity."

"A what?" I asked, gaping at the grin on Arthur's face. He actually looked thrilled!

"An opportunity. Jane, you'd be entering a realm Becker, Bishop and Deane has never had access to before. Entertainers have significant assets that need protecting, not to mention other legal needs, and it could open up a whole new client base for us."

Arthur reached over and picked up the *Sun-Times*, rereading the brief article. "I want you to talk to Teddy Rock," he told me, handing over the newspaper.

"I don't even really know the guy. I haven't seen him in over twenty years," I practically stammered. "Besides, I don't even know if Teddy Rock has any assets left from his 'Janey 245' days."

"Maybe not, but if he's really trying to reignite his career, this may be an ideal opportunity to get in before the other firms."

"Arthur, like I said, I don't even really know him."

"So, get to know him," he insisted.

"I don't think that's such a good idea. Rock stars aren't exactly my forte. Besides, I'd like to maintain my professional reputation. How would the others look at me?"

"Ever hear of Johnnie Cochran? Robert Shapiro?"

"Landing on an *E! True Hollywood Story* was never one of my professional goals."

Arthur crossed his arms over his chest and shook his head at me. "True, but becoming a partner is." Arthur had made his point and managed to put me in my place. And that place was one of an associate approaching her review. "Kitty's a significant client, Jane, but given the lawsuit and the fact that sometime in the near future her son will take over where Kitty leaves off, it would be in your best interest to diversify your client base, don't you think?"

I was thinking that Arthur wasn't giving me a choice.

"Come on, Jane," he continued, more jovially. "I think you're making a bigger deal out of this than it needs to be. I'm not asking you to compromise your professional integrity. I'm just asking you to make a little phone call, talk with the guy. How bad could it be?"

I guess I was about to find out.

Olivia was waiting for me by the hostess stand when I arrived. Despite the large lunchtime crowd waiting for tables, we were seated almost immediately. I suspected that the boys' animated descriptions of the cheesecakes in the display case helped move us to the front of the line. Really, how many times could the hostess put up with George declaring, *It looks like poopie,* while pointing to a double chocolate mousse cheesecake?

The boys climbed into the booth and Olivia and I flanked them on either side, creating a formidable barrier designed to keep them contained.

"What's that?" I asked, pointing to the thin, white paper-wrapped tube Ethan was waving at George.

"My sword," Ethan announced, proudly.

I removed the Tampax weapon from his hand and passed it across the table to Liv, who tried to explain why the paper-wrapped cylinder was not an appropriate toy.

Ethan quickly lost interest and moved on to the next distraction. Liv stuffed the Tampax back in her purse and hung her head in her hands for a few seconds before looking up again.

"You know the difference between me and my parents?" she asked with the defeated tone of a woman outnumbered by her children. "I feel the need to explain to a three-year-old why he can't play with feminine protection."

We waited for Natalie and watched the boys color their placemats with the crayons Liv kept stashed in her purse. I knew Olivia was silent on purpose, trying to wear me down. Every few seconds she'd stare at me, as if attempting some Jedi mind trick. She wanted to hear about Teddy and Sam's, and while she'd promised not to talk about it, that didn't mean she couldn't try to get me to bring it up.

And I wasn't going to do that. I was still trying to digest the idea that Arthur expected me to find Teddy Rock. I wanted to put the whole fiasco out of my mind, not rehash last night minute by minute. In less than twenty-four hours, Teddy had permeated every part of my life, and the last thing I wanted to do was talk about him for the next hour.

And it must have been killing her. Liv must have warned Natalie, too, because she arrived shortly after we'd gotten the boys settled into their booster seats and didn't mutter a word about Janey. She just offered an apology for keeping us waiting. As usual.

Natalie always apologized for being late before glancing down at her beeper as if to remind us that doctors shouldn't be subject to the punctuality expectations of mere mortals. But I knew that her tardiness was less medical miracle and more a tactic she used to ensure that the boys were appropriately restrained and under control before she had to share their air space. Children made Natalie nervous, which would make one think that a career as an ob-gyn was an ill-conceived choice, but that never seemed to occur to her. You'd also think that all that time spent in the delivery room coaxing babies out of the womb would make her immune to the chaos kids create. Instead she still

saw them as slippery little creatures not to be trusted unless they were swad-
dled within an inch of their lives.

As usual, Natalie's straight auburn hair was held back with a navy
bandana—I suspected a last resort should the boys need to be restrained or
gagged. Her standard day-off outfit consisted of jean overalls and a short-
sleeved polo shirt that was so old the logo had unraveled to a point where it
was a headless horseman beating a two legged animal with a piece of kin-
dling. Instead of looking like a preppy country club doctor, Natalie was a
glaring *Glamour* DON'T with a beeper and privileges at Northwestern Memorial Hospital.

We gave the harried waitress our order and Natalie filled us in on her life,
which meant mostly her job, all the while keeping an eye on George and
Ethan.

"What's going on with that secret agent you were dating?" Liv asked, removing a straw that George was pushing up his nose.

Natalie hesitated before answering.

"First of all, he was a federal marshal," Natalie clarified before reaching to
take a bread knife out of George's hand. "Second of all, he's missing in action."

"Oh my God, what happened? Witness protection? Undercover assign-
ment?" Ever since she had the twins and handed in her resignation at the firm,
Olivia listened raptly to Natalie's dating escapades and my legal entangle-
ments. She demanded that we share every detail of an experience, every facet
of a conversation, until she could picture exactly what she'd missed out on,
like a teenager with mono who had to skip the school dance.

"He should have such an excuse. Nope, he just never called me after our
second date." Natalie reached over to take the salt away from Ethan, who was
shaking it into George's hair like a dandruff commercial gone bad. "Are you
sure they're okay in those booster seats?"

"Yeah, they're fine," Olivia assured her. "So, why don't you just call him?"

Natalie shrugged and stabbed a fork into her Caesar salad. "Are you kidding me? No, thanks. If I'm going to waste my time with a guy, he better have
something to offer besides the Tommy Lee Jones autograph he snagged during filming of *The Fugitive*." She pointed to George. "Liv?"

Olivia wrestled the ketchup away from George, who was about to use the
condiment for finger paint.

"My winkie has to go," Ethan whined, holding himself with an urgency that meant Olivia had about two minutes to get him to the bathroom or face the unpleasant and public consequences.

"Winkie?" Natalie repeated, shaking her head at Olivia. As a doctor she had little patience for anyone who didn't take a purely clinical approach to bodily functions.

"Sorry. I'm not quite ready to arm them with another word they can shout at the top of their lungs in the grocery store. The last thing I need is a chorus of *penis* sung repeatedly in the produce aisle."

Natalie took another piece of bread from the basket. "Remind me never to go shopping with you."

While Liv took Ethan to the bathroom, we shared supervision of George, who, under the watchful and intolerant eyes of Natalie, squirmed in the booth like an ant under a magnifying glass.

"Do you want to talk about last night?" Nat asked, briefly taking her gaze off George.

"No."

She went back to staring at the squirmy three-year-old, while George looked at me with big brown eyes, probably hoping I'd say yes and give him a break. He wasn't that lucky.

Natalie had actually delivered George and Ethan, although she didn't seem to have any particular affection for either one of them beyond the fact that they were Liv's kids. It wasn't that Natalie was detached from the idea that there were children running around that she'd helped bring into this world, so much as she saw her job as done once their pink little bodies were shrieking as they gasped for air and their bottoms were covered in Pampers.

I introduced Natalie to Olivia shortly after I started at Becker, Bishop & Deane. Olivia was three years older, and my first "real world" friend. Instead of bonding over a package of ramen noodles or five-dollar pitchers of beer, our friendship was sealed the day Olivia expressed the international sign of friendship, an olive branch shared between women, if you will—she passed me a roll of toilet paper under the stalls and spared me the unpleasant task of drip drying.

When Liv and Ethan finally returned from their trip to the bathroom, George was thankful for the reinforcement, and the boys kept busy building log cabins with their French fries.

"Drew didn't tell Arthur," I finally announced. "He saw the article in the *Sun-Times*."

Liv nodded cautiously, waiting to see whether I was ready to talk about my night at Sam's. "Well, that explains it, I guess."

"So, what was with all the warnings about Drew Weston?" I asked her. "You were totally off base."

"Why, is he bald and paunchy now?"

"No, you were right on with the physical description, but he never had sex with the temp in the copy room."

"How do you know?"

"I asked him."

"You asked him? How did that topic come up, if I may ask? A quick, *Hey, Drew, how's that motion to dismiss going, and, by the way, when you fucked the temp on the copy machine did you refill the toner?*"

"No, I brought it up after he mentioned that I had something of a reputation around the office, too."

Olivia rolled her eyes at me. "I'm sure your reputation pales by comparison."

"He called me a workhorse and practically made it sound like my idea of fun is watching C-SPAN while I alphabetize my spice rack."

"You don't watch C-SPAN, do you?"

"Only if there's nothing else on, but it's not like I enjoy it. And I don't even own a spice rack, but that's not the point. He made me sound so serious."

"That's a good thing, right?" Natalie asked. "Isn't your review coming up?"

Liv's shoe bumped Nat's shin a little harder than necessary, and she reached down to rub her injury. Nat turned to Liv and mouthed *What?* Liv responded with a discreet swipe of an index finger across her throat, the universal signal for someone to shut up.

They really were trying so hard to be good. I took a bite of my chicken salad sandwich. "Six weeks from Thursday."

"God, I remember that whole waiting game," Olivia remarked wistfully after she saw I wasn't freaking out. "Trying to figure out what the committee is saying about you when you're not around and wondering whether or not the last seven years of your life were a complete waste of time."

"Please, you had it made after the Arctic Springs merger. You were always an overachiever. Even when it came to kids you couldn't be like everyone else. One baby just wasn't good enough, you had to have two."

"Yeah, and look where it got me." Olivia waved her hands in the direction of two little boys on the verge of using their hot dogs as dueling instruments. "Do you think they care if I was a partner in a prestigious law firm? Or that people used to ask for my opinion on things besides whether or not their macaroni and cheese tastes funny?"

"Don't blame the boys. Blame it on the six martinis you downed at Gibson's and the drunken belief that as long as a diaphragm is in the same room with you, it works."

"Can we please talk about something besides my drinking habits and unprotected sex?"

George and Ethan weren't exactly planned. In fact, Olivia had done her best to plan *not* to have children, the drunken incident after dinner at Gibson's notwithstanding. Not that she and Bill wouldn't have gotten married anyway—they'd been dating for almost five years—but she seemed to have so much to accomplish on her to-do list that kids weren't even on the first page. And I knew for a fact that a shotgun wedding definitely wasn't something Olivia wanted announced in her Princeton alumni magazine.

"So, what do you two think? Is Drew right? Am I just a boring lawyer with no life?"

"Is that what he said?" Natalie asked.

"Not exactly, but I think it was pretty obvious that's what he meant."

"I wouldn't say you're boring, just"—Nat paused, searching for a word—"focused."

"Directed," Olivia added. "You're very directed."

"Those aren't exactly thrilling endorsements." I watched George and Ethan taunt each other with pickle spears and tried to remember one of my better nonboring moments.

Liv nodded and gave me a satisfied smirk. "Ah, now I get it."

"Get what?"

"Why you asked Drew to go to Sam's. You wanted to show him that he was wrong about you."

"He *was* wrong about me," I answered, not denying Liv's observation. I turned to Nat. "Right?"

She wasn't rushing to my defense.

"I took belly dancing in high school, you know," I offered up as evidence.

Liv wasn't believing any of it. "You did not."

"Yes, I did. Actually it was called Middle Eastern dance, but that's what it was—belly dancing. It was part of my first-semester senior seminar on world cultures."

"Somehow I can't see you in harem pants shaking your ass to the rhythm of finger cymbals."

"The finger cymbals were backordered, so we had to go without for a few weeks. I made my own with the lids of two Starkist cans and rubber bands. They sounded pretty good." It was true, they did sound pretty good. They also garnered me a captive audience with my cat, Pumpkin, who rubbed against my leg and purred when I practiced my dancing in my room. No matter how hard I tried, I couldn't get rid of the tuna smell completely. "And I didn't have harem pants. I tied a bunch of my mom's scarves around my waist instead."

"Let me get this straight. You fastened tuna can lids between your fingers with rubber bands, made a makeshift skirt out of scarves and belly danced like something out of *I Dream of Jeannie*?" Nat attempted to process the information. "Okay, you've proved your point. You're not boring. You're weird."

Not weird. Resourceful.

"So, what, you don't think I'm the Janey from Teddy Rock's song?"

Liv paused midbite and looked up from her turkey club. "Is this where we stop pretending that last night didn't happen?" she asked me.

"Yes."

"Finally!" Liv exclaimed. "Jesus, I was beginning to think I'd never get the whole story."

"Andy probably told you everything already."

When she heard Andy's name, Natalie stopped monitoring Ethan's sodium intake. She may have had little patience for children, but Natalie had an unexplainable fascination with the biggest child of all—my brother.

"He was watching a show and Teddy Rock was talking about the girl who inspired the song," I continued. "Andy seems to think that it sounds a lot like me."

Natalie leaned in and patted my hand, like she was talking to a delusional patient. She didn't suffer hypochondriacs well. "I know this guy, Drew's, comments bugged you, but don't you think that's a little wishful thinking, Jane?"

"Wishful thinking?"

"Sure," Liv agreed. "Who hasn't wanted some guy to sit bent over a guitar composing a love song about her?" Natalie and I stared blankly at Olivia and she shrugged. "Well, I have."

"I can assure you both, I've never wanted to be a notch on some rock star's bedpost."

Olivia leaned forward and lowered her voice so the boys couldn't hear her. "Have you seen Teddy Rock?" she asked, raising her eyebrows. "If I was going to be someone's notch, he'd be at the top of my list."

"Really?" Nat dismissed the idea with a wave of her fork. "I was more of a Bon Jovi girl."

Liv considered this for a minute. "Bon Jovi? I guess I can see that, but he's only like five foot six, you know."

"That's okay. I'm only five four. What about you, Jane?"

"What about me?"

"Bon Jovi or Teddy Rock? It has to be one or the other."

"Why?"

"Because that's just the way it is. You either like chocolate or vanilla. Mary Ann or Ginger. Shawn Cassidy or Leif Garrett. The Brady Bunch or the Partridge Family. Teddy Rock or Jon Bon Jovi," Liv explained, as if this was a universally accepted duality.

"Does this really matter right now?" I asked, even though Liv was still waiting for my answer.

Olivia wiped a gob of ketchup from the corner of Ethan's mouth. "Fine."

"So why would Teddy Rock write a song about you?" Nat asked. "Were you living some double secret life as a groupie that I wasn't aware of? Studious math major by day, big-haired rocker chick by night?" Natalie grinned, apparently trying to picture me wearing suede fringed boots and an I ♥ TEDDY ROCK tattoo.

I repeated the supporting evidence behind Andy's theory.

"Wait a minute, here." Liv held up her hands like a cop at an intersection. "If what Andy's saying is true, how could you have not known you were Janey 245?"

"I was still a little out of it my freshman year."

They nodded. My explanation appeased their implication that I was clueless, and they both looked a little chastened by my reminder. After all, my dad had died only ten months before I left for college. I couldn't be expected to be infatuated with rock music's flavor of the day when I was still trying to come to terms with the idea that my father wasn't coming back.

"Do you think Andy's wrong?" I asked.

"Look, does it really matter? Andy got his publicity for the bar, you'll smooth this over with Arthur and your life will resume its regularly scheduled programming." Liv wiped her hands on her napkin. "It's over."

"No, it's not. Arthur wants me to find Teddy Rock and see if he needs any legal services."

"So, now Arthur's pimping you?" Nat joked. "Didn't you give all your feather boas and vinyl miniskirts away to Goodwill?"

"I'm glad you find this so amusing, but I'm serious. He wants me to see if there's any potential business. This whole thing is just unreal."

Olivia sat back in the booth and studied me. "Why do you find this so unbelievable?"

"Come on, look at me. Look at how Drew sees me. Look at how Andy sees me. Even Arthur's reaction to this whole thing. *Jane's up onstage removing articles of clothing and belting out the chorus to a song about some wild woman—quick, see if she can get us some more business.*" I shook my head. "Obviously I'm not exactly the type of woman people write songs about."

"And what type of women *do* they write songs about?"

"You've seen the videos, Liv. They're the doe-eyed, adoring types who hang on a guy's every word. Or they're straddling the hood of a Jaguar in a spandex miniskirt. They're the types who dig their stilettos in a man's thigh while they're having sex. Against a wall. In an alley." I shook my head. "The whole idea that maybe Teddy saw me like that is a little disconcerting, to say the least. Not to mention the slight crimping effect this could have on my career. There isn't big demand for a lawyer with stars in her eyes."

Olivia reached across the table and removed a French fry from Ethan's ear. "Hey, a little spontaneous sex never killed anyone, although an alley wouldn't be my first choice. Would you prefer that Janey 245 was respectable and responsible?"

I didn't know what I preferred. Last night, up onstage, this all seemed like such a great idea. I was in control of Janey. Now Janey was in control of me.

"Would you have preferred he wrote a song about the smartest girl in class who finished her work on time, was always first in line, and never took a sick day?" Liv asked.

"Come on, Liv. *Wanton thighs?*"

"What?"

"You know, the lyrics—*reached to touch your wanton thighs, look into your melting eyes?*"

"I always thought it was *I want your thighs.*"

Natalie looked up from her salad. "You know that Prince song?" She hummed the tune until we nodded. "I always thought he was singing, *She wore raspberries and grapes*."

Liv laughed. "I thought it was *She wants raspberry sorbet*."

"That doesn't make any sense. Why would she buy raspberry sorbet from a secondhand store?"

"Hello," I interrupted, tapping my fork on my water glass. "Can we please focus here?"

Liv turned her attention back to the matter at hand. "In any case, I'd be flattered."

Maybe Olivia had a point. There had to be inspirational women who had more going for them than their abnormal breast-to-waist ratio and an ability to pole dance. Wanton thighs weren't that bad. They were certainly better than jiggly thighs. Or dimply thighs. I remembered reading somewhere that Alanis Morissette had written her first angst-ridden, man-hating anthem about that nerdy blond guy on *Full House*, the one who did the Bullwinkle impersonation. We're talking about a guy who imitated a moose and played a supporting role to Bob Saget and the Olsen twins, and yet he managed to inspire lyrics in Alanis Morissette—an independent, modern woman with obvious talent—that had her questioning whether the Bullwinkle impersonator's new girlfriend was giving him a blow job in movie theaters. Obviously, musicians got their inspiration from all types of people. "So, you don't think Andy's just making this up?"

"It is a little coincidental, isn't it? The guy lived across the street from you. And there's the name," Natalie pointed out, as if running down a list of symptoms. "But Jane is a common name, right?"

"Not really," I answered a little too quickly. "I was the only Jane in my school."

"And then there's your address and the fact that he said it was about a girl he knew when he was a boy."

"Not just a girl he knew. A girl who lived in his neighborhood," I added, beginning to wonder why I was defending the very idea I'd dismissed three days ago.

"Your address was 245 Memorial Circle?"

I nodded. "Yep, 245. Just like the song."

"And we're sure that Theodore Brockford is Teddy Rock?"

"Absolutely. Andy said the show did a whole segment on how Teddy changed his name and moved to LA hoping to make it big."

Listening to Natalie tick off the facts like that, I was almost convinced Andy was right. There were an awful lot of coincidences.

I let my fingers brush my cheek under the guise of patting my mouth with my napkin. I'd never thought about it before, but one could certainly describe my skin as satiny if they wanted to stretch the metaphor a little, although I thought my lips were more rosy than ruby.

Liv and I waited for Natalie's scientific conclusion, but all she did was shrug and continue to munch on her Caesar salad while she pondered the idea. "I can't imagine you with stars in your eyes, but maybe."

"You really think so?" I asked, my voice sounding more hopeful than I'd intended.

"I said maybe," Natalie reiterated.

"It's got to be you," Olivia announced, a little too loudly. George and Ethan looked up from their French fry construction projects and stared at me.

"Who is Jane, Mommy?" George asked.

"She's famous," Olivia told the boys.

"She's like Elmo," George told Ethan, and they started giggling.

"You're our very own Elmo," Olivia repeated. "Our Janey, the girl Teddy Rock couldn't forget. Imagine that."

Yeah, imagine that.

Is Teddy Coming Between Julia and Kiefer?

That's the question everyone's asking. It all started when Julia Roberts attended a launch party for Kick Records' newest act, Famous Last Words, and was seen huddled in a corner with Teddy Rock. Reps for the actress and fiancé Kiefer Sutherland deny reports that the rocker and America's sweetheart left the party together, but onlookers say the two seemed like more than just friends. "There were defi-nitely sparks flying," says a Kick Records source, who asked to remain anonymous. "If I were Kiefer, I'd be worried."

Roberts and Sutherland met on the set of *Flatliners* and announced their engagement last August. The couple have a June 14 wedding planned. But Rock and Roberts have been seen around LA together in past weeks, and word is, the two are getting too close for comfort.

"From the way Teddy and Julia were carrying on, I'd be surprised if the wedding went off without a hitch," says the source. "With Teddy Rock, where there's smoke, there's usually fire."

CHAPTER EIGHT

It was one thing for Andy to come up with this whole idea about being Janey, and even for Arthur to want me to try to leverage the opportunity. But Liv and Nat were rational people, and if they thought there was something to this, then there had to be. And it was confusing the hell out of me. From one minute to the next my feelings about Janey changed. It was like balancing on a teeter-totter—one minute I was up in the air waving my hands and telling everyone to look at me, and the next I was smacking my ass on the ground and crying foul. Lunch with Natalie and Olivia had helped. Not a whole lot, but enough. And one thing was clear. I was going to have to find Teddy Rock.

Instead of jumping into a cab and rushing back to the office, I decided to walk back and let it all sink in. As I got closer to my block I started to notice how different everything looked. Cafés that usually had CLOSED signs hanging in darkened windows when I arrived for work were packed with people ordering lunch. Stores that shielded their empty windows with metal bars at night now displayed shoes and clothes and luggage, inviting people in to browse.

The shoeshine stands that had only ever been empty red leather chairs to me were now filled with businessmen reading newspapers while their loafers got a polish. This was the downtown I never saw anymore, the one that was more than just empty brick facades, darkened windows and closed signs. In the mornings, the few people I passed on the sidewalk were rushing to early meetings while they talked into ear pieces curled around their ears, every one attached to a cell phone wire. But in the middle of the day it was different. People walked more slowly and carried on conversations in pairs or trios. They sat on benches and ate sandwiches out of white paper bags while laughing with friends. I felt like a bear coming out of hibernation.

Was I so focused and directed, in the kind words of Liv and Nat, so unwilling to be distracted, that I'd stopped noticing life going on around me?

As I passed the Starbucks attached to my building, knuckles rapped on the window and caught my attention. I stopped and peered inside, cupping my hands around my eyes to avoid the glare. And what I found were two brown eyes staring right back at me.

Come in, Drew mouthed, pointing toward the door. I couldn't ignore him, we were practically touching noses. Suddenly I hoped that mine wouldn't leave some greasy skid mark behind. Besides, I owed him an apology for this morning. It wasn't his fault Arthur and everyone in the office found out about Sam's. It was mine.

I found the door and went inside, where I spotted Drew at the window table, sipping a tall coffee while he picked through a bag of Doritos. I guess there was only so long a guy could subsist on leftover pastries.

"Look, I'm sorry about this morning," I apologized when I reached him. "I shouldn't have assumed you told Tara."

Drew finished sipping his coffee and placed the cup down on the table in front of him. "Come on, you really didn't think I'd tell Tara of all people, did you?"

"I just figured you were the only one who could have said anything."

"I told you I'd keep it to myself. Although I have to admit, seeing you up onstage like that—it was a whole side of you I never thought existed." Drew held out his bag of Doritos. "Want one?"

"That's a pretty odd combination. They don't even sell Doritos here."

"I know. I snuck it in. It's contraband." He removed another large, cheesy triangle from the bag. "Last chance before I polish these off by myself."

I shook my head. My first kiss with Chris Booker had been a nacho cheese–filled experience that I'd never quite gotten over. He'd led me down Liz Buffino's basement stairs after the neck of the Orange Crush bottle landed on me. We were sitting on the bottom step in the dark, the cold cement floor quickly working its way through the soles of my Keds, when Chris slipped his tongue between my lips. Instead of thinking about tipping my head to the side so our noses didn't knock or wiping the spit beginning to dribble down my chin, all I could think about was the tangy taste of his Dorito breath and how I'd never be able to eat the snack chips again. Even Cool Ranch still gave me the shivers.

"No, thanks. I'm full. Had lunch with some friends today." I patted my stomach. "You know how it is when you have lunch with friends; you always eat more than you want to."

I was sure he got the message. The only way I could have been more obvious was if I brought him the leftovers and a signed affidavit that said, yes, Jane Marlow did leave her desk and have lunch with friends.

"I'm surprised you could find the time."

That was me, a one-woman surprise party. I stopped short of demonstrating a Middle Eastern belly roll. "Well, I should be getting back. I just wanted to apologize."

"Apology accepted, but there's something else I wanted to talk to you about. Darcy's attorneys have presented a motion to freeze the assets of the Farnsworth Foundation."

My lunch turned over in my stomach as the teeter-totter once again plunged to the ground.

"What do they think Kitty's going to do, drain the funds of her own foundation?" I heard my voice rising and caught a few stares from waiting customers. I lowered my voice. "She established that foundation. She gives out hundreds of millions of dollars in grants with that foundation."

"It's not black-and-white, Jane. It never is. Unfortunately, everything is left up to interpretation."

But it's not supposed to be, I wanted to say. If you couldn't count on the law being cut-and-dried, then what was the point? Either the trust documents were valid or they weren't. Either Darcy is right or she isn't. Either you cared enough to take care of your family before you died or you didn't. It all sounded pretty black-and-white to me.

"In any case, we should meet with Kitty and tell her what's going on," Drew continued, wiping the orange dust off his fingers.

"I'll set something up for Monday."

I turned to leave, but Drew stopped me. "Hey, hold on."

"Was there something else?"

"No, not really. I just wanted to say that I'm looking forward to playing softball on Saturday. You're our mascot, right?"

"Right. I'll be the one in the big fuzzy bear costume doing back hand-springs across the infield."

Drew crumpled up his Doritos bag and laughed.

"I was just kidding about the handsprings," I told him.

"Does that mean you weren't kidding about the bear costume?"

This time it was my turn to laugh.

Drew smiled. "Anyway, thanks for letting me join the team."

"You don't have to thank me; it's Andy's team."

"Still, you probably weren't planning on having anyone from the firm on Sam's Sluggers."

"That's okay." There were a lot of things I hadn't planned on, but that didn't seem to matter anymore.

"Your phone's been ringing off the hook," Sandy told me when I returned from lunch. "Is everything okay?"

"Yeah, I think so." I took the stack of pink message slips she held in her hand.

"Most of those are just local media wanting to interview you—the *Reader*, *Chicago* magazine, some TV stations. I told them you were unavailable. And Kitty called; she was wondering if you could reschedule for Monday at her house. She's still a little under the weather. I put all the other calls through to your voice mail." Sandy watched me tentatively, waiting to see whether I'd offer to give her some sort of explanation.

"I guess you're wondering what's going on."

"Not if the *Sun-Times* article posted on the bulletin board in the coffee room sums it up."

I nodded. "That's pretty much the whole story."

"Why didn't you tell me sooner?"

"I didn't know."

Sandy wasn't quite buying it. "How could you not know you were the subject of one of the biggest hit songs ever?"

I shrugged. "You know me. Would you have thought I was Janey?"

Sandy didn't answer. I'd made my point.

"You didn't happen to remove the article from the bulletin board, did you?" I asked.

"I figured even if you were Janey you wouldn't want that article up there for everyone to see." Sandy reached into her desk drawer and handed over the torn page. "I think I was a little too late, though. Tara asked me if I thought you'd be willing to do a lunch and learn. I asked her what she expected us to learn and she said, *Everything about Teddy Rock, of course.*" Sandy tossed her hair back in a pretty convincing imitation of Tara. If only she had the two-inch acrylic fingernails with tiger stripes.

"That would be one lunch without much learning." What did I really know about Teddy? That he caught the school bus on the corner of Memorial Circle and Pepperidge Lane? "I hope you told her no."

"Of course."

I took the paper and examined the picture of me taken less than twenty-four hours ago. I hoped that Drew wasn't just being nice when he said that I looked better in person. It wasn't possible to look any worse. Why couldn't the photographer have waited a little while until the shock of Big D and the crowd wore off? If he'd snapped a picture just ten minutes later he would have captured someone settling into the role of Janey—or maybe even someone who looked like she was actually well suited to the part.

"Thanks for the warning." I folded the article in half and stuffed it in my pocket. "If you see any more of these floating around, can you do me a favor and take them?"

"Sure."

I thanked Sandy and retreated to my office, where I took the article out and placed it in a manila folder I labeled JANEY with a black Sharpie. It wasn't so much that I wanted to save the article, even though if Drew or Andy saw me they'd think I was preparing to archive the page between acid-free paper, after which I'd catalog it along with my other keepsakes. And it wasn't so much that I wanted to keep people from reading the article. What with the radio interview and newspaper and now all the reporters calling, word was already out. I didn't have a folder big enough to keep everyone from finding out. No, what bothered me more than the article was that damn picture.

I hated it. It looked nothing like Janey. And I hoped—I really did—that it also looked nothing like me. Because the idea that that frightened woman even vaguely resembled me was more unsettling than the possibility that I inspired Teddy's song.

I sorted through the messages—Sandy wasn't kidding, there had to be at least fourteen of them—and read the names and phone numbers of people who just yesterday wouldn't have given me the time of day. It was mind-boggling to think that even though I was sitting in the same black leather desk chair, behind the same desk, in the same office, everything was different. *I* was different. I was newsworthy. I was someone a radio station wanted to interview, someone Teddy's fans wanted to meet, someone the mail room staff thought was cool. It was like trying to fathom the idea that even while you're waiting in rush hour traffic at the O'Hare tollbooth, the earth is rotating at over one thousand miles per hour.

When had it all changed? The night Andy called about *Off the Record*? That first meeting with Drew? The morning the paper hit the newsstands? The moment I stepped out onstage?

A single moment. Is that all it took to change your life?

I grabbed a pencil and drew a straight line across my desk blotter, the flat, finite line immediately giving me a sense of control. This was where being a math major came in handy, not so much because I wanted to resolve a mathematical equation as because I liked the idea of having answers. English, psychology, sociology—they all left the answers up to interpretation. They're subjective. In one class I took we were expected to interpret the symbols and abstract concepts in Blake's poetry, and it frustrated the hell out of me. "Tyger, tyger burning bright?" How could I even begin to deal with a poem when the writer didn't even spell *tiger* correctly? But math provided absolutes. Three plus three will always equal six. A circle will always be three hundred and sixty degrees. An isosceles triangle always has two equal sides. Speculation and interpretation had no place in math.

I attempted to graph the events, to pinpoint the exact moment things changed, but instead of a neat and clean answer, an identifiable point at which Jane and Janey intersected, I wound up with a jumble of conspiring circumstances.

The red blinking light on my phone reminded me that, even though I was immortalized in Teddy Rock's only hit song, I still had voice mails waiting. I punched in my password, picked up the pencil to take notes and listened.

"Jane, this is Mrs. Winston across the hall." She stopped talking and spent the next few minutes clearing the phlegm from her throat. "I'm calling on behalf of the condo board. I ran into Mr. Hanson in the lobby this morning and he was telling me about the cabaret show you put on last night. We're a little concerned about—"

My finger found the star key and deleted Mrs. Winston's concern. As far as *my* concerns went, Mrs. Winston was at the bottom of my list right now.

I listened for the second message. "Hi, Jane. It's Sam. Saw the paper this morning. I know you're busy so I'll let you go. I just wanted to say thanks. I hope we didn't create too much trouble for you at work."

Trouble; is that what this was? It sure seemed that way this morning when Michael Sullivan was checking out my ass. But now it was something else. Arthur thought it was an opportunity. Liv thought it was flattering. Robert and the guys from the mail room thought it was cool. But Darcy was probably the one who summed it all up the best—it was unbelievable.

I saved Sam's message and starting dialing the phone. I'd dealt with the repercussions of last night all day, and Andy was probably still in bed unaware of the commotion he'd caused. It was time to call the person who started all this in the first place.

"Do you have any idea what you did last night?" I asked, not even giving Andy a chance to say hello.

"I know that Sam's Place had its best night in fifteen years, if that's what you mean."

"That's not what I mean and you know it. Arthur knows about Teddy Rock. The receptionist knows about Teddy Rock. The guys in the mail room are high-fiving me, for God's sake. Have you seen today's paper?"

"Jane, I'm still in bed. It's barely one o'clock and my phone's been ringing all morning." Andy paused. "Shit, I'd better go. I just heard the toilet flush."

"You have a girl there?"

"Yeah, Shelly—or Sheila, maybe?"

"Well, you're not the only one who's been getting calls. Sandy's been taking messages from reporters all morning, and now Arthur wants me to find Teddy Rock."

"You don't have to do that," he told me with an air of confidence that seemed awfully cocky for a guy who'd managed to demonstrate just one night of initiative and ingenuity in the last twenty-nine years.

"Yes, I do, Andy. Arthur made it clear that that's exactly what I have to do."

"That's not what I meant."

"Then what did you mean?"

"You don't have to find Teddy Rock," Andy repeated. "He's already found you."

Teddy Rock / Better Ted Than Dead

KICK RECORDS ★½

Teddy Rock's debut album, *Rock Hard*, combined sharp vocals, tumbling riffs and resonating lyrics that promised to change the musical landscape for a new generation of fans. Unfortunately, Rock's sophomore effort doesn't live up to that promise. There's little originality and no surprises here. From the seriously pretentious "You Know Me" to the bloated "No Way Out," Teddy Rock sounds too much like he believed his own press, and too little like the artist we all hoped he could be. Rock is at his best on cuts such as "Not Now" and "Into the Sun," where he lays off the minor-key hysterics and kicks out a groove that's honest as well as propulsive. But too much of *Better Ted Than Dead* sounds like the kind of album a musician makes when he's used up all his best stuff. Sadly, for Teddy Rock, that just might be the case.

CHAPTER NINE

I stared at the seven-digit phone number I'd scribbled on a legal pad. A legal pad filled with notes about Darcy Farnsworth's suit and the two hundred million dollars she was suing for. Notes that supported our claim that Kitty's actions were reasonable. Notes with the names and phone numbers of Darcy's legal team. And yet the one piece of information that stood out now was the name I'd written hastily in red in the margin. Ian White.

This wasn't a local journalist who wanted to interview me for a spot on some public access channel. This wasn't some local DJ broadcasting from a bar. This was Teddy Rock's New York publicist.

Apparently, a friend of a friend of a friend of Ian's heard Big D's broadcast and started making phone calls. When Ian was finally able to hunt down the radio station's promotion person, he was given Andy's number and told to speak with Janey's manager. My manager! Andy thought this was just too funny.

"Now I'm your manager," he'd told me while waiting for Shelly or Sheila to emerge from his bathroom. "And to think just two days ago I was merely a bartender merrily mixing Long Island iced teas at Sam's Place. What do I get? Like fifteen percent."

Fifteen percent of what? Was Andy already planning to farm me out to endorse products for well-worn groupies, perhaps flavored condoms and self-heating motion lotion? "You're not my manager Andy," I'd told him. "You can barely manage to match your socks on a daily basis."

"Hey, if you can be Teddy Rock's muse, I can sure as hell be a manager," he'd assured me, apparently confident in his ability to make Janey Marlow a household name.

So now I had Ian White's phone number in front of me. And he was expecting my call. Andy suggested we set up a joint meeting so I had someone there to represent my interests, but I was able to convince him that three years of law school beat ten years of making woo-woos when it came to representing my best interests.

It was just that at this point I wasn't sure what my best interests were anymore. On the one hand, there were rumors swirling around the office hallways wreaking havoc on a reputation I'd been meticulous in creating. But on the other, nobody seemed too disappointed to see that reputation bite the dust. In fact, they all seemed to be rooting for Janey. And she seemed to be winning.

When I introduced myself to Ian White, I thought he would wet himself. Apparently he wasn't really expecting me to call, because he started shushing what sounded like a crowd, and then asked if he could put me on hold while he cleared everyone out of his office.

When he returned to the line he was more composed but no less enthusiastic. "This is amazing." I could almost see him pumping his fist in the air in victory. "I wasn't sure you'd get back to me. Your manager said he'd try to convince you."

"Andy's not my manager. He's my brother," I clarified. "But I did think I should see why you called."

"Well, it's quite simple, actually. I'd like to meet the woman behind 'Janey 245.' With Teddy about to make a comeback, I thought it would make sense for us to talk."

"That's a good idea," I immediately agreed, picturing Arthur happily sucking a cream soda Dum Dum in celebration.

"Oh." Ian seemed surprised that I didn't put up more of a fight and floundered for a minute while he figured out his next move. "I can be in Chicago on Monday. Would that work for you?"

"Why don't we meet at the offices of Becker, Bishop and Deane around one o'clock. It's on Wacker Drive."

"Great." Ian yelled for his assistant to clear his calendar for Monday. "And Jane?"

"Yes?"

"We really can't wait to meet you."

"Thanks," I answered, even though I knew that wasn't what he really meant. He meant that they couldn't wait to meet Janey.

Rocker Behind Bars

Teddy Rock spent the night behind bars late Thursday after being charged with disturbing the peace for allegedly inciting a crowd at his concert. Three members of Rock's crew were also arrested.

Police met with Rock's management prior to the concert and repeatedly warned that rowdy behavior similar to his 1990 appearance would not be tolerated. The 1990 concert was interrupted when a crazed fan attacked Rock onstage and was followed by minor destruction of property.

Police arrested Rock around midnight after a fight broke out between his crew and police, The three crew members were also arrested and the four men were then transported to the Clark County Detention Center.

Rock was booked on a charge of provoking a breach of the peace, while crew members Chris Smith and CJ Deane were both charged with obstructing a police officer, and Larry Croyne was charged with battery on a police officer. All four were released early Friday morning.

CHAPTER TEN

"Hey, what are you doing here?" I carefully stepped through the freshly mowed field, trying to avoid the discarded clumps of grass that stuck to the sides of my sneakers and made it look like I was wearing Chia Pets on my feet. "I thought I was going to be the only mascot."

"You didn't think I'd miss the opening game, did you?" Sam asked, rising to his feet. "They're warming up."

I watched Drew throw a ground ball to Andy, who caught it in his base hand before tagging out an imaginary runner on second. Drew caught me staring and waved.

"I can't believe Andy made it. It's not even ten o'clock yet."

"Andy was here before I was," Sam told me and patted the empty seat next to him. "Sit down. The grass is still wet."

I joined Sam on the double nylon folding chair and rubbed the goose bumps pimpling my legs. In Chicago we watched the calendar instead of the thermometer. Over the walking bridge on the other side of Lake Shore Drive, Lake Michigan was still a slate blue, the sand a dark, wet brown, but next weekend the beach would open and lifeguards in red jackets would be shivering on the spindly white wooden stands. Andy always thought it would be cool to be a lifeguard at North Avenue beach, although his opinion was probably influenced more by *Baywatch* and the idea of performing mouth-to-mouth on Yasmine Bleeth than by a strong desire to save lives.

"You cold?" Sam asked. "Here, take this." He removed his navy blue windbreaker and laid it over my shoulders.

"You don't have to do that," I protested, even though I gratefully accepted the warm flannel lining against my bare arms. I'm sure Andy would have liked me to show up in a cheerleader sweater and pleated skirt, but I'd opted for shorts and a polo instead.

"Don't be silly. I was getting a little hot in that thing anyway." The wirey gray hairs on Sam's arm stood on end, betraying him. He was just as cold as I was.

"Are you sure?"

"Absolutely. Next weekend's the official start of summer, it's almost hard to believe." He crossed his arms and tucked his hands under his armpits. "The sun's warming up."

It wasn't worth arguing with him. He'd never admit he needed his jacket back, just like my dad never admitted he was still hungry when I'd ask for his last French fry. When my dad died, Sam had inherited Gordon Marlow's fathering gene, which is why, even though we weren't really family and the bar wasn't doing much business, he'd asked Andy to help him out. Sam was probably the only single, childless bar owner who thought of his place as a family business.

"I talked to your mom the other day. It's funny how she always manages to call when I'm due for a cleaning."

"I'm sure that's not exactly a coincidence. I'm probably the only person in the world who gets anonymous packages of dental floss in the mail."

"You're not the only one. She sends me the mint-flavored floss and doesn't even bother to enclose a note. Audrey gives the tooth fairy some stiff competition."

Almost by reflex, I ran my tongue along my front teeth, feeling for leftovers from my morning bagel. Talking about my mom tended to have that effect.

Never has a woman embraced dental hygiene like my mother. Between the dangling toothbrush earrings, shoelaces imprinted with a continuous row of smiley faces with braces, and the stationery adorned with dental witticisms, you'd think her foray into the world of dental hygiene was more out of a preoccupation with incisors and molars than necessity—although the obsession had quickly followed. She'd needed a way to support herself after my dad died, so she answered an ad for a receptionist in Dr. Lang's office. Apparently she had a knack for all things dental, because after just a few months of answering the phones, Dr. Weldon Lang offered to send her to school to pursue a career in the dental arts—you would have thought he'd offered to send her on a trip around the world, the way she carried on. Two years later, she graduated first in her class, and two years after that, Dr. Lang made her another offer she couldn't refuse, which is why Weldon is now my mother's husband.

My mom didn't expect me to attend their wedding. She kept stressing how it wasn't even a real wedding, just a small ceremony at the courthouse. But I liked Weldon—I really did—and I was afraid that if I didn't attend the fifteen-minute ceremony and the small reception at my aunt Vicki's house, Weldon would think it was a form of protest. So, while other college seniors were off in Cancún or Jamaica getting their last wet T-shirt contest and beer boat race out of their system, I was back in suburban Chicago pinning a corsage of pink roses to the lapel of my mother's day suit and watching her say *I do.*

It was weird, because in some strange way I guess I wished Sam and my mom would get together somehow. When Sam came over to our house on Sundays to eat pot roast and watch the Bears game with my dad, my mom was always right there in the family room with them, trying to convince Sam to date some woman she met in line at the grocery store. After the game we all stood at the front window waving to Sam as he pulled out of our driveway, and my mom always remarked that it was such a shame Sam never married. *He's such a catch,* she'd say on her way into the kitchen to wash the dishes, and I'd always picture some lonely widow reeling Sam in on a big hook like Charlie in those Starkist commercials.

"I hope you know how much I appreciate you helping out at the bar," Sam said, turning his face to the sun and squinting at me. "Business has really picked up since that Janey thing. If it keeps up I'm hoping to bring Bruce back and maybe hire some real waitresses—not that Natalie hasn't been helpful, but you know what I mean."

Sam hadn't shaved this morning, and I watched as the sun filtered through the short gray whiskers sprouting from his chin and cheeks, turning them into tiny prisms of light.

"Yeah, I know what you mean."

A softball rolled through the grass toward us and Drew trailed behind, chasing it down. "It's amazing what your brother's done. First the radio show, now this." Sam stuck his foot out and stopped the ball beside our chair.

"Thanks, Sam," Drew said when he caught up to the ball and bent down to pick it up. He'd rolled up the sleeves of his T-shirt, and as he reached for the ball I noticed a small vaccination mark on his upper arm, a perfectly round indentation, like he'd slept on a button. "Hey, Jane."

I managed to take my eyes off his arm long enough to say hi, and then watched Drew jog back to second base in a Nike T-shirt vaguely similar to the one Arthur wore when I ran into him in the movie line. But that was where the similarity with Arthur ended. The legs running onto the field were nothing like the thick, shapeless trunks filling the space between the hem of Arthur's Bermuda shorts and the leather straps of his Birkenstocks. No, these legs were definitely more my type.

Not that Liv would ever consider Drew my *type*, which is why she probably warned me about him in the first place. She was just saving me time. If Liv thought I'd go for Drew she probably would have been the first one to encourage me to explore his talent with office equipment. But she'd only seen me with guys like Perry. Not that there was anything wrong with Perry, just that he was like most of the guys I dated throughout college and law school. They were the ones who were just enough—good-looking enough, smart enough, successful enough—but never *right* enough. It wasn't poor judgment, contrary to what Nat and Liv thought. It was by design. One guy pulled his pants up a little too high, one wore the type of all-white sneakers that looked a little too much like nursing shoes, and another used just a dollop too much hair gel so you could see the comb tracks separating the chunks of hair. In John Hughes movies, my type was the decent guy in khaki pants who never got the girl. The guy who could be easily left without much discussion or regret, the one who didn't cause much distraction.

That was the only type of guy Liv and Nat had ever seen me with, so, even if they didn't understand it, they learned to accept it. No, Drew wasn't the type of guy I'd go for now. But he used to be.

In high school there was a guy, John. I loved him. Not like let's-run-off-and-spend-our-lives-together love, but the kind where you know where he is every second of every minute of every hour. I knew when he had geometry with Mrs. Huffson, knew which seat he slunk down in at the back of the class, and knew that if I passed by the room and walked close enough to the

lockers, I could get just the right angle to see him through the slim rectangu-
lar wire-webbed glass in the door window. John was all my type, and all not
my type. He smoked pot and listened to the Grateful Dead. During lunch
he'd stand around in a circle with his friends, kicking a rainbow needle point
Hacky Sack while he dug one hand in the pocket of his Levis, as if he
couldn't even be bothered to take it out. I could spot John coming down the
hall from a mile away. He didn't walk so much as he meandered, strolled and
ambled. His brown hair, streaked almost blond at the tips from hanging out
in the summer instead of getting a job, hung over his right eye no matter how
many times he pushed it away. Even on the soccer field, where I'd watch him
jog after the ball, his hair flopping up and down, he was never in a rush. He
didn't have to be first in line, and wherever he was headed, they could wait to
start until he got there.

We were completely opposite. I was researching colleges, his future plans
didn't go beyond the Dead show in Saratoga. Not that he wasn't smart, he was.
He just didn't care whether you knew it or not.

It wasn't that I thought I couldn't get John, because I did. Get him, that is.
We went out for pizza, hooked up at parties, talked on the phone. Not that
he was a big talker, because he wasn't. We didn't ponder the meaning of life or
debate the value of taking the SATs more than once. Nobody ever thought of
us as boyfriend and girlfriend. He wasn't the guy everyone wanted to be with,
the one the guys took their cues from or the girls fought for attention from,
like Jimmy Shaw. But he was my Jimmy Shaw. He was my distraction.

Drew didn't have the floppy hair, and I couldn't quite picture him dancing
in the mud at a Dead show, but there was something about him that reminded
me of John. Maybe it was the way he didn't seem to care what other people
expected of him. The way he could leave the conference room in the middle
of working on a huge case and head to a strange bar with a woman he barely
knew, or join a softball team without worrying he'd be the worst player on the
field.

"Earth to Jane." Sam tapped me on the arm and laughed, following my
stare until he stopped on the object of my distraction.

"So, who else is playing?" I asked, pulling the windbreaker around me.

"Well, I think Andy asked a few guys who've started coming into the bar,
and then there's your friend Drew, and Natalie and Olivia."

"Natalie and Olivia?"

"Yeah, didn't you know they were on the team?"

"No, I didn't." They never mentioned anything at lunch. "Why are Nat and Liv playing?"

"Ask them yourself." Sam pointed across the field toward the parking lot, where Liv and Nat were headed in our direction. They certainly looked like they were old pros. Liv was decked out in her athletic finery, which included white and pink Adidas shorts, a matching warm-up jacket, and peds with pink pom-poms. I could swear even her sunglasses had a pink tinge to the lenses. Nat's outfit was more sweat than color-coordinated suit, but she was wearing a baseball cap, her ponytail threaded through the hole above the back strap.

"I'll be right back." I left Sam and went to greet the all-stars. "I didn't know you were softball fans."

Liv pretended to swing a bat and then covered her eyes from the sun as she watched the imaginary ball float into space. "I've swung a few bats in my day."

"And your being here has nothing to do with the all the twenty-year-old guys flexing their muscles out here?"

"Oh, please. I'm an old married woman now. These days fitting into my jeans turns me on more than watching a bunch of sweaty guys—although I'm not complaining."

"What about the kids?"

Liv started twisting from side to side and jogging in place. "Bill's going to bring the boys around to watch the game after they go to the park," she huffed midstretch.

"Andy called yesterday," Nat explained. "I guess he needed a few more people."

"First you're waitressing for him, and now you're joining his softball team?"

Nat shrugged. "He asked."

Liv stopped straddling the ground long enough to look up at me, her eyebrows raised suspiciously. Natalie doesn't exactly fit Andy's criteria for female companionship, not that his screening process is all that stringent. Proximity to his bedroom seems to be the main consideration.

I probably wouldn't have thought anything of it if we all didn't already know that Nat had something of a crush on my brother. Not that I thought anything would ever happen between Nat and Andy. They reminded me of the way our cat, Pumpkin, used to stand outside our neighbor's sliding glass door, completely fascinated with their pug, Warhol. Warhol would stand inside the house, his nose pressed up against the glass, while Pumpkin stood outside, her nose directly across from his, as if kissing. They could stay like that for hours, just staring at each other with bemused expressions on their little faces, their whiskers twitching as if sending silent signals back and forth. If they'd ever run across each other on the street, there probably would have been some shrieking meows and fevered barks, but as long as there was no chance of actually coming into contact with each other, Pumpkin and Warhol felt safe with that transparent obstacle between them. And that's how it was with Natalie and Andy. I was the impenetrable barrier between them that made any actual contact impossible.

"He's asking, but why do you keep saying yes?" I asked, and Liv went back to stretching.

"I'm just helping out, it's no big deal," Nat told me and then added, "Besides, he's not as bad as you make him out to be."

I covered my eyes with my hands and kept them there, trying to erase the disturbing image forming in my head. "Please, stop before I have to stab myself in the eye with a baseball cleat." I rubbed a few more times, until I was seeing stars. "You can't be serious, Natalie. I don't think there's a waitress or aspiring actress in all of Lincoln Park that he hasn't slept with."

"Please. Do you think that intimidates me? I've seen more vaginas than Andy could ever dream of. I think I've got him beat in that department." She turned to Liv, who was rolling her head around in circles like something out of a Stephen King movie. "Come on, Andy's waiting for us."

They left me on the sidelines and walked onto the field, where Drew and my brother and three of his friends waited on the pitcher's mound. I walked back to Sam and we watched as Andy clapped his hands together three times, propped them on his bent knees, and gathered his six players together for a huddle.

"What do you think he's saying?" I asked Sam.

"The standard go-team rah-rah stuff every coach says before a game. Don't worry, you're not missing much."

But if I wasn't missing much, how come I felt like I was the odd one out? Why was I bothered by the hushed voices and the backs turned to me?

And that's when I realized, sitting there on the sideline, that Andy had asked my coworker and my two best friends to be on his team. And he'd never even asked me.

It never mattered before. I was always the one who made the choice to sit out. When Andy and my mom and Sam were all huddled together on our couch politely accepting condolences, I was the one on the phone in my dad's office canceling his magazine subscriptions, removing his name from the phone listing and organizing the bills that had already started to pile up. I was the one who salted the front walk so our neighbors wouldn't slip and drop the armfuls of tuna noodle casseroles, lasagnas and sympathy cards that arrived like clockwork every day for weeks. Why should I care that Andy didn't ask me?

"We're still missing someone," Drew pointed out five minutes before Sam's Sluggers were scheduled to take the field. Andy had distributed the team uniform—a green T-shirt with SAM'S SLUGGERS in big block letters on the front and a number on the back—and everyone was loitering along the third baseline, waiting for the game to start.

Andy didn't seem fazed. "Mike's late, but he'll be here."

But at ten o'clock Andy was on the verge of freaking out, which is something I can admit I've never witnessed. My brother is a *shit happens* kind of guy. Not the type of person who wigs out over the idea of forfeiting a softball game.

"Where is he?" Andy kept asking as he dialed and redialed his cell phone. "This is so typical of Mike."

I didn't point out that just a few weeks ago, it was also typical of Andy.

"I am not going to lose our first game," he said to no one in particular.

"We're not losing, we're forfeiting," Liv pointed out.

"That's worse. It means we can't even field a team."

Andy looked over to Sam. "Unless Mike shows up in the next minute, we're going to have to forfeit. I'm sorry, Sam."

"That's okay, Andy." Sam gave him a shrug that was supposed to show it was no big deal, but Sam's flat smile gave him away. "At least you tried."

The umpire yelled *batter up*, and Andy kicked the ground, the force of his sneaker sending a rock skidding through the dirt toward third base. "Damn it," he swore and kicked the ground again.

Still, Andy never looked over at me. Even on the verge of forfeiting, it never occurred to him to ask me to play on his team. Didn't he think I'd want to help out? My dad used to play baseball with us. Surely hitting a ball was like riding a bike—something you never forgot. How hard could it be? Then again, if I was horrible I'd make an idiot out of myself in front of everyone.

And, come to think of it, I hadn't ridden a bike recently, either, so that theory had yet to be proven accurate.

I could either risk looking like a fool in front of my family, friends, a coworker and numerous strangers, or I could take a chance and hope that the skills I'd learned on the front lawn weren't too rusty. I felt like I should be wearing one of those WWJD bracelets—what would Janey do?

Finally, I raised my hand—not because they needed me, but because I wanted to be on the team.

"I can play," I offered.

Andy looked up. "Really?"

I nodded. "Sure."

Andy must have been feeling pretty desperate, because he didn't bother asking me twice and instead tossed me a team shirt. "Here. Put it on and get out in left field. Everyone else take your positions."

I stood up and shook off Sam's jacket. The uniform was a little snug going over my shirt, and Sam helped pull it down over my head.

"Wish me luck," I called over my shoulder, running to my place in the outfield.

"Good luck!" he shouted as Sam's Sluggers took the field and the umpire yelled *play ball.*

About fifteen minutes into the game, Bill showed up with the boys and we had our own little cheering section. We were down one-nothing after the first inning, but things were looking good. Sam taught George and Ethan to taunt the opposing team by singing "We want a pitcher, not a belly itcher," which cracked them up.

Unfortunately, when my turn came, I stood over home plate and let the belly itcher get the best of me. It was humiliating. I looked like an idiot up there, swatting at the air. And it wasn't like the pitches were curveballs at Mach speed. No, the ball was lobbed. I'm talking full-on arc, practically stopping to stare at me and stick out its tongue as it crossed home plate. So, why couldn't I hit the damned thing?

Every time I swung the bat, the only thing I managed to connect with was air. I waited for the laughs and boos and catcalls. At the very least I expected Andy to threaten to kick me off the team if I didn't get with the program. But even Andy didn't say anything. Sam didn't throw his hands up. Liv and Nat didn't make fun of me. Instead my teammates yelled encouragement—*Keep your eye on the ball, Swing slower, Swing faster, Step back, Move up.* What they didn't yell was what I thought was pretty apparent. I sucked.

"Sorry, guys." I handed my bat to Nat, who, it ends up, swung like the long-lost daughter of Mickey Mantle.

"It takes a lot of eye-hand coordination to deliver babies," she said, as if that was supposed to make me feel better. "You'll get 'em next time."

Only next time it was the same thing. And the next time and the next. It was humiliating. I changed my grip, switched my stance, attempted to copy everything Nat did, and still, nothing.

"Want some pointers?" Drew asked after my fourth strikeout.

I knew they were just trying to help, but all it did was highlight the fact that I was the worst player on the team. Me! I wasn't used to being the worst at anything. Even Liv could hit the ball, and she wasn't shy about letting everybody know it. She high-fived everyone but the soda vendor every time she stomped on home plate and scored a run. But I wasn't ready to ask for help. I wanted to figure it out on my own. There were five-year-olds playing T-ball who could get a hit. I was just out of practice.

"No, thanks, I think I'm getting the hang of it," I assured Drew.

I got up to the plate six times in the first five innings. And I struck out every time. I was gaining a whole new respect for five-year-old T-ball players.

When I reached the sideline after my sixth strikeout, Drew was waiting for me. He grabbed my bat and stood behind me, positioning my feet into the correct batting stance.

"Really, you don't have to do this," I objected, but Drew wouldn't move.

"You do know that George just told Ethan you couldn't hit water if you fell out of a boat?"

"He did not!" I yelled.

"Well, in his defense, I think they heard the other team say it first, but yeah."

I glanced over at George and Ethan, who were mesmerized by Sam's ability to magically pull quarters from their ears.

"Fine," I agreed, not willing to be ridiculed by two little boys who couldn't even figure out that the quarters were hidden in the palm of Sam's hand. "Teach away."

"Here, let me show you." Drew moved in closer until I could feel the waistband of his shorts graze my back. "Now, bend here," he told me, reaching around and placing his hand on my stomach, which I promptly sucked in and squeezed tight.

"Like this?" I asked, folding a little at my waist.

"That's it. Now hold the bat," he instructed, his fingers firmly wrapped around my forearm.

I followed his orders and concentrated on gripping the bat. Not because I wanted a major league swing, but because if I didn't the only thing I'd be thinking about was the idea that if we were naked, we'd be about three inches from needing some latex.

Drew helped me bring the bat back and then told me to follow through until my swing was complete. "And that's how you do it. What do you think?"

I think I need to pull up the covers and have a cigarette. "That was great. Thanks."

The next time I got up to bat I stood over the plate and tried to remember exactly what Drew told me—bent waist, bent knees, bent elbows. And I didn't strike out. I got a hit—or more accurately, the ball hit me. As I rubbed my elbow and made my way down the first baseline, my teammates cheered me on. If I'd known getting hit would get me on base, I might have sacrificed my body earlier.

But I didn't give up. And I kept on swinging. Even though we managed to hold our own, and I caught two of the six pop flies hit in my direction, we still ended up losing 7–5. My team lined up to congratulate the winning team and show we weren't sore losers, and I joined them despite my earlier altercation with the cheating Guinness rep during the Pins & Pints tournament. Even though I knew it was my fault, and I knew my team knew it was my fault, on our way back to the sideline to pack up and get ready to go to the bar, nobody mentioned that I was the weak link that cost Sam's Sluggers the game. Drew even gave me an *A* for effort.

"Not so bad out there, Marlow," Drew acknowledged.

"Thanks."

"So what's this I hear about Teddy Rock's publicist calling Andy?" he asked.

"He told you?"

"I'd think by now you'd realize that your brother isn't very good at keeping secrets." Drew stopped next to a small canvas duffel bag and sat down on the grass.

"You're right. Teddy and his publicist are coming to the office on Monday to see me," I explained, not unaware that I was telling Drew a once-famous rock star was traveling halfway across the country just to see little old Jane.

"Teddy must really want to see you again after all these years."

Yeah, he must. And I was warming up to the idea of seeing him, too. I was ready to end the speculation about why he wrote about me and get the real answer.

"I hate to even think about how sore I'll be tomorrow," Drew moaned and reached to unlace his sneakers—which were blue, red and white Adidas and looked nothing like nursing shoes.

"Are you coming to Sam's?"

"Can't, I already had plans before this came up. But after the next game, I promise."

"Do you need a ride somewhere?" I asked, moving out of the way as the next team started to arrive for its eleven o'clock game. Sam's chair was folded up, and Liv and Bill were over buying the boys a soda from the refreshment stand. Still, I wasn't ready to leave.

"Nope." Drew held up a pair of Rollerblades he'd removed from the duffel bag. "What about you? Are you going to Sam's?"

I looked over behind the backstop, where everyone was already walking toward their cars. George and Ethan were arguing over who got to hold a Coke can, and my brother and Sam were shoulder to shoulder, the nylon chair slung over Andy's arm as they talked.

"Yeah, I think I will."

"Not heading into the office today?"

I looked over at Sam surrounded by Andy and my friends. "Not today."

"Hey, you're Janey 245, right?" A player from the eleven o'clock team called over to me, and several heads turned in our direction.

"Yes, I am," I answered, not even hesitating.

She walked over to me and held out a softball and ballpoint pen. "Can you sign this for me?"

"Go ahead," Drew urged, pointing to the pen.

I took the ball and did my best to write legibly on the round, grass-stained surface before handing it back. "Here you go."

"Thanks." She took the ball back to her team and showed it around.

"Watch, it will end up on eBay," Drew whispered.

"You think so?"

He shrugged. "Maybe."

"Hey, Jane, let's go!" Andy yelled from halfway across the fields.

"They're waiting for me."

Drew stuffed his sneakers into the duffel bag and stood up on his wheels. "I guess I'll see you on Monday, then. Have fun."

I left Drew on the grass and jogged over to join my team. "Shotgun!" I called out to Andy and ran my fastest toward the car, all the while wondering just how much a softball signed by Janey Marlow was worth, anyway.

JULY 1, 1991
BERLIN, Germany

European Leg of Teddy Rock Tour Canceled

Teddy Rock has canceled the opening dates of his first European tour in two years due to technical problems.

The tour had been due to start in Cologne on June 5, with a second concert in the city the following day. Marek Liesterberg, the rock star's German concert manager, said both had to be canceled and future dates for the European tour are on hold.

He gave no explanation of the nature of the technical problems that have hit the shows, but speculation about the poor sales of Rock's second album, *Better Ted Than Dead,* and a lack of sold-out shows have many wondering if the tour will resume.

Tour organizers and concert promoters are "faced with several million dollars of losses, and the very tough decision of whether or not to even continue the tour," according to an undisclosed source. "Teddy Rock just isn't pulling them in like he used to."

CHAPTER ELEVEN

"I thought we were meeting in your lawyer's office. I didn't realize that *you* were the lawyer," Ian admitted, following me down the hall. His head kept bobbing from side to side as he attempted to catch glimpses inside each of the offices we passed. Ian White may have been surprised by me, but Teddy's publicist was pretty much what I expected. The only person who'd wear a black mock turtleneck, black pants and a black blazer in May was obviously all about image.

"Why would I need a lawyer?" I asked, showing him into my office and gesturing to the chair across from my desk.

"Nice place," he complimented before taking a seat. "No reason, really. It's just that sometimes people have their own agendas. With the new album coming out we expected there might be a few skeletons in Teddy's closet, people hoping to seize the opportunity to capitalize on his comeback."

"Isn't Teddy joining us?" I asked. We'd stood in the lobby exchanging niceties for a few minutes and taken our time getting to my office. If Teddy was going to show up, I'd thought he'd have been here by now.

I'd be lying if I said I hadn't spent more time than usual getting dressed this morning. Every suit I selected, every blouse I held up, every pair of pumps I placed at the foot of my bed, were all put through the Janey test.

And most picks failed the test miserably. After nixing six options that would have been fine on any other day, I decided it was time for drastic measures.

Teddy may remember the little girl in leg warmers, but he wasn't meeting a little girl. He was meeting the woman she'd become, and even though I wouldn't have admitted it to anyone, I didn't want him to be disappointed.

So I pushed aside my tried-and-trues, reached back into the darkest corner of my closet, and connected with Liv's cast-offs. Several options were immediately ruled out. A leopard print skirt. A black suede skirt with a zipper running from the hem to the waistband. A Pucci-inspired wrap dress. I may be meeting a rock star, but I wasn't that delusional. I was still me.

I finally settled on a winter white pants suit and hot pink button down shirt. A perfect compromise.

"Teddy's in New York," Ian told me.

No Teddy?

I glanced down at the slashes of hot pink poking out from inside my winter white sleeves. And I felt ridiculous. I was the girl in the rainbow leg warmers playing dress up.

So what was Ian doing here? And what was I going to tell Arthur? Better yet, what was I going to tell Drew—that Teddy couldn't even be bothered to see me, so he sent some metrosexual PR guru instead? "Oh."

"I'm sorry. Did I give you the impression that he'd be coming with me? I thought that until we had a chance to meet it would be best if Teddy wasn't involved."

Involved? Involved in what? It was just a brief meeting, not foreign espionage. Maybe Ian was here on some reconnaissance mission, sent to gather information before returning to mission control and reporting on what—or who—he found.

I attempted to tuck the hot pink cuffs back inside my suit jacket sleeves, but they refused to hide. "So Teddy doesn't know you're here?"

Ian shook his head. "Um, no. Not yet. Didn't want to get his hopes up. You understand, right?"

Not really. "Sure. Right."

"So you haven't seen Teddy in, what, twenty years?" Ian kicked his foot onto his knee and sat back, settling in.

"Twenty-one. He moved away in sixth grade."

"That's so sweet," Ian practically cooed. You could tell this man was well versed in the art of making nice. "So, bring me up to speed on what you've been doing since then."

I doubted Ian really cared about the details of my life over the past twenty-one years, so I gave him the abridged version. "Well, I went to college out East, and then came back to Chicago for law school."

"Okay, that's good." Ian's expression became serious and he started down his mental checklist. "Did you make law review, head of the class, that whole thing?"

"Yes, that whole thing." Ian made it all sound so simple, like I'd joined an extracurricular glee club instead of beating out everyone in my class. "Then I came here to Becker, Bishop and Deane."

"Nothing scandalous in your past?" Ian continued his interrogation. "No sexual experimentation, no dalliances with amateur porn, arrests for shoplifting, anything I should be aware of?"

"No, Ian. Nothing like that. It's just like I told you."

Ian attempted to run a hand through his heavily gelled hair, but it stalled about halfway through. "I've got to tell you, Jane; you're not exactly what I pictured. In the past, Teddy's taste in women, well, let's just say the girls he liked were more likely to *need* a lawyer than *be* a lawyer. Besides, he usually goes for platinum blondes."

"It's dirty." I pointed to my head and held out a few strands of hair before realizing that I'd just implied a lack of personal hygiene. "I meant the color, it's dirty blond, not that my hair is dirty."

Ian laughed at me, as if appreciating my stand-up act. "I knew what you meant."

"No platinum. Sorry to disappoint."

"Disappoint? God, no. You're perfect." Ian paused, taking a few minutes to silently size me up, almost debating what to do next. Finally, he stood up and pulled a cell phone out of his blazer pocket. "Can you excuse me for a minute?" Ian speed dialed a number and casually made his way over to my window, where he faced the glass and pretended to admire the view. Despite his attempt to appear enthralled by the air-conditioning units on the building next door, it was obvious that the change of locale was intended to keep me from overhearing his conversation.

Was he calling Teddy? Was the famous rock star down on the street sitting in some limousine, waiting for Ian to give him the all clear? Maybe Ian was flashing some secret reflective signal out my window, telling Teddy it was okay to come up, that I wasn't some psycho stalker.

While I waited for Ian to finish his urgent call, Arthur passed by my door for the second time since Ian arrived. When he spotted Teddy's publicist by the window, he gave me a thumbs-up. I attempted to give him a reassuring look in return.

After a series of animated assurances that he would *get it done*, Ian rejoined me at my desk.

"All set?" I asked.

"We have an idea that we'd like to throw by you."

Since it was just the two of us in my office, I couldn't help but wonder what *we* he was referring to. "Sure, go ahead."

"We've got Teddy scheduled for Letterman tomorrow night and we want you to be there."

My head was shaking no even before the words were out of my mouth. "I don't think I can make it. Besides, I can watch Letterman from Chicago."

"We don't want you to *watch* Letterman, we want you to *be on* Letterman. With Teddy. We want you to be reunited with Teddy on live TV."

What was with all this *we*? *We want this* and *We want that*. Did Teddy have a whole team behind him pulling the strings?

"I don't think so, Ian."

"Come on, it's a great idea. Letterman's producers will eat it up. We were even thinking Teddy could sing an acoustic version of 'Janey 245' with you looking on."

So I was going to be a prop? "Do they want me to sit there mouthing the words while wearing an I ♥ TEDDY ROCK T-shirt, too?"

"That'd be perfect!" he exclaimed. "You must be reading my mind."

"Ian, I was kidding."

I could see it already. They'd make fun of me on Tuesday night's Top Ten list—The Top Ten Reasons Janey Marlow Flew to New York to See Teddy Rock.

Reason number three: Janey's got a nipple shield under her cashmere cardigan, and she's dying for Teddy to help with her *wardrobe malfunction*.

"This is a great opportunity, Janey," Ian reassured me, as if reciting the speech Arthur gave me in his office.

Reason number two: Janey's already put an auditorium of lawyers to sleep with her seminar on irrevocable trusts, and now she wants to try her hand at a national audience.

"I don't know, Ian," I continued to object, and then noticed a paisley bow tie and lollipop pass by my door for what seemed like the fifth time.

And the number one reason Janey Marlow Flew to New York to See Teddy Rock: Janey's always done what's expected of her.

"Okay. Fine."

Ian's face lit up. "Really?"

"Really."

"That's great. Teddy will be thrilled when he finds out. I'll take care of all your travel arrangements, you just show up and be yourself."

Sure sounded easy enough, only lately I was starting to wonder who that really was.

"Teddy Rock's publicist wants me to go to New York to meet Teddy," I announced before flopping down in the chair across from Arthur.

He removed the grape lollipop from his mouth. "That's super, Jane. I knew you could do it. Want one?" Arthur offered, holding out the jar filled with rainbow flavors.

"No, thanks."

"They're sugar-free," he sang and fanned out a few flavors in front of me like the Child Catcher in *Chitty Chitty Bang Bang*.

I shook my head. "He wants us to go on TV together."

"What did you tell him?"

"What were my choices, Arthur? I said I'd go. He gave me his word that it wouldn't be a free-for-all or anything. I'll fly out tomorrow afternoon and the show starts taping at five."

"Wow. You must have done quite a convincing job."

"Actually it didn't take much convincing at all."

In fact, it hadn't taken any. Which, now that I thought about it, was strange considering Ian had flown all the way from New York to make sure I wasn't trying to steal Teddy's spotlight. If Ian was so worried that I had ulterior motives for going public, you'd think he'd be a little more skeptical of me. But he was so quick to believe everything I told him, like he wanted to believe I was telling the truth.

"So when are you going to have a chance to talk with Teddy? I mean, his publicist is all well and good, but it's Teddy we want to get on board."

"Ian, the publicist, said we'll have dinner or something after the show."

"You'll bring your laptop and bill on the plane, right?"

"Absolutely," I assured him. The opportunity to snag Teddy as a future client was one thing, but billing paying clients today was another. "Drew and I are meeting with Kitty this afternoon."

"Sounds like you know what you're doing. Make sure you tell Tara to send out an e-mail with the show's information. I'm sure everyone would love to watch you on TV."

"I'll be sure and do that," I told him, knowing that Tara was the last person in the world I'd tell. She'd probably hold screenings for the office staff and charge admission; she'd probably even offer popcorn for five bucks a pop. At this point, nothing would surprise me.

"I'm going to New York tomorrow to see Teddy Rock," I told Drew in the cab on the way to Kitty's house, not entirely unaware of the shock value in my statement.

"I'm not surprised."

Now it was my turn to try and sound not surprised. "You're not?"

"I heard Arthur gave you some speech about getting Teddy on board with the firm. I figured it was just a matter of time until you met with him."

Drew may have expected me to meet with Teddy, but I could bet he didn't expect our meeting to take place on TV. "We're going to be reunited on Letterman."

Drew laughed.

"What's so funny?"

"That's just so rock star, you know? Most people would meet over lunch or something."

The cab turned left off Michigan Avenue and stopped in front of Kitty's house.

Drew let out an appraising whistle as he looked out the window. "Nice place."

I used to feel intimidated by Kitty's street. Astor Place was a throwback to a time before the generic square high-rises started pricking the Chicago skyline. The carefully planted trees and shrubs that dotted the narrow street gave it a residential feel completely in contrast to Michigan Avenue, a few blocks away. Although Kitty's townhouse blended in seamlessly with the other graystones, brownstones, and brick Georgians, you could tell that there was something a little different about the four-story mansion. Maybe it was the sense of history left behind by generations of Farnsworths that once occupied the twenty-room home, or maybe it was simply Kitty's penchant for decorating the wrought iron fence out front according to the season—pumpkin lanterns and straw scarecrows at Halloween, garland and red berries at Christmas.

"Is there anything you want to tell me about Kitty before I meet her?" Drew asked as we made our way through the iron gate leading to Kitty's front door.

How could I describe Kitty? She was part Dale Evans, part Maude, and part Ethel Kennedy. "Not really. She's pretty self-explanatory."

Bernard answered the door and led us through a maze of rooms until we reached the glass-enclosed solarium overlooking Kitty's garden, where she was waiting for us with a pitcher of lemonade and chocolate chip cookies.

It was odd having Drew in Kitty's house with me. Even though Arthur and a few of the more senior partners knew Kitty, I was the only one from the firm ever invited into her home. In a way it made our association less like the traditional client-attorney roles at Becker, Bishop & Deane, and more like a relationship between friends. Of course, that would be assuming one friend paid the other by the hour for her advice, but, still, there was nothing stilted or forced about the time we spent together. That was probably why, of all my clients, I enjoyed her the most. Although Arthur probably assumed that, even more than our friendship, I enjoyed the year end bonuses.

The first time I went to Kitty's Gold Coast home, she greeted me wearing a pair of Gap khakis, a man's striped oxford (although from the impeccable tailoring I could tell it was from Paul Stuart) and a blue paisley doo rag tied on her head. She'd been working in her garden, which explained the green rubber clogs on her bare feet but didn't explain the walkie-talkie clipped to the waistband of her pants.

"Hello, Jane. Come, sit down." Kitty patted the cushioned wicker chair next to her and held out the plate of cookies. "You'll excuse me if I don't get too close. I definitely think I'm coming down with something. At least I hope so. I'd hate to think I'm becoming allergic to horses at my age."

"Kitty owns a horse farm out in Barrington Hills," I explained to Drew.

"I love it out there," Kitty told Drew as she stood up and reached for the pitcher of cold lemonade. "All that grass and the crisp air. But you know, I'm really a city girl at heart. My husband used to say that if there wasn't a horn honking at two in the morning and a garbage truck outside my window at six a.m., I didn't feel at home."

I took the cookies, and the seat next to Kitty. She baked amazing cookies from a recipe a friend supposedly paid one hundred dollars for at Neiman Marcus's café. The friend asked for the recipe and then discovered the obscene charge on her Neiman's card so she passed the recipe on to everyone she knew just to get even.

I never had the heart to break it to Kitty that the story was actually urban legend, like the rumor that little Mikey from those LIFE commercials died from the explosive effects of mixing Pop Rocks with Coca-Cola. She loved to make the cookies, and told me that every time she baked them it was her little rebellion.

"Hello, Mrs. Farnsworth." Drew extended his hand. "It's a pleasure to meet you."

Kitty met his hand with a cold glass of lemonade. "And you, too, Drew."

"The garden looks beautiful," I observed, stroking the purply blue petals of the grape hyacinths clustered beside my chair. "I wish this was just a social visit."

"Our meetings aren't as much fun as they used to be, are they, Jane? We used to talk about charitable gifts and where the foundation was allocating funds and awarding grants. Now it's just this lawsuit all the time. I must say, it's getting tiresome."

"We can start getting William involved in the details, if you'd like," Drew offered, referring to Kitty's only son and Darcy's father.

"That's not necessary. No reason to burden him with all this when he's the one who has to live with Darcy, after all."

"Jane and I wanted to see you and tell you what's going on with the suit. We don't want anything to take you by surprise."

"Surprise? At this point there's nothing that Darcy can do to surprise me." Kitty held on to the arms of her wicker chair and lowered herself onto the floral cushion. "I still can't believe this is happening. Darcy's confused the judicial system with the family dinner table, a more appropriate place to deal with family matters, don't you think?" Kitty asked, her voice more sad than accusatory.

Between helpings of chocolate chip cookies, Drew told Kitty about the petition to freeze the foundation's assets. And she was right. She didn't even register a bit of surprise.

"Tell me, Drew. What would happen if I wanted to settle this mess now instead of going through a nasty lawsuit?" Kitty asked, taking a tissue out of her pocket as she stifled a cough.

"We could certainly go to Darcy's attorneys with an offer, if you'd like to settle the suit. Did you have anything specific in mind?"

Did I just hear Drew offer to settle? I thought he liked to win. Giving in would be like holding up a white flag. And waving that white flag would be like admitting I made a mistake. And like Andy said, I don't make mistakes. I stopped midchocolate chew and waited to hear Kitty's answer.

"I'm not sure I want to continue fighting Darcy on this. There's more than enough Farnsworth money to go around."

"It's not about the money, Kitty," I interrupted before Drew could agree with her, and before the cookie had made its way completely down my throat. If it came down to choosing between choking and settling, I'd take choking any day. "It's that what she's doing is wrong. What she's accusing you of is wrong. And Drew thinks we have a shot, right?" I turned to Drew for reinforcement.

He nodded.

"So, I'm not sure we have to be talking about this just yet," I continued. "There's no need to rush into anything. Why don't we let Drew continue doing what he's doing and see where it gets us?"

Kitty let out a long, deliberate sigh. "If that's what Jane thinks is best, then I guess we can do that."

"Then it's settled." I told her, not choosing my words very wisely. "Well, you know what I mean."

I'd managed to avert disaster, and we stayed just long enough for Drew to finish off two more cookies before he stood up to leave.

"You go ahead without me," I told him. "I think I'm going to stay and go over a few more things with Kitty."

Bernard escorted Drew to the door and left us alone.

"There's something else I wanted to tell you," I told Kitty, stirring my lemonade with my fingers so I wouldn't have to look at her. "I'm going to be on TV."

Kitty started to say something but began coughing instead. "Excuse me, Jane. I just can't shake this cold. Did you say you were going to be on TV?"

I nodded and handed her a fresh glass of lemonade. "That's what I said."

"It's not one of those horrible reality shows where you compete for a husband, is it, Jane? I always thought you were too smart to fall for that prime-time love thing."

"No, it's nothing like that. It's a long story, but suffice it to say that there's a guy I grew up with who wrote a song about me." I couldn't believe how easily the sentence slipped off my tongue. Last week I was vehemently denying Andy's theory and here I was talking about it as if it was an undisputed fact, like gravity. "This guy has a new album coming out soon and so he's been getting a lot of attention lately."

"A song about you? Would I have heard of it?"

"I don't think so. It came out when I was in college. The Janey he remembers is a little livelier than me, to say the least."

"Why's that?"

"She's gregarious and uninhibited," I explained. "That sort of thing."

Lord knows Kitty didn't hire me because I was gregarious and uninhibited.

"His publicist asked me to fly to New York to be reunited with him on the Letterman show."

"Reunited? Were you that close?" Kitty knew how to cut to the chase. Nobody else thought to question whether or not Teddy and I were close enough to warrant a teary-eyed televised reunion—or even whether or not we were worth reuniting in the first place.

Sure, I knew we weren't close, but between making up stories to amuse Sam's customers, autographing sporting equipment, and absorbing everyone's enthusiastic reaction to Janey, I was almost starting to believe Teddy and I were Westover, Illinois's version of Joanie and Chachi.

"Not really, it's just that there are some people who think it would be . . ." I trailed off without finishing. What was it going to be? A boost to Teddy's album sales? The clincher for my partnership review? "I just wanted you to know so you're not surprised if you hear about it. This is a onetime thing. I'm still absolutely focused on Darcy's lawsuit."

"I don't doubt that, Jane." Kitty gave me a reassuring smile.

"Thanks."

"Darcy's birthday is coming up, you know. She'll be eighteen. Officially an adult." Kitty reached out and stroked a hydrangea resting against her chair. "Do you remember what you did for your eighteenth birthday, Jane?"

My eighteenth birthday was spent eating a frozen chocolate Pepperidge Farm cake while I went through the yellow pages looking for moving companies who were willing to throw in the cardboard boxes at no extra charge.

My mom had tried to make it a special occasion, but the purple streamers strung haphazardly across our dining room only seemed to highlight the fact that the gift-wrapped presents piled at the head of the table were merely filling the void where a father used to sit. Turning eighteen had been less of a milestone to adulthood than the unexpected and uncelebrated event that occurred four months before on Thanksgiving.

"Nothing as exciting as Darcy has planned, I'm sure."

"Unfortunately, I don't know what she has planned. It's sad, isn't it? I remember when all she wanted for her birthday was to spend the day riding Clover." Kitty stopped midstroke. "So why does this man want to meet you now?"

"We're not meeting," I reminded her. "We're being reunited."

"Oh, that's right. *Reunited*," Kitty repeated, making fun of me. "I remember that song. Peaches and Cream was it?"

"Peaches and Herb."

Kitty nodded. "Ah, yes. You're right. They were very popular once. Was your friend as popular as Ms. Peaches and Mr. Herb?"

Comparing Teddy Rock to Peaches and Herb. I'd love to see how Ian could spin that one. "Even more so."

"Really?" The idea seemed to intrigue Kitty. "I can't wait to see what happens."

"Yeah," I agreed, taking a long sip of my lemonade to help me wash down the idea a little more easily. "Me, too."

DECEMBER 12, 1991

Teddy Rock Dropped by Record Label

Singer and musician Teddy Rock has been dropped by Kick Records.

The singer—who had a chart-topping hit with "Janey 245" in 1989—was axed by his record label because his most recent music releases failed to ignite the charts.

A music insider revealed that "Teddy Rock was great right out of the block, but he wasn't consistent and Kick decided to cut its losses."

When Rock's second album from Kick was released last March, the al-

bum did not fulfill the label's prophecy. It opened at number 30 on the *Billboard* chart, with a non-huge 54,000 copies sold, and slid from there.

Kick did not return calls for comment Tuesday, and instead issued a statement citing "less than acceptable sales performance" for Teddy's second album as the reason the label dropped the onetime platinum-selling singer.

But Rock isn't fazed. The 21-year-old predicts he still has a bright future ahead of him. The source adds, "Teddy was surprised about the recent news, but he feels it's Kick's loss and if they're not willing to step up and support him, he'll go it alone."

CHAPTER TWELVE

Apparently Olivia's greatest concern wasn't that I was about to go on national TV and tell the world that I was Teddy's Janey. No. She was worried that I'd announce I was Janey while wearing something wrong for the occasion.

"You can't wear that," she'd cried when I told her I was going to wear my beige suit.

"Not just the beige suit," I'd told her. "My beige suit with the black ribbed turtleneck." Black turtlenecks were artsy and hip, right? Wrong.

"Stay put," she instructed. "I'm coming over to help."

An hour later I buzzed in Olivia and discovered that she'd also recruited reinforcements. Dressing Janey was a two-person job.

"I didn't know this was going to be a group effort." I stood aside as Liv and Nat pushed past me carrying armloads of clothes. "What is this, a fashion intervention?"

"Come on, a beige suit?" Nat repeated. "Even I know better than that."

If Natalie thought it was necessary to join in on my wardrobe rescue, I was definitely in need of help. This was a woman who lived in green scrubs, clogs and overalls.

"Just because I can't enjoy them doesn't mean somebody else shouldn't," Olivia explained, organizing the pieces she hasn't been able to fit into since the boys were born. "These are perfect for your televised coming out."

Liv had impeccable taste. She also had expensive taste.

"Here." She held out three options to start with. "We have a white Dolce and Gabbana tuxedo-style suit with satin lapels and satin side strips down the pants, a pair of black leather pants and a Missoni mosaic print miniskirt with this beaded top."

"They're interviewing Janey, not Demi," I told her. "Didn't you bring anything a little less flashy? I was thinking of something more tasteful."

"Come on," she cried. "Embrace your Janey-ness!" She handed me a red Escada pencil skirt.

I slipped out of my sweatpants and pulled on the skirt. "I don't want to look like I'm trying too hard."

"You're going to be on TV, Jane. You're supposed to try hard," she informed me while she rifled through my drawers.

Liv was right. I examined my reflection in the full-length mirror. The skirt did look nice. No, it looked better than nice. It looked hot.

I turned sideways and scrutinized my profile in the mirror. Why hadn't I worn something like this before? There was definitely some Janey there. Sure, the red was a little brighter than what I was used to, and the way the material hugged my thighs—my wanton thighs—I wasn't sure I'd be able to sit down, but all in all, pretty nice.

I ran my hand along the waistband that managed to accentuate my curves without making me look too hippy, and then smoothed the front of the skirt down over my flat stomach, which would stay flat as long as I didn't exhale.

"I like it, but I think it's too dressy."

Liv would not be deterred in her quest for sartorial perfection. "If you want to go casual but cool, how about my Seven jeans, a white top and your black blazer with the high-heeled boots? It'll be very Gwyneth. And take this." She threw a scarf at me.

"And what am I supposed to do with this?"

"Where are you staying?"

"The Carlyle."

"Then you use that to tie Teddy to the bed at the Carlyle."

I tossed the scarf back to Liv. "I'm doing this to show Arthur I'm a team player, not to get laid."

"Why not kill two birds with one stone?" she asked, completely serious. "Besides, admit it. You can't wait to see Teddy."

I stepped out of the skirt and found the jeans among the pile of clothes on my bed. "Maybe I'm a little curious."

"You're more than a little curious. You can't fool me. You're dying to find out why he wrote a song about you."

Liv had me there. You could bet I'd be asking him why. Why me? Why was I someone he remembered after so many years? But there was also the question that Teddy couldn't answer, the question that wormed its way into my head every time I thought about being, about *becoming*, Janey—why was the girl in the song so different from the woman I became?

And what about Teddy, the quiet little boy who went on to become a household name and then fell from grace? He expected to meet Janey, but I had no idea who'd be waiting for me in New York. The cocky rock star who affectionately named his tour bus the Port-o-Party, or someone else entirely?

Natalie found the blazer she'd been searching for in my closet and brought it over to me. "Here, take this one. Do you have a white tank you can wear under it?"

I pointed toward the closet. "I think so. Look on the second shelf, next to my sweaters."

She tossed me the tank top and I pulled it over my head before slipping into the blazer. I stood there like a mannequin as they circled me for inspection. "So, this is it?" I asked. "Do I have your stamp of approval?"

"You have more than that," Liv answered, grabbing my tank and tucking it down into my pants so that my boobs were prominently displayed. "You have my lucky jeans."

"Why does that worry me?" I stood in front of the full-length mirror and surveyed the results of their hard work.

"You like?" Liv asked, peering over my shoulder until she could see our reflection. "You look very Janey."

"Janey is a noun, Liv. Not an adjective," I corrected her.

"Actually, it's a person," Natalie pointed out. "It's you. Will Teddy even recognize you when you meet him?"

"I don't know." The girl in the mirror didn't exactly resemble a bowlegged eleven-year-old dancing like a maniac in her favorite Flashdance sweatshirt.

"Were you cute?" Nat asked, folding the discarded outfits.

"I was cute," Liv offered. "Not Cindy-Brady-banana-pigtails cute. More like Kristy McNichol cute."

Funny, I'd always pictured Natalie as the Kristy McNichol tomboy type. Not Olivia.

"I thought you'd be the girl who always called first dibs on playing Farrah Fawcett during a game of Charlie's Angels."

"Oh, I was," Liv confirmed. "I didn't have the blond hair or cleavage, but I had the attitude. What about you?"

"I always wanted to be Jaclyn Smith," Natalie told us.

"Me, too!" I cried.

"Kelly?" Liv wrinkled her nose. "But everyone always said they wanted to play Kelly. I definitely pictured Jane as more of a Sabrina—all book smarts and no bikini shots."

"Yeah, they always had Kate Jackson pretending to be a librarian while Farrah and Jaclyn got to play race car drivers and cocktail waitresses. Why didn't anyone ever want to be Sabrina?" Natalie asked.

"I bet Teddy liked Farrah," I said to no one in particular, thinking my black blazer and jeans weren't very Jill Munroe. Now a tube top, that was probably more Teddy's style.

"Come on, all the guys liked Farrah," Nat pointed out, placing the red skirt back on its hanger and hanging it up in my closet instead of returning it to the pile with the rest of Liv's clothes. "Was Teddy Rock cute?"

I tried to remember if anyone had a crush on Teddy back then, but I couldn't recall a single girl who went out of her way to sit near him on the bus or ran-walked across the music room in a race to snag him for a square dance partner. He was just sort of average. "I guess, but not more so than anyone else."

"There are the kids who peaked when they were young—once again I'll use Cindy Brady as an example or even that kid who played Nicholas in *Eight Is Enough*." Liv kicked off her shoes and sat cross-legged on my bed. "And then there are the kids who have buckteeth and gangly bodies and grow up to be stunning. Ever seen a picture of Tyra Banks as a child?"

Nat made a face. "Eesh. Homely."

Interesting concept, but it begged the question, Had I already peaked? "Do you think everyone has a peak?"

"I think the key is to keep peaking."

"Do you think that Teddy peaked when he was eighteen?"

"I'd call going from sold-out arenas to the lounge at some Holiday Inn a big peak and a huge fall."

"He's not playing at Holiday Inns."

"Only because Dan Fogelberg and Debbie Gibson probably come cheaper."

"Okay, enough with the fairy godmother act." I handed Liv her shoes and waved her off the bed. "It's almost seven thirty; you'd better go. Andy's on his way over to wish me luck." It occurred to me that if I'd known about Liv's jeans, I could have saved him the trip.

"So, why do we have to leave?" Nat collected the discarded clothes and stuffed them in a Bloomingdale's shopping bag.

"With the three of you around here it will be Janey overload."

Liv took the shoes and dangled them from her pinkies as she planted her hands on her hips. "Honey, I have one piece of advice for you: Get used to it."

"Can't I come, please?" Andy begged for the billionth time. "I promise I'll be good." He took an imaginary key out of his pocket and locked his lips, but I pushed him out the door and shoved a parting gift in his hands—a tray of frozen Stouffer's lasagna.

"I'm just going for the night, Andy. Besides this is business, not pleasure."

"Well, hello, Mrs. Winston." Andy stopped short and practically bowed to my neighbor as she walked toward us. "Can I help you with those bags?"

"Thank you, Andy." Mrs. Winston handed Andy her grocery bags while she fished around in her purse for her keys. "So, what's this I hear about you being a famous go-go dancer, Jane?" she inquired without even bothering to look in my direction.

"Not a go-go dancer, Mrs. Winston. Someone I knew wrote a song about me," I explained, although it probably wouldn't do any good. From this day on Mrs. Winston would tell everyone that the girl across the hall danced in a cage and let men stuff dollar bills down her G-string.

"Well, I don't want those paparazzi people hanging around the entrance to the building all night," she cautioned, as if I was rivaling Princess Diana for media attention. "We don't want to have to call a meeting with the condo board, now, do we, Jane?"

"That's not going to happen, Mrs. Winston."

She took her grocery bags from Andy and stepped inside her apartment. "You keep your sister in line now, you hear me, Andy?"

"Every word, Mrs. Winston."

Mrs. Winston shut her door and the sound of six dead bolts locking into place immediately followed.

"She's probably watching us through her peephole," I muttered, doing my best ventriloquist impression to keep my lips from giving me away.

"She's harmless." Andy lifted the lasagna up and down as if trying to determine whether or not the family-sized aluminum tray really held the five pounds of food it promised. "Well, have fun in New York. Be good," he called over his shoulder before disappearing down the hall muttering *Go-go dancer, I love it.*

NEW YORK DAILY NEWS JANUARY 14, 1992

Rock Paternity Suit Dismissed

The pending paternity suit against musician Teddy Rock was dismissed on Wednesday when medical tests proved that Rock did not father the one-year-old child named in the suit.

Rock was hit with the paternity suit as he turned up to face criminal charges in a New York court last September. Minutes before the 21-year-old rock star pleaded guilty to operating a motor vehicle under the influence of alcohol, he was served with paternity papers. An angry and shocked Rock hurled abuse at the process server who handed him the papers outside court, and had to be persuaded to calm down by his attorney. In the court papers, a woman from upstate New York alleged the rocker fathered her one-year-old son and hasn't paid child support. The rocker insisted he wasn't the father of the child involved in the paternity suit.

"While Teddy Rock feels badly for the child in question, he's relieved that he can put this matter behind him and focus on his music career," said Max Pope, Rock's manager.

Last month Rock was dropped from his label, Kick Records.

CHAPTER THIRTEEN

My flight was delayed, but a driver was patiently waiting for me by the luggage carousel, a discreet sign with my name in bold black letters held up to his chest.

"Are we going to make it?" I asked, watching the minutes tick by on the dashboard clock as we wedged into line behind the crawling traffic.

"Don't worry, I'll have you there in plenty of time. Just sit back and enjoy the ride."

I took my driver's suggestion to heart and let my body sink into the slippery leather seat. As we drove, I watched the dingy gray warehouses pass by, giving way to larger buildings until we crossed the bridge into Manhattan. Teddy was somewhere on that island waiting to meet me—or at least waiting for the girl he remembered. The fact of the matter was that Teddy probably wouldn't recognize me if he ran over me with his car.

I had to wonder—the song was fourteen years old, so why now? Sure, there was Teddy's impending album, but why was Andy only now realizing the resemblance between me and the girl in the song? Why was everyone so willing to accept that I was the girl Teddy sang about—the radio station, everyone at

Sam's, Arthur, even Mrs. Winston. Admittedly, I was growing more accustomed to the idea every day, but it was like going from a raging ulcer to a mild case of acid reflux—I still wasn't quite able to digest the idea without some discomfort.

It was like the movie *Trading Places,* when two rich brothers decide to take a homeless Eddie Murphy off the streets of Philadelphia and see whether, given all the benefits of a privileged life, he could change who he was. A real-life experiment of nurture versus nature. Was I always destined to turn out as ultrareliable, überdependable Jane? Or did I actually have a choice somewhere along the line? Had I been given a chance to take a different path and instead decided that I was better safe than sorry?

I almost believed I had a choice, once, when I left Westover and went to college. My first semester I walked around in a fog. You do that for a while, wake up and think that maybe you imagined it all. *Maybe today things will return to normal,* you think before you open your eyes and see the same beige walls with the Big Green poster tacked above your roommate's bed. It takes only a few minutes for you to realize things will never be normal again, to realize that normal now means you don't have a father and your mother is living in a strange house she can barely afford with the job she got answering the phones at a dentist's office in town.

But during my second semester I decided that wasn't working. So I made a choice. I decided to try and have fun. There were times at parties when I'd force myself to forget about my dad for a minute and let myself be happy, let myself enjoy what I was doing at that exact moment rather than putting it in the context of the timeline that seemed to have a large black divider in its center marking when everything changed—before Dad died, and after Dad died.

And it worked, until something took the place of the sadness. Something that I found even harder to live with than the pain of remembering—the guilt of forgetting.

When the car finally slipped between the cabs and pulled up to the curb in front of the studio, the driver opened my door and waited for me step out, to make a choice.

I could tell the driver to take me back to the airport and catch the next flight back to Chicago. I didn't have to ask for Teddy's business. I didn't have to stay in New York. I didn't have to go on TV and meet Teddy. And I didn't even have to be Janey.

But a part of me wanted to.

I took the driver's hand and let him help me out of the car.

"Good luck," he said, handing me my overnight bag.

Standing on the sidewalk, looking up at the marquee announcing LATE SHOW WITH DAVID LETTERMAN, it almost seemed as if luck did have something to do with my being there. Then again, maybe it was just Liv's Seven jeans.

Once I checked in at the front desk, they kept me and Teddy apart. The producers thought it would heighten the drama of the moment if we met for the first time onstage. Although it wasn't really the first time we were meeting, it may as well have been. When Teddy last saw me, I was still wearing my Bonne Bell root beer Lip Smacker.

But there was no Lip Smacker tonight. I'd been ushered into the makeup room, seated in a swiveling barbershop chair and covered in a paper bib designed to protect my clothes from the powders and gels and creams about to be slathered on my skin. A makeup woman applied foundation, eye makeup and MAC Pink Poodle LipGlass before the stylist ran a straightening iron through my hair, creating a slight bend and more body than I'd achieved in thirty-two years of abuse at the hands of curling irons, hair dryers and even chemical perms, back in the good old days. I was looking more like Janey with every passing minute.

"Voila!" the hair stylist cried when she'd pumped the final mist of hair spray. "What do you think?"

I stared in the mirror and took a deep breath before answering. It was still me, but I was somehow transformed—like they say in *Spinal Tap*, it was me turned up to eleven. In some ways it reminded me of when we had to sell the house on Memorial Circle. Once the moving men removed the sofa and chair from the living room, we stood in the empty space and noticed for the first time how faded and worn the carpet had grown right under our feet. The areas once concealed beneath furniture stood out in stark contrast, the carpet's pile brighter and more vivid from years of hiding. If you hadn't seen the *before*, you would never have realized how different it was from the *after*.

"I think I look like someone Teddy Rock would write a song about."

I figured Ian had probably drilled Teddy until he had all of his perfect rock-star responses down pat, so while I waited in the greenroom I rehearsed answers to every possible question Dave could ask. This sounded easy in theory. In reality, Teddy had an entire team of people in a private room with him somewhere while I sat in the greenroom next to the nine-year-old winner of

Nebraska's annual fiddle tune competition and the owner of a German shepherd who could bark the theme songs to 1970s sitcoms. Forced to listen to Thor rehearse the theme from *Laverne & Shirley* while a third-grader polished his trophy with a chamois cloth, I felt seriously outnumbered.

In law school I'd spoken in front of an auditorium filled with people, and four minutes talking to Dave had to be easier than two hours debating the merits of tort reform. At least there were no desks they could put their heads down on for a nap. So why were my hands practically misting? And why was my stomach as hollow as Andy's piggy bank? Because I hadn't eaten anything since breakfast or because I was about to meet Teddy Rock?

I was beginning to feel like the prize on *The Price Is Right*, waiting for the curtain to be pulled back and for Bob Barker to announce, *And behind curtain number two, we have Janey 245!* What if the curtain didn't reveal what Teddy was expecting? What if he took one look at me and asked to see what was behind curtain number three instead?

It was just Teddy Rock; I knew shouldn't care what some has-been rocker thought of me. But I did. And I hated it! I hated myself for even caring enough to hate it.

I stood up and attempted to shake the feeling of impending humiliation, alternately picking at the sandwich platter and pacing the room, which, contrary to its name, wasn't even green.

Right after my canine friend left for his moment in the spotlight, the greenroom door swung open and Ian stood there smiling at me. "Janey, you look great. Are you nervous?"

I wiped my hands on Liv's Seven jeans—and not for good luck. "I'm just ready to get this over with."

Ian pointed to the TV mounted on a bracket in the corner of the room. "Dave's going to introduce Teddy next, so I wanted to come in here and check on you. And I also wanted to do this." He reached up and shut the TV off. "We want you to see Teddy for the first time when Dave calls you onto the set."

I was beginning to wonder whether there was more to this than Ian was letting on. Maybe Teddy wasn't the hot rock star I remembered. That episode of *Off the Record* could have been filmed years ago, and for all I knew, Teddy could be sporting a comb-over and one hell of a beer belly. After all, this was Teddy's first live television appearance in a decade.

"Before you go out there, I wanted to mention a few things." Ian moved the fiddler's trophy aside and sat down on the couch next to me. "After the success of Teddy's first album, there was kind of a backlash. Not many guys come on the scene and have a hit right off the bat. And to say that Teddy took advantage of the *opportunities* his celebrity afforded him would be an understatement. I know his second album wasn't quite up to par, but people had it in for Teddy. They were jealous. This is his first live interview in a while and we're not sure how it will go, but I hope you'll do what you can to help make it a good one." Ian patted my knee. "I think you'll see that he's not the old Teddy everyone's expecting."

I knew it. Back acne and unruly nose hair.

For some reason, I started to relax. Was it pathetic that the thought of Teddy's poor skin condition and unkempt nostrils made me feel better?

"I'll try my best."

Satisfied that I was on Teddy's side, Ian led me to the set, where I waited offstage while one of the show's staff wired me for sound.

"Here, can you slip this mike up your shirt? Then we'll clip it to your lapel." The sound woman handed me the small black microphone and I obediently lifted my tank top and snaked the thin black cord inside until it reached the opening at my neck.

"Now we'll just clip the body pack on the back of your pants like this and we're all set." She stepped back. "Can you say something? We need to test the sound."

"Testing, one-two-three." Isn't that what they always said on TV? Look at me, an old pro already.

"Perfect. You're on in about two minutes."

"Ladies and gentlemen, Janey 245."

At the sound of Dave's voice, my ribcage seemed to contract, allowing only short shallow breaths that made me wonder whether I was hyperventilating for the first time in my life. And that thought practically had me gasping for air.

I took one last gulp and stepped out under the lights just in time to see Dave and Teddy rising from their seats to watch me. As I started toward the raised platform where Teddy awaited my arrival, I couldn't help but glance out at the audience, which was reduced to a blur of faces and clapping hands as I strode across the stage to meet the man who had taken me from relative obscurity to a guest on one of the most watched late-night talk shows. When I

turned back to get a good look at Teddy, he was grinning. I tried to stop it—
I really did—but without even thinking, I found myself matching his grin
tooth for tooth. It was just too ironic, almost as if Ian had planned it. We
were dressed almost identically in dark denim jeans, white shirts and black
blazers.

When I reached him, Teddy held out his arms and embraced me, burying
his freshly shaven face in my hair. I found myself closing my eyes and inhaling the clean scent of shaving cream and guava shampoo. This wasn't the
balding, bloated Teddy I'd prepared for. And it wasn't the stubbly, grimy
Teddy from *Off the Record*. Gone were the vintage T-shirts and the broken-in
leather pants. There wasn't a baseball cap hiding his hair, and although the
dark strands falling just above his shoulder were shiny enough to reflect the
overhead lights, it seemed to be done on purpose rather than the result of forgetting to shower after a five-day bender.

No, this wasn't the Teddy from the days of "Janey 245." It wasn't even *Off
the Record* Teddy. He'd managed to surprise me with new and improved Teddy.
But as his hands rested lightly on my hips and he pulled away from me to
once again face the audience, the biggest surprise of all was that I really kind
of liked the way this Teddy looked.

I took Teddy's lead and stepped up to my seat, noticing for the first time
that the scenic nighttime view of New York City behind Dave's desk was really created with small bulbs resembling Christmas tree lights. The skyline
that towered behind Dave on TV was all an illusion.

"Did you two plan this?" Dave joked, pointing to our outfits.

Teddy grabbed my hand and laced our fingers together before lifting it to
his mouth for a kiss. "She obviously has great taste."

I was still looking at the small moist spot on the back of my hand when
Dave turned to me.

"So, Janey. What do you think?" he asked. "Is this who you remember?"

"Not exactly," I admitted. "I think Teddy's traded up from his Toughskins
and Chuck Taylors."

Dave laughed and the audience followed his lead. The tightness in my chest
started to melt away, allowing my lungs to fill with air again. If I was going to
introduce Janey to the world, I may as well try to enjoy it.

"Well, we're glad you could join us tonight, Janey. This is a little piece of
music history happening before us, folks," he told the audience. "Teddy, what
about you?"

"What can I say, she's beautiful," Teddy answered, not taking his eyes off me as he studied my face. I couldn't tell whether he couldn't get over how much I looked like he remembered, or whether he was trying to remember me altogether.

"What do you remember most about Janey? I mean, she had to be quite memorable to stick with you for almost seven years before you wrote 'Janey 245.' "

Teddy continued staring at me and I started to feel uncomfortable. His eyes were even clearer in person than they were on TV, practically verging on turquoise. They reminded me of the huge saltwater fish tank in the foyer of the Chinese restaurant my parents took us to as kids.

"It's not really one specific thing I remembered all those years," he finally answered. "It was the whole package."

The whole package? He was talking about an eleven-year-old girl. How much of a package could I have been?

"It was the way her ponytails would bounce behind her when she chased her dog across the lawn."

"I think Teddy means my cat," I interrupted, thinking that Pumpkin was a little on the rotund side. She could have easily been mistaken for a small dog from across the street.

"Of course, your cat," Teddy corrected himself. "Fluffy, right?"

"Pumpkin."

"Of course," Teddy agreed. "And she had this pink bike with a bell and streamers hanging off the handlebars."

Actually, my bike was purple, but he got the bell and streamers right.

"So, what happens now?" Dave asked.

"I'd like to get to know Janey again. Maybe spend some time together getting reacquainted."

There were a few whistles from the audience, just in case we all missed the innuendo. For a rock star, *reacquainted* probably meant *naked*.

"What do you say, Janey?" Dave asked. "You interested in going out with Teddy?"

The red beacon light atop the camera in front of me lit up and I had to think of an answer fast. What would Janey do if a rock star just insinuated that he wanted to fuck her? She'd probably play along and have fun with it. I turned to Teddy. "Does that mean you're paying for dinner?" I joked, and again laughter rippled through the audience.

Dave waited for the audience to quiet down. "So, we know all about Teddy, but what about Janey? You don't strike me as a full-time groupie."

"No, not even a part-time groupie. Actually I'm an attorney in Chicago."

"Impressive. You know how to pick 'em, Teddy."

Teddy squeezed my hand and Janey squeezed back.

This wasn't at all what I'd expected. Where was the chain-smoking wild man who used to punctuate every sentence with *fuckin' A*? What happened to the Teddy who trashed hotel rooms and dove off of balconies into swimming pools, only to later claim that it wasn't him, it was Jack Daniels?

"So, Jane. I hear you had no idea that you were the subject of Teddy's song. How'd you react when you found out?"

"I was surprised, to say the least. But I guess I'm warming up to the idea. I think Teddy took some liberties with the lyrics, because I don't exactly remember my skin doing any taunting back in sixth grade, unless it was the Clearasil."

The audience laughed at me. At me! Janey Marlow was funny.

Dave turned to Teddy. "So, Teddy, how much of the song is true?"

"Dave, as you know, reality is only a foundation, a canvas, upon which we, as artists, paint our own picture," Teddy explained, becoming serious. I thought he was being a little over the top with that one. I mean, he wrote a rock song, not a symphony. "Of course, I think you can see why I'd remember Janey. Who wouldn't find her memorable?" Again with the long gaze in my direction.

"But she was eleven years old at the time. Are you telling us that you two . . ." Dave let his question trail off, but we all got the hint. Was Teddy molesting a preadolescent Janey?

Teddy looked stricken, and I could just imagine Ian freaking out in the wings. Teddy Rock—a pedophile. How would he spin that one?

Teddy needed my help. "I think what Teddy means is that while we didn't have carnal knowledge of one another, there was definitely a connection between us," I jumped in. "We had an innocent flirtation—maybe it was my Wonder Woman Underoos."

Teddy regained his poise and joined me. "Right, it's just like Janey said. There was no carmel knowledge."

Did I hear that correctly? Did Teddy just say *carmel* knowledge? If he did, Dave let it slide.

Instead he pulled a CD case out from under his desk and held it up for the audience to see. The cameraman focused on the CD cover, which featured a simple black-and-white photograph of Teddy holding an acoustic guitar. "Teddy Rock's new self-titled CD will be in stores on July fourth. What can we expect from this album, Teddy?"

"Well, Dave, it's been almost ten years since my third album."

"And from what I remember—actually I don't remember that one." Dave scratched his chin and prompted a wave of chuckles through the audience.

Teddy laughed at himself. "Not many people do, unfortunately. Anyway, things have changed since then. I've changed since then. And I think the music on this album reflects that."

"So, none of the screeching guitars we all remember?"

"I think we might have one or two of those for you," Teddy teased, and the audience applauded. "But on the whole, I'll think you'll be seeing a different Teddy Rock."

"Does this mean we won't be reading about you raising hell like the old days? Have you given up on biting the heads off of baby bunnies?"

"That was a chocolate bunny, Dave. And it was an Easter show. Come on, give me a break." Teddy gave the audience a sheepish grin, but you could tell he was loving every minute of this. "We're going to be doing some small shows in the next few weeks to get ready for the tour, which begins in July right after the album's released."

"Well, Janey, it's been great seeing the woman behind the song. When we return, Teddy will play the first single off his new self-titled CD."

The center camera pulled in for a tight close-up of us. Teddy and his muse together at last. It was like something right out of a song.

When the cameraman signaled that he'd stopped filming, I stood to leave the stage.

"So, you're Janey." Teddy looked me up and down, pondering the stranger before him.

"The one and only," I confirmed.

Teddy nodded his head and grinned at me. "Ian was right."

Before I could ask what Ian was right about, an assistant appeared from out of nowhere and directed me off the set, where Ian was waiting with a smile even bigger than Teddy's.

"Janey, that was great! You were great. Go wait in the greenroom and I'll come get you when Teddy's finished."

The TV in the greenroom had been turned back on, and right there, projected from a stage not fifty feet away, was Teddy Rock with a cranberry red Gibson guitar strapped across his body. There were minimal hip gyrations while he sang, but he still managed to sway to the music and move in a way that suggested he had skills away from the microphone as well.

Olivia had to be freaking out at home. Bill was definitely getting lucky tonight.

I listened intently to Teddy singing the lyrics and tried to imagine, to truly understand, why Teddy remembered me so vividly when I could barely recall a single conversation we ever had.

Was he the boy who pulled the fire alarm and had us evacuated from the school just in time to avoid our science test? It could have been, but I thought I recalled Greg Schiller apologizing over the intercom after the fire trucks drove away, their sirens still blaring. Did Teddy and I stand together in the cafeteria line every Tuesday, waiting for our sloppy joes and lime Jell-O with Cool Whip? When the light was on in his bedroom, was he waiting for me to stand in my window and look back at him?

I wanted to remember. I really did.

When the song ended and the TV went black, I sat down and waited. And waited. Until finally the greenroom door flung open and Ian heralded Teddy in like a returning conqueror.

"Janey, this is Teddy Rock."

"Hey, thanks for coming." Teddy hung back, almost using Ian as a shield between us. He wasn't reaching to touch me or hold my hand like the affectionate guest I'd sat next to on the show. But at least he hadn't transformed into obnoxious rock-star guy, either. "I hope it wasn't too bad."

"No, not at all."

Ian clapped his hands together like a coach trying to psych up his team. "Okay, it's almost six o'clock. What are you in the mood for? You have the entire city at your disposal."

I glanced over at the disheveled sandwich platter on the side table. "To tell you the truth, I'm not that hungry right now."

Ian wasted no time suggesting an alternate plan. "How about we have the car take you to the hotel, you check out your rooms, get comfortable, and meet in the bar for a drink."

Teddy looked at me expectantly, waiting for my answer with all the excitement of someone who'd just been diagnosed with athlete's foot.

What happened to the guy who couldn't keep his hands off me? The guy who found me so memorable he practically declared himself a pervert on national TV? Without even realizing it, during the ten minutes I waited in the greenroom I'd built up Teddy and Janey to mythical proportions—private jokes, shared histories and innocent flirtations. So what was with Teddy's sudden change of heart? Was he the attentive, amicable Letterman guest or the standoffish rock star? Was I memorable, or just some girl Ian made him hold hands with on TV? I wished Teddy would make up his mind.

"Sure," I replied curtly, when what I was really thinking was *Bring back my Teddy Rock!*

Rock's in a Hard Place

BY JAMIE TYNE

(2/20/92)—Teddy Rock has sometimes come across as someone who doesn't quite live in the same world as the rest of us, with all those million-dollar-budget videos filled with blimps, dolphins, lavish recreations of gothic ceremonies, pyrotechnics and the like. Some have even thought that the singer is crazy to try to recapture the success he once achieved with the release of his debut album, *Rock Hard*. Well, Rock continues to live up to his image as an out-of-touch rock star with the latest report that he's self-producing a third album after his label, Kick Records, dropped him. He seems perfectly confident that he can learn in a year or so what seasoned producers have mastered over the course of a lifetime.

CHAPTER FOURTEEN

Apparently Teddy wasn't just a rock star. He was quite an actor as well.

His interest in me diminished as soon as the cameras stopped filming and Ian was out of earshot. As the car wound its way in silence up Madison Avenue, Teddy was more concerned with retrieving his voice mail than making conversation with Janey. A credit card–sized cell phone was plastered to his once-pierced ear the entire ride. After what I thought were some obvious clues that I found his constant button pushing and cell phone beeping rude, including some overzealous throat clearing and tapping of feet, I decided to just ignore him. I tried not to listen, but in the stillness of the limousine's backseat it was hard not to catch a few of the conversations, which of course revolved around Teddy, Teddy's comeback and Teddy's career.

Now, this was definitely what I expected—an egotistical rock star who didn't even have the common courtesy to talk to the person sitting two feet away from him in the backseat of a car. To him I was just another girl in his limo, like all the groupies who'd gotten nothing more from Teddy than a pounding against some backstage door, his pants around his ankles, their underwear stretched like a rubber band around their knees.

Only I wasn't just another star-struck groupie. I was Janey. And you'd think that would mean something to Teddy. It had started to mean something to me.

I turned my back on him and stared out my tinted window at the people rushing by. If Teddy was going to ignore me, I was going to ignore him right back. After all, why should I care what Teddy thought of me? I was the one doing him a favor. I was the one Ian needed to make Teddy's Letterman interview a true media event. He was just lucky Arthur was so gung ho about this "opportunity."

And Teddy had gotten his media attention, his live reunion with Janey. Now it was my turn to get what I came for—a new client. So much for the trip down memory lane.

In the smoky window, a dim image of Teddy reflected off the glass so that I could watch his every move unnoticed. I spied him toying with the vent above his head, trying to redirect the circulating air while he listened to the person on the other end of the phone. The mirrored version of Teddy masked the signs that showed any time had passed since "Janey 245," softening the lines around his eyes and masking a receding hairline that was perceptible only up close.

As the top of the Carlyle Hotel emerged from between the shadows of neighboring buildings, its top pointed and illuminated like the tip of a pencil, Teddy's cell phone snapped shut. The car stopped in front of the hotel and uniformed doormen greeted us before walking around to the back of the car to retrieve our luggage.

The whole scene seemed a little stuffy for the likes of Teddy Rock. The polite yet dutifully reserved uniformed doormen. The ornate overhang with elegant script protecting the heavy brass revolving doors underneath. The lobby's black polished floors setting the stage for pristine tangerine couches under a crystal chandelier. Thick, carved crown molding wrapping around the lobby like a piece of ribbon candy. This wasn't a place that would look kindly upon Teddy's well-publicized rock-star antics.

"Ian already checked us in," Teddy told me, heading straight for the elevator. "You can get your key from the desk and I'll meet you in the bar in half an hour."

"Fine," I replied, but Teddy was already on his phone with an editor from *Rolling Stone*. I should have known better. Teddy was exactly what I'd imagined.

Teddy was already waiting for me in the bar. I had to admit, I was a little surprised. I'd loitered longer than necessary in my suite, but only because I figured Teddy would be still be attached to his cell phone. But there he was, seated on the snaking leather banquette hugging the length of the wall, still dressed like my identical twin. There was no phone pressed up to his ear and he wasn't making conversation with a couple seated at the table next to him. In fact, it really looked like he was just waiting for me.

The bar was all mood, with candle lamps glowing softly on the nickel-trimmed black glass tables dotting the banquette. Glass columns illuminated in gold light added drama to a room already adorned with a gold leaf ceiling. I followed every curve of the wall until I reached his table, delaying the inevitable.

"I was starting to think you weren't going to show," Teddy commented, not even bothering to stand up and offer me a seat.

I *could* have told him that he was rude. I *should* have told him that he was obnoxious. I *wanted* to tell him that I had better things to do than be ignored by some guy on his cell phone.

But what I *had to do* was ask him if he had a good attorney.

"I'm here now." I flagged over the waiter and ordered a glass of wine. If I was going to get through an evening with Teddy Rock, superstar, I needed some help. Preferably from a good cabernet.

While we waited for my wine, I looked around the room and avoided any direct eye contact with Teddy.

"You want an autograph or something?" he asked, circling a finger around the rim of his water glass while he spoke.

An autograph? Did I look like I was eighteen and this was 1989? "Thanks, but I think I'll pass."

My wine arrived and I took a long, grateful sip.

Teddy exhaled a long, bored sigh. "So, you want to go back to my room and fuck?"

"What?" I choked, trying to keep my wine from spraying down the front of my white tank.

Teddy shook his head, puzzled. "Isn't that why you're here?"

"God, no."

"Really?" Teddy seemed genuinely surprised.

Did I truly look like I had all the willpower of a bobble-head doll? "Yes, really," I repeated. "Why would you think that?"

"Well, Ian said maybe . . . No. Forget it. Forget I said anything."

The more I learned about Ian, the less I liked. I pushed my glass away and waited for Teddy's explanation. "No, tell me. What did Ian say?"

"You've got to admit, you coming all the way to New York to meet me on TV and all. Ian thought you might think there was something in it for you."

"Sex? I'd take the afternoon off from work, fly two hours to New York, take a shitty ride from LaGuardia to midtown during rush hour, just to have sex with you?"

Teddy looked up at me through a thick fringe of dark lashes. "Women have done more."

"Not this woman," I informed him.

Teddy looked down at the ice cubes melting in his glass. "Okay, my bad."

"Yeah, your bad."

We both reached for our drinks and spent way too much time and care taking sips, or, in Teddy's case, sucking on ice cubes.

"I'm starting to get the idea that you don't want to be here."

"Maybe you should get out your cell phone and call someone who cares," I couldn't help answering. Sure, I was here to see if he had any business, but I wasn't going to let him treat me like crap in the process.

Instead of telling me I was acting like a bitch, which is what I expected at this point, Teddy truly looked apologetic.

"You're right. I probably should have waited until I got to my suite. I'm sorry." His face softened and Teddy looked almost relieved. But about what? That he could drop the cool rock-star act? Or that he didn't have to sleep with me? "Ian's got me so paranoid about missing any media opportunities I feel like those prisoners with ankle bracelets that beep every time they leave their houses. If I don't return calls right away Ian practically sends a posse after me."

"So Ian's your parole officer?"

"Worse. He's my warden—Ian the Enforcer." Teddy laughed and I couldn't help but join him. Maybe he wasn't a total asshole.

I pointed to his clean-shaven face. "So, what happened to the goatee?"

He reached up and stroked his smooth chin. "Ian suggested I shave it off for the show. Do you like it?"

"I do. It's different."

"That's the idea." Teddy took a sip of his ice water and smiled at me. "But enough about me, what about you? You're a lawyer?"

"I'm a trusts and estates attorney."

"Like wills and that kind of thing?"

Without intending to, Teddy had given me my opening. "It's more than that. It involves financial projections and analysis of the income and tax con-sequences of assets and holdings—" I could tell I'd lost him. Maybe this was something I'd have to work up to. "Yeah, wills and those kind of things."

Unfortunately, Teddy seemed satisfied with the more simplistic explana-tion. Maybe he wasn't the one I should be talking to about this. Maybe I should be talking with his personal manager.

"It's beautiful here," I remarked, noticing the fluted mahogany facing against the black granite bar.

"Yeah, I guess. Ian picked it."

"It seems a little"—I paused, trying to think of the right word without in-sulting Teddy in the process—"*refined* for a rock star."

"I know. When I used to travel I'd stay in the hottest places, trendy bou-tique hotels, that sort of thing. But Ian thought this would be more fitting with my image as the new and improved Teddy. Nobody wants a drugged-up rock star pissing on the lobby carpet, right?" Teddy laughed, but I almost got the feeling that he missed his days of public urination.

"Have you always worked with Ian?"

"Are you kidding me? He was barely out of diapers when 'Janey 245' came out. He can be a little annoying, but he's supposed to be the best at what he does."

"And what does he do?"

"Ian likes to say he's in charge of my image, but I think he just gets off on telling me what to do. He figures out how to get me more press, makes sure the Teddy Rock people see is the Teddy Rock people want. You'd think a Grammy winner wouldn't need someone to tell him what to drink, but ap-parently image is everything these days." Teddy held up his ice water.

"You don't have to drink water on my account. Order whatever you want."

"Yeah, we'll see." Teddy crunched on the cubes as he spoke. "Look, I'm sorry I said that about going to the room. I mean, why else would you come all the way here to see me?"

"Maybe I just thought it would be interesting to see someone I knew a long time ago. Take a stroll down memory lane, that sort of thing."

"Sure. We could do that if you want," Teddy agreed, signaling for the waiter.

"Why don't you order a real drink," I suggested.

"Really? You won't tell Ian, will you?" He looked up at me with wide eyes and for a minute I could picture him as the little boy in the last seat of the school bus.

I shook my head. "It will be our secret."

A tuxedoed piano player sat down at the baby grand over in the corner and started tickling the keys before launching into a familiar Frank Sinatra song. Even though old standards weren't really Teddy's speed, his fingers began tapping along with the tune.

"You know, when my brother first called me and suggested that I was 'Janey 245,' I thought he was crazy," I told Teddy once his hands were wrapped around a glass of scotch.

"You have a brother?"

"Well, yeah. Andy. You must remember him, he was always creating some sort of neighborhood commotion. He used to stand in the middle of the street and wait for cars to drive by so he could run next to them and pretend he was the Six Million Dollar Man."

Teddy stared blankly at me.

"You know, he'd bring his arms back really slowly"—I raised my arm to show Teddy what I meant—"and make that noise—*na-na-na-na-na*—just like they had on the show whenever Lee Majors did something that required his multimillion-dollar strength."

Teddy nodded and slowly seemed to recall the incident. "Oh, yeah, right. Andy."

"You didn't play much with the neighborhood kids, did you?"

Teddy shook his head. "Nah, they were always running around playing army guys or Frisbee, and all I wanted to do was sit in my bedroom and figure out how to play my brother's crappy guitar."

"Your efforts obviously paid off. I can attest to the fact that Andy's imitation of Steve Austin didn't exactly lead down the path to riches."

"So is your family still in Westover?"

"My mom is still there, but now she lives over on Steeplechase, by the high school."

"I don't remember many of the street names. We moved to Saint Louis."

"I didn't even know you were planning to move."

Teddy swirled the ice cubes in his scotch with his finger while he talked. "Me neither. My mom just sprung it on me one morning and next thing I knew we were packing up. Why, did I miss anything exciting?"

"My dad died" slipped out before I even realized I'd been thinking of the words. My revelation hung in the air for a moment, mingling with a Nat King Cole tune floating our way.

Teddy stopped stirring his ice and lightly touched my hand, his still-wet finger leaving a droplet of water on my skin. "He did? Hey, I'm sorry. Obviously, I didn't know that. When?"

"Senior year. That's why my mom had to move."

"Too many memories in the old house?"

"No, the bank was on the verge of foreclosing on the house, so she didn't have much of a choice."

For some reason, sitting across from someone who knew my dad made it easier to talk about. It was as if we had an unspoken understanding. Teddy may have gone on to be a rock star who went below stage between sets to get blow jobs from willing female fans, as legend has it, and I may have chosen a more conventional path, but our shared history gave us something in common. Even if it was a history that I couldn't quite piece together.

"Do you go back there a lot?" Teddy asked.

"Not a lot. My mom remarried and I go back for holidays and special occasions, that sort of thing."

"I never went back. When we drove down the street in that rented U-Haul I remember thinking, *I'm never coming back. I'm going to move to a big city far away and play my guitar.*"

"So you always wanted to be a rock star?"

"As long as I can remember. Doesn't every guy? Ever since I picked up my brother's acoustic guitar and tried to imitate what I heard on his Led Zeppelin albums, there hasn't been anything else I've wanted to do."

"I guess when you're young being a famous rock star seems glamorous. Nobody ever dreams about being a lawyer."

"What about you? Did you ever have star ambitions?"

I shook my head.

"Not even a tiny bit?" Teddy held his fingers close together, measuring an inch.

"No, never," I quickly insisted, and then really thought about his question. Maybe that wasn't entirely true. "Okay, a tiny bit."

"See! I knew it! Everyone does."

"I used to wonder what it would be like to be one of those kids on *Zoom*.

I even practiced speaking Ubbi Dubbi, but it wasn't like I seriously considered it was possible."

"*Zoom?* Your brush with stardom was going to come from doing science experiments on public television?"

Teddy make it sound so positively uncool. "I loved that show."

"You got good grades in school, didn't you?"

I nodded. "Yeah."

"Hey! Now I remember!" Teddy exclaimed, pointing his finger at me. "Were you the one who freaked out when Mrs. Duffy dropped your plaster coliseum on the floor?"

"It was the Parthenon. We were studying Greece, not Rome."

"Now I totally remember!"

I thought Teddy's enthusiasm was a little over the top for my sixth-grade social studies project, but it was one damn good plaster reproduction. And Teddy was right; Mrs. Duffy did inadvertently let all my hours of hard work go to hell when she dropped the Parthenon on the floor on the way back from the principal's office.

"That was me."

The waiter returned and offered us another round of drinks.

I snuck a peek at my watch. Eight thirty Chicago time. "It's getting late," I pointed out.

"Come on, Jane. You won't turn into a pumpkin or anything, will you? Just one more drink."

"One more drink," I agreed. "And how about a menu? I'm hungry."

"This isn't as bad as I thought it would be," Teddy admitted while we waited for the waiter to return with our menus.

"Did you expect me to be that terrible?"

"Not terrible, but, well, it's not like I really know who you are."

"Me, too. I expected the guy I remembered from MTV."

Teddy grinned. "That was one hell of a guy."

"Yeah, but not someone I'd usually want to have drinks with."

"You never know."

Teddy was right. If someone had told me I'd be sitting in the bar at the Carlyle Hotel enjoying myself with Teddy Rock—or even Theo Brockford, for that matter—I'd have said they were crazy.

Like Teddy said, I guess you never know.

"So, are you excited for your new album to come out?" I asked.

"It's going to be great. Ever hear of Mark Kasper?"

I shook my head.

"He's an amazing producer."

I decided to just take Teddy's word for it. "Have you missed playing?"

"More than anything. After 'Janey' came out there were so many people involved, it got to the point where I couldn't take a piss without four people telling me where to aim. So, after my label dropped me I went in the other direction, thought I could do it all by myself. And we know how that turned out."

"So, you stopped playing music altogether?"

"I may as well have. I went from doing sold-out arenas to playing shit bars where all anyone wanted to hear was 'Janey 245.' Nobody cared about any new stuff I was writing. They'd just stand there pounding their fists in the air chanting *Ja-ney, Ja-ney*."

I imagined people chanting my name. Didn't sound so horrible to me. "And that's a bad thing?"

"Look, I had one huge hit and it's ended up defining my life. Don't get me wrong—it paid for a lot of indulgences, some of which eventually got me into trouble. It's just that at times it's been like a leash around my neck. I can't escape it."

Any awkwardness between us seemed to fall away when Teddy talked about his music. Listening to the enthusiasm in his voice, I could tell that he truly believed that this time around it would be different. He wouldn't have one hit and then fade into music oblivion. And seeing this Teddy, the one who wasn't pretending to be the cool rock star profiled on Music One, or the practiced personality who was a guest on Letterman, I wanted to believe it, too.

"Are you ready for your big comeback?"

"You bet I am. Ian keeps comparing me to John Travolta. He says all I need is my *Pulp Fiction* and everyone will be ready to take me back."

"There are worse things than being lumped in with John Travolta. Ian could have compared you to that guy who played Arnold Horshack."

"True." Teddy smiled. "I just hope Ian's right. Do you mind if I have a cigarette?" he asked, pulling a pack of Camels out of his blazer's inside pocket.

"I don't think you can smoke in city bars anymore. It's the law."

Teddy tapped the Camels on the table and sighed. "Shit. Ah, it's just as well. Smoking is another of my nasty habits Ian is trying to curb, along with swearing and various other socially unacceptable behaviors. I think it's this whole Justin Timberlake, Nick and Jessica thing. Nobody gets in trouble anymore."

Teddy Rock would certainly never be confused with some hip-hopping Bally's theme-song-singing kid, no matter how well behaved he managed to act.

It was the question I had to ask sooner or later, and I was tired of waiting. "So, why me?" I ventured.

"Why not?" Teddy asked me right back.

"Because I'm nothing like the girl in the song, for starters."

"That may be true, but I think you're the first woman to ever turn down my offer to . . . well, you know."

"Yeah, I know."

Teddy leaned in over the table and looked into my eyes. "Besides, who says you're not like the girl in the song?"

"Pretty much everyone I know."

Teddy reached for his drink and took a long, slow swallow of scotch. "Well, I always thought you were nice. Isn't that enough?"

You know, at that moment, sitting there with Teddy in the bar at the Carlyle, it was enough for me.

Teddy Rock / Rock On / Rock Records

Three strikes, you're out. Teddy Rock's third effort, the self-produced follow-up to the lackluster *Better Ted Than Dead*, is dead upon arrival. This odd collection of poorly produced and executed tracks includes "Me, Myself and I" and a self-important cover of Led Zeppelin's classic "Gallows Pole." Zeppelin got it right the first time, and Teddy should have left well enough alone. The wrongful assumption that Rock could improve upon a classic typifies what's wrong with this entire album. Teddy has forsaken substance for showmanship. With *Rock On*, Teddy Rock is way off.

CHAPTER FIFTEEN

All this Teddy Rock business had seriously curtailed my billable hours. So much so, that I hadn't even bothered to keep track of my time in my leather desk calendar, where the satin ribbon still marked last Thursday as if indicating the end of Jane Marlow and the beginning of Janey.

Between leaving early for Sam's, having lunch with Liv and Nat, meeting Ian White, and my trip to New York, the past two weeks were falling severely short of my typical output. Sure, Ian and New York would fall under the category of *business development*, but in the end my partnership review was about results, and so far I still didn't have Teddy as a client. Our rocky start aside, I actually ended up enjoying my time with Teddy and forgot to bring up the subject of his legal representation until I was back in my hotel room. I wasn't planning to tell Arthur that, of course, but I hoped to talk to Teddy again soon.

I was about to start in on my timesheets when what sounded like a herd of elephants stampeded down the hall and stopped in front of my door. Their zookeeper wasn't far behind.

"What are you doing here?"

Olivia grabbed the boys' hands and directed them into chairs. "I couldn't wait to hear what happened in New York. So spill. Was he totally obnoxious?"

"Actually, he wasn't as bad as I expected," I admitted.

"So he didn't try to get you into bed in the first five minutes?"

"Oh, no. He did. But after that he got better."

"Jane, Natalie's on the line," Sandy announced over the intercom.

I picked up the phone. "Liv's here."

"I know, she told me she was going to see you. I've got fifteen minutes before my next appointment, so put me on speaker and start talking."

I pressed the SPEAKER button and returned the handset to its cradle. "You there?"

"I'm here. I didn't get to watch you last night. I got called in for an emergency C-section."

"Where do you want me to start?"

"From the beginning," they instructed in unison. And so I started from the moment I spotted the sign in baggage claim with my name on it—Janey Marlow.

"So, do we all have to start calling you Janey now?" Natalie asked when I finished the story.

"Of course not. I just got sick of correcting everyone—the driver, the producer, the makeup woman. Everyone wanted me to be Janey, and eventually they wore me down."

"So, what now? Did you convince Teddy to become a client?"

"Not exactly. He's coming to Chicago in the next couple of weeks, so we're going to have dinner. I'm hoping we can talk about it then."

"Dinner?" Liv repeated. "Sounds like you're trying to land more than just a new client."

I dismissed her suggestion with a wave of my hand. "No interest."

"Really? Not even just a teensy little bit?"

In the seconds I hesitated before answering, Olivia jumped on me. "I knew it! You want Teddy Rock."

"I do not want Teddy Rock. He's just not as bad as I thought he'd be."

"Okay, ladies, I've got to run," Nat interrupted. "*Do not*, I repeat, *do not* continue this conversation without me."

After Natalie was gone, Liv immediately started in on me. "You looked great, by the way."

"Did I?"

"Yeah. You should have seen Teddy Rock's face when you walked out. They had the camera focused on him to catch his reaction. He almost looked relieved."

Again with the relieved look. What had he been expecting? I couldn't have changed *that* much, could I?

"We didn't look dumb in our matching outfits or anything?"

"Not really. I was actually kind of impressed. Teddy probably had a whole team of high-priced stylists selecting his clothes, and here we dressed you all by ourselves."

"And I'll be forever indebted to you."

"You know what we should do? Have a girls' night and watch the show together, I taped it. How about Friday night? Bill will watch the boys and we can all meet at Natalie's around seven."

I had to admit, I was curious to see what the interview looked like to millions of television viewers. I'd been so worried about making it to my seat without tripping or looking like a fool that I totally missed Teddy's first impression of me. I wondered if he was as surprised as I was.

"Olivia!" Arthur boomed, barreling into my office and wrapping his arms around Liv. "I heard that you were wandering the halls."

Liv returned Arthur's embrace and then pulled away. "More likely you heard my little monsters wandering the halls." She pointed to George and Ethan, who were doing a remarkable job of sitting still in their seats. "I told them that if they behaved themselves we'd go to the Children's Museum."

"They look just like Bill," Arthur observed, moving in closer to the boys for a better look before kneeling in front of them so he was at eye level. "You're both getting so big. Are you taking good care of your mommy?"

George nodded silently.

"I also told them that if they were quiet we'd get ice cream," Olivia explained.

"You certainly have some incentive program working at home," Arthur joked and stood up. "Would you boys like a treat from my special stash of lollipops?"

"Yes, please," George and Ethan sang in unison.

"Polite, too." Arthur reached for their hands and they hopped down from their chairs. "And what did you promise them for exhibiting such impeccable manners?"

Olivia shook her head, surprised. "Nothing. I guess that was a freebie."

Arthur held the boys' hands and led them out of my office.

"So, what do you say?" Liv asked when they were gone. "Friday night at Natalie's?"

You don't get to watch yourself on TV every day. And the segment had lasted only five minutes—I could watch it twice before my fifteen minutes of fame were up.

"Okay," I agreed, "Friday night at Nat's."

Olivia was thrilled. "Great. It's a date."

"How was your client meeting in New York?" Drew asked when I entered the conference room.

"He's not a client yet," I reminded him, taking a seat at the table.

"If I know you, he will be." Drew smiled. "I didn't get a chance to watch the show, I'm sorry. I heard you were great."

"Really?" I couldn't help asking, even if it sounded like I was fishing for a compliment. "Who told you that?"

"Everyone around here who saw it. They couldn't believe it was really you."

I could interpret that as everyone either not believing I'd be on a nighttime talk show, or not believing that I could be the hot chick that made the audience laugh. I preferred the former.

"It really wasn't such a big deal. The whole thing couldn't have lasted more than five minutes. It was Teddy they really wanted."

"So, did he put his rock-star moves on you, ask you up to his hotel room to see his tattoos?"

"Not exactly. It was relatively painless."

Drew pounded the table with his fist. "Damn."

"What's wrong?"

"I was hoping you'd give me a few more reasons to hate him."

"You hate Teddy Rock?"

"Not Teddy Rock personally. Just any guy who gets to go up onstage and play rock star while women look up adoringly and cry out his name. I'd trade places with him in a minute."

"So, you're jealous?"

"Oh, it's not just me. It's every guy. We all wish we could have been the rock star / pro baseball player / race car driver we thought we'd be when we grew up. Underneath our respectable pin-striped suits, we're all rock stars at heart."

I thought about Teddy saying he'd wanted to be a rock star for as long as he could remember. Apparently his feelings were widely shared among the male population. "After talking with Teddy, I think you're right."

"Of course I'm right. You know what else?"

"What?"

"I'm hungry."

I looked up at the large round clock above the door. It was almost six o'clock. "I'd have Sandy order you dinner, but she's already gone."

"It's just as well. The idea of eating another dinner out of a plastic container isn't exactly appealing." Drew pushed his chair back and faced me. "What do you say? Want to go get some dinner with me?"

His invitation didn't include anything about going over documents or talking about Kitty's case, which meant that there was a possibility that his dinner request wasn't all business.

"Come on. It's just dinner," Drew said, as if reading my thoughts. "For someone who had her body praised in song on radio stations across the free world, I don't think dinner with a colleague will jeopardize your reputation at this point."

He was right. Jane Marlow may have a policy not to date coworkers, but as far as I could tell, Janey 245 would have no problem with it.

"Okay. Meet me by the elevator in ten minutes."

We walked down Dearborn until we came to Trattoria 10. The sun was still high in the sky, lingering longer with every passing day, and the after-work crowd that hurried to catch their trains were shedding suit jackets and blazers as they walked.

When we reached the restaurant, the theater crowd had already emptied out to catch opening curtains, and the maître d' led us across the orange terra-cotta floor to a quiet table for two.

Seated across from Drew, I remembered the stories Olivia told me. Last week I was convinced that Drew would make a move on me, maybe ask me over to the fax machine under the guise of some paper stuck between the rollers. I'd been hell-bent against letting him succeed, yet here I was reading a menu in a quaint Italian restaurant without worrying about so much as giving him the wrong idea. And if anyone was having ideas, it was me.

I reached for the bread basket and removed a crusty heel before passing it across the table to Drew.

"Take some while it's hot," I suggested.

"Thanks." Drew took the basket and placed it beside his plate. "So, what's the story behind the song? Why'd he pick you?"

"Teddy says that he just never forgot me because I seemed nice."

"Come on, there has to be more to it than that." Drew drizzled some olive oil onto his bread plate and waited for a more plausible explanation. But I didn't have one to give him.

"There's no more. That's what he told me."

Drew tore off a piece of bread and set it down. "I don't believe it. I remember lots of girls growing up but not because they were nice. In second grade, Lizzie McCarthy showed me her underwear behind the tire swings to prove that they really did spell out Bloomies in bold letters; Courtney Mitchell and I had an elaborate plan to sneak out of our houses at night and meet by the big elm tree for a make-out session in fifth grade—a plan I'm afraid never came to fruition. In high school, Letitia Dunn even had my class photo hanging up in her locker next to a picture of that Soloflex guy. Those are the girls you remember, not someone who's just *nice*."

"I guess I'm proof that nice girls don't always finish last."

Drew didn't look convinced. "So, what's it like being on TV?"

"Not bad."

"Come on, admit it. You loved it," Drew teased.

"I wouldn't say I *loved* it."

Drew didn't let up. "Well, I would. You loved it. Come on, say it."

"Fine, I loved it," I confessed. "It was great."

"See, that wasn't so hard, was it?" Drew sat back, satisfied with my admission. "I told you I like to win."

But I couldn't help think that it was Janey who'd won, because I wouldn't be sitting here right now if Drew still saw me as the tedious, uninteresting lawyer he thought he was sitting next to when we first met. He wasn't talking to a colleague or someone about to be reviewed by the partnership committee. He never mentioned a word about work or Kitty's case. If I didn't know better, I'd almost think we were on a date. I *did* know better, and still I almost wished it was a date. Sure, it had something to do with Drew, but it was also something else. It was as if I'd been given permission to want things I couldn't want before, to do things I wouldn't do before. Although I wouldn't admit it to anyone, I was starting to see the person Teddy Rock wrote about. I wasn't exactly what everyone expected. And now I had a song to prove it.

APRIL 21, 1994

Teddy Rock Sues Ex-Manager

By William Beck,
Post Staff Writer

Teddy Rock filed a lawsuit in New York alleging that his former manager, Max Pope, took more than $7 million from him over five years.

The lawsuit claims Pope charged unreasonable fees and manipulated Teddy's finances for his own financial gain. Rock is seeking an unspecified amount of money because his attorney claims they don't know how much above and beyond the $7 million is gone.

"It would appear that his manager didn't always act in a manner consistent with Teddy's best interests," Lawrence Lott, Rock's attorney, told The *New York Post*.

Pope's lawyer says the accusations are "completely false" and his client's compensation was fair. "I can only imagine that after failed attempts to achieve the success he experienced under Max Pope's management, Teddy Rock is merely trying to figure out ways to continue supporting his rock-star lifestyle," Kirk Wright said.

The lawyer for Rock's former manager said Teddy Rock owes him money, not the other way around. "Max Pope is the one who has been wronged here," Wright said. "This effort will not be successful."

CHAPTER SIXTEEN

"**W**hat are you doing here?"

Teddy leaned against the door frame, his lanky figure straddling the entry to my office. "I told you I was coming to Chicago. I thought I'd stop by and say hi." He crossed his arms over his chest and smiled. "Hi."

"Yeah, but you didn't tell me you'd be here in the next forty-eight hours." Seeing Teddy standing there, waiting for an invitation, I felt the surprise of his visit start to be replaced by something verging on excitement. It was like having the captain of the football team show up at your locker. "How'd you get past the receptionist?"

"Let's just say she's a big fan." Teddy peered inside my office, the rim of his black baseball cap shielding his eyes. "So, can I come in or are you too busy?"

"No, come on in. I was just looking over client files." I slipped some documents back into a manila folder and pushed the files aside.

Teddy accepted my offer and came over to my desk, where he folded himself into a chair and pointed to my manila folder. "Must be something top secret."

"Not top secret, just confidential documents," I told him, realizing that he'd just given me an opening that was too perfect to pass up. Arthur had handed me my marching orders, and here was Teddy Rock practically feeding me my opening line. "I mean, you wouldn't want your attorneys leaving sensitive documents out on their desks for all to see, would you?" I asked.

"I guess not," Teddy agreed.

Here was my chance. I almost wished Arthur was here to witness this. "Who represents you anyway? Someone out in LA?"

Teddy removed the baseball cap and raked his fingers through his hair before replacing it. "I didn't come here to talk about my lawyers. I came to see you."

Maybe it was better that Arthur didn't witness my failed attempt. "What are you doing here anyway?"

"Here, as in your office, or here, as in Chicago?"

"Both."

"I'm singing during the seventh-inning stretch at Saturday's Cubs game, and I figured as long as I was in your neighborhood, I should stop by and say hello. I guess that stroll down memory lane was more fun than I expected."

"Me, too," I blurted out a little too quickly. And way more enthusiastically than I'd intended.

Teddy grinned, and I half expected the second-period bell to ring so he could offer to walk me to my class. I needed to get a grip. So what if we ended up having a good time the other night. It was still just Theo—even if he was also the rock star I needed to land as a client.

"I'm surprised Ian let you out of his sight. I'd think he'd have you all booked up with local media or something."

"Not yet. Ian doesn't want to saturate the market too far in advance." I could tell Teddy was repeating Ian's explanation word for word. "He's waiting until the first single is released in a few weeks. Then it will be chaos for a while."

An inordinate amount of foot traffic passed outside my door. "I think Tara told a few people you were visiting."

"Hey, the more the merrier. If they're old enough to buy an album, they can walk holes in the carpet for all I care." Teddy stood up, came around to my side of the desk and sat right on top of my daily planner. "So, what do you say? Want to go do something?"

"I can't. I'm working, Teddy."

"How about I go out, take a walk around the city, and come back around six. Maybe we could go see that brother of yours. Doesn't he own a bar somewhere in Lincoln Park?"

"Our friend Sam owns the bar. Andy's just a bartender."

"We could stop by and see him."

Teddy didn't even remember Andy the other night, and now he wanted to go see him? My Six Million Dollar Man story couldn't have been that intriguing. "You want to see Andy?"

"Sure. Come on," Teddy coaxed. "I had a good time with you the other night and I just thought it would be nice to meet another blast from the past."

"I don't know if he's working tonight."

Teddy picked up the phone and handed me the receiver. "So, call the bar and find out."

It might be fun to spend one more night with Teddy, there was so much more to talk about. We'd barely said anything at all about the kids we went to school with, and he had to be curious about what happened to everyone after he left. And I did still have to bring up the idea of his joining the ranks of clients at the firm. Not to mention that Andy would absolutely lose it if I walked into the bar with Teddy Rock. The look on his face would be priceless.

I took the receiver and replaced it on the cradle. "You know, it doesn't really matter. We could just stop in for a drink anyway."

Teddy clapped his hands together and hopped off my desk, wrinkling my blotter and knocking over a stack of folders in the process.

"Super. See you at six."

It was almost seven o'clock by the time we made it to Sam's, and although the place wasn't nearly as crowded as it had been the other night, almost half the tables were filled with people sipping drinks while munching on bowls of free popcorn. Andy's back was to us as he counted the bottles lined up behind the bar and ticked off hatch marks on an inventory sheet. He didn't even see us until I reached over the bar and tapped him on the shoulder.

"Andy, you remember Teddy, don't you?"

Teddy tipped his baseball cap and nodded in Andy's direction. "Hey."

Andy spun around and, for the first time in his life, his mouth was open but there was nothing coming out. I couldn't tell what shocked Andy more— the fact that Teddy Rock was standing right in front of him or the fact that Teddy's arm was draped over my shoulders.

"Wow, of course I do," Andy recovered and reached across the bar to shake Teddy's hand. "Man, Teddy Rock in Sam's. This is so cool."

Yeah, it was pretty cool. "Is Sam here? I wanted Teddy to meet him." I looked around for Sam's familiar figure.

"He's not here tonight."

"So, who's in charge?"

Andy thumped his chest. "Yours truly."

"You're kidding me."

"Nope. Sam's been letting me kind of fill his shoes lately. He says he's getting too old to be standing behind a bar for hours."

Was Sam really that old? It was almost hard to believe that Sam and my dad were thirty-two when I used to sit at the bar eating maraschino cherries out of the garnish tray. It didn't seem possible that Sam was now almost sixty. Or that, if he were alive, my dad would be almost sixty, too.

Andy wiped his hands on a dish towel and pointed to the far end of the room. "Jane, can I see you over by the popcorn machine for a sec? I think there's something wrong with the heat lamp."

Before I could answer, Andy was on our side of the bar, firmly directing me to the popcorn machine.

"What are you doing? I don't know anything about heat lamps," I told him, placing my hand on the imitation butter-coated glass and burning my fingertips. "Besides, this is working fine."

"Shit, why didn't you tell me you were bringing Teddy?" Andy whispered. "We could have set something up with a local TV station or something."

"What, and miss you getting all starstruck? Not on your life."

"I was not starstruck. You caught me off guard."

I did. And it was great.

A table of four called over to Andy for another round of drafts.

The tables on either side of them were also full. "I thought business was dead."

"It was, but ever since last week's event, more people have been dropping in after work."

"So, is Bruce coming back?"

"It's still too soon to tell if this is going to keep up, but"—Andy rapped his knuckles on the warm buttered glass—"knock on wood, this continues."

I didn't bother pointing out that knocking on wood for good luck probably only worked when you actually knocked on wood, not greasy buttered glass.

One of the guys waiting to order looked over at us impatiently. "I better find out what they want before they walk out."

"Why don't I take their order and you can go talk to Teddy," I offered.

"Really?" Andy almost had the same look on his face as when he'd turned around and seen Teddy Rock.

"Sure." I took the pencil and pad of paper Andy had poking out of his shirt pocket and left him standing there wondering what alien had possessed his sister's body.

It turned out the table just wanted a pitcher of beer. Easy enough. As I headed back toward the bar to place the order, one of the women sitting at a table of six reached out and tapped me on the arm.

"Excuse me. Isn't that Teddy Rock you walked in with?" she asked, pointing over at the bar where Teddy was talking with Andy, who appeared to have bought him a drink.

"Yep. That's him."

"And are you Janey?" the other girl asked.

I nodded without so much as a moment of hesitation. "Yes, I'm Janey."

"Wow, that's so cool." She turned to the guy on her left and took out her cell phone. "I'm calling Sharon and telling her to get over here. You're not leaving, are you?" she asked me.

"Not yet. I think we're going to have a drink first."

"Good." The whole table already had out their cell phones and were punching numbers on the keypads.

It looked like Andy may get the crowd he was looking for after all. He certainly seemed to be having a good time with Teddy at the bar. It was almost hard to believe that Teddy didn't remember Andy; they were laughing and drinking and sharing stories like old friends.

Maybe it was talking with Andy, someone who knew him before he'd transformed into Teddy Rock, or maybe it was that he was sitting in some neighborhood bar instead of an elegant hotel selected by his publicist, but Teddy seemed different. The bottle in his hand definitely wasn't springwater, and he didn't seem to care that it clashed with the carefully fabricated image of the new and improved Teddy Rock.

"I need a pitcher of Bud," I called out to Andy as I approached the bar. "And I think the bar is going to be filling up pretty quickly."

I took the stool next to Teddy and watched Andy fill the pitcher. "That table over there knows you."

"Nah, they just think they know me." Teddy finished his beer and pointed to the picture frame on the shelf above the cash register. "Isn't that your dad up there?"

Andy and I looked up at the photo and then at each other. "You remember him?" Andy asked.

Teddy nodded. "Can I get another beer?"

Now it was Andy's turn to nod. "Coming right up."

I had no idea why Teddy would remember my father and not Andy, but the thought made me smile.

"Here." Andy tossed a rolled-up apron across the bar. "If this place is really going to fill up, we'll need a waitress."

"And I'm assuming I'm her?"

"You assume correctly." Andy slid the pitcher toward me and wiped away the wet trail it left behind. "Now, take this pitcher back to the table and ask if they'd like some shots."

Handing me an apron was one thing, but now Andy was teaching me how to sell up to my customers? Was it possible that Sam knew what he was doing when he put Andy in charge?

"Do I have to split my tips with you?" I asked, tying the apron's strings into a bow around my waist.

"I think we'll wait and see how you do before I worry about sharing in your fortune."

"Hey, if you can be a bar manager, I can sure as hell be a waitress," I replied, paraphrasing Andy's own words. I took the pitcher and went to sell some shots.

Apparently Sharon called a friend, and she called a friend, and so on and so on, because within half an hour all the tables were occupied and there wasn't a free stool at the bar. Although nobody rushed up to Teddy asking for an autograph, it was obvious that everyone was aware of his presence. When it came time to order a drink, nobody flagged me over, choosing instead to sidle up to the bar next to Teddy and mention that they loved "Janey 245" and couldn't wait for his new album. Teddy was always gracious, accepting the compliments and making small talk until they left with fresh beer bottles in hand.

"I think you have a few fans here," I observed between interruptions.

"Let's hope there are more than just a few," Teddy answered back.

The girl who had grabbed me earlier appeared behind us and held up her camera phone. "Hey, can you take a picture of me and Sharon with Teddy?"

"I want to e-mail it to my sister," Sharon explained.

"Sure." Teddy draped his arm across Sharon's shoulders and grinned at the camera like he'd done this a million times. Which he probably had, in the old days. It amazed me how easily he shifted from one fan to another, making small talk and cracking self-deprecating jokes that made it hard to believe that this was the same guy who used to overturn tables and set floors on fire with the grain alcohol he'd pour from a bottle and light with the flick of a cigarette butt.

"Are you going to sing something?" Sharon asked Teddy, viewing the picture on the small color screen while she typed in her sister's e-mail address.

"I wasn't planning on it."

"Aw, come on. The stage is still set up from the other night." Andy pointed over to the trusses against the far end of the bar. "I keep calling the rental company to pick it up but they insisted I keep it a little longer."

"I have an acoustic guitar in the trunk of my car," the guy one stool down offered. "I could run out and get it if you want."

"Maybe just one song." Teddy looked at me. "Would that be okay?"

What was I going to do? It was as if the stars were aligned and Teddy Rock was meant to play a few songs—the stage, the guitar waiting in some guy's trunk, the rapid spreading of the news that Teddy Rock was at Sam's Place. I had six people gathered around me waiting for an answer. I was his muse. How could I say no?

"Sure, go ahead."

Guitar in hand, Teddy took the stage and made himself comfortable on the stool Andy placed under a single overhead spotlight. While he plucked the strings and tuned the guitar, the bar grew quiet. The mood in Sam's was decidedly different from the other night, when Big D provoked the audience to a noise level that verged on frantic. There had to be at least fifty people in the bar, but it was still practically half the number that were squeezed into Sam's last week. This time the crowd had room to move and carry on conversations while they waited for Teddy to begin. I imagined this was exactly what it was like when Teddy was still making a name for himself in small clubs and bars, before he hit it big with "Janey 245." Even Teddy's mood was more low-key than I would have expected. Once he was satisfied with the sound of the guitar, he simply segued into a song I'd never heard before. I assumed it had to be off his new album—the album that was supposed to relaunch Teddy's career.

The crowd listened to the unfamiliar song, but because they didn't know the words and couldn't sing along, they just tapped their feet or nodded their heads to the rhythm once they started to become comfortable with the recurring chords.

When he finished singing, applause rose from the audience that had spontaneously gathered as a result of phone calls and word that traveled around the neighborhood.

Teddy acknowledged the positive reaction with a slight tip of his head, and then launched into the song he knew they were waiting for, the song that they'd all tell their friends they'd heard sung live at some local bar on Southport.

Although the acoustic version lacked the blaring guitar riffs that announced the inimitable beginning of "Janey 245," there was no mistaking the song that made Teddy Rock a household name.

Every eye in Sam's was on Teddy, and I couldn't help but acknowledge that he was the real thing. Teddy Rock had talent.

As I listened to him sing the words that everyone in the crowd knew by heart, I was reminded of my first few months at college, when Teddy's song would drift out of dorm windows or from the porch of a fraternity in the throes of a party, and for three brief minutes the fact that my dad was gone would fade into the background and I'd be like every other freshman experiencing independence for the first time. As Teddy carried me along from one verse to another, I relived walking to class while the New England leaves seemed to turn colors around me like a crimson, orange and gold kaleidoscope. I could recall the exact afternoon I met Natalie in the Courtyard Café at the Hopkins Center and watched her methodically dissect her meal, unable to figure out why she'd be scraping all the tomato seeds out of the red sauce ladled over her pasta. "It's like eating little pits," she'd told me as I placed my tray next to hers, not even waiting for me to ask what she was doing. "What about you? What's your dirty little secret?" And without thinking, I'd told her, right there, with "Janey 245" wafting out of the speakers embedded in the waffled ceiling and the clinking of dishes coming from the cafeteria's kitchen. "My dad died and I can't forgive him."

After playing four more songs, Teddy said good-bye and stepped off the stage, only to be replaced by Andy, who seemed to be taking his role as the master of ceremonies a little too seriously.

"Teddy Rock, ladies and gentlemen," Andy announced, clapping his hands as Teddy made his way through the impromptu audience.

The crowd joined Andy's applause, stopping only when they attempted to shake Teddy's hand and pat him on the back as he made his way over to me.

"Come on, let's get out of here." Teddy took my hand and led me toward the front exit.

As the door was about to close behind us, I heard Andy proclaim, in his best Las Vegas announcer's voice, "Teddy has left the building."

"I hope you didn't mind that," Teddy said, hailing a cab.

"Who was I to mind? With the stage, the crowd, the guitar in that guy's trunk—it was meant to be."

A yellow cab pulled up to the curb and Teddy placed his hand on the door handle. "Now what?"

I shrugged.

"Would it be too much if we went back to your apartment, maybe for some coffee or something? The thought of going back to another hotel room is just too depressing."

I could have said no and sent Teddy back to some high-priced suite at the Peninsula. And I could have gone home, alone, and spent the rest of the evening going through my nightly routine as if life was exactly like it was before Teddy Rock. But I liked that Teddy wanted to spend more time with me. I liked the way he saw me, and I liked people's reactions when they learned I was Janey 245.

So, I could have said no. But I didn't.

Teddy pulled the door open and I climbed into the backseat of the cab.

"The corner of Wrightwood and Lincoln," I told the driver, and then watched as Teddy slid into place next to me and smiled, almost as if he knew I'd take him home with me all along.

* * *

"Nice place," Teddy commented, running a finger along the fireplace mantel as if checking for dust. "How long have you lived here?"

"Three years." I handed him a mug of decaf and he followed me back to the couch.

"Three years? It looks brand-new."

"Nope, I bought it the year I landed my first big client."

"Those CSI guys would have a hell of a time proving anyone lives here. The place is immaculate. I think it's neater than my hotel room." Teddy took a sip of coffee before continuing. "Do you fold your toilet paper into little triangles at the end like the housekeepers at the Peninsula?"

Now he was starting to sound like Drew. "No. And before you ask, I don't give out complimentary toiletries, either."

Teddy laughed and made his way over to my bookshelf. "I don't see any Teddy Rock here," he commented, flipping through my CD collection.

Teddy didn't look surprised, but, still, I felt bad. "My roommate had *Rock Hard* on cassette," I started to explain.

Teddy waved away my answer. "No big deal. You alphabetize your CDs by artist?" he asked, turning to me. "Why stop there? I kind of expected you to also organize them by album name."

"Actually, each artist's albums are organized chronologically. That was quite a show you put on tonight," I told him before he noticed that the next shelf of books was organized according to the Dewey decimal system.

"Thanks. I've been practicing for the tour. It can get pretty grueling on the road after a while, but playing in front of a live crowd—there's really nothing like it."

"Is it weird?"

"Is what weird?"

"The way all those people sing along with you. The way they watch you with all that expectation?"

"It's the greatest feeling in the world."

"But what happens if the new album doesn't sell? What if your new label drops you, too?"

"I don't think about everything that could go wrong, Jane. If I did, I probably wouldn't be able to get up in the morning. I just think about making my music."

"But you could probably make a decent living playing your old songs, right? I mean, there are clubs and bars and stuff that would probably love to have you play. Look how many people showed up tonight and they didn't even know you were going to play until five minutes before you went up on-stage."

"Just go around to shitty little gigs where everyone sings your songs and then when they leave they talk about how sad it is that you never went on to do anything else? No, thanks."

Teddy didn't have to convince me. I'd witnessed a scene like that firsthand.

"When I was a first-year associate, the firm hired KC and the Sunshine Band to play at our summer outing. KC came out dressed in these spandex pants, his gut hanging over the waistband. When he started singing 'Shake Your Booty' and demonstrated his own booty shake, I thought our managing partner was going to have a heart attack."

I'd thought how sad it was, this guy who was once riding high, now relegated to singing at corporate outings or for the Jerry Lewis telethon, or head-lining some dinner theater in Indiana. But what Teddy was trying to do was even harder—totally break away from his past and become who he wanted to be, regardless of what everyone else expected.

"But you won a Grammy," I pointed out. "That's a big deal."

"Are you kidding me? Winning Best New Artist is the kiss of death. Do you know who's won in the past?" Teddy started rattling off the names. "Men at Work. Jody Watley. Culture Club. Sheena Easton."

"Okay, you may have a point."

"They might as well escort you right off the stage and into a car waiting to take you to the set of *Hollywood Squares.*"

What was I going to say to that? Maybe he'd get the coveted middle square?

"Did it ever get old, playing the role of rock star?" I asked.

"Sure it did. By the time the third album came out I was trying so hard to be *the rock star* that I didn't know who the hell I was anymore."

"So why'd you do it?"

"I thought that was what people expected of me."

"And what would have happened if you stopped being Teddy Rock, *rock star* and just let yourself be Teddy Rock, *musician?*"

"I don't know. I figured we all have our roles to play in life, right?"

"Tonight, when you were up there playing, you looked more like a musician than a rock star to me."

"Thanks." Teddy grinned. "That's nice of you."

"And when you were playing at those so-called shit bars, you were probably just like you were tonight."

"You're probably right." Teddy was silent for a minute. "You know, Ian wants me to start wearing one of those red Kabala strings around my wrist."

"Why, are you into Kabala?"

"No, but I guess a bunch of celebrities are, and Ian thought it might get me lumped into their circle or something."

"Is that what you want?" I asked.

Teddy thought about my question before answering. "You know, I don't," he said slowly.

"So, then, don't."

Teddy slapped his hand against his thigh as if he'd come to some sort of conclusion. "You're right, Jane. You're absolutely right. I'm going to tell Ian no."

I smiled at Teddy and enjoyed the idea that, if it wasn't for me, Teddy Rock would be wearing a meaningless red string around his wrist. And I also had to admit that a little part of me liked the fact that Teddy wasn't going to listen to Ian for once. "Good."

"So, what about you?" he asked, coming back to the couch.

"What about me?"

"What role have you been playing?"

I shrugged. "None. I'm not a rock star."

"Everyone thinks they have a role to play, Jane." Now I didn't know whether he was talking about him or me. "You're still wearing your apron, you know."

I looked down. "Doesn't quite go with my suit, does it?"

"You have any old yearbooks hanging around?" Teddy asked, changing the subject. "I thought you could show me what happened to everyone. Remember that kid who used to pretend he was Bruce Lee? He used to try and cut his tuna sandwiches in half with karate chops. It was so gross, tuna fish everywhere."

"Marty Engle. In eighth grade he ended up with both hands in casts after he tried to show Ginny Taft how he could break the railing on her back deck."

"He wasn't the brightest kid, was he?"

"I might have a few yearbooks in a box in my closet. My mom gave me a bunch of stuff when she moved. I'll be right back."

Instead of waiting on the couch, Teddy followed me into my bedroom. Now, my one-bedroom apartment isn't the biggest place, but as we walked down the ten-foot-long hallway to my room it seemed to take on mythical proportions. I listened to every one of Teddy's steps land on the hardwood floors behind me and attempted to figure out whether he was just really curious about the yearbooks or whether this was just his way to get me nearer a bed. But instead of closing the gap between us and making his move, he lagged behind at a safe distance.

"They should be in here." I knelt in front of my closet and crawled under the pant legs hanging like the cloth strips at a car wash.

"I can help," he offered.

"Here." I slid a box out of the closet toward Teddy. "You can start with this one."

He knelt on the floor and untucked the cardboard flaps holding the box top closed. "You sure saved a bunch of crap," he noted, sifting through old term papers, report cards and camp medals. "What was this one for?" he asked, holding up a gold medal dangling from a thick red ribbon.

I twisted around and took the medal. Instantly, I recognized the faux coin with roman numerals and embossed YMCA logo. It was hard to believe that my brother and I could cooperate long enough to ever win anything, no less a contest that required we be tied together. "I think that was when Andy and I won the three-legged race at Y camp."

I tossed the medal back into Teddy's box and resumed my own yearbook search.

"What are these?"

This time when I turned around, Teddy wasn't holding a medal. Instead he had two small circular metal cymbals held up against his chest. "Brass pasties?" he asked, attempting not to laugh.

"They're not pasties, you idiot." I grabbed for the finger cymbals, but Teddy moved back out of my reach.

Teddy laughed at me. "My, my, who would have guessed that Jane Marlow had a pair of pasties. What else do you have hiding in these boxes?" he asked.

"They're finger cymbals," I told him, trying not to laugh at the sight of Teddy Rock with brass pasties over his nipples. "Okay, enough. No more boxes for you. Now I am officially the only one looking in these." This time I grabbed the finger cymbals and stuffed them back into the box, way at the bottom.

While I opened boxes looking for the yearbooks, Teddy wandered around the room as if looking for clues.

"Hey, remember Jimmy Shaw?" I asked, making a Herculean effort to push aside a box of law school textbooks.

"Sure I do; whatever happened to him?" Teddy called back.

"He owns the Sherwin-Williams store in town. Wears painter's pants every single day. How's that for irony?"

Teddy lifted the top of my jewelry box, picked out a hoop earring and held it up to his ear. "Ironing? He irons his painter's pants?"

I looked up to see if Teddy was kidding. He wasn't.

"Not *ironing, irony*. It's ironic that he works there because, well, you know he always used to wear those painter's pants." Having to explain my funny little anecdote about Jimmy Shaw made it not so funny anymore.

Teddy closed the jewelry box and reached for a sterling silver picture frame on my windowsill. "A dance?"

"I can't find the boxes with my yearbooks," I told him and crawled out of my closet. I joined Teddy by the window and took the sterling silver frame from him. "That was my dad and me before my date picked me up for junior prom."

"Nice dress."

"Mauve polyester. I thought it was gorgeous."

Teddy looked around. "No pictures of senior prom?"

I shook my head and grazed the corner of the frame with my fingertip. "I didn't go."

Teddy returned the photograph back to its spot on the windowsill, and for the first time I noticed the calluses the guitar strings built up on his fingers. "He was a great guy."

He confused my cat with a dog, forgot I had a brother and yet knew enough about my dad to call him a great guy?

"You talked to him?" I asked.

"One afternoon I was sitting outside on our lawn trying to figure out a Hendrix song and your dad came home early from work. He must have heard me because he came over and stood on the sidewalk and watched me for a little while—he didn't even say anything, although I probably sucked. He just stood there until I figured that damn song out. Before he walked away he waved good-bye and told me that I reminded him of a young Eric Clapton. Then he said he used to play the drums."

"I never knew that."

"I'm not surprised, it's not like we had a nice long chat or anything."

"I meant I didn't know he played the drums." I reached for the picture and held it, taking a new look at the man standing beside a seventeen-year-old girl in a mauve strapless gown. He was just as I remembered, the way I'd always see him. Sam continued to age and change, but my father would always be the forty-ish guy in an Izod shirt and Dockers. Instead of Sam's graying strands, the tips of my dad's light brown hair were tinged gold from spending hours in the yard seeding the tire tracks left by Andy's mountain bike. The highlights contrasted with his dark lashes and accentuated his eyes—the same green-gray hazel eyes as the girl he had his arm around. There was nothing remotely drummer-like about him.

Teddy moved over to my dresser and slid open my top drawer about an inch before pulling it out all the way and exclaiming, "Man, what's with all the scarves?"

"Impulse purchases. The saleswomen at Saks love me."

He held up a black and tan leopard-print scarf. "This one is pretty cool. Why are the tags still on?"

"It's never been worn."

"That's too bad. I bet you'd look good in it." Teddy held the scarf out and stretched it taut, strategically positioned in midair, exactly where my breasts would be. "So you've never worn any of these?"

"Nope."

Teddy shook his head and reached for a photograph tucked into the frame of my mirror.

"Was this some sort of family vacation?" he asked, turning over the picture to look for a date or description. "Where was it taken?"

"A Cubs-Cardinals game. Huge rivalry. Every year Sam and my dad would take us to the game."

Teddy smacked the picture down on my dresser. "Then it's decided. You've got to come with me to the game on Saturday."

"I can't."

"Sure you can; Ian will get you a ticket."

I picked up the photograph and placed it back on the mirror. "I can't. I should really make up the work hours I've missed the past week."

"Jane, it's Saturday. Don't tell me you work on the weekends, too."

"Okay, I won't tell you."

"Don't you get any free time?"

Andy had asked me that same question once, a few years ago. I'd given him the same answer I wanted to give Teddy—that my time wasn't free. It was billed out at three hundred dollars an hour. When I'd told Andy that he'd laughed. But looking back, it wasn't really funny any more.

"Come on, I bet the crowd would love to see the girl behind 'Janey.'"

"Thanks anyway."

"Well, if you change your mind, here's my cell number." Teddy picked up an eyeliner and wrote his number on a magazine subscription card he pulled from my *Marie Claire.* "Save this. I'll be expecting a call."

I took the card and read the number. Even the model imploring me to *subscribe now* seemed to think I was nuts for turning down Teddy's invitation. But it would just be too weird to go to a game with him. I'd only ever gone with my family.

"I'll think about it."

Teddy frowned and flopped down on my bed. He lay sprawled out in the middle of the now off-center bedspread, my two throw pillows pitched awkwardly against his head. He actually looked bummed out.

I folded the subscription card in half and tucked it inside my drawer. "Hey, do you play softball?" I asked, thinking I'd offer Teddy a consolation prize.

"Sports aren't exactly my thing. Remember what happened with Mr. Feely in gym class?"

I didn't remember, but from the look on Teddy's face it obviously wasn't a pleasant experience.

"Well, Andy got together a team for the bar and we have a game on Sunday. Why don't you play with us?"

"I'll think about it." Teddy sat up and leaned back on his elbows. "I guess I should get going." He rolled off the bed, taking half the covers with him. "Walk me out?"

I had two choices. I could follow Teddy or I could fix the pillows and Egyptian cotton bedding now draped on the floor beside my bed.

"Yeah, I'm coming," I answered and followed him down the hall.

PEOPLE MAGAZINE OCTOBER 10, 1994
PASSAGES

Update

On October 18, a Manhattan judge threw out a $7 million lawsuit filed by musician Teddy Rock. The former platinum-selling rocker sued ex-manager Max Pope, citing financial wrongdoing (PEOPLE, April 16, 1994). "We're very pleased with the judgment and feel it reinforces the sound management Mr. Pope pro-vided to Teddy Rock during the length of their relationship," said Kirk Wright, Pope's attorney. "Although Teddy Rock hasn't been able to achieve the level of success he experienced under Mr. Pope's management, Mr. Pope wishes Teddy the best of luck with his career and holds no ill ill toward his former client."

Rock doesn't have a publicist or representative, so it wasn't clear how to reach him Thursday.

CHAPTER SEVENTEEN

Olivia was already on her second margarita when I arrived at Natalie's apartment. She'd wasted no time getting out of the house when Bill walked in from work, and by the time Nat's clock read 7:01, Liv had commandeered Nat's KitchenAid blender and a bottle of tequila.

I sat on the kitchen counter and watched Liv whip up another batch of neon green drinks, dramatically combining ice and margarita mix and tequila as if the task was more art than science.

"Since it's a holiday weekend I thought we'd have some margaritas and celebrate the official start of summer," Liv told me, although I knew that she never needed an excuse to wield a blender and bottle of tequila.

As the blender's steel blades churned through the ice cubes, Liv poured in the margarita mix and tequila, completely ignoring the recommended amount of Jose Cuervo and substituting her own more generous measurement.

Natalie watched her pour until the bottle had just a shallow reservoir of brown liquid left in the bottom. "You sure you've got enough in there?" she asked dryly.

"What? You and Jane don't have to get up early tomorrow. I'm the one who'll be up at six o'clock making blueberry pancakes and chocolate milk."

Nat didn't look convinced. "You make blueberry pancakes?"

"Make, microwave, what's the difference?"

Natalie arranged tortilla chips on a platter. "I can't believe I handed those innocent children over to you."

"Who are you kidding? You couldn't get rid of them fast enough." Olivia dipped a finger in the blender, declared the green slush *perfect*, and turned her attention to me. "I saw in the paper that Teddy showed up at Sam's and put on a little concert last night. Did you join forces with Andy and lure him there under false pretenses?"

"Not exactly. Teddy showed up at my office yesterday."

"Out of the blue?"

"Yep. He'd mentioned something about coming to Chicago, but we didn't make plans or anything."

Nat poured salt into a saucer. "That's strange."

I thought it seemed odd at first, too. When I left him in the lobby of The Carlyle he'd mentioned he was coming to Chicago, but he didn't mention that he'd be there two days later. It wasn't like he had to arrive early to prepare for the game. He could have shown up the night before, unless Ian decided Teddy go to Chicago early for a reason. Or Teddy decided I was reason enough.

So even though I thought it was odd at first, now it didn't feel weird at all. It almost felt like it was meant to be, like Teddy and I were supposed to reconnect for some reason.

"So, he went to Sam's with you? Is that all that happened?" Liv asked suspiciously.

I slid a paring knife through the rind of a lime and sliced three thin wedges. "He did end up coming home with me afterward," I confessed, keeping my eyes on the slender blade in my hand while they processed the fact that Jane Marlow had had a rock star in her apartment.

"He was in your apartment?" Nat repeated.

"And my bedroom," I added, just for fun.

Olivia smacked the bottle of margarita mix onto the counter. "Don't even tell me you slept with Teddy Rock."

"No, we just talked. He wanted to see if I had any old yearbooks."

"That's a line if I've ever heard one." Nat reached into the kitchen cabinet and handed me a round, shallow margarita glass. I turned it over and ground the rim into the plate of rock salt.

"Teddy's singing at the Cubs game tomorrow. He invited me to go with him."

"And you're going, aren't you?" Liv asked, as if the right answer was a no-brainer. "If you say no, I'm not going to share my margaritas with you." She huddled over the blender, shielding it from my grasp.

"No, I'm not going." I pushed her aside and took the blender off its stand to pour my own drink.

"But you've got to go, right, Nat?"

Natalie grabbed the tray of salsa and chips and carried it into the living room. Liv and I collected the glasses and blender and followed her.

"I don't know. This whole thing still seems a little odd to me. It's like all of a sudden Teddy's all over Jane, but where was he fourteen years ago when the song actually came out? He wasn't all that interested in going on TV with her or taking her to baseball games back then."

"Andy thinks that when 'Janey 245' came out Teddy was too caught up in the whole thing to stop and find me," I explained before realizing that I was using Andy's logic to rationalize the situation. A frightening idea to say the least.

"And you don't think that his interest in you is a little timely?"

"It's actually kind of cool," I admitted. "He remembers everything the way I do, it's like pressing rewind and watching your childhood play back all over again."

"This doesn't sound like the same woman we were dressing Monday night. What happened?"

"Nothing. He's just not the asshole I thought he'd be."

The three of us settled onto the couch with our wide-rimmed glasses, the plate of salt and the blender conveniently waiting on the coffee table for refills.

Natalie held her margarita in one hand while she pressed the remote control's FAST FORWARD button with the other. "Well, let's see for ourselves."

As the video played, I watched the nine-year-old fiddle tune winner go by in double time; the sitcom dog's mouth moved so fast it looked like he was barking in tongues. When a commercial break ended and Teddy Rock walked out to meet Dave, I yelled, "Stop."

"What?" Nat paused the tape.

"I didn't get to see this part. His publicist turned off the TV in the green-room." For the first time I was going to get to see what transpired before I made it onto the stage. And I didn't want to miss a second.

Nat rolled her eyes. "The greenroom. Would you listen to her? She goes on one lousy TV show and all of a sudden she's Oprah."

Liv laughed and Nat pressed play.

Dave was tapping a blue index card on his desk while he prepared to introduce Teddy. "You all know my next guest for his wild antics and his hit, 'Janey 245.' But just in case you forgot, take a look at this."

A video montage filled the TV screen and the three of us watched concert footage of a younger Teddy, his hand gripped tightly around a half-empty bottle of Jack Daniels. Another clip showed Teddy diving into a concert audience, where he was passed over the heads of ecstatic fans until he ended up at the other end of the stage, a black lace bra clenched between his teeth. Still another showed Teddy's fingers bending the strings of an electric guitar, his eyes shut and his head tipped back as if in a trance.

"Are you thinking what I'm thinking?" Olivia asked, her eyes not leaving the TV.

It was so blatantly sexual, the way his expression changed when his fingers pressed against the metal strings on the neck of the guitar, the way his fingers plucked, bent, pushed and prodded those strings fast and then slowly until they emitted the sounds he wanted them to make. You couldn't help but imagine how those same nimble fingers would work on a woman's body. *I couldn't help but imagine it.*

You'd have to be brain-dead not to.

"Not a bad way to earn a living; how do I get that gig?" Dave joked after the montage ended. He stood up and gestured to the side of the stage. "Ladies and gentlemen, Teddy Rock."

It was probably a good thing Ian wouldn't let me watch Teddy from the greenroom. If I'd seen how charming and gorgeous Teddy was, how he filled the stage with his presence like a balloon expanding with helium, I probably would have been scared to death.

"So what are you expecting when Janey comes out?" Dave asked Teddy after exchanging a few lighthearted welcoming remarks.

Teddy shrugged. "I don't know if she remembers everything the way I do, it was a long time ago."

"Why haven't you tried to find Janey until now?" Dave asked, once again tapping the blue index card.

"I figured she wouldn't remember me, that she'd probably moved on. I was a little kid who used to listen to Journey albums in my bedroom, I wasn't exactly all that memorable." Teddy turned away from Dave and faced the audience. "I mean the cool Journey, not that sappy ballad crap."

The studio audience applauded and Teddy grinned.

"Well, let's see what she remembers. Ladies and gentlemen, Janey 245."

Polite applause punctuated my entrance. I was second runner-up to his Miss America. It didn't even come close to the cheers that welcomed Teddy's entrance. It was almost embarrassing.

The camera panned past Dave and Teddy until it found me walking purposefully across the stage. Although I didn't remember feeling all that calm, the expression on my face was pure relaxation. And I'd had no idea I was smiling so big.

"I can't believe that's you. You look amazing," Natalie cried, elbowing me in the side.

Liv smirked. "I told you."

Natalie wasn't just being nice. I did look good. I looked damn good. And from the expression on Teddy's face it was evident he thought so, too.

The rest of the segment was pretty much as I remembered. Even though I knew what questions were coming up, my answers still seemed witty— although I may have been a little biased.

When Natalie flipped off the TV I almost wanted to watch again, to go through it frame by frame until I'd committed every moment to memory. It'd been like watching some enhanced version of myself—Janey Marlow in high-definition TV, where everything sparkled a little more, had a little more depth and color.

"I can't believe that was me." It wasn't just the professional makeup job or even the outfit. It was the way I moved across the stage, the way I joked with Dave and Teddy and the way the audience responded to me, laughing at the right moments and sitting at rapt attention when I spoke. It was the way Teddy's face changed when he saw me for the first time. A look that verged on apprehension and anticipation turned to delight. If I didn't know better, I'd almost think he looked a little too thrilled.

"Believe it." Nat tossed the remote control onto the coffee table. "What would you have done if you'd known when the song first came out?" she asked.

"I can't even begin to imagine," I answered honestly.

"I doubt you would have been as good for his image back then. The whole bad-boy rock thing was big. Fucking everything in sight was big. Waking up with a needle in your arm was practically de rigeur," Olivia pointed out.

"Ah, the good old days, right, Liv?" Natalie teased.

"And then grunge came along and fucked it up for all of us. Bye-bye, Jon Bon Jovi. See you later, Poison. Adios, Guns n' Roses. I mean, really, do I want to watch a guy who hasn't changed his underwear in weeks and looks like he washed his hair in orange juice sing about depressing crap? Nirvana, my ass. It was hell."

I reached for a chip and scooped up some salsa. "I wonder when he started calling himself Teddy Rock. Theo Brockford wasn't that bad a name, was it?"

Liv made a sour face, and not from the margaritas. "Theo? Come on. He wouldn't have made it past the Knights of Columbus talent show with that name."

Nat refilled her glass from the pitcher. "My mom thought everyone would think of Natalie Wood when they heard my name. Instead they thought of the fat girl on *Facts of Life*. Not exactly the elegant movie star she had in mind."

"We all associate names with people we crossed paths with at one time or another. When Bill and I were trying to come up with names for the boys, everything we came up with had connotations of some sort. I loved the name Sean, but Bill wouldn't go for it."

"Wasn't that the name of the guy you lost your virginity to?"

Liv nodded. "Like I said, Bill wouldn't go for it. Eighteen years later, and he thinks I'm naming my kid after someone whose idea of foreplay was changing the radio station in his Rabbit."

"Pam," I suggested.

Liv didn't even hesitate. "Jesus freak in tenth grade who used to talk to herself in the halls and laugh. She said God told her knock-knock jokes."

"Christie."

"Seventh-grade bitch who wore Calvin Klein jeans and velour tops—every single day. She was obsessed with Brooke Shields and used to draw in these big bushy eyebrows with brown eyeliner. By the end of the day she had the stuff smudged all across her forehead, so everyone called her *skid marks*. She actually thought Eliot Goldstein came up with that nickname after Christie got a case of the runs at our Valentine's dance."

"Look at John Cougar—think he would have made it big if he started out as John Mellencamp?" Nat shook her head. "No way."

"I guess Theo is kind of geeky for a musician."

"Not if he's playing the oboe, but if he expects to be in *Rolling Stone*, definitely." Liv swiped her finger along the rim of her glass and licked the salt. "You're a perfect example. One minute you're Jane—responsible, well-educated woman who wouldn't think of wearing white past Labor Day, and then the next minute you're Janey—fun-loving, good-time girl who not only wears white all year round, she does it without underwear."

"I always wear underwear," I insisted.

Liv drained her glass and stood up to take the empty pitcher into the kitchen. "We know. I was just saying . . ."

"Can we watch the tape one more time?" I asked.

"Sure. Just can't get enough of yourself, huh?" Nat joked, watching the numbers on the video counter tick backward.

"I just can't believe that's me up there."

"It's Janey," Nat reminded me.

I watched the tape again by myself while Olivia and Natalie were in the kitchen replenishing our snacks and blending more margaritas. The second time around it was just as unbelievable as the first, only more so. I noticed how I leaned into Teddy when he talked, almost inviting him to reach over and touch my arm. When Dave asked me a question, I tipped my head to the side and watched him out of the corner of my eye, almost flirting. The funny thing was, they both seemed to enjoy it.

I stood up and went to get my purse from the foyer table.

"What are you doing?" Nat asked, returning with a full platter of cheese-covered Tostitos.

I unfolded the subscription card and was greeted by an enthusiastic model that looked like she'd been expecting me. "Calling Teddy. I'm going to the game with him tomorrow."

Make an Offer

Teddy Rock is selling his Malibu home. Six years ago Rock created a stir in the private enclave of celebrities when he moved into the 4,000-square-foot modernistic marvel. The striking Mies Pooten–designed home was host to many of Teddy Rock's infamous parties. The former platinum-selling musician hasn't had a hit since the release of his debut album, *Rock Hard*. Sources say the rocker is selling his Malibu home because he felt it was time to "downsize" to a house that better suited his needs.

Vital Stats The home features four bedrooms, a slate-floor media room, an ash and steel kitchen and a master suite adorned with a CaesarStone tub and Bisazza steam shower. An infinity-edge pool overlooks the Pacific Ocean.

Cost $4.7 million; call Lee Dennis at International Property Consultants, 310-555-7516.

CHAPTER EIGHTEEN

Wrigley Field is plunked right in the middle of a north-side Chicago neighborhood. Fans wait on Waveland Street in lawn chairs to catch home runs over the back wall and rooftop decks with bird's-eye views of the field and host keg parties complete with bleachers and catered meals. On game day fans milled around the streets crisscrossing around the stadium, and after the ninth inning they'd spill out into the surrounding bars. And there were plenty of bars. Sam's Place was less than a mile away, but he'd never seen a crowd like the drunken fans at the Cubby Bear or Murphy's Bleachers.

Saturday morning I took the el to the Addison stop, making my trip all of ten minutes door-to-door. When I was little, the drive into the city seemed to take forever, a long, painful process that no travel-sized Yahtzee or game of I Spy could make bearable. Andy and I were constantly asking *Are we there yet?* until my dad had to threaten us with something worse than physical brutality or bodily harm—no cotton candy.

Back then Andy and I would get all decked out in our red, blue and white Cubs gear, just in case the visiting team had any question who we were rooting for. But this morning I didn't paint my nails blue and stick on little Cubs decals, or put my hair up in blue and red ponytail holders. Instead, I picked out a pair of shorts and the same white tank I'd worn on Letterman. It had served me well the first time, and even though I wasn't the superstitious type, I wasn't necessarily averse to the idea of my own piece of lucky clothing.

I told Teddy I'd meet him on the corner of Addison and Sheffield, and as I waited there among the ticket scalpers and vendors selling programs and overpriced Cubby memorabilia, I expected some shiny black limo to pull up and discharge its passenger, along with an entourage of Ian and maybe a few of the people who made up Ian's infamous *we*. I figured Ian would come up with the sort of fanfare befitting a rock star on the rebound.

Instead, while I watched a seven-year-old throw a fit because his father wouldn't spring for a seventeen-dollar snow globe of Wrigley Field, Teddy walked up behind me and tapped me on the shoulder. "I'm glad you decided to come."

"I thought you didn't do sports." I pointed to Teddy's Cubs jersey. "Have you reconsidered?"

He shrugged and looked down at the team name written across his chest. "Nah, Ian gave me this and told me to put it on. I figured it was the least I could do considering they were giving me an audience of almost forty thousand people. A little polyester never killed anyone, right?"

"Not unless they lit a match." I looked around for Ian, or at least a few hangers-on. But Teddy was alone. "What, no limo? No police escort?" I kidded, following Teddy toward the turnstile.

"Ian's already upstairs in the broadcaster's box talking with some people about how this works. Here." He handed me a ticket. "We're sitting along the first baseline, and when it's time I'll go up to the booth."

"Sounds good."

The ticket taker looked at us funny, like he knew Teddy from somewhere but couldn't quite place the face. As I slipped through the turnstile behind Teddy I noticed fingers pointed in our direction, followed by whispers.

"They recognize you," I told him.

"Maybe they recognize you," he replied, and even though I knew he was just being nice, it made me smile.

Anyone from Chicago knows the words to "Take Me Out to the Ballgame" by heart. I grew up thinking that everyone stands and sways while bellowing the tune in unison with forty thousand strangers. But even though Teddy was wearing the jersey, and even though he had prime seats down the first baseline, he didn't exactly look like he belonged. His eyes kept glancing

down at the tickets in his hand, as if trying to figure out if they bore any resemblance to the concert passes he was used to. "Have you been practicing?"

"Believe it or not, yes."

I spotted Ian's familiar black figure walking toward us, still looking like an
Armani-clad Johnny Cash despite the fact that we were at a Saturday afternoon baseball game.

"Jane, I'm glad you could make it," he gushed, air kissing both of my
cheeks. "Has Teddy asked you about the radio show?"

I shook my head. "What radio show?"

Teddy almost looked embarrassed. "Jesus, Ian, she just got here. Give her a
break, would you?"

"Oh, I'm sorry." Ian feigned apology and backed away. "I thought it was
my job to promote you. But if you don't want me doing my job, well then,
that's just fine with me," he whined, practically pouting.

God, that guy got on my nerves. He must really be good at what he does
if Teddy was willing to put up with this crap.

"Jane, Ian wanted me to ask if you'd consider going on a radio show with
me Monday morning." Teddy rolled his eyes at the melodramatic publicist.
"It'd be just a quick interview, I'd play a song, that sort of thing. You don't
have to work on Memorial Day, do you?"

I'd planned to go into the office and catch up on some work, but I didn't
want to give Ian the satisfaction of blaming Teddy for not asking me sooner.
If I was going to side with anyone, it sure as hell wasn't going to be Ian.

I shook my head. "Nope."

"So, you'll do it?" Teddy asked.

"Yeah, I could do that."

"See." Ian practically stuck his tongue out at his client. "Nine o'clock
Monday at WMXX. Now, I've got to take Teddy upstairs for a few minutes,
you'll be okay?"

"Yeah, I'll be fine." I spotted the beer line and turned to Teddy. "I'm going
to go get something to drink. I'll meet you at our seats."

Teddy managed to give me a thumbs-up before he was shepherded off
by Ian.

I followed the crowd snaking along the corridor, catching brief glimpses
of the brilliant green field through the open aisles. It was amazing how little
the stadium had changed since I came here with my dad and Sam. There were

still no rotating ads on the walls surrounding the field, and no digital Jumbo-Tron on the scoreboard blinking corporate logos. The numbers on the scoreboard were still changed by hand by people hidden inside the green board like the wizard of Oz.

The ivy on the back wall was almost filled in and would be completely green in a few weeks, totally obscuring the brick wall behind it. The bleachers just behind the center field wall were already dotted with fans, and I knew that by the seventh inning a few guys would have their shirts off, maybe even with blue and red letters painted on their chests so that when the camera panned their way they could stand up and spell CUBS, later bragging that they were on TV. Andy always like to be the *S*; he said it made him feel like Superman.

Unlike last year's Memorial weekend, when it rained for three days and I ended up going with Olivia and the boys to see *Shrek 2* just because I was dying to get out of the house, today was gorgeous. The trees were green with newly sprouted leaves, the sky a watery blue, and with the sun's warm rays beating down on the emerald outfield, they all conspired together to create the illusion of summer.

The smell of hot dogs and beer and peanuts swirled around the cement corridors running along the rim of the stadium and I followed the scent into line like Elmer Fudd in those old Bugs Bunny cartoons that showed swirls of fragrance lifting him up and carrying him gently along.

"Jane!" A hand waved frantically at me from the front of the line. "Jane, over here!"

The hand motioned for me to join it at the front of the line, which would mean I'd be cutting ahead of the twelve people in front of me. And I wasn't a cutter. I always waited my turn.

Then again, I was thirsty, and the Old Style dribbling from the taps looked awfully refreshing.

I was about to enter uncharted waters. I took a step to my left and gauged the crowd's hostility. It would be at least another fifteen minutes before I'd make it to the head of the line. Fifteen minutes watching people walk away with the cold beers I could already practically taste. And then there was the cotton candy.

Quickly, I made my way up front and slid into line beside the hand.

"What are you doing here?" Drew asked, moving aside to make room for me. I glanced over my shoulder expecting to see thirsty fans preparing to wrestle me to the ground. Instead nobody seemed to notice. "Teddy invited me."

Drew took a step back and fixed his eyes on the menu behind the counter.

Was it my imagination or did Drew's eager reception just cool down a few degrees?

"Oh."

"He's singing during the seventh-inning stretch."

"That should be interesting. Where are you sitting?"

"Along the first baseline, I think." I showed Drew my ticket. "Where are you?"

"The bleachers. You can come visit if you get bored."

"I figured you for someone who'd be right behind home plate."

"Nah. I'm a bleacher bum at heart. Besides, out there the umpire can't tell me to shut up when I'm yelling too loud. You can't miss me. I'll be right in the middle."

I wondered if he'd be the one with his shirt off. "Maybe I'll stop by."

"What do you want?" Drew asked, stepping up to the counter.

"Two Old Styles," I answered. "And a cotton candy."

I paid for my order and waited for Drew to finish up.

"Well, you know where I'll be," he reminded me before starting off for his seat. "Enjoy your cotton candy." Drew waved and disappeared into the crowd.

"Here, I brought you a pretzel." Teddy handed me a stack of napkins and the pretzel before sitting down.

"You must think I'm a cheap date."

He took his beer from the plastic cup holder on the seat in front of us and held it up as if toasting me. "Nothing but the best for you, babe."

"*Babe?*"

Teddy looked down at his knees, embarrassed. "For some reason that sounded better in my head."

"Does that really work on some women?" I asked.

"Believe it or not, yeah."

I tore off a piece of my pretzel and passed it to him. "You need to hang out with a classier crowd."

"I thought that's what I was doing."

Our seats were right behind the visitor's dugout, and every time I noticed a camera pan in our direction I wondered if it was focused on the opposing team's players or Teddy Rock and Janey. I was sure we looked like a couple sitting together, sharing a pretzel while we drank our beers. Teddy even let me have the armrest all to myself, which is something Andy used to refuse to do. Usually my dad and Sam would sit next to each other so they could talk, but by the end of the first inning that always changed. After watching Andy and me elbow one other mercilessly in attempts to claim sole ownership of the armrest, a battle that stopped only long enough for us to rub the funny bones that inevitably collided and sent pins and needles shooting up our arms, my dad would give up and make us switch seats. I always ended up next to my dad, and Andy ended up next to Sam. And I'd spend the rest of the game feeling like I'd won.

"Hey, aren't you Teddy Rock?" a guy in the row behind us asked after debating the issue with his friend for fifteen minutes. I'd considered turning around after five minutes to tell them that they were right. It was Teddy Rock. But I was enjoying the speculation too much—*isn't he taller? Shorter? Older? Younger?* And so was Teddy.

Teddy turned around to face him. "Yeah."

He pointed to me. "Is this your girlfriend?"

"That's Janey," Teddy told him, which didn't really answer the question, but seemed to satisfy the asker.

The game was pretty uneventful and right before the start of the seventh inning Teddy stood up to leave. "I better go upstairs now. If I'm late Ian will send down a brigade to find me. You'll be okay?"

"I'll be fine. I think I'm going to head over to the bleachers and try to find a friend," I added, for some reason hoping Teddy wouldn't ask me to elaborate.

He didn't. "I'll look for you. You can see this whole place from up in the broadcasting box." Teddy stood in the aisle and waited for me to follow him. "Any idea where you'll be?"

"Right in the middle."

"Excellent. I'll meet you back here when the inning's over. Wish me luck!"

I took my beer and walked around the stadium until I came to the entrance to the bleacher section—and the guard who looked armed and ready to kick the ass of anyone attempting to get by him without a ticket. The seats faced south, directly in the sun, and it had to be fifteen degrees warmer than our seats on the baseline.

I showed him my ticket stub and started to push by, but he held out an arm and stopped me midstride. "Sorry, you need a bleacher ticket to get by."

"I'm just meeting a friend," I explained, adding my best smile.

"Sorry. No ticket, no entry."

I stared directly across the field toward home plate and looked up until I spotted the broadcasters' box and Teddy and Ian. And thats when it occurred to me—maybe if I told the usher I was with Teddy Rock he'd be a little more understanding.

And that's when I saw my opening. The ticket taker was busy tossing out an inebriated trio of college students, and with his hands full and back to me, I dodged past the fence and snuck inside the gate. It was like something out of *Escape from Alcatraz*, my back pressed against the chain link, my hands feeling for the point of no return. I was baseball's version of Clint Eastwood. Me! So it wasn't exactly like I was crawling over barbed wire or facing a firing squad, but from the way my heart was pounding, you wouldn't have known it.

I kept looking over my shoulder expecting the long arm of the law to reach out and grab me, but instead all I spotted was a peanut vendor. I was free and clear. Now I just had to find Drew.

Which ended up being easier than I thought.

"Hey, you made it," he cried out when I passed him in front of the men's room.

"Barely."

"We're sitting down there." Drew pointed to an opening on the third row of bleachers. "I'm with those three guys there. Just go squeeze in and I'll be right back."

I followed Drew's directions to the empty spot and introduced myself to his friends. The no-nonsense metal bench wasn't nearly as comfortable as the seat I had with Teddy, but you couldn't beat the atmosphere. We had an un-obstructed view of the broadcasters' box, and, in one more out, a perfect view of Teddy singing during the seventh inning stretch.

When he returned, Drew handed me a large blue foam finger just like the ones a few people were waving while they yelled "We're number one."

"Here, this is for you."

"Thanks." I slid over and made room for him on the metal bench. Next to me.

"Andy told me you used to love waving the finger when you guys came to a game."

"So did he, but it was a different finger."

"Somehow that doesn't surprise me." Drew laughed. "So, where do we stand?"

"The batter's got two strikes, one ball, and there's one out remaining."

"Listen to you. You know your stuff."

I might not remember how to hit a softball, but apparently all those years coming here with my dad made something rub off on me.

"Why don't you start a wave and get this guy out?" Drew suggested.

"You want me to single-handedly start a wave?" I asked, slipping my hand into the foam finger's pocket. It fit perfectly.

"Sure."

"I've never so much as participated in a wave, no less started one."

"So, here's your chance."

Me starting a wave. I hoped Andy was watching from Sam's. "But what if no one joins in?"

Drew pointed to his friends. "You've got four other people right here."

What was the worst thing that could happen? We had a five-person wave? The guard saw me stand up and threw me out? Andy and Sam and everyone in the bar laughed at me? Um, yeah! All of the above.

I decided to take my chances. I stood up and raised my arms, foam finger and all, into the air. Drew followed me, and then one by one everyone in our row rose to their feet. By the time the wave reached the upper deck, entire sections were rising and falling until a huge wave rippled past home plate and made its way around the stadium back in our direction.

Drew elbowed me. "Nice job. He struck out."

"I don't think I can claim credit for that."

"Hey, why not? Somebody's got to."

I decided Drew was right. So what if the pitcher threw a ninety-mile-an-hour curveball. I started a wave.

As the Cubs left the field the announcer introduced Teddy and the crowd stood up, ready to sing along with him.

Fifteen minutes ago I was sitting next to Teddy, sitting close enough to smell his guava shampoo and to knock knees with him when one of us shifted in our seat. And now he was across the field, three decks up, where I could just make out the block lettering on the front of his jersey, a rock star distanced from his fans. And from me.

Didn't Janey belong up there, too? I was sure that if I'd asked, Teddy would have let me join him in the broadcasters' box, would have let me share his spotlight, maybe even let me share in his song. But I didn't ask, and he didn't offer. And even though Janey probably should have wanted to be by Teddy's side, I wanted to be in the bleachers. I wanted to sing with the crowd, to sway from side to side with each verse, just like I used to. With my dad.

Teddy leaned out of the broadcasting box and began the traditional count down—*a-one, a-two, a-three*—before launching into "Take Me Out to the Ball-game."

It was ridiculous, and I knew it, but for some reason I kept waiting for him to catch my eye or make some gesture that was meant only for me. I was standing in a stadium full of singing fans and yet all I heard was the little voice in my head calling out *Me! Look at me!* It was crazy. I didn't need to be ser-enaded. I needed to be figuring out how to suggest that Teddy should become my newest client.

And that's when I noticed it—a leopard-print scarf tied to the top of Teddy's microphone, its silky ends fluttering in the light breeze blowing off the lake. My leopard-print scarf. A gesture that I knew was meant only for me.

"I better get going," I announced when Teddy finished.

"You could stay, you know," Drew offered.

I wanted to stay, but I couldn't. I'd always been taught that you leave with the person who brought you. And I was with Teddy Rock, just like everyone wanted. Even if I wanted to stay with Drew Weston and make waves.

I waved good-bye with my twelve-inch foam finger and went to find Teddy.

"Nice decoration on the mike stand," I told Teddy when he returned halfway through the eighth inning.

"I figured you wouldn't miss one scarf, considering you've never even worn it."

I wasn't letting him off that easily. "You could have at least asked me."

"I wanted it to be a surprise."

"But you didn't know I'd come to the game."

"Oh, I knew," he boasted. "I know you better than you know yourself, Janey Marlow."

"Don't be so sure of that," I challenged. "So, what are we going to do when the game's over? Does Ian have some superspectacular media opportunity for you?"

"Not until Monday's radio show."

"Do you want to head over to Sam's for a few beers?"

"Sounds good." Teddy leaned over and cupped his hand next to my ear.

"You know, we could leave now. I don't really care if we see the rest of the game."

I turned my head and whispered back, "Why are you whispering?"

"Because I don't want anyone to hear me and lynch us on the way out."

I nodded and stood up. "Come on, I'm ready to go," I announced so everyone within earshot could hear me. "I know you'd like to stay, but we have to get to that thing."

I brushed in front of Teddy and made my way toward the aisle. "Yeah, sure, if that's what you want," he replied, following my lead.

When we reached the corridor he turned to me. "Hey, thanks for doing that."

"No problem. I wouldn't want to ruin your image as the cool guy." I led the way toward the exit. "Did you happen to catch that wave?"

Teddy nodded. "Yeah. Who started it?"

"I did."

"What are you doing here?" I asked Drew, accepting his offer of a Long Island iced tea.

"I heard this was the hottest spot in Lincoln Park so I thought I'd bring my friends by and have a few drinks." Drew looked over at Teddy. "Aren't you going to introduce me to your friend?"

"Teddy, this is Drew Weston; we work together."

Teddy moved closer to me and looked Drew up and down before managing to say, "Hey."

"Where are your friends?" I asked. The bar was at least half-full, but I didn't recognize the three guys from the Cubs game.

"They're in the back getting a lane." Drew pointed down the hallway past the bar. "Why don't you come with me and say hi? I told them all about Sam's Sluggers."

"He's on your softball team?" Teddy asked, pointing to Drew.

I nodded. "Yep."

Teddy draped an arm over my shoulder and squeezed me. "You know, I was thinking that I'd take you up on your offer."

I had no idea what Teddy was talking about or why he was pulling me against him so that I couldn't move. "What offer?"

"Janey asked me if I'd like to be on the team, too," Teddy told Drew. "I think I'm going to play. When's the next game?"

"Tomorrow at noon."

"Tomorrow at noon," Teddy repeated. "It's a date."

Teddy let his hand fall and held it there against the small of my back. "We're going to sit at the bar," he told Drew, leading me away. "See you later."

"Sure. Well, you know where you can find us." Drew turned and went to join his friends.

Before I could ask Teddy what his problem was, he excused himself and headed for the bathroom.

"What's up with that?" Natalie asked, appearing behind me with a tray of margaritas.

"What's up with that?" I asked back, pointing to the margaritas. "Are you turning this waitressing gig into a full-time job?"

"Gig?" she laughed. "I think you've been spending too much time around rock stars. So why does he got his hands all over you, and why is Drew giving him the evil eye?"

"What?"

"Come on. If they were dogs they'd be peeing on you to mark their territory."

I took a long sip of my drink and felt the sweet mix of rums warm my throat. "That's ridiculous."

"I think somebody likes Janey," she teased, walking away to deliver her order.

I stood there slurping down my drink, wishing she'd stayed long enough to tell me who the *somebody* was. Did she mean Teddy or Drew? Maybe later she'd pass me a note in gym class.

"Hey, you're done with that already?" Teddy asked when he found me sucking on a piece of rum-coated ice.

"All gone," I told him. "Want another one?"

"That would be my first," Teddy reminded me as we headed for the bar. "I think I've got some catching up to do."

And catch up he did. By the time Andy served us our third round—well, that would be my fourth—I'd walked Teddy through most of the years he missed in Westover. Eventually I ran out of stories, not that he was all broken up over it. I almost got the feeling that Teddy had grown tired of nodding every time I asked if he remembered somebody.

"You sure do remember a lot," Teddy commented when I finally stopped regaling him with tales of our youth—well, my youth.

But at that point I didn't care whether I'd bored him. I was on my fifth

Long Island iced tea, my bare feet were propped up on the stool next to me, and a warm, fuzzy feeling had settled around me like a down comforter. Sam's was feeling cozy again. I didn't know whether it was the rising alcohol content in my blood or the rising nostalgia, but I was feeling good. Not some *I'm having a nice time* good, but an *all is right with the world* good. I felt like I was exactly where I was supposed to be. And as I sucked down the last drops of my drink, I knew exactly what I was supposed to do.

"I'll be right back," I told Teddy, and hopped off my stool.

I passed by the waitress station on my way to the bowling alleys and Nat shook her head at me. "You're bombed."

"Am not," I sang, sounding about eleven years old.

"Yes, you are," she insisted and pulled Andy over to get a look at me.

"No, you are," I sang. I started down the hall toward the noise of crashing pins.

"Excellent comeback, Jane." Nat took her order off the bar and left Andy to deal with me.

"You can't go back there in bare feet," Andy yelled at me from behind the bar.

I ignored Andy and kept walking.

Drew's friends were sitting down with a pitcher of beer while they watched him throw the ball down the lane.

"Nice shot," I called out, the words a wee-bit slurred. "Can I play?"

Drew looked over at me and smiled. "I thought Andy said you weren't allowed back here anymore."

"No," I told him. "Andy said I wasn't allowed to bowl in the tournament anymore. He didn't say anything about bowling against you."

Drew picked up a bowling ball and handed it over to me. "If you don't mind, I'll be sitting down over there out of your way. I bleed easily."

"I like to win, too," I told him, and set myself up at the top of the lane. Where I stood until the room stopped spinning. Just when I felt steady enough to attempt to walk toward the line, Teddy appeared.

"Here you are," I heard him exclaim as he made his way over to me. "I thought you said you'd be right back."

"I'm bowling," I told him, squinting at the lines on the alley as I attempted to figure out where to line up. But no matter how hard I squinted, or which eye I closed, things weren't lining up right. Perhaps I shouldn't be throwing a nine-pound ball if I couldn't even see a straight line.

Teddy came and stood next to me. "I'm ready to go."

"Let her bowl, Teddy." Drew stood up and brought over his beer. "She's having fun."

"It's been a long day, I'm just ready to leave," Teddy repeated, reaching to take the ball out of my hands.

"Just one game. Then you can go." Drew turned to me. "You want to stay, right, Jane?"

"Come on, Janey. Make up your mind," Teddy demanded before I could answer.

But I couldn't. How could I? The floor was swaying beneath me, the music was so loud that, combined with all the loud voices and the crashing pins, I could barely make out what Teddy and Drew were saying anymore. Drew wanted me to stay; Teddy wanted me to go. And my stomach was telling me that if I didn't make it to the bathroom in one minute they were both going to end up with three gallons of Long Island iced tea on their shoes.

The last thing I remember, I was standing between Drew and Teddy, trying to choose. And then everything went black.

Ex-Girlfriend Files Palimony Suit Against Teddy Rock

One-time rock sensation Teddy Rock was slapped yesterday with a $5 million palimony suit by an ex-girlfriend who alleges that Rock had promised to support her for the rest of her life. In the Los Angeles Superior Court complaint, Ashlee Breeland, a centerfold model and aerobics instructor, alleges that Rock, 25, reneged on promises to pay her expenses and purchase a Los Angeles home. Breeland, who says she dated Rock for 11 months before splitting from him in June, also contends that the musician promised to marry her and have children.

"I dated Ashlee for less than a year, and she expects people to believe that I'd promise to support her for the rest of her life?" Rock answered, when questioned about Breeland's claim. "Do I really look that stupid?"

Although still relatively rare, palimony suits have been growing in popularity since the first palimony suit was brought by Michelle Triola, a girlfriend of the actor Lee Marvin, back in 1976.

CHAPTER NINETEEN

The first thing that came into focus when I managed to peel my eyes open was my Sam's Sluggers T-shirt hanging from the closet doorknob.

The second thing I noticed was a foot nestled up against my ankle. Under the covers. Of my bed.

Somehow I'd made it home last night. But I didn't do it alone. And now I had no idea who was lying next to me.

Condoms. I squeezed my eyes shut and silently pleaded to the powers that be. *Please don't let there be an empty condom wrapper on the floor.* No. Scratch that. If I was going to have sex, I sure as hell hoped he used a condom, whoever *he* was. Please let there be an empty condom wrapper on the floor. Better yet, please let there be no need for a condom wrapper, period.

I attempted to lift my head off the pillow to see whether there were any souvenir wrappers (yes, plural, due to my high desirability quotient after consuming all those Long Island iced teas) from last night scattered on the rug. Bad idea. Waves of nausea rose in my stomach and my dry mouth started filling up with what little saliva it was capable of producing. Drooling on the pillow. Very nice.

I'd seen *The Perfect Storm*. I knew what happened when you tempted fate. I heeded the warning. There would be no abrupt movement anytime soon. I took a deep breath, gagging from the cigarette smoke steeped in my hair.

I lay there for four minutes, attempting to be still but restlessly moving anything that didn't ache—which left the tips of my pinkies, my nose and my left earlobe.

The sheets were twisted around my waist, providing a convenient cover, considering that, for some unfathomable reason, I was wearing the pale pink lacy camisole I bought for Liv's wedding. In the four years since my purchase, I have never, ever worn the camisole to bed, and now I knew why. The thin strap was in the process of cutting off the circulation of my left shoulder, and what I assumed was the matching underwear was crawling up my ass. At least I hoped that was my underwear.

How could my bed partner sleep through this? Between the dry heaves, morning breath and all that naked skin, you'd think he'd be awake by now. Nobody could be that tired.

Sleep. That was what I needed. If it wasn't for the spaghetti strap slowly amputating my left shoulder and the fact that my stomach was feeling like I'd done shots of Drano, I might be able to nod off. Then again, the fact that there was a strange body in my bed was a little hard to sleep through.

Okay, the body wasn't exactly a *stranger*. It had to be one of two people. One of two mistakes. A rock star or a litigator.

If it was Drew, he'd find out that I squeezed my toothpaste from the bottom and methodically folded the empty tube until every last bit of Colgate Tartar Control was neatly delivered onto my toothbrush. Although at this point, if the toxic fumes escaping from my mouth were any indication, he'd probably be thankful for any minty fresh gel I could get within brushing distance of my tongue.

And then there was Teddy. I had to admit, in the two weeks since I first met him on the show, he'd become less of a caricature of a has-been rock star and more of a real person. But Teddy still wasn't someone I'd go for if we hadn't been thrown together by an attention-hungry brother and an image-conscious publicist, even if he wasn't as detestable as I first thought. Teddy was a pretty decent guy, but he wasn't Drew.

Wouldn't Janey want to go to bed with a rock star? Wouldn't Janey want the sleeping body to be Teddy? So why, if Janey would want Teddy, was I hoping that it was Drew's slow and steady breathing beside me?

I slid my hand across the sheets until my fingertips rested lightly against a thigh, hoping I'd be able to tell whether it was the same thigh I'd had pressed up against me during my batting lesson.

"Are you making a move on me?" a groggy voice asked, pulling the covers down off its face. "Man, you look like crap."

"Nat!"

"Yeah, who were you expecting?"

Instead of answering I rolled onto my right side and listened to the contents of my stomach slosh in waves until they settled on my bladder. "Please tell me what happened last night."

"You mean before or after you made the cab driver stop so you could throw up on Lincoln Avenue?"

"Oh, my God." I covered my mouth, which was beginning to water again.

Nat yawned, as if I was boring her. "So, you don't remember Drew hoisting you over his shoulder and carrying you to the cab?"

"Stop!" I cried, pulling the sheet up over my face.

"Don't worry, I'm sure the cab driver's seen that happen a million times."

It wasn't the cab driver I was thinking about, although that idea didn't thrill me, either.

I peeked one bloodshot eye out from under the sheet. "That still doesn't explain why I woke up in bed with you."

"It was one o'clock in the morning and I'd been on my feet all night. I practically had to go through an obstacle course trying to find a freaking lamp to turn on in your living room. You ended up knocking over the table by the door, so don't blame me when you find it on the floor. At that point I just wanted to go to sleep."

"And this?" I lifted one of the spaghetti straps. "Why?"

"That one I can't answer. I was just going to let you go to sleep in your T-shirt, but you insisted on wearing that getup. You kept saying *Janey wants to wear pink*, talking about yourself in the third person and stuff—it was out of control."

"So what was Teddy doing while I was carried out of the bar?" I asked, envisioning a heated battle as he fought Drew for my comatose body.

"He just kind of tailed behind Drew looking like he didn't know what to do. Drew scooped you up pretty quickly and got you the hell out of there before Teddy could do anything."

I closed my eyes and massaged my throbbing temples. "My head is killing me."

"You're not looking that great, either."

"Gee, thanks." I reached for the half-full glass of water on the night table and gulped down the room-temperature liquid.

"Stop!" Natalie yelled, reaching for the glass and pulling it away just as I finished its contents.

I wiped my mouth with the back of my hand. "What?"

Nat looked like she couldn't decide whether she should laugh or cry. "You just drank my contact lenses."

"That's just great. I need coffee." I managed to plant both feet on the floor and felt my way along the wall with one hand while I held on to my head with the other.

"Do you want a cup?" I called from the hall, sounding like I was yelling through a bullhorn. If I didn't know better I'd think those Long Island iced teas were swimming around in my ears.

"How about some orange juice?" Nat asked when she appeared in the kitchen. "You better get well soon; we have a softball game in two hours."

"No way."

"Yes way. Drink lots of water and take a nice hot shower."

"Yeah, at this point I'm really going to take your advice. Where were you last night when I really needed your help? How could you let me drink so much? You're lucky I don't throw up on you."

Natalie plunked down some Alka-Seltzer and the Tylenol she found in my medicine cabinet. "Take these and you'll be as good as new."

I dropped my head onto the cool granite countertop and pressed my cheek against its smooth surface. "I will not be as good as new."

"You're not the first person to get drunk and go a little overboard."

"Thank you, Dr. Rowley. Is that your professional opinion?"

"Hey, I'm going to charge you for a house call if you're not careful." Nat finished her juice and placed the glass in the sink. "I'm heading to my place to change. I'll see you at the fields at noon. And you'd better be there, Andy's counting on you."

How about that, Nat was lecturing me about letting my brother down. Shouldn't it be the other way around? Since when was Andy Marlow the one in charge?

"Move," I mumbled, covering my mouth with one hand and pushing Natalie aside with the other. "I think I'm going to be sick."

CHAPTER TWENTY

"What's he doing here?" Nat asked as we walked toward field three.

"I asked him to play," I answered, walking slowly behind Nat in hopes that she'd just let me pass out on the grass. I wanted to sleep. "I thought you said all I needed was a shower and some water."

"So, I was wrong. What are you going to do, sue me for malpractice?" Nat grabbed my hand and pulled me along behind her at a pace I wasn't quite comfortable with given the precarious state of my intestines. "You're spending an awful lot of time with Teddy. Are you sure he's not getting the wrong idea?" she asked, her tone tinged with accusation.

"Come on, it's not like that."

"So, then if you found the time to ask him to play softball, I'm also assuming you've managed to ask him if he's in the market for a new lawyer?"

"Not yet," I told her, tripping over my own shoelace. I couldn't quite get myself to bend over this morning without making my head feel like a water balloon about to explode. "But I'm working on it."

"Really?"

"Yes, really," I insisted, but Nat just gave me a look that said *Who are you kidding?*

I wiggled my hand out of her grasp and traded in our tandem marathon race for a more leisurely stroll. "Look, I can't really explain it, but it's nice hanging out with someone who remembers me from so many years ago," I attempted to explain. "Trust me, it's nothing like you're thinking."

"Does Teddy know that? Because he sure seems to be putting in an inordinate amount of time with someone who isn't interested in him."

"We're just getting to know each other again. We have a lot of catching up to do."

"So, you're not a couple like all those articles are making you out to be?"

"You can't believe everything you read, Natalie."

"Oh, God, look at you, the seasoned media expert. Who are you, Paris Hilton?" Nat stopped walking and turned to me. "It's funny," she observed.

"What's funny?"

"That you never once mentioned that you're spending time with Teddy because Arthur expects you to. I thought that was why you started all this in the first place."

"Look, we're almost there, so can you stop grilling me for two seconds?" I asked, this time walking ahead of her. Natalie followed and quickly caught up, not too difficult when the person you're chasing feels like she has lead weights in her shoes. And not because she's trying to build her leg muscles.

As we got closer to field three, I noticed that Teddy wasn't the only one waiting for us on the sideline. He was talking to a very familiar white-haired woman while Andy, Sam and Drew tossed a ball around the infield. And sitting on the grass I spotted Liv, Weldon and a woman wearing a Colgate Tartar Control T-shirt.

What was this—a bad episode of *This Is Your Life*?

"Hey, everyone," I called out and tried to look like I was waving and not testing out the range of motion of my fingers to make sure at least one part of my body was in working order. I walked behind the backstop and gave my mom a hug. She pulled me in close to her and squeezed, giving me a noseful of her scent of choice—Scope. "What are you all doing here?"

"Well, Sam invited us to come watch his team," my mom explained.

"And I thought some fresh air would do me good," Kitty added, coughing into an ivory linen hankie she held in her hand. "Lord knows staying cooped up in that house isn't helping any."

Teddy was hovering about five feet away, watching us bashfully from under the lid of his black baseball cap while Drew, Andy and Sam loitered around the infield.

"Jane?" Liv came over to me and waited for an introduction.

I pressed my hand across my stomach, trying to hold my coffee down. "Teddy, this is my friend Olivia."

"Hi." Teddy stepped forward and awkwardly reached for Liv's hand.

"And you remember my mom, and this is Weldon, and it looks like you've already met Kitty," I added as, one by one, they stepped forward. "Everyone, this is Teddy Rock."

"Wow, Teddy, you're all grown up," my mom observed, moving in closer for inspection. "It's hard to imagine you're even the same little Theo from across the street. Andy told me you're a famous rock star now. I'm sorry I'm not familiar with any of your work."

Teddy shrugged. "That's okay. My mom can't even name one of my songs—besides the one about Janey, of course." Teddy touched me lightly on the shoulder. His gesture didn't go unnoticed by Natalie.

"I can't believe that's Theo Brockford," my mother reflected as Liv moved in on Teddy and started grilling him about the good old days. "The Brockfords moved to Saint Louis or somewhere when his parents divorced. Apparently it wasn't an amicable decision."

"How come I didn't know all this?"

"Well, it's not like you played with him or anything. He wasn't really interested in sports, so naturally Andy thought he was retarded. I was friendly with Beth but Theo's father, David, worked a lot. I got the impression that had something to do with their splitting up."

"What was the song about?" Weldon asked. "Can you sing it for us?"

I tried to think of the lyrics I'd feel comfortable singing in front of Weldon and my mom, but as I ran through the words in my head, they all started to sound a wee bit on the sleazy side. I may be thirty-two years old, but this was my mom. I didn't think she needed to hear about *taunting Teddy to begin*. She was smart enough to imagine exactly what Teddy was beginning. "Suffice it to say he sings about a girl who likes to have a good time."

My mom shook her head. "I don't know. It seems odd. He wasn't all that interested in the things the rest of you kids did. I've got to say, I'm a little surprised."

The look of doubt on my mom's face irked me. "And why is it so surprising? You don't think I like to have a good time?"

Before my mom could answer, Kitty picked up a wicker basket waiting on the ground beside her lawn chair and held it out. "Bernard packed some muffins, if anyone's hungry."

Muffins? All of a sudden I was ravenous. Maybe all I needed was a blueberry muffin to make me feel better. Alka-Seltzer and Tylenol were not the breakfast of champions.

While Liv monopolized the conversation with Teddy, I took Kitty up on her offer and attacked the basket of muffins. Mounds of warm poppy seeds and nuts and cinnamon greeted me, and the moan from my empty stomach seemed to echo across the park. I figured it was just my imagination, because at that point everything was a wee bit overamplified in my ears. Which is why, when I started to get the feeling I was being watched, I figured it was just my imagination. Surely it hadn't been that loud. But when I turned around, Drew was studying me from the pitcher's mound.

I held up an almond poppy-seed muffin. "Would you like one?" I offered.

He nodded and I walked out to the mound with the muffin in my hand and my tail between my legs. Here we go again.

"Sorry about last night," I apologized. Why did it seem like I was always apologizing to Drew for doing something stupid? "I was totally out of hand and I'm sorry."

"Hey, happens to the best of us." He took the muffin and tore off a piece. "How are you feeling?"

"Pretty lousy. All the batting lessons in the world won't help me today, I'm afraid."

"Your friend over there could sure use some." He looked over at Teddy but didn't offer to provide any instructional assistance.

"Did you invite Kitty?" I asked.

"Yeah, I called her last week to see how she was feeling and I told her we'd be just down the street if she wanted to stop by."

"That was nice of you."

"I don't think she's feeling any better, but when Bernard dropped her off he said she insisted on coming. I'm glad she did." Drew took another bite of his muffin. "With all this Darcy crap going on, I thought she might like the break."

I reached for a small piece of muffin and savored the almond poppy-seed flavor. "She makes a mean muffin, doesn't she?"

"Well, yeah." Drew laughed. "That, too."

After last week's loss, Andy had turned our little pregame warm-up into military boot camp, and I was willing to do anything to get out of the sprints he had Natalie running between bases. It turned out that Liv had only shown up to tell us she couldn't stay for the game. I seized the opportunity and offered to walk her to her car.

"What do those two have against each other?" Liv asked as we walked past first base toward the parking lot. Teddy had joined the practice throw with Andy and Drew, and he wasn't kidding when he said he wasn't into sports. Every time Drew threw the ball in Teddy's direction, Teddy practically stepped aside to avoid having to touch it. Not that there wasn't some reason for him to be afraid. Drew was hurling the ball pretty hard and fast in Teddy's direction. Actually, a little *too* hard and *too* fast for a game that didn't use mitts. And the ball almost seemed to be aimed more at Teddy's head than his hands. And Teddy never returned the ball to Drew, always tossing it to Andy instead.

"I don't think Drew likes Teddy."

"Gee, you think?" Liv laughed as we watched a ball dribble through Teddy's legs toward the neighboring field.

"It's hard to believe that someone could be so good with a guitar and so bad with a softball."

"You should have seen them at Sam's yesterday if you think this is bad."

"Natalie filled me in. It's because of you, isn't it?"

"I don't think so," I denied, although it was pretty obvious at this point. Was it so wrong to find the thought mildly enjoyable?

"Really? You should have seen them when Teddy strolled up this morning and saw Drew. I thought they were going to challenge each other to an arm wrestle right then and there."

"I'd actually like to see that," I told her, and we both laughed.

"So, why didn't you tell me you invited Teddy to play with us?" Liv asked me.

"Don't start," I warned. "I already got an earful from Nat."

"She's just afraid you're going to get hurt, that Teddy's not all he's cracked up to be. I have to admit, meeting him in person, he's not what I expected."

"See, I told you."

"Well, I'm glad he's here because he can take my place. I just came to tell you guys I wasn't going to be able to play, the boys are sick."

"Like stuffy-nose-sick or sick-sick?"

"We're talking full-on vomiting-smelly-chunks-sick. Kids aren't like cats, you know. They don't hide their dirty business in the corner behind the curtains. They find the center of the room, the one spot you could never hide with a strategically placed end table or lamp, and then they heave." I must have turned green, because Liv laughed. "It was actually kind of funny—disgusting, but funny in a sick, twisted way. Ah. The joys of motherhood."

"Let's not talk about getting sick, please." I stopped beside Olivia's car and rested my head against the shiny steel roof trim while she dug around in her pocket for car keys.

"Can I tell you something?" I asked, not looking up.

"Anything," Liv assured me. "Shoot."

I lifted my head up and leaned against the car door.

"I haven't asked Teddy for his business yet."

"So? Is there a statute of limitations on new client development?"

"There is if I want it to have an impact on my review in two weeks."

"So, why haven't you asked him?"

"That's just it. I don't know. It just doesn't seem all that important anymore."

Liv reached over and laid her hand across my forehead. "You must be delirious with fever, my dear, because I just thought I heard you say that becoming a partner isn't important anymore."

"I didn't say it wasn't important, it's just not as important as it used to be. Or maybe because I know that's what Arthur expects of me and I'm tired of doing what's expected of me."

"I swear I don't know who you are anymore, Jane Marlow," Liv confessed. "You're on TV, you're serving drinks at Sam's, you're taking batting lessons from Drew Weston, who you obviously would like to get to first base with—"

I didn't let her finish. "Don't say that!"

"Please. I'll admit you certainly needed the batting instruction, but the old Jane wouldn't take help from anyone, no less let a partner wrap his arms around her from behind."

"He was just helping," I told her. "Andy was going to kill me if I didn't get a hit."

Liv opened the car door. "Oh, you got a hit all right," she repeated, pointing over to the field, where Drew and Teddy were squared off over home plate, bats in their hands. "In fact, I think you scored a double."

Rockin' On

BY JAY FELLOWS, COLLEGIAN
CORRESPONDENT

The highlight of this year's Spring Concert had to be the sensational performance by Teddy Rock. Although the former platinum-selling performer was relegated to the position of opening act, he didn't pull any punches. To say that Teddy Rock surprised the crowd is an understatement. Armed with some new material as well as the hits off *Rock Hard*, including "Janey 245," Rock got the audience, well, rocking.

In addition to his arsenal of electric guitar riffs, Teddy also included some unexpected songs on a 12-string acoustic guitar. The diversity of material, which ranged from crowd favorites "Janey 245" and "One Too Many" to new songs that captured the edge of old-time Teddy Rock, was a nice change from the usual rehash of old material played the same old way. Although at times he was a little rough around the edges, Rock, a self-taught guitar player, played with a passion and feeling not many have seen since his debut album almost ten years ago.

After fading away to near obscurity, Rock seems to be serious about his talent and entertaining the audience. If he keeps this up, let's hope we get to see more of Teddy Rock in the future.

CHAPTER TWENTY-ONE

"Feeling better today?" Teddy asked, watching me while I read the magazine in my lap.

I nodded and made sure the receptionist couldn't hear our conversation. "Much."

Teddy continued talking even as he strummed an acoustic guitar to pass the time while we waited to be called into the radio station's studio. "I don't know what Natalie told you, but I tried to get to you before Drew did."

"It's okay, Teddy. I know you tried to help."

"I just don't want you to think I'd let you pass out on a bowling alley and not do anything."

"It's fine, Teddy. Really. I'd just rather forget the whole incident."

Teddy's fingers slid along the neck of the guitar as he sang a few verses and the chorus to a song that sounded a lot like a track off his first album. When he finished, the receptionist clapped and Teddy seemed pleased.

"Well, what do you think?" he asked.

"It's good," I offered, trying to muster the enthusiasm I knew he was hoping for.

He laid his hands across the frets and silenced a lingering chord. "Okay, what's wrong with it?"

"Nothing. It's fine."

"I'm not going anywhere until you tell me what you really think."

If I told Teddy what I really thought he wouldn't be thrilled, but what was the point of lying to him? He was used to being surrounded by people who did that all day long. Ian would tell Teddy it was the best thing he'd heard since the words *black mock turtleneck sweater*. Ian was so concerned with *selling* Teddy Rock that he didn't even bother looking at his merchandise. Teddy didn't need another another Ian; he needed a friend.

"Okay, I'll tell you. It's just that it sounds a lot like 'No Way Out.'"

"Oh, shit." Teddy plucked a few strings, replaying the chorus. "You know, you're right. Why didn't anyone just come out and tell me that before?"

"It's not *exactly* like 'No Way Out.' The part where you had your fingers up there"—I pointed to the top of the guitar neck—"that sounded different. Why don't you do more of that?"

"Like this?" he asked, his fingers moving along the neck.

I nodded. "Yeah, and then maybe do that chorus thing, but a little slower."

Teddy did what I explained, only he took my suggestion and added a few new chords as well.

"Wow, that sounds great," he exclaimed, continuing to play. "Why didn't I think of that sooner? Thanks, Janey."

The producer called us into the studio, and we were seated on stools at a high table that reminded me of a breakfast bar. Microphones were attached to the ends of long, spidery metal poles and hinged so we could position them near us.

Teddy was right at home in the studio, but I needed some help.

"Put these on," the producer told me, handing me headphones with soft rings of black, cushioned vinyl that surrounded my ears. They reminded me of the headphones that came with the stereo my dad bought me from Sears one year, although the graphite instrument console was nothing like the wood-paneled tape deck I used to play my *Grease* soundtrack.

"We all set?" the producer asked, but before I could ask what I was supposed to do, the commercial playing in my ears ended and the DJs sitting across from me were talking.

"Hey, we're back with Vicki and Dave, and sitting here with us now is someone we all remember from his rockin' first album, *Rock Hard*—Teddy Rock."

Dave paused and Vicki joined in.

"And Teddy's not alone. Welcome, Janey."

"Look at you two, reunited after all these years. What's it like?" Dave asked.

"It's pretty nice," Teddy admitted.

Vicki smiled at me. "What about you, Janey? There are a lot of girls out there who'd love to be sitting where you are right now. As a matter of fact, our lines are lit up with them. Dave, can we take a call?"

"Absolutely, Vicki." Dave pressed a button and I could hear a new person breathing in my ear. "Teddy, we've got Sabrina on the line and she's got a question for you. Go ahead, Sabrina."

Sabrina let out a squeal. "Hi, Teddy. I can't wait for your new album. I was just wondering if you and Janey are getting back together now that you found her?"

Getting back together? That would be a little difficult, considering we were never together.

Teddy cleared his throat. "First, let me say hello, Sabrina, and thanks for calling. I don't know that I'd say Janey and I are *getting back together* so much as getting reacquainted. It's been a long time, you know."

"Is that true, Janey?" Vicki asked.

"I think I'd agree with that," I answered, nodding at Teddy. "It's not like Teddy and I are *together* together." *Together* together? Did I really just use the vocabulary of an eighth-grader to describe my relationship with Teddy?

"In that case, we have another caller on the line." Sabrina's heavy breathing was replaced by that of Barbie from Evanston. "Barbie, you have a question for Teddy?"

"I sure do," Barbie answered. "As long as Teddy's not dating Janey, I was wondering if he'd like to go on a date with me." *Or me,* a girl yelled out in the background. Who was that, Skipper?

What woman would be crazy enough to call a radio station and ask Teddy Rock out on a date? Especially when he was sitting next to Janey. Was this woman into public rejection? I hoped Teddy let her down easy.

"What did you have in mind, Barbie?" Teddy replied.

What? I whipped around and looked at Teddy, who instead of circling his finger around his temple to show me he knew this girl was cuckoo, was intently waiting for Barbie's answer. Whatever happened to dancing with the one who brought you? I might not want the world to think I was getting together with Teddy, but I sure as hell didn't want Barbie from Evanston asking him on a date in front of me, either. Besides, what could she possibly offer Teddy? Her Barbie townhouse and a dune buggy ride?

"I thought we could maybe have some drinks, go out for a nice dinner, maybe hit a blues club and listen to music," Barbie babbled on, planning their romantic evening together. "And then we could just see where we end up."

I found myself holding my breath as we waited for Teddy's answer. I didn't want to date Teddy, but I wasn't expecting him to say he wanted to date someone else, either.

"That sounds nice, Barbie," Teddy answered. "But I'm afraid I'm going to have to say no. I'm leaving tonight and heading back to New York for an interview with *Rolling Stone* tomorrow. But thanks anyway."

That's my Teddy. I knew he wouldn't let me down.

"I see you've got your guitar there," Dave pointed out when Barbie was gone.

Teddy patted the guitar lying across his lap. "I've had this six-string since before I cut my first album."

"You're a lefty," Vicki observed. "We don't see many left-handed guitar players."

"Actually, I'm amphibious, so I can play either left- or right-handed," Teddy explained, holding up his hands for Vicki and Dave to see.

Vicki and Dave looked at Teddy's hands, then at each other, probably trying to figure out who would take that answer and make it part of their morning comedy routine. An amphibious guitar player—who could have imagined?

Before they could take Teddy's answer and run with it, I jumped in. "I think Teddy meant he's ambidextrous." I nudged Teddy. "Right?"

"Yeah, sure. That's what I meant. Anyway, I learned to play on my brother's guitar, and he was a lefty, so it's the way I'm most comfortable."

"What are you going to play for us today?" Vicki asked.

"I was going to play something off the upcoming album, but I've decided to play something new instead." Teddy picked up his guitar and I could picture

Ian kicking himself for flying back to New York last night. I was sure he gave Teddy explicit instructions on what to say, and definitely on what to play. He was here to promote the album, not pick random songs at whim.

"Actually, this is something new that Janey helped me with." Teddy began strumming the strings and I instantly recognized the song that we'd been talking about in the lobby not five minutes ago.

"Is this one named after Janey, as well?" Dave asked.

"It doesn't have a name yet, but we'll see." Teddy winked at me. "Right now it's just a collaboration between old friends."

"I can't believe that song isn't on the new album," Dave commented when the last chords of Teddy's guitar faded away. "It's fantastic."

"That was amazing," Vicki echoed. "What did the listeners think? Why don't you all give us a call and let us know."

Teddy nudged me. "Well, it's different from how it was originally written. It's much better than it was, actually."

The lights on console in front of Vicki and Dave flashed frantically. "Let's see what our first caller has to say." Dave pushed a button and I heard a click in my ear. "Caller? Who are you and where are you from?"

"This is Brian from Evanston. Teddy, man, that was great."

Teddy smiled to no one in particular. "Hey, thanks."

"Are you going to release that as a new single?" Brian asked.

Teddy looked over at me and shrugged. "I hadn't planned on it."

"We've got Carl on the line from Oak Park," Vicki cut in. "Carl?"

"You've got to make that into a single," Carl ordered. "Or at least put it on your web site. What was the name of the song? Old friends?"

The studio was quiet as Vicki, Dave and Carl waited for Teddy's answer.

"What do you say, Janey?" Teddy finally asked. "Old friends?"

Vicki and Dave turned to me.

"Yeah," I agreed, watching the console light up with callers. "That sounds about right."

Taking a Chance that Rock will Roll

Twelve years after his first label, Kick Records, dropped him, Teddy Rock has joined the Roundabout Records roster. Rock was playing at a bar last month on the same night that a talent scout from Roundabout Records happened to be there. Although Rock hasn't had a hit since "Janey 245," Roundabout is confident that Rock can re-ignite the musical fire that once burned bright.

"Teddy Rock has grown as an artist and musician and we believe that he has a tremendous future ahead of him

with the label," said a Roundabout Records spokesperson.

After a rapid rise and fall, Teddy Rock has been repaying his dues for the past nine years, performing at a slew of off-the-eaten track venues all over the country, most notably in college towns that have earned him a new generation of fans as he performed new material and honed his craft.

"I look forward to working with Roundabout and appreciate the support they've demonstrated on my behalf," Teddy Rock told Record Industry News.

Rock is expected to release a new album next summer.

CHAPTER TWENTY-TWO

"**C**all in sick."

I cradled the phone on my shoulder and attempted to slip my other arm into my suit jacket. "What?"

"Call in sick," Teddy repeated.

"I can't call in sick."

"Sure you can. It's easy. Just talk like this." Teddy cleared his throat and spoke in a low, gravelly voice that sounded like an attempt at laryngitis. "Hello, I think I've come down with something, it may be malaria, and it's definitely contagious. I wouldn't want to get everyone sick, so I'll be staying home today. Bye."

"You sound like you've done this before." "School was never quite my thing. So, what do you say?"

"Who are you, Ferris Bueller?"

"I guess that would make you the geeky kid who's afraid to take out his dad's sports car."

"My dad had a Buick, remember?"

"Come on, just make the call."

"I've never called in sick."

"All the more reason to do it right now."

"I can't. Arthur and everyone are expecting me."

"And what would happen if you didn't do what Arthur expected?" he asked, pausing just long enough to make me wonder the same thing. "Come on."

"I don't know." In elementary school I'd fake sick days. It hadn't been that hard. I'd rub the tip of the thermometer to make the mercury rise and jump around my room until my face was red and sweaty. I loved those days at home with just my mom, eating tuna sandwiches off TV trays while we watched *The Young and the Restless.* My mother would take care of me, always touching the palm of her hand to my forehead to see whether I was cooling down, as if a mother's hand was a better gauge of my health than a medical instrument. That was before things changed, before I took over and became the one who took care of everyone because it was something I could do to keep busy, something to keep my mind off what was really going on.

"We can do whatever kids around here do when they play hooky," Teddy continued, trying to convince me.

For a minute I thought he was suggesting we make out behind the 7-Eleven. "I guess we could go to Navy Pier and ride the Ferris wheel," I suggested, starting to warm up to the idea. "Then we can head over to the zoo and ride the paddleboats."

"Sounds perfect. Now, call Sandy and tell her you've got the measles or something. I'll meet you at Navy Pier at ten o'clock."

"I thought you were flying back to New York for that *Rolling Stone* interview."

"I figured, why fly all the way to New York when they could just as easily fly the writer here? Been here at the Peninsula the whole time getting pampered. Have you ever had a lavender salt glow?"

"I haven't."

"Well, it's a little frightening. They take these lavender petals and start rubbing them into you—doesn't sound so bad, right? It's the salt that's a bitch. I thought this little Japanese woman was rubbing shards of glass into my skin. Not exactly my idea of relaxation."

"Sounds painful."

"You're not kidding. Now, put on some shorts and meet me at Navy Pier. I'll be the one who's pretending to be Matthew Broderick."

"Does that make me Sarah Jessica?"

"God, I hope not. Met her. Total bitch. Besides, to me she'll always be that skinny, gawky girl from *Square Pegs.*"

"See you at Navy Pier, Ferris."

It was the Tuesday after Memorial Day and kids were back in school after a three-day weekend. Navy Pier was practically empty, but the few people we walked by did double takes when they noticed us on the pier, as if the guy in the black baseball cap and jeans looked vaguely like some rock star they once saw on MTV.

"They didn't have places like this when we were kids," Teddy commented as we walked passed the souvenir carts on our way to the Ferris wheel.

"There was that cheesy place with the go-carts," I reminded him. "The one with the bales of hay surrounding the track, as if a pile of straw was going to stop a thirteen-year-old behind the wheel of a motorized vehicle going thirty miles per hour."

"Oh, yeah, I remember that. They didn't even make us wear helmets."

"Or shoes."

"Whatever happened to that place?"

"Remember John Dennis?"

Teddy shrugged. "Vaguely."

"Well, our freshman year in high school John Dennis was drunk one night and he and a bunch of guys decided to break in and take the go-carts for a spin. He ended up losing control and crashing into the snack shack, where someone had left the hot dog grill on—you know, the kind with all those hot silver rods rotating the hot dogs under heat lamps? Anyway, the grill fell onto a box of paper napkins, which tumbled onto the paper plates, and the rest, the fire department says, is history."

Teddy laughed. "That's a funny story."

"Mr. Dennis didn't think so. He was the fire captain."

While Teddy paid for our tickets I noticed a couple watching us from the fried dough stand.

"Hey, I think those are photographers over there," I told Teddy, pointing them out.

"What gave them away?" He handed me my ticket and led me toward an open, waiting car. "The telephoto lens or the fact that they've been following us since we got here?"

"They've been following us?" I asked, stepping inside as the car continued to slowly move across the loading platform. "How'd they know we were here?"

The car rocked as Teddy's weight shifted, and the Ferris wheel operator locked the door behind him. "That's their job."

As the car rose into the air along the arc of the wheel, the city seemed to grow in front of us. I noticed the top of my office building peek out from behind the smaller high rises. "Look." I tapped Teddy's arm and pointed to the glass-encased offices. "That's my office, on the thirty-second floor."

"Are you having pangs of guilt?" he asked.

When I called Sandy and told her I wasn't feeling well she said my ears must have been ringing. Arthur had the review committee in a meeting at exactly the same moment I was in my living room planning to meet Teddy for a day of hooky. Next week I'd find out what they decided. The wheels were in motion. I just wasn't sure anymore if I wanted them to keep moving.

I shook my head emphatically. "Not even one itty-bitty pang."

"I have a question to ask you," Teddy announced when we'd reached the top of the wheel. "You can say no, there's no pressure or anything. It's just that I promised Ian I'd ask you."

"Okay. What is it?"

"This is Ian's crazy idea, so don't hold it against me."

"I won't."

"Would you consider coming out on tour with me?" he asked and then rushed on before I could answer. "You don't have to say anything now, just think about it. Ian thought it would be fun for the audience to see you and all. You wouldn't have to go everywhere, maybe just a few of the larger cities."

"Teddy, I don't know," I started, but Teddy wouldn't let me finish.

"Just think about it. I promised Ian I'd get you to at least think about it."

"Okay," I finally agreed. "I'll think about it."

Teddy squeezed my hand and looked out over Lake Michigan. "Thanks."

"So, you're doing this for Ian?"

"Actually, it was my idea, but Ian thought it was great." He took his eyes off the lake for a minute and glanced over at me. And there it was. The look I didn't even realize I'd been waiting for. The look that clearly showed Teddy

Rock had considered me *that way*, even if he didn't act on it. Not because I was awestruck by his rock-star status or because I had the body of a centerfold. And not because Ian told him to. But just because I was me. "You've been good for me, Janey, and I hope you know how much I appreciate that."

As our car slowly made its descent toward the ground, I realized that this was my opportunity. Teddy had asked me to consider his question, and now I could ask him to consider mine—would he become my client? I could ask him right now, get my answer, show up at work tomorrow with my big news and put all this Teddy Rock / Janey Marlow business to rest. I could get on with my life and return to normal.

But as our car slid down and the glass windows of Becker, Bishop & Deane disappeared from view, I didn't say a word.

The sea lion pool was our first stop when we reached the zoo. Teddy and I stood together at the edge of the wrought iron fence surrounding the pool and watched the sea lions glide effortlessly through the water.

"This place is pretty cool," Teddy admitted.

"Your parents never took you here?"

Teddy shook his head and led me away from the exhibit.

"My dad used to take us here on weekends when my mom was visiting friends," I told him.

"Before you go strolling down memory lane yet again with stories about class field trips to the zoo, I'm going to get myself a pretzel."

I followed Teddy to the closest concession stand and waited while the vendor handed Teddy a large soft pretzel drizzled with mustard.

When the pretzel exchange was over, I ordered. "I'll have a rocket pop, please."

"A Popsicle?" Teddy asked.

"Yeah, maybe it'll bring back those ruby lips you remember."

Teddy bit into his pretzel. "Maybe."

After I paid for my Popsicle, we wandered toward the Farm in the Zoo. "You know, I've been wondering about that."

"What?"

"The ruby lips. The melting eyes. I don't remember us wishing upon any stars."

"It's creative license, Janey. You don't think all songs are that literal, do you?"

"No, but it seems like the entire song is creative license."

"Come on, there really isn't a stairway to heaven. Bob Marley didn't really shoot the sheriff."

"I know, but those songs weren't written about real people."

"Well, I guarantee you this one was."

We walked until we reached the Farm in the Zoo, one of my favorite places because you could get up close to the animals and even touch them if the zoo staff wasn't looking. For Christmas one year my dad even adopted one of the zoo's pigs for me. I didn't get to take the pig home, which was a surprise to me, but I did receive an eight-by-ten glossy of a gray spotted pig and his adoption certificate. My dad told me he had his choice of adoptee, a cow or a pig. Andy thought it was hysterical that my dad picked the dirty, mud-covered pig over the sweeter, cleaner alterative. At first I was a little confused myself. This wasn't some pink little piglet right out of *Charlotte's Web*. My pig weighed over two hundred pounds and sprouted razor stubble from its snout. It wasn't until we were finished opening our presents and my mom and Andy were out of the room that it all made sense.

"Turn over the picture," my dad suggested.

I flipped over the pig portrait and read my adoptee's vitals.

Born: September 27. Sign: Libra. Weight: 204 lbs. Height: 2'10". Favorite food: Grain mash. Name: Andy.

"I thought you could take this out whenever your brother starts to get on your nerves."

My dad was right. Holding that picture was a big help when Andy would steal my bras, stuff them with socks and put them on his head like rabbit ears, exclaiming, *Silly Rabbit, tits are for kids.*

But Andy the pig was long gone by now, off to the big pigpen in the sky and he'd been replaced by a whole new generation of hairy-snouted swine who still made me think of my brother. As we circled around the barn and made our way back to the main exhibits, I had the distinct feeling that Teddy and I were being trailed. When we stopped in front of the monkey cages I pretended to stretch my arms out and twist from side to side. And there they were again, about ten feet away, lurking around a peanut cart. The man attempted to look interested in a bag of popcorn while the woman swapped the lens on her camera for a longer one she pulled from her fanny pack.

"There are those photographers again." I tipped my head toward the cart.

Teddy turned and looked over at the couple. "Probably just paparazzi trying to snag a photo of Teddy and Janey. The least we can do is give them what they came for." He reached for my hand and pulled me toward him. "Give me a kiss."

"Why?"

"That's what they want to see—a Teddy that's settled down, a Teddy that kisses his girlfriend in front of the giraffes."

"But I'm not your girlfriend."

"They don't know that." Teddy cradled my face in his hand and leaned down to kiss me. Reason went out the window and instinct kicked in. On cue, my eyelids closed and my lips pressed against Teddy's mouth. Instead of pursing together into the type of kiss usually reserved for mothball-scented great-aunts or cheeky air kisses, they parted easily. A little too easily.

A knowing look on the Ferris wheel was one thing. Making out in public was another. Still, I didn't pull away. I wanted the photographers to see the girl Teddy wrote about, and I wanted to see whether I felt like the girl in the song, the girl who wanted Teddy.

The kiss couldn't have lasted more than a minute, but when it was over I had my answer. I didn't feel any overwhelming urge to keep kissing Teddy, even though a part of me really wished I had. Teddy's Janey should feel something, shouldn't she?

"You taste like a rocket pop," he told me when the shutter of the cameras finally stopped clicking in the background and he pulled away. "And your lips are blue."

I wiped my mouth with the back of my hand and looked over at the photographers, who were already walking away. "Do you think they got what they wanted?"

"I think so." I was almost afraid Teddy would ask the next logical question—did Janey get what she wanted? "Let's go check out the lions."

"Do they always follow you everywhere?" I asked, walking ahead of Teddy to keep some space between us before he reached for my hand.

"You think this is bad. After 'Janey 245' came out I had photographers camped outside my house every day. I couldn't get the mail without a shot of me in my underwear appearing in a magazine somewhere."

"I guess it doesn't get any worse than that."

Teddy ripped off a piece of his pretzel and handed it to me. "It can definitely get worse."

I flicked off the white grains of salt and took a bite. "How?"

"They could stop snapping pictures altogether."

I looked over to see whether Teddy was kidding, but I sensed he wasn't. Instead he'd stopped in front of the lion's grassy habitat and watched as two tawny cats stretched their long frames out on a rock and turned their faces to the sun.

"I'm surprised they weren't camped out at our softball game on Sunday." I joined Teddy at the wrought iron railing and we watched the lions in silence for a while. "Do you ever wish you could go back to when 'Janey 245' first came out?" I finally asked.

"Every day. I'd handle it a lot differently. How about you?" Teddy turned to face me, his weight leaning against the railing. "Ever wish you could go back to when your dad was alive?"

"I think that's a little different, Teddy."

"How?"

"Well, you at least have a shot at getting your career back. My dad is gone forever."

"Not really. I think you relive your dad's mistake every day."

"I help people plan for the future, Teddy. I hardly think that qualifies as trying to relive the past."

"You act like preparing a strategy in advance will make it easier when the time comes, Janey, but it won't. There are some things in life you just can't prepare for—like achieving fame, or losing it."

"Well, being prepared sure would have made it easier on my mom and Andy and me."

"You really believe that?"

"Yes, I do."

A group of school kids ran toward us and lined up along the railing next to me.

Teddy let it drop, but I could tell he thought he was right. I could tell that he didn't think I was that different from him. But I was. There was no way he could compare losing a spot on the Billboard top twenty to losing your father.

"There's a reporter from the *Tribune* who wants to go back to Westover next weekend and have me show him around—sort of like *local boy makes good.*" Teddy turned to me. "Would you like to come with me?"

"Would you like me to?"

"I would, but I'm afraid my reasons are more selfish than anything else." Teddy laughed. "I'm afraid I won't be able to find my way around without you."

Entertainment Section

Here's Janey!

Last night, just in time for faded star Teddy Rock's comeback attempt, Chicagoans made a startling discovery—the inspiration for Rock's hit, Janey 245, wasn't just some girl he met in some dingy bar. She's our very own Jane Marlow, a Chicago attorney. Marlow, a childhood neighbor of Rock's in Westover, IL, walked on stage during a ROK96 promotion and gave the audience a show to remember. In front of over one hundred onlookers lucky enough to make it into the standing-room only crowd at Sam's Place on Southport, Marlow answered questions about Rock and their relationship before belting out the chorus to her namesake song.

"It was great," noted Louisa Mul-drew, who showed up hoping to catch a glimpse of the woman who helped Rock soar to number one back in the fall of 1989. "I know the lyrics to that song by heart."

And she's not the only one.

Even without touching, I felt your skin
Calling me, taunting me, time to begin
I took your hand, let you lead me astray
Willingly let you have your way
And now I close my eyes, bringing you back to me
Like the stars we wished upon, only a memory

Janey 245 made a name for Teddy Rock, who was unable to sustain his success after his first album went platinum. After being out of the spotlight for years, Rock re-signed with Roundabout Records. Rock's comeback fourth album will be released in July.

CHAPTER TWENTY-THREE

Drew looked up when he heard the conference room door open. "Feeling better?" he asked.

"I am."

"I can tell." He eyed my outfit. It had been a last-minute decision, and all of a sudden I wondered whether it had been a good one. I'd paired Liv's red Escada pencil skirt and chain belt with a plain white oxford. It was understated chic, kind of like when Sharon Stone paired her husband's shirt with a Vera Wang ballroom skirt to the Academy Awards. Okay, maybe not exactly.

"Calling in sick after a three-day weekend? You look pretty healthy to me. What happened? Did you have a hot date?"

I didn't have to explain myself; it was so obviously a question that wasn't meant to be answered honestly.

"I spent the day with Teddy," I admitted, and waited for Drew's reaction.

"Oh." Drew looked away, picked up his pencil and resumed making notes. "Did you see this?" He handed me a *Time* magazine without looking up. "Turn to page fifty-six."

There she was. Darcy Farnsworth.

"What is with this girl?" I read the caption below a photo of the poor, aggrieved Darcy: *Feeling cheated by her own flesh and blood, Darcy Farnsworth, 18, is taking her grandmother, Kitty, to court looking for money and answers.* "This is such bullshit."

"She knows how to play the game. If this were going to be tried in the court of public opinion, I'd say Darcy had a shot." Drew reached for the magazine and placed it back into the accordion file. "Your filing system is turning out to be very helpful."

"If my greatest contribution to your defense is an accordion file, then I'm starting to get worried." The table was covered with documents and motions and legal reference books. Drew didn't have to be busting his ass like this. There were associates and paralegals he could unload some of this work on. "I appreciate all you're doing for Kitty."

"It's obvious how important she is to you." Drew held my gaze for a minute before turning away. "Don't worry. We're doing just fine."

Since Drew first arrived, not much had changed around the office. He still worked in the conference room and called me in when he had a question or wanted to throw an idea past me. But something had definitely changed between us. And something had definitely changed in me. I just wasn't sure if I was ready to admit it to anyone except myself.

I could spend an entire day with a rock star and yet the idea of being alone with Drew scared the crap out of me. At least with Teddy I knew what I was getting; I felt safe. Nothing was ever going to happen between us, because even though the world knew him as Teddy Rock, to me there was still a part of him that was Theo, the little kid from across the street. Teddy was all about the past, but Drew was all about an uncertain future. Who would have imagined that being with a rock star would feel like the safe choice?

On the way back to my office it finally happened. I mean, he'd been so patient, so understanding every time I gave some vague answer about Teddy. This time, Arthur wanted to know what was going on.

"Are we any closer to getting Teddy?" Arthur asked when I passed him in the hallway.

"Everything's good. I think we're almost there," I called over my shoulder, hoping he'd continue on his way. Instead of accepting my response, Arthur turned around and followed me.

"I didn't think it would take this long, Jane. It's been almost four weeks."

"I know, Arthur. It's just not as easy as we thought." I tried to come up with a plausible explanation for stretching out what should have been a relatively quick task. "Teddy's leery of lawyers, and, given his history, I think we need to be sensitive to that."

"Still, this wasn't what I expected from you, Jane."

I stopped in front of my door and turned to face Arthur. It had just become too exhausting trying to please everyone, trying to be what I thought they wanted me to be. I was like a magician pulling rabbits out of hats and tissue-paper bouquets from my sleeves. And now the curtain was closing, and the act was over.

"You're right, Arthur," I told him before turning around and heading back to the conference room. "This wasn't what I expected from me, either."

I didn't even step into the room, instead I cracked the door open a little and poked my head in. "Why don't we go get some dinner and I can tell you all about my day of hooky," I suggested.

Drew hesitated, considering my offer. "Should I bring my laptop?" he asked.

"Nope. And we're not going anywhere around here, so make sure you bring enough for cab fare. You're treating."

"Are you sure you can risk it? I might try to have my way with you on the postage scale," he ribbed.

"I think I'll take my chances. Meet me by the elevator at six o'clock."

Before I actually had a real job, I read somewhere that a woman should always keep a pair of sassy heels in her desk—just in case. Of course, I probably read that in some *Cosmo* article that also espoused the virtues of swallowing versus spitting. But in my seven years of full-fledged, adult employment, I never once received a surreptitious phone call asking me to attend a last-minute cocktail party at a trendy art gallery or whisked off to Paris for dinner, and so I never had occasion to pull out my lower-left desk drawer and slip on my stilettos, unbutton my shirt to expose a little cleavage, and slick on a coat of glossy lipstick before strutting out the door, transformed.

Until now.

There they were in the bottom drawer, three-inch black heels with a thin ankle strap that was supposed to keep me from toppling over. Needless to say, Olivia had picked them out. As someone who used to actually receive the aforementioned surreptitious phone calls, Liv kept the shoes in her bottom drawer, until her feet started swelling and never returned to her pre-pregnancy size eight.

At five minutes before six, I slipped on Liv's shoes, smoothed down my skirt, and went to meet Drew at the elevator.

He was waiting for me when I got there.

"You grew taller," he observed and pointed to my shoes.

"Let's just hope I can walk, or you'll be carrying me to the cab."

"I've done that once before if you'll recall. Wait here, I'll run and get my weight-lifting belt." He pretended to walk away, but I grabbed his arm and pushed him through the open doors.

"Thanks to your Long Island iced teas I can't recall much from that night. Just get in the elevator."

The cab ride up Michigan Avenue to Capital Grill was different from the last time we shared a backseat. Instead of feeling cramped, it was comfortable. Maybe because this time we left our briefcases behind at the office.

"I'm sorry, we don't have any tables available without a reservation," the maître d' told me, running his hand down the reservation book. "I could get you in around ten o'clock if that works."

Yeah, just what I wanted to do; wait around for three hours. Now I really needed to pull a rabbit out of my magic hat.

"You know, I was really hoping you could find us a table"—I leaned in over the reservation book and lowered my voice—"for Janey Marlow."

"You're Janey Marlow?" he repeated.

"Yes, I am." I backed away from the hostess stand and shrugged. "But if you don't have a table . . ."

"Well, let me take another look here and maybe we can do something." He disappeared into the dining room and returned carrying two menus. "Right this way. I have a lovely table for two right by the window."

"Nice move," Drew whispered as we made our way between the crowded tables. "Normally I wouldn't ask you to throw your weight around, but I'm glad you did. I'm starving."

I took a deep breath and reached for Drew's hand, pulling him close behind me. "Me, too," I told him, not even looking back to see his reaction. "Me, too."

* * *

"Why do you even still keep a license to practice in Illinois? You haven't lived here in years," I asked Drew after the waiter took our orders.

"At first I was convinced it was just a temporary move, that once the office was up and running I'd be back. I kept saying it wasn't a permanent situation. Of course, I was kidding myself. And now, well, it still makes practical sense for when cases come up that I'm best suited for, but I'm not holding out hope of returning anymore. If it happens, it happens."

"Well, I'm glad you're the one handling Kitty's case."

"Thanks." He glanced at his watch. "That should do it. Now we can write off the dinner to the firm and not feel guilty. Enough about work. Tell me about yesterday."

Over our appetizers I told Drew about Navy Pier and the zoo, describing how the photographers followed us around from place to place.

"It sounds like you and Teddy are spending a lot of time together."

"I guess so."

"You guess so?" Drew grinned. "The newspapers certainly think so."

I hadn't told anyone about Teddy's offer to go on tour with him, but I wanted to tell Drew. I knew what everyone else would expect me to do—you'd have to be crazy to turn down an offer like that. "He asked me to go on tour with him to a few cities."

Drew put down his fork. "Wow. That's pretty big news. What did you tell him?"

I shrugged and kept occupied with my stuffed mushrooms. "I didn't tell him anything. I know it's an amazing opportunity, but I can't go, can I?"

"Do you want to?"

I'd been asking myself that same question. Maybe that's why I hadn't told anyone yet, because I wanted to make up my own mind without thinking about what everyone else thought. "No, I really don't."

"Then, there's your answer."

There was my answer. Janey didn't want to go on tour with Teddy. How would I explain that one? Janey was supposed to want to live the life of a rock star. She was supposed to want to be with the guy who wrote a song about her. So why would I rather be here having dinner with Drew than in some foreign city with Teddy Rock? And why did spending time with Drew make me feel like I was cheating on Teddy?

"Enough about Teddy Rock," I told Drew. "I thought we weren't going to talk about work anymore."

"I wasn't asking about Teddy as a partner in the firm, Jane," Drew answered. "Am I competing against a rock star here?" he asked, his voice low and serious.

"I told you, it's just business."

"I suppose you have all sorts of personal policies about seeing coworkers, probably a whole volume of regulations—Marlow's Rules of Order or something."

"You're not a coworker. You're a partner. Which makes it even more complicated."

"Not if you're about to make partner," he pointed out.

"I don't know that yet."

Drew sat back, sliding his knee farther against my leg. "You know, I lied."

"About what?"

"I watched you on Letterman."

"You did?"

"Yeah, I just didn't want you to think I was overly interested in the girl in the song. You already seemed leery of me."

"Not leery," I clarified. "Just unjustly forewarned."

"You know what I was thinking when they showed those clips from Teddy Rock's past performances? What would my montage be? What would be the defining moments that I'd have shown in some sixty-second clip?"

"And what'd you come up with?"

"Nothing as sensational as Teddy's, I'm afraid. I've never had thousands of people chanting my name."

"I have." I looked up at Drew and smirked. He laughed at me.

"I guess you have, haven't you?"

"Does it still count if they don't really know who they're chanting for? Because I'd hate to lose this popularity contest on a technicality."

"No, I think it counts. I guess you win."

I grinned triumphantly. "Good."

When the waiter placed the check in the center of the table, I realized this was the moment of truth. I could slip my credit card into the billfold and make this whole evening one big friendly gesture or I could let Drew pick up the tab and take the chance of seeing where this went.

"This was nice. You didn't grill me about the case once." Drew shifted in his seat and our legs touched under the table. I could feel the sharp surface of his knee against my thigh but didn't move to avoid it. Instead, I let it stay there, resting against me.

"You know what they say, all work and no play makes Jane a dull girl."

"Not dull, just not exactly someone I'd want to have a real dinner with."

"We've had dinner before."

"No; we've had dinner, but it was merely a change of venue. You were still working. Tonight was different."

"I think I'll take that as a compliment."

"You should."

Drew placed his hand on the billfold and slid it toward him. He kept it there, not even opening the black leather folder to look at the check.

"So, are you getting nervous for your review?" he asked, placing his credit card—his personal credit card—on top of the bill. If I'd had any questions about the nature of our dinner, he'd just answered them.

"Should I be?"

"I don't think so."

"Olivia told me it's relatively painless if all goes according to plan."

"Things rarely do, don't you find?"

Despite myself, I flinched. "Do you know something I don't?"

"No, but that's just the way life is, isn't it?"

"Yeah," I nodded. "I guess it is."

"So, now what happens?" Drew asked as we left the restaurant and walked toward Michigan Avenue, where just a few blocks away Teddy was probably watching TV in his hotel room.

We were meeting at my mom's house on Saturday before giving the *Tribune* reporter a tour of Westover. And the reporter would want what every else wanted. Teddy and Janey, the rock star and the muse, reunited after all these years, frozen in time like the lyrics of a song. Only I didn't want to be frozen any more. *So what happens now?* Drew wanted to know. Him and me both.

I was about to reply when Drew leaned in to me and in one fluid movement placed his soft lips on mine and parted them with his tongue. The taste of gin and lime was foreign, the smell of his cologne unfamiliar. Drew brought his hands up to my face and held them there, not letting me turn away. And I didn't. It didn't even occur to me to try.

If I felt like I was cheating on Teddy before, now I was doing the real thing.

NEW YORK POST MAY 26, 2004

LIZA BASSET-LUND,
ENTERTAINMENT REPORTER

Turns out that one-time rock 'n roll phenom Teddy Rock reconnected with an old friend last night in New York. Expected to hype his new album due out July 1, Rock instead turned the clock back to 1989 and introduced a thrilled Late Night with David Letterman audience to "Janey 245," the woman who inspired the namesake song. Rock looked as shocked as the rest of us when Janey, aka Jane Marlow, walked on-stage. As for Janey, she seemed a bit smit-ten with the rocker herself. After lots of hand-holding and reminiscing, the two were seen later on that night sharing a cozy table at The Carlyle.

"It looked to me like Teddy and Janey had a lot of catching up to do," joked a source close to Rock. "I wouldn't be surprised if they started spending more time together."

CHAPTER TWENTY-FOUR

"**M**om," I called out. "Where are you?"

"I'm in the kitchen," she answered from down the hall. "We've got appointments this morning," she told me when I found her standing in front of the sink in her standard blue scrub pants and a white pullover top with Daffy Duck brushing his beak—she always tried to make her uniform a little less threatening to her pint-sized patients. Her head was down, and her fingers were hard at work trying to undo the knotted drawstring at her waist. "Darn drawstrings; you'd think by now I'd figure out how to work these things."

"Do you need my help?" I asked, already reaching into the kitchen drawer for a fork. I moved her hand aside. "Here, I have it."

She dropped her hands to her hips and let me take the knot. "I enjoyed watching the softball game the other day," she told me while I worked the tines through the drawstrings. "It's nice to see you spending your time on something besides work."

I pulled out one long spaghetti-like string and the knot loosened. "I've almost got it; if I can just get this one, I think it will come undone."

My mom kept her head down, watching me work. "You know, you remind me so much of your father," she told me, placing a hand on my head and running her fingers through my hair.

I froze, the fork intertwined between the drawstrings like a knitting needle. "Why would you say that?"

"Well, because you're so busy taking care of other people you forget to take care of yourself. You're always worrying about your clients, your partners, your friends, and your brother, of course. Even me."

"That's not true," I told her and went back to the knot.

"Sure, it is. You always think it's up to you to fix everything; you don't want help from anybody. You know where I'd be if I did that? Wearing a lot of knotted drawings." I made one last pull of the fork and the knot slipped apart. "I used to be afraid that you were missing out on being just a normal teenager," she added, pulling the drawstring tight around her waist and tying a perfect bow. "At the time I thought it was how you decided to deal with the situation. I'm not always sure I did the right thing. You were probably the only eighteen-year-old girl who had a preference in laundry detergent."

I bought only Tide, not because I liked the smell or the color of the packaging, but because it smelled like my dad. Even when I noticed other brands on sale, I picked up the familiar red container, unscrewed the cap and inhaled. And once I smelled him I could never bring myself to screw the cap back on, replace the Tide on the shelf, and buy the sale brand, because the entire time I was wondering how we got there, how our lives could change in less time than it took for my dad to ask who wanted dark meat.

"Teddy's going to be here with the reporter any minute," I told my mom, running the fork along my leg and watching the neat, even lines it left behind.

"We should get going, too. *Weldon*," she called upstairs. "We're going to have patients lined up outside our door if we don't get out of here right now."

A white car pulled into the driveway and I watched Teddy emerge from the passenger's side. He walked up the brick pathway to the kitchen door, peering through the blue gingham curtains before knocking.

"Hi, Teddy." My mom held the door open and invited him inside.

"Hello, Mrs. Lang."

"Will you still be here later on? We could have dinner," she offered.

I shook my head. "I don't think so. We'll be heading back into the city."

"Isn't your review coming up, Jane?" she asked, before calling for Weldon one more time.

"Thursday."

"All this big news," she remarked, slipping into the white clogs she kept on the mat by the garage door. "First Teddy's song, then your review, and now Sam is selling the bar."

I watched my mom to see if she was joking, but she just reached for her jacket.

"What? He's selling the bar?" I repeated. There was no way I'd heard that right. "He can't do that."

"Sam says he's ready to retire and take it easy. I guess in some way, he has you to thank for that."

"Me? What did I do?"

"I guess the bar's been doing better since that stunt Andy pulled, and Sam thinks he should sell while he can." My mom grabbed the big awning-striped canvas beach bag she used as a purse and pecked a kiss on my cheek. "Tell Weldon I'll be in the car. Teddy, it was lovely seeing you again. Give your mother my best."

"I can't believe that," I mumbled before taking a seat at the kitchen table.

"I know." Teddy joined me and looked as disturbed by my mother's news as I felt. "This isn't good," he told me.

A look of distress settled across his face, and for some strange reason it almost made me feel a little better. Teddy understood. He knew how important Sam's was to me. As I watched Teddy chew his lip in deep concentration, it occurred to me that maybe he'd resurfaced for a reason. Maybe with Sam's gone Teddy was going to be one of the few things I had left to remind me of the past.

"It's nice that you're so concerned."

Teddy leapt out of his chair and started pacing laps around the kitchen, which, given the small size of the room, meant he was practically turning in place. "I'm sorry about Sam's, Janey. Really. It's just that when Ian finds out, he's going to shit."

"What's this have to do with Ian?"

"Do you have any idea what will happen if people find out that a bar was essentially sold after I played there? That doesn't look so good—for either of us," he added.

"Will you stop moving for one second," I ordered, getting dizzy just trying to trace Teddy's circular steps. "You're being ridiculous. This has nothing to do with you."

"Of course it does, Janey," Teddy snapped back.

Now he was really taking this rock-star thing a little too far. "Not everything is about your comeback, Teddy."

He shook his head at me, as if pitying my poor, disillusioned suggestion. "If you only knew."

We decided that I should drive. Paul, the *Tribune* reporter, sat in the backseat and took notes while I drove through town and showed him where we grew up. I started out on Main Street, going by the Dairy Queen and 7-Eleven—all the local hot spots. Teddy didn't have much to say, even though Paul tried his best to get some material for his article.

"Do you remember the first time you met Janey?" he asked Teddy.

"Not exactly," Teddy replied.

"He remembers how I used to play with my cat in the front yard," I offered, but Paul didn't seem that interested in the information I provided. He wanted Teddy's recollections, not mine.

"Did you ever play the guitar for Janey before you moved away?" Paul tried again.

Teddy shook his head.

"Take me to some of your favorite hang outs," Paul suggested, but we just ended up driving to the places I used to go. The miniature golf course, where my dad used to talk in a low whisper and British accent, like the commentators on TV. The town pool, where Andy had all the little kids convinced they put a special dye in the water that created a red ring around anyone who peed in the pool.

But Teddy never offered his own memories, and the only time he had anything to say was when he could piggyback on mine.

After an hour Paul seemed like he was ready to give up, and Teddy reached for the radio, turning up the volume. "Are we almost there?" Teddy asked, still in a bad mood after the news about Sam's.

I pointed up ahead. "It's that street up there on the right."

I pulled the car onto Memorial Circle and the years flooded back to me. The houses looked smaller than I remembered, the street a little narrower. Trees that once had branches I could reach if I stood on my tippy toes now towered above the rooftops offering shade. Even though my mom still lived in Westover she may as well have moved away. In fact, once we moved into the house on Steeplechase, I never revisited our old neighborhood, never went back to our old house. Until now.

"This is where it all began. That's Teddy's old house, over there." I pointed to the white Cape set back from the street.

We parked the car along the curb and got out to walk around.

"It looks good, doesn't it?" Teddy asked, kicking a stone on the sidewalk as we approached the house. "I think the shutters used to be green, though, weren't they?"

"You know, I think you're right. My mom said Mr. Feely's son lives there now." I turned to Paul and explained. "He was the middle school gym teacher. I loved him."

"Mr. Feely and I didn't have much fun together," Teddy continued. "He was always yelling at me to climb that fucking rope like my life depended on it. Once, we were getting changed in the locker room and he overheard me call him Mr. Freaky. I was running laps for months after that, which I pretended to hate but actually didn't mind. It beat having Feely blow that whistle at me every time I dropped a football."

"But Mr. Feely was so nice. He used to give you a piece of Bazooka if it was your birthday and he never yelled if you forgot your sneakers."

"I never got any Bazooka," Teddy told Paul. "At least it looks like his kid is taking care of the house."

"Which room was yours?" Paul asked.

Teddy pointed to a window toward the end of the top floor. "Up there. Man, it was small."

The reporter jotted down Teddy's answer in his notebook.

The sun reflected off the glass, creating a slash of white down the length of the dormered window. "At least it got a lot of sunlight," I told Teddy.

"I guess."

"Did you two hang out together much? Play games, walk to school, that sort of thing?" the reporter asked.

I watched Teddy for a reaction, but he just turned to me.

I shook my head. "We took the bus."

"Hey, do the Sargents still live in that house?" Teddy pointed to a gray ranch tucked behind a row of manicured hedges.

"I don't know. Remember how every Halloween they used to cover their front yard with gravestones and Mr. Sargent would rig the front door so when you rang their bell all those ghosts would leap out from behind the hedges?"

Teddy shook his head and Paul kept scribbling, trying to keep up with our conversation. "Maybe. I remember that they used to give out green apples instead of candy. That sucked. I mean, what kid would want fruit over a

Marathon Bar or Charleston Chew, right? It was almost as bad as that house that gave out those plastic baggies with pennies."

"That was my house," I informed Teddy, who quickly backpedaled.

"No, it was cool, really. I didn't mean it sucked. It's just that back then I really wanted candy, you know?"

"We also gave out Charms Pops and Snickers and SweeTarts, so I don't know why you only remember the pennies. Besides, all the other kids loved the pennies."

Teddy turned to Paul. "Janey's right. I guess it was pretty cool. Everyone loves money, right?" Teddy took a few steps up the driveway and then turned back toward the street. "See that rock over there, by the mailbox?" He pointed to the end of the driveway. "That's where my dad was standing when he waved good-bye. My mom pulled out to follow the moving truck and I was kneeling on the front seat watching my dad waving at me until eventually I couldn't make out his hand or his body anymore and he just faded away."

The reporter stopped writing and looked up at Teddy. "That doesn't sound like fun."

"It wasn't. I couldn't wait to get the hell out of here. Looking back, it was the best thing that could have happened to me."

"Why?"

"I didn't belong here. I wasn't the all-American kid, I didn't care about playing flashlight tag or riding bikes to Dairy Queen for crappy ice cream."

"They don't call it ice cream," I corrected. "It's DQ soft serve. The chocolate Blizzards with M&M's were awesome."

"Come on, Janey." Teddy made a face. "That place always smelled like fried fish."

"You make everything around here sound so horrible."

"I guess it depends on how you choose to remember it. If I'd stayed here, who knows what would have happened."

For a minute I thought he meant us—who knows what would have happened between us. But then I realized that Theo was wondering if he ever would have become Teddy Rock.

"Don't you remember anything good about living here?" I asked.

"Not much." Teddy grinned. "Although your dad telling me I reminded him of Eric Clapton was pretty damn good."

We continued walking past the other houses, past the bikes in the driveways and the basketball nets waiting for a game of pickup and the swing sets in the side yards. I didn't know the place that Teddy remembered. I loved growing up here.

"So, what's next for you, Teddy?" Paul asked. "The single is released in three weeks and then the album comes out and you spend the rest of the year on the road?"

"That's right." Teddy smiled just thinking about it. "Janey may come with me, too. Right, Janey?"

"Is that true?" Paul asked. "Are you going to go on the road with Teddy?"

Before I could answer, Teddy's cell phone chimed and he glanced at the digital display. "It's Ian, I'd better get this."

While Teddy listened to Ian, I kept thinking about what he'd said. He hated our neighborhood. He hated growing up here. And yet he wrote his only hit about a girl he knew here. It just didn't make any sense.

Before Paul could ask me for an answer to his question, Teddy came back to us, his mouth hanging open.

"What's wrong? You don't look so good."

"I'm better than good, Janey. I'm fucking fantastic." Teddy grabbed me and spun me around. "And I don't even care if you print that, Paul—Teddy Rock said he's *fucking* fantastic. They're putting me on the cover of *Rolling Stone. Rolling Stone,* Jane!" he screamed and then pointed to the reporter. "Make sure you put that in the article. Teddy Rock is going to be on the cover of *Rolling Stone.*"

"That's great," I told him, pulling away. "But I thought it was just going to be an article."

"It was, but the reviewer loved the album and I guess the photos they shot came out better than expected. Do you know what this means? It's happening, Janey. Just like I knew it would."

Teddy started walking toward the car. "Come on, Janey, let's head into the city to celebrate. We're done here."

Paul joined Teddy, asking questions about his upcoming tour, but I hung behind and just looked around at everything I'd left behind. While my mother and Andy mourned, I took the responsibility for erasing the memory of my dad, of the family we once had. I cancelled his magazine subscriptions, called the University of Michigan to remove his name from their list of alumni. I was the one who checked the phone book when it arrived at our new house and made sure his name had been removed. I was the one who called the movers and packed up his tools in the garage, and, eventually, the last one to close the front door.

Teddy thought we were done here, but if we were really done here, then why was I standing next to Teddy's mailbox thinking about the little boy waving to his dad from the back of a station wagon? And why was I jealous that at least Teddy got to say good-bye?

We dropped Paul back at his car, in the center of town, and Teddy and I headed back to Chicago. Teddy was in another world. He held his arm out the window, feeling the air rush by as if wanting a physical reminder of this moment. He flipped through the radio stations until he found something he liked and then sang along to an Aerosmith song, hitting every note and not missing a word.

Once the jutting skyscrapers of downtown Chicago came into view, Teddy was ecstatic, alternating between singing at the top of his lungs and repeating his conversation with Ian word for word. But as we approached the city, I couldn't help thinking that it wasn't a celebration I wanted. It was an explanation.

"If you hated growing up there so much, how come you remember me so fondly?"

"What?" Teddy asked and continued singing.

"You could hardly remember a single thing about growing up in Westover." I reached for the radio and turned down the volume. "So why'd you write a song about me if you were miserable every minute you lived across the street from me?"

"Come on, Janey, it was, like, twenty years ago. Does it really matter anymore?"

"It matters to me. I made an impression on you and I want to know why."

"Look, it was forever ago. You're here now, the buzz on my comeback is huge, and *Rolling Stone* is putting me on their cover."

"Yeah, but you wrote a song about me. You told Music One I was your inspiration, that you'd never met anyone like me before."

I drove along and waited for his answer, the yellow dotted lines bleeding together into one blurry line.

"Janey, come on, can't we just enjoy this?"

I kept my eyes on the road, blinking at the yellow lines as they skipped past us. My foot eased up on the gas pedal as we edged toward the exit ramp. I wanted an answer. Because now it all made sense. It'd been too easy.

"I'm not Janey." It wasn't even a question. It was a statement. It was what I should have known all along.

"What?" Teddy stopped singing. "Of course you are."

"You made it up."

The light at the end of the ramp turned red and I dropped my foot onto the brake pedal. Teddy grabbed the dashboard to keep from hitting his head on the windshield.

"Tell me, Teddy," I demanded. "I'm not Janey."

"Look, you're being ridiculous."

"I want the truth," I told him, getting angrier. At both Teddy and myself. "Say it right now or we're not moving."

"Fine. You're not Janey 245. You're not her," Teddy repeated.

I sat there staring at the steering wheel, half expecting the airbag to inflate under the impact of Teddy's words. *You're not Janey.*

The light turned green, but still I didn't move. I'd been so stupid. All this time wanting to believe it, when I knew it couldn't be true.

"Who was she?" I asked over the blowing horns.

"Why are you doing this now, Janey?" Teddy pleaded. "Come on. We're holding up traffic."

But I didn't take my foot off the brake. I didn't care about stopping traffic. I wanted an answer.

"Fine. She was a hooker I met in a hotel when I was still trying to land a label for my first album."

I stepped on the gas pedal and the car lurched forward. Teddy continued talking.

"I mean, at first I thought you could be her, I swear, but she had this long, pale blond hair that used to fan out on the pillow while she slept. Not to mention the most amazing tits. You're not exactly endowed in that department, if you know what I mean." Teddy glanced down at my chest in case I'd missed his point. "Then when Ian met you he thought it would make great press, that you'd be good for my image as the grown-up, more mature Teddy Rock."

"What about all those interviews, all the time you spent with me? My address was 245 Memorial Circle. How do you explain that?"

"Des Moines, Iowa, Red Roof Inn. It was actually room 247, but the only word that rhymes with seven is heaven and that chick was anything but angelic, so I picked the room next door."

"The hooker's Janey?"

Teddy nodded.

I knew it couldn't be true. There was just no way I was Janey 245. I couldn't be. Because if I were, then my life had ended up all wrong.

"Then who am I?" If I wasn't Janey 245, then I was just plain Jane. And while that used to be fine, it was no longer enough. I jammed on the brakes and this time Teddy did hit his head. I reached across the front seat and pushed his door open.

"Get out."

"Come on, Janey; what are you doing? You can't just leave me here. *People* magazine wants to do a piece on us when the album comes out."

"How could you lie to me this entire time, Teddy? If nothing else, you owed me the truth."

"Believe me, Janey, I wanted to tell you. I never thought I'd see you again after New York, and then the whole thing just kind of snowballed. I had to go along with it, and then you didn't seem to mind being Janey, so I figured we'd both just have a little fun.

"Come on," he pleaded above the noise of the highway traffic overhead. "I remembered that plaster labyrinth you made. Doesn't that count for something?"

"It was the Parthenon, Teddy," I yelled. "The fucking Parthenon."

Teddy didn't move. He didn't try to make a joke or give me some cocky one-liner. He just looked scared. "Don't ruin this for me, Janey—Jane. I worked too hard for it."

"Get out," I repeated, my voice steady and calm. It was the voice of someone who knew the game was over.

Teddy let out the breathy laugh. He knew he was screwed. "Okay, fine, if that's what you want. Go ahead and kick me out. Leave me right here under a fucking bridge in the middle of nowhere. You think I'm the one who used you, but who are you kidding, Jane? You used me right back. The last few weeks were the best you've ever had." Teddy slammed the car door shut and almost seemed surprised when the wheels kicked up loose gravel and I drove off without even once looking back in my rearview mirror.

I hated him. I hated the way he always smelled like stale cigarette smoke. I hated that he always wore that damn baseball cap to cover up his receding hairline. I hated everything about him. And I especially hated that he was right.

Teddy Rock Shows Sam's Place a Good Time

By Grace Bronson
Tribune entertainment reporter

Just as she was unwinding after work with some friends at Sam's Place on Southport, Francie Conroy noticed a familiar couple enter the bar. "I couldn't believe it. I was like, 'That's Teddy Rock and Janey!'"

Conroy, 26, was among the lucky few who got to mingle with Rock and his companion, local attorney Janey Marlow. Although their appearance was unexpected, Sam's Place patrons were treated to a personal concert by the former—and maybe, future—rock star.

"We immediately started calling our friends," said a beaming Agnes McDonald, a 25-year-old graduate student at DePaul University.

McDonald wasn't the only one. By the time Rock took the make-shift stage, the bar was half full with fans waiting to hear a live concert.

It seems that Sam's Place is the new North side hot spot—and Teddy and Janey are the new hot couple. Two weeks ago Chicagoans learned that hometown girl Jane Marlow was the inspiration for Rock's hit "Janey 245," a family friend of Sam Harris, the owner of Sam's Place.

CHAPTER TWENTY-FIVE

I was in no mood to deal with the person I found sitting on my couch shelling peanuts onto my coffee table. "What are you doing here?"

"I called Mom, and Weldon said you were probably on your way back into the city." Andy peered over my shoulder, as if expecting someone else to follow me through the door. "Where's Teddy?"

"He's not here."

Andy must have sensed my mood, because all of a sudden he attempted to sweep the discarded shells into a tidy pile on the table. Of course he only succeeded in making a bigger mess when half the skins ended up on the floor. "I was kind of hoping I could talk to both of you."

"Whatever it is, forget it. Forget everything. It's over." Even as the words escaped, I wasn't sure what I meant. What was over? My starring role as Janey? The illusion of me and Teddy? He never really wanted anything to do with me. I was just the means to an end.

Andy sat back on the couch and watched me. "What do you mean, it's over?"

"I'm not Janey."

"What?" Andy stood up and came over to me. "That's impossible."

"Apparently not. Janey was a hooker."

Andy laughed. "Come on, you're kidding, right?"

"Do I look like I'm kidding?"

"You look like you're pissed."

I glared at Andy, the boy genius.

"So why'd he say you were her?" Andy wanted to know. "Why go through all the trouble?"

"I was going to help him make his comeback. They needed a fresh image to show that Teddy was new and improved, and I fit the part."

I walked into the kitchen while Andy slowly grasped my explanation. "This is unbelievable."

"As unbelievable as me being Janey 245? I told you it wasn't true. I told you!" I practically screamed.

Andy followed me into the kitchen but I couldn't even look at him. Sure, he'd come up with the ridiculous idea, but I'd swallowed his Janey Kool-Aid like some Jim Jones convert. I'd wanted to believe it was true.

I stood over the sink washing the dirty plate from Andy's peanut butter and jelly sandwich, while in the living room, the melody from a Clapper commercial provided background music.

"Shit, Jane, this isn't my fault. I wasn't the one who lied to you about all this. I just thought maybe you were Janey. Don't blame me because Teddy turned out to be an asshole." He put his hand on my shoulder and turned me around, flinging lemon-scented dishwashing suds across the breakfast bar in the process. "Besides, was it so bad being Janey for a little while?"

I shook Andy loose and pushed past him, wiping my wet hands on his shirt as I passed by. It was probably the closest his shirt had come to soap in weeks.

The least he could do was finish washing the dishes, but instead Andy trailed me into the living room. "This makes my visit sort of pointless now," he told me, my wet handprints smeared across his chest. "I was going to tell you that Sam is selling the bar."

"I know. Mom already told me. So what? You wanted one more free Teddy Rock concert to fill the place? His publicist planned the whole thing, you know—the guitar in the trunk, the rental company leaving the stage up, the fact that news spread so quickly around the neighborhood. Everything."

"That's not what I wanted to talk to you both about. If Sam sells the bar, I could be out of a job, Jane."

"So, what are you going to do about it?"

"I'm going to buy the bar from Sam."

"With what, your collection of Indian head nickels and baseball cards?"

"With the little money I've saved and a loan from a benevolent lender."

"And who would that be?"

"Well, I was hoping Teddy would be interested, but maybe my lovely sister would like to take his place?" Andy gave me a hopeful grin.

"No way."

"Jane, I have to buy it. We can't let Sam sell the bar. It'd be like losing a piece of family history."

"Our family history isn't that great, Andy."

Andy shook his head at me. "That's not true, Jane."

"Besides, we lost it years ago," I pointed out.

Andy let out an exasperated sigh. "Jesus, Jane, will you just let it go and move on already?"

"Move on? Me? Who are you to talk? You still act like you're sixteen years old. I wouldn't be surprised if you still slept on your *Hong Kong Phooey* bedsheets. I'd be even more surprised if you ever washed them. You're the one who's stuck, Andy. I did move on. I went to college. I went to law school. I have a career and can support myself. What do you have?"

"A life," Andy deadpanned.

"Oh, please. Is that what they call it these days?"

"It's more than you have. You just exist."

"Don't give me that crap, Andy. I have a life. I'm planning for the future."

"No, Jane. You're planning for the moment it all ends because you think that will give you control over the inevitable. There's a difference."

I didn't have to take this from a guy who treated my home like a cafeteria. I pointed to door. "Just leave, okay?"

Andy grabbed an apple off the breakfast bar and headed to the door. "Thanks for all your help, Jane," he tossed over his shoulder sarcastically before opening the door. "Once again, you've been a load of fun."

Why was Andy always making me out to be the bad guy when all I ever tried to do was set everything right? "You're going to end up just like Dad, you know," I called out before he could close the door.

"I sure as hell hope so."

"How can you even say that?" I demanded, running after Andy and grabbing the door before he could close it behind him. "That is the dumbest thing I've ever heard come out of your mouth. And that's saying a lot, considering the ample competition."

Andy stopped in the doorway and stood there for a minute facing Mrs. Winston's apartment. "You want me to say it, Jane? I'll say it." Andy whipped around to glare at me. "Dad fucked up. He blew it. He was wrong. Does that make you feel better?"

"Of course it doesn't make me feel better. He should have known better. Every day he went to work and took care of his clients. Why couldn't he do the same for us? Why didn't we matter enough?"

"It was a mistake, Jane. He was forty-two years old. He didn't expect to die. It just happened."

Right. Shit happens. I didn't need Andy's bumper sticker wisdom. "Didn't you learn anything when he died?"

"Dad didn't die to teach us a lesson, Jane."

"Well, I sure learned something."

Andy watched me, a frown flattening his lips. "Unfortunately, it was the wrong thing."

"Fuck you, Andy," I spat, and the door slammed shut before I could catch his reply.

My hands were still shaking as I held the garbage can against the lip of the coffee table and cleaned up Andy's mess. That was my job—cleaning up other people's messes. Taking care of details so nothing fell between the cracks. Putting the broken pieces back together. It was easy for him to preach the word according to Andy when he knew that there'd always be someone there to pick up his slack.

While I collected the peanut shells in my hand the light on my answering machine blinked at me from the breakfast bar. I knew it was Teddy. He was probably scared shitless that he'd have to tell Ian that Janey wasn't going to play their game anymore. He'd probably beg me not to tell anyone, not to ruin his *Rolling Stone* cover story. But no matter what he had to say, it wouldn't matter. On

Monday morning I'd get the numbers of Andy's radio and TV contacts and set the record straight. No explanation he could provide would change that.

Still, on my way into the kitchen I pushed the button and listened. As much as I hated Teddy, I wanted to hear him apologize.

But instead of the groveling I was prepared for, a man's hoarse voice started speaking. "Jane, it's William Farnsworth. My mother's in the hospital. Northwestern Memorial. It's not looking good."

I didn't even wait to find out what room number. I grabbed my keys and ran out the door to hail a cab, still clutching Andy's peanut shells in my left hand.

When I was finally directed to the correct waiting room, I found William talking with a nurse. He looked shell-shocked, one hand nervously jingling the change in his pants pocket while the other hand rubbed his temple as if trying to erase the very news he was trying to absorb.

I hung back and watched.

It was all too familiar. The same uncomfortable metal-framed chairs and plastic end tables with old *National Geographics* and *Time* magazines, their covers frayed and their pages rippled from the tears that dribbled onto them while visitors pretended to read the outdated articles. Were they afraid that if the furniture was comfortable and the reading material current, visitors wouldn't leave? Did they really think that people would choose to sit in a waiting room surrounded by drab, tweedy textured wallpaper with shiny black plastic picture frames screwed to the wall, as if while waiting to find out if your dad is dead the only thought going through your mind is whether or not you could make off with a faded reproduction of Van Gogh's *Irises*?

The antiseptic smell, the sound of the sliding doors opening and closing as doctors and nurses came and went—it was as if no time had passed, as if just hours ago I was having Thanksgiving dinner with my family.

"How is Kitty?" I asked William when the nurse walked away.

"She's hanging in there. She has pneumonia and the doctor says he'll know more after getting back some test results, but she's eighty-two years old, Jane. I don't know how much we can expect."

"Can I go see her?"

"She can't talk very well, she has tubes in her nose and she's tired." William took a breath, attempting to steady his voice. "She's in the second room on the left."

* * *

When she heard me, Kitty slowly turned her head toward the door. She looked so small lying on the bed, her white hair crushed haphazardly against the pillow. The thin outline of her body barely rumpled the sheets.

I dragged a chair beside her bed and sat on the cracked vinyl cushion.

"See, I was right. It's not allergies." Kitty reached for my hand and a thin smile creased her dry, cracked lips. A few spots of Kitty's shimmery pink lipstick clung to the flaking skin, reminders that just yesterday she was at home applying makeup. "I told you I was too damn old to get allergies."

"How are you feeling?" I asked, the words barely managing to make it over the lump already forming in my throat. It was hard to believe that this was the same woman who sang to her flowers while she watered her garden. The woman who never once, in the four years I'd known her, regretted a choice she'd made, whether it was deciding which causes the foundation would fund or which entrée to order in a restaurant.

A gurgled cough echoed in Kitty's throat. "I'd rather have a room at the Four Seasons, but they didn't offer me that option."

"William says they're doing everything they can for you." I caressed her cold hand, my fingers softly rubbing her papery skin, careful not to touch the IV poking out of her vein like a stem holding on to a delicate flower.

"They've all come to visit, you know. The entire family. Every one of them." Kitty looked away at the respirator pumping up and down like an accordion. "Except Darcy."

"Her lawyers probably advised her that coming to see you right now wasn't a good idea."

Kitty ignored my explanation. "Fighting Darcy on this was a mistake."

"But she's wrong, Kitty."

Kitty looked up at me, her watery blue eyes attempting to hold my gaze. "Is being right so important, Jane? Sometimes being at peace is more important than being right."

She sighed and then let her lids slowly cover her eyes. I reached for Kitty's hand and watched her chest rise and fall under the white and gray polka-dotted hospital gown. Her fingers were thin and creased, the excess skin gathering around her knuckles in loose folds. The pale pink polish Kitty wore on her nails had peeled away to expose yellowed nail beds beneath the artificial enamel. I remembered reading that nails continue to grow even after you die, which made me think of that guy in the Guiness book of world records, his nails thick and curling under.

"Wait here," I told her. "I'll be right back."

Kitty opened her eyes. "I'm not going anywhere."

I took the elevator down to the lobby gift shop and found what I was looking for on a corner shelf holding travel-sized toiletries. I grabbed a bottle of moisturizer, a package of six emery boards, nail polish remover, cotton balls, baby oil and one of those pocket-sized black plastic combs they used to give out on photo day at school.

When I returned, a nurse was scribbling something on the chart at the foot of Kitty's bed while another replaced a bag of clear fluid hanging limply from a metal pole.

I took the baby oil, nail polish and cotton balls out of the plastic gift shop bag and reached for Kitty's hand. She watched as I gently removed her makeup and nail polish.

"That feels nice," she told me, a weak smile on her newly soft and shiny lips.

I worked in silence as Kitty watched me file her brittle nails and then rub the baby oil into the cuticles.

"Why'd you pick me?" I asked, turning her head to the side and carefully pulling the comb through her hair.

"Why?"

"You could have chosen anyone to work with you. Why me?"

"The first time we met, when we were at the gallery looking at that model of downtown? I remember watching you intently as you peered inside the little windows of the buildings. All the lawyers who always approached me just saw the Farnsworth money, the real estate portfolio, the buildings. But you didn't just see concrete and steel. You were looking for something else."

"So you picked me because I looked inside the models?"

"No, I picked you because you saw the people inside the buildings."

When I finished combing Kitty's hair, the fine strands were lying neatly against the pillow, and she'd slipped into a heavy sleep. I stayed there like that, one hand on her head, the other holding on to her cold hand.

"That's right, Kitty," I whispered, still stroking her hair. "Get your rest. I'll take care of everything else."

It wasn't until I dialed the number that the reality hit me and tears started flowing down my face. Somewhere in me I knew it was the end.

"Can you meet me?" I sniffled into the phone.

"Where are you?" Drew asked.

"The Starbucks at Rush and Oak."

Drew didn't even hesitate. "I'm on my way."

I bypassed the cozy armchairs and comfy sofas and went right for a straight-backed chair. I stared down at the black Formica table and tried to calm down while I waited for Drew.

"Kitty's in the hospital," I said when his shadow finally crossed the table.

"How's she doing?" he asked, taking the seat across from me.

I looked up to face him. "Not very well."

"How are you doing?"

"Not very well." I repeated, attempting a smile. Warm drops slid down my cheek and Drew reached over to wipe them away with his sleeve even though there was a stack of paper napkins on the table.

"I'd prepared for this, you know. For four years I've done nothing but make sure that when this time came, I'd be prepared. And now, even though I've meticulously dotted the Is and crossed the Ts, it doesn't matter." I shook my head at the futility of my efforts. "It still doesn't make it any easier."

"Of course it doesn't, Jane. It's not supposed to be easy." Drew reached for my hand and we sat like that until I didn't think I had any tears left to cry.

With every tear-soaked napkin I started to feel lighter, like I was letting go of something that had been bottled up inside me for years, weighing me down. It was time to let go, not of Kitty or my dad, but of the feelings that no longer had a place in my life. Being angry with my dad had given me something to cling to, an anchor that kept me in place, kept me from moving on. And in some way, given me a way to hold on to him. I'd wanted to hurt forever because I was afraid that once the pain was gone, he would be, too. But I didn't need to be mad to remember. Although I hadn't realized it until now, my father did leave a legacy. And she was sitting at this table about to do something I never thought she'd do.

"The review committee meets on Thursday," I reminded him, balling up the wet napkins piled on the table. "And you know what? It doesn't matter to me anymore. It doesn't make sense."

"What doesn't?"

"What I do. Andy's right. I'm like the grim reaper's groupie."

Drew laughed. "Groupie, muse—I wish you'd make up your mind."

"I have made up my mind. I just wanted you to know before I went ahead and did it." I dried my eyes before continuing. "I don't know what the fallout of this is going to be, but I wanted you to know what I'm about to do."

When I finished explaining, Drew was silent.

"I know, it's not exactly what you'd expect from me. I know Arthur certainly wouldn't expect it from someone who once wanted to make partner."

Drew nodded. "That's true. I probably would have thought the same thing once. But now that I know you Jane, I wouldn't expect anything less."

"Jane, what are you doing here?" Darcy stood in the doorway, not inviting me in.

"I was just at the hospital with Kitty and I wanted to talk to you."

Darcy stepped aside and closed the door behind me. I followed her through the foyer to the living room, where we sat on opposite ends of the couch.

I was about to do something that verged on malpractice, something that just a few weeks ago would have gone against every fiber of my being. Yet here I was, sitting in Darcy's living room, the living room of the girl who was suing my client. And it felt one hundred percent right.

"I think you should go see your grandmother," I told Darcy.

"Don't you think I want to see her?" Darcy drew her bare feet up on the couch and wrapped her arms around her knees. "I'm the only person in my family who isn't at the hospital."

"So, go see her."

"You're an attorney, Jane. You know what my lawyers are telling me."

I looked at the girl on the couch, the girl with the polished and jeweled toes, the girl who wouldn't be celebrating her eighteenth birthday with her grandmother. A young girl who needed a chance to do what I didn't do.

"Don't listen to them. Go see her before it's too late."

"Why are you here, Jane?"

"Because I want you to have the chance to say good-bye."

Darcy looked at me to see if I was serious. "So, you think I should go right now?"

"Go get your shoes on. I'll hail you a taxi."

CHICAGO SUN-TIMES JUNE 2, 2004

Rock and Janey on a Roll

By Don Decker, Sun-Times
Columnist

Sharing a pretzel at Wrigley Field? A softball game in Lincoln Park? Riding the Ferris wheel at Navy Pie? Now comes word that **Teddy Rock** and **Janey Marlow** were spotted kissing at Lincoln Park Zoo. Is this the way today's rock stars behave?

Apparently so, according to sources close to Rock. It seems that Rock's relationship with Janey Marlow is living proof that Teddy is ready to put his bad boy days behind him. And after two failed albums and over-the-top antics that put Rock's career into a nose dive, many believe that Teddy's turn-around is coming at just the right time.

"Just friends" and "close pals" is the official word from the rocker's spokesman, which yours truly tends not to believe. After all, the two sure sounded like a couple during their radio interview yesterday with WMXX's Vicki and Dave. Even though Rock skirted the issue when a listener called in and asked if the two were getting back together, I hear that Janey is preparing to go out on the road with Rock when he begins touring in July.

"I bet we'll see Janey on stage with Teddy," confides a source close to Rock. "Teddy's asked her to be by his side, and seeing the two of them together, I think she'll be there."

CHAPTER TWENTY-SIX

"**D**rew told me that Kitty's very sick. I'm sorry." Arthur came around to my side of the desk and kneeled in front of my chair, just like he'd done with Ethan and George. If only there was a cotton-candy-flavored lollipop that could make everything all better. "I don't want to seem insensitive, and I know this is bad timing, but with your review scheduled for Thursday we all thought it should be one less thing you needed to worry about."

"And?"

"And we'd like to offer you a partnership in the firm, Jane." Arthur spoke softly, adding, "If that's what you'd like."

If that's what I'd like. Six weeks ago that was exactly what I would have liked. Now I wasn't so sure.

They'd made me partner even without a big rock-star client. I'd made partner in spite of Teddy, in spite of Janey. Not that it mattered anymore, because I never expected to see Teddy Rock again.

"With everything going on, I need some time to think about this," I told Arthur, forgetting even to thank him for the offer. But I was tired, tired of jumping through hoops, worn out from trying to exceed everyone's expectations—including my own.

"Certainly. You take all the time you need." Arthur stood up. "We'll be here when you're ready."

As I walked the halls, passing the larger, brighter, more ornate offices I once coveted, I realized that for the first time I had a choice. Not because Arthur was willing to give me time, but because I was willing to give myself time as well.

I'd chosen to devote the past four years to ensuring that Kitty's estate was neat and tidy and foolproof. And in the end there was still devastation and disbelief and sadness. I made a choice to be the Jane that everyone could rely on, the Jane that was sure and steady, because I'd always thought that sure and steady would win the race. But then I'd chosen to believe I was Janey and realized that running a race is no way to run a life.

Are we really the person we were meant to be, or do we just become who the people in our lives want us to be? The daughter who pays the funeral director with a check from her mother's checkbook while her family waits for her in the car, crying. The sister who keeps quarters in a jar under the kitchen sink so her brother can't use a lack of change as an excuse not to go to the Laundromat. The friend, the neighbor, the coworker and the attorney—I'd been taking my direction from offstage and reciting my lines as instructed without even thinking.

Kitty passed away early Monday morning, a few hours after Darcy arrived at her bedside. Darcy called around eleven to tell me.

"She's gone," Darcy practically whispered when I picked up the phone.

I grasped the hollow I felt forming in my stomach and tried to keep my voice steady. I knew it was coming—maybe not that morning or that minute, but soon. And I'd known what I had to do, for Kitty, for Darcy and even for myself. Because Kitty was right, maybe being at peace was more important than being right.

"Did you get to say good-bye?" I asked.

"I did," Darcy sobbed. "Thank you, Jane. Really. Thanks."

* * *

I took the rest of the afternoon off and went home, the long way. I walked up Michigan Avenue until I reached Oak Street beach, and then continued walking along the lake. Joggers and dog walkers and mothers pushing strollers passed by me, their nylon shorts and tank tops and capri pants making my suit and heels look ridiculous.

When I made it home I changed into gym shorts and my ratty green Dartmouth T-shirt and lay on the couch, watching the minutes tick by on the VCR until the green digital numbers were the only light in the room.

At seven thirty my buzzer rang.

"Who is it?" I asked, leaning against the wall and pressing down the intercom button. I wasn't exactly in the mood for company.

"Land shark," two nasal voices chimed together in a horrible impersonation.

I pressed the buzzer and waited.

"What are you two doing here?" I asked, holding open the door.

"We come bearing gifts." Nat held out the flat, square box she'd been hiding behind Olivia's back and Liv produced a six-pack from under her arm. "Pizza from Café Luigi and a six-pack of Miller Lite—nothing but the best for our girl."

They brought their gifts into the living room while I went to the kitchen for plates and napkins.

"So, what's with the surprise visit?" I asked, handing the napkins to Nat in exchange for a slice of pizza.

"Arthur called me," Liv explained. "We're so sorry about Kitty."

I attempted an appreciative smile but it flatlined. "Thanks."

"How's her family?"

"Hanging in there. I keep telling myself she was an eighty-two-year-old woman who tried to enjoy every day she was alive, but it doesn't help."

Nat laid her hand on my knee and squeezed. "We're here if you need to talk."

"I know."

"Arthur also shared some other news with me," Olivia added.

Natalie tossed her crust in the box and sat back on the couch, reclining next to me. "Are congratulations in order for Becker, Bishop and Deane's newest partner?"

I shrugged. "I don't know. I guess now that Kitty's gone it's not such an obvious choice anymore."

Nat glanced over at Olivia and was silent.

"What do mean, you don't know?" Liv gasped. "You've always known."

"Not anymore. I don't know much of anything anymore." I finished my beer and reached for another. Since I'd already burst one bubble, I figured I'd burst one more. "I'm not Janey."

Instead of reacting, they didn't seem all that shocked. "We know. Andy told Natalie."

Now I was confused. I didn't think Andy would tell anybody; it would just make him look like he'd made another stupid mistake, not to mention the fallout if ROK96 discovered it was all a put-on. "When were you talking with Andy?"

"We went out for drinks the other night. He's really bummed out about Sam selling the bar, Jane."

"I know. He came over the other night looking for Teddy to bail him out."

"I don't think he's looking for someone to bail him out," Nat defended. "He wants to keep the bar going. I really think he could have, too, if Teddy was willing to give him the money."

I turned to Nat, trying to figure out what the hell was going on. This didn't make any sense. "Since when are you and Andy having heartfelt discussions over drinks?"

Natalie looked away and pretended to use her napkin to clean an invisible spot of pizza sauce off a chenille cushion. At least I hoped it was invisible; there was only so much pizza sauce those pillows could take.

"Please tell me you're not sleeping with Andy," I half joked, hoping that Natalie would tell me I was crazy. Instead she looked to Liv for reinforcement, but Olivia just held her hands up and shook her head, a signal that she wanted nothing to do with this conversation.

I covered my mouth with my hand and held my breath. "Please tell me you're not sleeping with my brother, Natalie," I exhaled.

"I'm not sleeping with Andy," Nat echoed.

"Then what are you doing with him?"

"We've been spending time together, that's all."

"Are you *dating*?"

"I don't know that I'd call it dating. It's not like he's taking me to the opera or anything."

"Nat, the only theater Andy could take you to is the dollar Brew 'n' View on Thursday nights."

"That's fine with me, Jane."

I reached for a pillow, buried my face in its soft, velvety cushion, and screamed until I couldn't scream anymore. "Is there a full moon or something?" I asked, lifting up my head. "Please tell me there's an explanation for everything that's happened these past few weeks."

Natalie took the pillow away from me and passed it to Liv. "I didn't tell you because there really wasn't much to tell, and, well, you were so busy with Teddy and everything."

"So, you're not sleeping with Andy?" I reiterated, just to make sure I got it right.

Natalie shook her head.

"Is that a no or a not yet?" I wondered aloud, not knowing whether I really wanted the answer.

Liv decided it was time to jump in and help Nat. "I don't think Natalie and Andy know what it is yet."

"Well, when you know, will you please remove any sharp utensils from the vicinity when you tell me? I may need some time to get used to the idea."

Nat crossed her heart. "Promise."

"So, what are you going to do about the partnership?" Liv asked now that we'd swept the topic of Andy off the table.

"I have no idea. I feel like I went to sleep and woke up and everything around me changed," I mumbled into my beer. "One minute everyone thought I was Jane, conscientious, dependable attorney. Then all of a sudden I was Janey the muse, Janey the woman who does unexpected things. And now I don't know who they think I am anymore."

"It's not who other people think you are that matters, Jane," Nat said. "It's who you think you are."

Liv stood up and started clearing away the remains of our pizza. "You don't have to give up your job just to prove you're not the same person you were before Teddy surfaced. It was never the job that defined you, Jane; it was how you defined your job."

"This is all so exhausting," I breathed.

Olivia laughed at me. "You think this is bad, try giving birth to two seven-pound boys without pushing out your intestines and creating a lifetime of hemorrhoids and incontinence in the process. Then you can talk to me about exhaustion."

Faces & Places

A few weeks before his comeback album is due to be released, **Teddy Rock**, 32, and Jane Marlow, the inspiration for his hit song, "Janey 245," were seen riding the Ferris wheel at Chicago's Navy Pier. "They looked like they were having fun," an onlooker told *Us*. Rock has been spending some time in Chicago, his boyhood home, while preparing for the release of his first record in twelve years.

CHAPTER TWENTY-SEVEN

"**D**o you hate me?" Teddy asked, this time not even waiting to be invited into my office.

I continued typing on my laptop, ignoring his entrance. "I'm going to have to tell Tara to stop letting assholes past the front lobby."

"That'd keep out a lot of your fellow attorneys, wouldn't it?" Teddy joked. I didn't take his bait, but I did stop typing. "What do you want, Teddy?"

"I just wanted to talk to you."

"Then talk. This whole game is getting old."

Teddy closed the door behind him but didn't make a move to come closer to my desk.

"I'm sorry. I'm sorry I didn't tell you and I'm sorry that Ian ever came up with this whole stupid idea."

"Are you sorry that it got you the publicity Ian was after?"

Teddy didn't answer.

"Look, I know you're just here because you're afraid I'm going to go around telling everyone that you lied. That the whole thing was a complete farce."

"Is that what you're going to do?" he asked, not even attempting to act like he was here for any other reason.

"Shouldn't I? Shouldn't I tell everyone what a fake you are, how you're so desperate to sell albums you'd lie about a song you wrote just to get publicity?"

"You're right. I lied. But it's not like you couldn't have been Janey."

That got a laugh out of me. "Sure."

"Look, I'm sorry. I never meant to hurt you or for it to end up this way. I just started to like it when we hung out together. You never saw me as this big rock star, you just wanted me to be Theo Brockford. And that was nice for a change."

"Well, you're not Theo anymore and I'm not Janey, so we're right back where we started, aren't we?"

"Shit, Jane. I made a mistake." Teddy held up a finger. "One mistake. And now you're going to hold it against me and continue punishing me for it? Make me pay every day from now on after I've worked so hard to get back here?"

"Why shouldn't I?" I asked, taking my hands off my laptop and crossing my arms. "Tell me. I can't wait to hear your answer."

"Um, well," Teddy stammered. His eyes darted around my office as if trying to find the answer somewhere on the walls. "I really hadn't gotten that far in the conversation. I thought you'd have tossed me out by now."

"I figured out why Ian didn't have any photographers at the softball game." I went back to typing on the computer. "It's because you suck at sports and he didn't want anyone to know. And you didn't go to New York for your *Rolling Stone* interview because the photographers were supposed to get pictures of us in the zoo and on the Ferris wheel, weren't they? But, don't worry, Teddy, I'm not going to spill your secret. I'm not going to tell anyone about the song."

"Really?"

"Like I said, you don't have to worry."

Teddy let out a relieved sigh and pretended to wipe the sweat off his forehead. "Whew! That was easier than I thought it would be." He walked over and sat down in a chair without an invitation. "As long as you're not throwing me out, I have one more thing I wanted to talk to you about. I know what I did was shitty, but when I ask you this, please be nice, okay? Because I'm serious."

"That's me, Teddy. Nice. That's why you said you wrote the song about me, remember?" I bumped my forehead with the heel of my hand. "Oh, yeah, that's right, you don't."

Teddy let my sarcasm slide. "Your receptionist told me they're making you a partner. That's great."

"I haven't accepted the offer."

"You have to, Jane." Teddy sounded panicked.

"Why do I have to?"

"Because I don't want to work with anyone else. I was thinking that it would be nice to have you on my side—not because you're Janey but because you're good at what you do. And I trust you."

"There are plenty of good attorneys out there who would jump at the chance to take you on as a client, Teddy."

"But I want you."

"I'm sure you'll be fine without me. You have Ian, after all."

"Ian doesn't give a shit about me. I'm his job, Jane, that's all. If he wasn't on retainer, do you think he'd be so worried about Teddy Rock's image? At least you really care about your clients."

"Good-bye, Teddy," I said, waving good-bye with one hand while continuing to type with the other.

Teddy threw his hands up in the air, but he didn't bother trying to convince me. "You know, I thought maybe you'd understand." He stood up to leave and I didn't stop him.

There was no way I could be Teddy's attorney when he'd lied to me, when I wasn't sure I wanted to be anybody's attorney any longer. I'd managed to put off giving Arthur an answer about my partnership offer, but eventually he'd want a decision. Eventually I'd have to make a choice. Until now I'd thought the only choice I'd have to make was what to wear to the dinner the partners would throw when I accepted their offer. I really did care about my clients. Not just Kitty and the Farnsworth family, but all the people I helped. Maybe that's why I went to see Darcy. No, that's exactly why I went to see Darcy.

So, why did I feel like now I was choosing between seeing the people inside the buildings and merely seeing the billable hours, the reviews and the promotions?

Even if the time I spent working with my clients didn't make the inevitable any easier, it was important to me. Not because I had to undo what I'd thought my father did wrong, but because it gave people the ability to get beyond the pain and get on with living. Because it was something I could do to help. I devoted myself to managing the details so I didn't have to worry about the big picture. Because in the big picture, my father was gone.

Teddy's song may have been about some hooker in a cheap motel, but that didn't mean I couldn't take away something more from his lyrics than the realization that my thighs weren't so wanton after all. It didn't have to be an all-or-nothing proposition. I picked up my phone and dialed the cell number that was once just numbers on a subscription card, and were now committed to memory.

When he picked up, I started talking. "Look, before you say anything, just let me finish. Remember that song from the radio station?" I rushed on, not waiting for an answer. "I was thinking that maybe it needed a different name, something that we could both live with. Instead of Old Friends, how about New Friends?" There was silence on the other end of the phone, and I took that as a good sign. "Look, you used me and I used you. Now why don't we use each other? Just listen to what I have to say and maybe we can work this out after all . . ."

Instead of going home after work, I had a cab drop me off in front of Sam's bar. The first thing I noticed was the fluorescent orange FOR SALE BY OWNER sign taped inside the front window.

I let myself in the front door and found Andy in the back room stacking empty kegs onto a dolly.

"You expect me to invest in a bar that doesn't even have Teddy Rock on the juke box?" I asked when he looked up and saw me standing against storeroom door. "Besides, I hear your softball team sucks."

Andy stopped loading the kegs. "Is that some sort of joke?"

I cracked a smile. "Maybe a tiny joke."

"Well, it's nice to know you haven't lost your sense of humor."

"Flattery will get you nowhere. I'm still not going to loan the money to you to buy the bar," I told him.

Andy held out a hand and sent me away with a quick wave. "Great, Jane. Thanks for coming all the way here to tell me that." He bent over and hoisted another keg off the floor and onto the dolly.

I inhaled deeply and let the familiar, reassuring aroma of stale beer, popcorn and white vinegar settle into my chest. "I won't lend you the money, but I will invest in the bar."

Andy paused, holding the keg in his arms like a newborn baby. "You will?"

I nodded. "I will."

He eyed me skeptically. "A silent partner?"

"As silent as I can be."

"That's not exactly an assurance, but I'll take it." He placed the keg onto the two already stacked on the dolly. "Thanks."

"This place sure doesn't look like the room I remember," I acknowledged, looking around at the neatly organized storeroom Andy and I used to pretend was a dragon's dungeon.

"This is just the beginning. I have all sorts of ideas and changes that I think can make a big difference. It's not going to be exactly the same Sam's Place we remember, but hopefully it will be even better."

"It won't be easy, you know. You really think you can do it?"

"I know I can," Andy vowed seriously and then held out his hand to me. "Pinky promise."

I gave him my pinky and we shook on it. "Me, too."

Teddy Bare
The Rolling Stone Interview

Teddy Rock is clean-shaven and the only bottle he's drinking from has an Evian label plastered to its side. Is this the Teddy Rock we remember? The guy who blasted onto the music scene only to fade just as quickly under the weight of his own rock-star image? Yes and no.

Rock's new album, simply titled *Teddy Rock*, may lack the catchy play on words and iconic image of an electric guitar-wielding hellion, but it brings Rock back to his musical roots. With its simple black-and-white photograph of an older and, may we assume, wiser Teddy Rock, the album isn't so much a departure from his "Janey 245" days as it is a return to them.

During two long conversations over two days in Chicago in May, his music took precedence over his decadence. Gone was the guy who once declared the postconcert motto: "Now that I've played, it's time to get laid." In his place is a musician who takes his music, but not himself, more seriously. "What I want is to make records, get respect, have fun and put out good music," says Rock.

With his fiery guitar leads and trademark throat-shredding vocals, the critics are saying that's exactly what he's done.

When his new self-titled album debuts at number one this week on Billboard, Teddy's fans and the music industry will both be saying the same thing—welcome back.

CHAPTER TWENTY-EIGHT

The rapping on my front door wouldn't stop, and I was already running late. Nobody had buzzed, and I wasn't expecting company, which meant it could be only one person. I peered through my peephole and got an eyeful of steely gray permed curls that wouldn't go away until the door opened. I turned the knob.

"Hello, Mrs. Winston."

She gave me her best smile, which sloped a little to the right, probably from an uneven application of Polident. "Hello, Jane. I hate to even ask you this, but my granddaughter was wondering if you could get her an autograph from that Teddy Rock friend of yours."

"I think that could be arranged. I have a meeting with his business manager next week. I'll see what I can do."

Mrs. Winston stood there uncomfortably, shifting her weight from one

246 • Jennifer O'Connell

orthopedic shoe to another. "That would be very kind of you, Jane," she painfully offered up in lieu of a thank-you. It was probably the closest we'd ever come to a pleasant conversation. And that's why I should have known it wasn't over.

"There is one more thing," she continued, turning slowly toward her door so she didn't have to face me. "I wasn't going to mention it, but would you mind turning down the radio? I think it's disrupting your neighbors. And I was also thinking that maybe you should replace this doormat, here. It's curling up at the edges and somebody could trip and hurt themselves. We don't want the condo association involved in any lawsuits."

"I'll get right on it," I promised, saluting her hunched back as she shuffled away.

Like they say, the more things change, the more they stay the same. Now I had one more item to bring up at next week's meeting. My number one priority was getting a better handle on Teddy's finances. Now that the album was out and *Rolling Stone* had hit the stands, somebody had to look out for Teddy. I figured it may as well be somebody who knew him when he was that little boy in the Toughskins corduroys, sitting under a tree in his yard trying to learn a Hendrix tune.

Although he'd probably deny it, there was a still a little bit of Theo in Teddy Rock, the part that just wanted to make music. And if Teddy was going to make music, he needed someone he could trust on his side, not just publicists and managers getting paid to act like they cared.

Arthur was shocked when I walked into his office and resigned, so shocked in fact that he stopped sucking on his lollipop and just stood there staring at me, the soggy white lollipop stick dangling from his open mouth. He'd really thought I was going to accept the firm's offer. And until the words were actually out of my mouth, until I heard them said out loud, I was almost sure I would. I'd seriously considered doing just that, even imagining what I'd do with the larger office, the bigger paycheck. But I wanted to try something new. So instead of accepting Arthur's office I gave him my two weeks notice. My new box of business cards had arrived yesterday and the plain, stiff white cards with raised black lettering looked pretty damn good—JANE L. MARLOW & ASSOCIATES. So what if I didn't have any associates yet. I had a rock star for a client.

In a way I owed Teddy. Not because he'd given me the freedom to be Janey, but because I'd finally given myself permission to be me. It'd been fun believing I was someone else's inspiration, but now it was time to find my own. Maybe I wasn't supposed to discover I wasn't Janey until Teddy had helped me remember the good things I'd forgotten, or, more likely, chosen to forget. It was just like he'd said; sometimes it's just how you choose to remember things that matters.

I'd been living at the end—the end of life, the end of relationships. Teddy helped me go back to the beginning, not to the starting line but to the moment after the gun pops and the adrenaline pulses through you and it's not the finish line you're thinking of, it's the next step, the way your foot falls to the ground and pushes you forward.

Even if I couldn't score an autograph from Teddy's business manager next week, I could always get one signed in person when I went to DC at the end of the month. Drew and I had tickets to Teddy's show at Constitution Hall. First row, of course. And backstage passes. Nothing less would satisfy a former muse.

Drew was leaving to go back to DC on Monday, so this was our last weekend together in Chicago. After talking with William, we'd decided to make Darcy a settlement offer, something fair that she could live with. It was what Kitty would have wanted.

I was meeting Drew down at Oak Street beach, where he vowed he could teach me to Rollerblade in one relatively painless lesson. I didn't bother telling him I'd been practicing every night after work. I could get a good hour or two in before the sun went down, which gave me enough time to test out my knee pads and wrist protectors once or twice. Rollerblading was easier than I thought it would be once I learned not to panic when I lost my balance. But maybe that was what happened when you stopped being afraid to fall.

Since I didn't need the lesson, I was going to suggest we skate down to Navy Pier and have lunch, maybe take a ride on the Ferris wheel. My treat, of course, now that I was the head of my own one-person firm. Drew could return the favor over dinner before we watched the Fourth of July fireworks over Monroe Harbor. I promised Andy we'd drop by the bar afterward to help plan the grand reopening of Sam's Pints & Pins. Besides, one of the benefits of silent partnership was unlimited use of the bowling lanes. And I had a trophy to win back.

I'd finished dressing and was in the hall closet grabbing my new Rollerblades when the song on my stereo faded away and Big D's familiar voice cut through the air. "It will debut at number one on the Billboard top twenty next week, and will surely send this guy back to the top of the charts. Here's the newest single from Teddy Rock."

The Jane in me knew I was going to be late, but the Janey in me couldn't resist listening to the song, which was actually really good. Besides, he wasn't just a client. He'd become a friend. Before he showed up and turned my life upside down, I'd truly believed I could control everything, that as long as every contingency was planned for, I could determine the outcome of every situation thrown my way. But I couldn't. And I didn't want to anymore. Instead of denying it, I'd decided to enjoy it. Sure, the pillows on the couch were still lined up at a forty-five degree angle, and the remote control was in its designated spot on the coffee table, but let's be honest. It just looked better that way. Luckily, though, there was one thing I had gained control over.

I clapped my hands together and the living room lights blinked off just like the Clapper directions said they would.

I grabbed my Rollerblades, flipped off the stereo and closed the door behind me.

Janey had left the building.